Too Little, Too Late

Portia A. Cosby

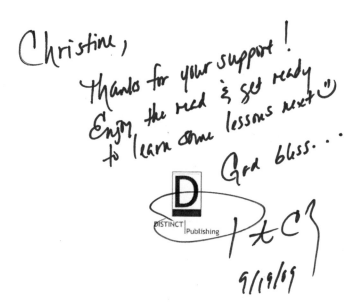

Christine,
Thanks for your support!
Enjoy the read & get ready
to learn some lessons next :)
God bless...

DISTINCT | Publishing

9/19/09

Portia A. Cosby

For more information, including special discounts for bulk
purchases, please contact DISTINCT Publishing at:

DISTINCT Publishing
PO Box 1034
Beaver Falls, PA 15010

PUBLISHER'S NOTE
This book is a work of fiction. Names, characters, places, and
incidents are either the product of the author's vivid imagination or
are used fictitiously, and any resemblance to actual persons, living or
deceased, business establishments, events, or locales is entirely
coincidental.

ISBN: 978-0-9823013-0-2

Cover design by Marion Designs

Publishing Consultation by Tracey Michae'l Lewis for Exodus
Media Group, Inc.

Printed in the United States

To my daughter, **Amari**. I can't explain how much of an effect you've had on me and how much of a driving force you are in my life. Trust that Mommy is doing this for us. I hope you see this and realize that you can do whatever you want in life. As long as you believe, nothing will stop you. I love you always.

Portia A. Cosby

Acknowledgements

Thank you, Jesus! Only God knows what this journey has been like—the stumbling blocks, the false starts, and the disappointments. But in spite of it all, I kept the faith and here I am. This opportunity to share my novel with others is definitely a blessing. Those who know me well remember the original version from high school...Can you believe I stuck with it after all these years? I tried to get this out to the world on my time, but I quickly realized that greatness can only occur on His time. God showed up and showed out, and I can wait to see what He has in store for me. I am truly humbled by this experience.

Mom, you finally started believing in my talent once you read my poetry and realized my writing was more than a hobby. Remember when you used to get frustrated because I was always writing in a notebook? Thank you for not ignoring my dreams. Dad, I appreciate your support. I have your hustler's spirit and when I believe in something, I go after it. You see that in me and have been in my corner from day one. Glenn, I did it my way, even when you doubted my strategy. I'm glad you see now. Thanks for the inspiration. Amari, Mommy's sorry for taking away some of our play time, sitting in front of the computer! You'll understand why when you're older.

To my "Advisory Board": Ericka, Rosie, Jamie, Cleveland, Danielle, Twydell, April, and Mama Wadlington—thank you for taking the time to read my work with a critical eye and offering your suggestions. Your honesty is what I value most, and none of you sugarcoat a thing! Get ready for Round 2 because the chapters for *Supposed to Be* will be rolling in. Janice, Shandra, and DeVawn, thanks for being in my corner from the beginning.

Ms. Tracey Michae'l Lewis...After all this time, it finally happened! Your patience, encouragement, advice, guidance, and sisterly love have made this process a smooth one. Thank you for everything. You are more than my consultant—you've become my mentor and a lifelong friend. Thanks to everyone else at Exodus Media Group who had a part in this. To my editor, Colleen Mullarkey...I appreciate your constructive criticism and thank you for giving me another perspective on some of the characters' choices.

Keith Saunders, my graphic designer…Thank you so, so much for bringing my new vision to life. I've already had a tremendous amount of positive feedback about the new cover. I look forward to completing the series with you.

In 1994, my 9th grade CP English teacher offered the class extra credit for creative writing. It was then that I penned my first poem and wrote my first script, and I haven't run out of ink yet! Mrs. Ryan, thank you for showing me how much of an impact my words have. Your praises and positive reinforcement lit a fire under me, and it's not burning out any time soon.

Sorry I couldn't mention every person who has believed in my writing career, but know that I appreciate the role you played and you're in my heart. I haven't forgotten you.

<u>A MESSAGE FOR MY READERS</u>

Open your mind and receive the message. Words are powerful. Focus on the right ones.

Portia A. Cosby

Chapter 1

You know, it's kinda hard being the girl in town that hardly anybody likes. And yeah, I guess a few people have their reasons for not liking me, but some stuff is uncalled for. Like the other week, I got into it with my best friend's cousin, Dap. Her and her sisters were standing in front of Express at the mall, and they wouldn't move so I could go in. We exchanged a few words, and as I pushed my way through they talked big shit about how they were gon' whoop my ass and how I'd better stay away from their men (as if I actually wanted any of their raggedy asses). In true Tameka style, I just waved my middle finger, making sure each one of them saw it and strolled into the store.

Dap's problem with me originated way back in high school. I used to deal with her now-boyfriend, Tyrone. Okay, I'll be honest. We used to bone. Pardon my language, but you'll learn that I'm a very blunt person. Anyway, Dap had a crush on Tyrone, but he wouldn't give her the time of day. She would stare us down every day in the halls while we talked and have her friends spread rumors that I was screwing somebody else. By our senior year, I'd dropped Tyrone, and she made her move on him. Even though they're still together, she's insecure as hell and takes every opportunity to mess with me when she sees me. I guess I add fuel to the fire sometimes. I figure if you're mad already, I'll give you a little more to be mad about. So to this day when Tyrone speaks, I flirt like I actually want his ass, just to piss Dap off.

I became cool with my best friend, Tielle, back in senior year of high school when we had to work on a group project together. She initially didn't like me because Dap is her cousin. You know how that goes. But during the project, we realized we had a lot in common. One thing I can say about Tielle is that she's a true friend. Like I said before, my fan club is damn near at zero, but she always had my back when somebody referred to me as "that bitch", "that ho", or whatever other creative names they could think of.

Portia A. Cosby

It used to bother me that people didn't like me, but at 24, I could think of more important things to worry about than somebody's opinion. I'm actually glad I have such a tight circle of friends. That way, I don't have to worry about phony bitches trying to take my man and stuff like that.

Speaking of which, I don't have a man. The dudes here are so pathetic. Most of them just wanna fuck and the rest are gay or married. True enough, I just want casual sex sometimes, too, but damn. Can a sista work a relationship into the equation at some point?

On the other hand, it's hard to entertain company since I have my tack-head sister, Alexis, as a roommate. Being confined to a bedroom is not my idea of privacy. I need the whole house when I have special company over. She doesn't have a problem with the restrictions, though. In fact, she has somehow convinced herself that the rooms are soundproof. I've walked in plenty of times, only to hear loud moans and orgasmic screams coming from her bedroom or bathroom. That's when I thank God for two-bed, two-and-a-half-bath townhouses.

For the most part, we get along, but we both have smart mouths so that causes a few problems. She's also cool with most of the people who don't like me, so we tend to have it out when I walk in the house and see my enemy sipping the last of the Kool-Aid and eating the leftover spaghetti I made.

We moved in together after our parents divorced and left town—I was 20 and she was 18. The marriage had been over, but they were just waiting for Lexis to graduate so they could officially go their separate ways. I took her in because she's wild, and if she's around the wrong people, she could end up in a world of trouble. When I say wild, I mean she's done everything from smoking weed, to selling weed, to tricking for cash (with her so-called boyfriends). This is the girl who didn't sneak out of her bedroom window at two in the morning—she walked out the front door and didn't care if Mom and Dad heard her.

I'm not claiming to be an angel, though. I worked as a stripper after I graduated high school, and I just stopped two years ago. It may sound cliché, but it helped me get through college. After I graduated, I became an assistant manager in the billing department of an insurance company. Alexis? Well, she's content at JC Penney for the time being, but if it is like any of her other jobs, she won't last long.

10

The only steady thing in that girl's life is her long-time boyfriend, Robert…and that's not saying much. They have one of those crazy relationships. You know, on for five months, off for one. That's why I live the single life. That break-up-to-make-up shit is played out. Me and my ex, TJ, used to be like that until I decided to grow up. He still calls every now and then and we do our thing, but I can't get back with him. I don't even go out in public with him because he's still involved in that thug shit. There are too many people who want to hurt him and anybody near him for me to be all up under him wherever he goes. That gangsta shit was cute when we met at the strip club, but it was time for me to find a man with goals—legal goals—that he was trying to attain.

***

The phone rang as I took my popcorn out of the microwave. "Hello?" I answered, trying not to sound out of breath after running from the kitchen to the living room.

"What you doin'?" Alexis asked on the other end.

I told her I was in for the night, and luckily picked up the last copy of *The Kings of Comedy* at Blockbuster.

"Well, you need to cancel those plans," she said matter-of-factly.

"And why is that?"

"Because we kickin' it over here at Tielle's."

"Who is we?"

"Me, Tielle, Kaelin, Carmen, Nina…Dap…"

"Umm hmm. I was wonderin' when that name was comin'. You already know I'm not comin' over there if she's there. I'm chillin' tonight, and I'm not in the mood for drama."

As I listened to Alexis ramble on about why I should get drunk with them, I popped in the DVD, grabbed my popcorn, and plopped down on the couch. I was barely listening to what she was saying. Finally, I cut her off. "Listen, Lexis. I'm comfortable here, by myself. I'll just see you when you come home."

"Aw, I see what's up. TJ 'bout to come over there, ain't he?" she asked excitedly.

"Bye, girl. Steve Harvey's about to start the show," I said before I hung up on her. I had to admit, though…Inviting TJ over didn't sound like a bad idea. It had been almost two months since I'd seen him.

"No, Meka. Don't call him," I said to myself as I laid the phone back on the couch. After three more repetitions of that routine, I called his cell. His voicemail picked up after two rings, which told me he'd pushed the "Ignore" button. I felt like an idiot for calling, and I took my frustration out on the phone as I threw it on the floor.

Ten minutes later, the phone rang. I paused the movie and answered it, pretending like I wasn't ecstatic that TJ called back and didn't take three days to do so.

"What's up, baby?" he responded with his sexy voice.

"Nothin'. Just watchin' TV. What you doin'?"

"Shit, I was about to go kick it wit' Carlos and them."

"Oh," I said, mad at myself for sounding so obviously disappointed.

"Why? What's up? What made you call?" he asked.

"I just wanted to see what you were up to. I thought you might've wanted to stop over for a little bit." We always went through that routine. I'd pretend like I didn't want anything, and he'd pretend like he didn't know why I called.

Twenty minutes later, there was a knock at my door. TJ and I finished watching the show and had a long talk about why I hadn't heard from him. He told me he'd been laying low because a couple of his old enemies had moved back into town, and he didn't want to get involved in no shit. (Evidently TJ had robbed them for some serious money and they were out for blood.)

"But I figure they've calmed down for a while. It's been two years since that went down, and they've been back here for two months, lookin' for me. They'll let it go," he said as I ran my fingers along the parts of his braids. He tried to act like he wasn't concerned about being someone's prey, but something told me he was trying to convince himself more than me.

Sitting there and holding him brought back too many old feelings. I really loved him and still could, but he hadn't released himself from that dangerous lifestyle. As he fell asleep in my arms, I turned off the TV and the lights and held him until I was asleep, too. I couldn't even be mad that I didn't get some.

When I woke up, TJ was gone. It figured. Reality hit once again. I could never get back with him, and little shit like that was a prime example of why. I looked at the clock. 6 a.m. I went upstairs and got in my bed. At eleven, I woke up to the smell of bacon, eggs, and pancakes. I walked downstairs and found Alexis and TJ sitting at the kitchen table.

"Mornin' sleepy head!"Alexis grinned. "I didn't think you was ever gon' get up."

12

"What are you doin' here, TJ?"

"I ran to the store with Lexis to get the food," he replied.

"He was up when I came in, so I asked him to go with me. A bitch was hungry after smokin' all night," Alexis explained.

"You need to slow down with that mess. Don't they give y'all drug tests at Penney's?" I asked.

"Girl, they say that just to scare us. They haven't tested nobody since they hired 'em, and that goes for them girls who've worked there over five years."

After we finished eating, TJ and I went upstairs and made love until we ran out of energy. It was like we both needed to feel each other's warmth and comfort. When we were done, we had the infamous after-sex talk. He told me how much he loved me and swore he was trying to get away from his thug lifestyle. I really didn't say much. I just let him talk. For a split second, I considered asking him if he wanted to get back together. I missed him so much, but couldn't bear the thought of lying to cops and peeping around corners again.

As soon as we got out of the shower, I heard Alexis screaming and running up the steps. I threw on my robe and ran into the hallway.

"What's wrong?" I asked.

"Some dudes just came to the door, lookin' for TJ," she replied, her voice trembling. "They said to tell him that he knows who sent them, he can't hide no more, and they know where else to look for him now."

"They didn't try to come in?"

"No. I told them that he left. They only know that he was here last night." Alexis paused for a few seconds. "Meka, he gotta go."

I already knew that. I went into my room and saw TJ quickly getting dressed.

"I'm sorry," he said, putting on his shirt. "I'm about to leave."

I couldn't even look at him. I had so many mixed emotions going through my head.

"I won't bother you no more," he said as he walked out of my room. Even though I didn't want him to leave like that, my lips couldn't form the words to stop him. I walked downstairs and watched him leave through the back door. Alexis ran down and asked me if I was okay. I played it off like I was cool and went back to my room to get dressed. While I was alone, I didn't have to pretend. I bawled like someone had just died and curled into the fetal position on my bed, wishing my pain would go away.

Tielle knocked on the door at 1:30. Alexis entertained her until I got downstairs.

"I'm surprised you made it out the bed this mornin', Miss Life of the Party," I teased Tielle.

"What?" she asked in her most innocent voice.

"Lexis already told me how you was actin', so don't front like you don't know what I'm talkin' about. How many shots did you have again? Seven?"

"You see she's wearin' her shades like it's sunny in here or somethin'," Alexis added.

Tielle gave us the finger and told us to hurry up before she left us. We were on our way to the mall to find outfits for the evening. A new club was opening, and everybody was gonna be there. I hadn't been out in a couple of months because I was working a lot of overtime and didn't have time to do anything but sleep when I was off. I couldn't wait to get to the mall so I could buy a cute little get 'em girl outfit. Not hoochie, but definitely something that would make even a gay man look twice. Two hours and nine stores later, all three of us had found outfits and shoes. After all that shopping, we needed to get something to eat. As we headed to the food court, Lexis stopped dead in her tracks.

"What's wrong with you?" Tielle asked.

"Shit! Robert's over there by the pizza place," Alexis replied.

"I thought y'all was back together," I said.

"We got into it when I got in last night. He was mad 'cause I got home so late."

"Well you can't just stand here in the middle of the walkway," Tielle said, walking off. "I'm goin' over here to get a steak sandwich."

"Hold up, girl," I called, jogging to catch up with her. "That sounds good."

Alexis walked behind us, hoping that Robert wouldn't see her. Her strategy didn't work, because when we got in line at the steakery, he followed us.

"Oh, so you had time to come to the mall, but you ain't got time to spend with me today, right?" he asked.

"Robert, get out of my face. I told you that I had shit to do today. I can't sit up under yo ass all day, every day."

The argument continued, and Tielle and I went to our seats to eat. Five minutes later, Alexis stormed over and sat with us. "I can't stand his ass," she complained.

We didn't have anything to say because we were too busy dogging our sandwiches. As we ate and joked around, a group of guys sitting nearby caught my eye. "Who are they?" I asked.

"They look like some of Robert's friends," Alexis said, rolling her eyes.

"Damn! Why don't he ever bring them to the house?" I asked.

"Look at you bein' hot," Tielle said.

"It ain't about bein' hot," I replied. "It's about meetin' new people," I paused. "Fine ass people!"

We all laughed, but Alexis and Tielle stopped all of a sudden. I noticed they were staring in the guys' direction. I turned around to see what they were looking at and noticed that one of them was walking toward us. He was about six feet tall, slim, but muscular, with slightly bowed legs. His skin was caramel with a hint of pecan, his eyes were a soft charcoal gray, and his goatee was trimmed to perfection. I prayed he was coming to the table to see me, and lo and behold, he stopped by my chair.

"How are y'all ladies doin' today?" the mystery man asked.

"Fine," we replied in unison.

"Aren't you Robert's friend?" Alexis asked.

"Yeah, I'm Romeo."

I laughed. "Romeo? Come on, now. What's your real name?"

"I'm serious," he said. "My name is Romeo."

"Okay Romeo, where's your Juliet?" I asked sarcastically. I was hoping he'd say he didn't have one.

"I think I just found her."

Tielle busted out laughing. "Man, let me get outta here. Y'all too corny for me." She stood up, and so did Alexis.

I was excited because he actually seemed interested in me. Robert must've told him to come talk to me. I would always tell him to hook me up with one of his friends, and he finally came through for me. If me and Mister Romeo worked out, I'd have to consider sticking up for him when Alexis was on the verge of cheating.

Just when I was about to ask what his plans were for the night, I heard him say, "Hey, Miss Lady. Where you goin'?"

"I'm not goin' far. I'm just givin' y'all a little privacy to talk," Tielle replied.

"How do you know I wasn't talkin' to you?" Romeo asked.

15

My heart fell right into my sock. That fine man wanted to holla at my best friend. I can admit I was a little jealous. Not of Tielle, but because it had been a long time since a guy had approached me with respect and looked as good as Romeo. Tielle seemed to get the good guys all the time. Her last boyfriend, Maurice, treated her like a queen.

Romeo and Tielle exchanged numbers, and she asked him if he was going to the club. He said he'd definitely be there if she was going. She didn't seem too impressed by him. She said he talked a good game, but she was waiting to see the follow-through. I always admired her patience and her ability to not linger on a man's every word. That was probably a big reason why she'd had mostly long-term relationships and only four sexual partners. Me? One long-term relationship, and we won't even get into my sexual partners. Let's just say the number is in double digits.

Before we went home, Alexis and I got our nails done. Once we were in the house, she fell on the couch and sighed. I walked over to the answering machine to check the messages.

"I hope Robert isn't on there, girl. That nigga is gon' be the end of me," she said out the blue.

"Whatever," I replied.

Robert, Carmen, and TJ were on the machine.

"See, girl! I knew he was gonna call. I promise he's a stalker," Alexis belted after Robert's message. "I should just drop him, huh? Well, maybe not, 'cause the sex is the bomb. But sex isn't everything..."

"Shut up!" I yelled, cutting her off. "Please, shut up. I'm not in the mood to hear this shit."

"Ugh," she replied. "The bitch has just entered the room, ladies and gentlemen. Let me leave you alone." She got up and headed upstairs. "Don't be mad at me 'cause you wanted Romeo to holla at you, and the only nigga you got is TJ's gangsta ass."

"Kiss my ass," I yelled.

The sad thing was that she was right. The whole situation with TJ had me in a bad mood earlier, but when we were at the mall, I was occupied so I didn't think about it. Once we listened to the messages, hearing his voice confused me again. I was so in love with this man, but I think it finally hit me that our monthly booty calls and games of phone tag didn't fit into my big picture. He was either going to be in my life or out, and I made my decision right then. He was out.

***

I woke up from my nap at nine o'clock and jumped in the shower. When I was done, I popped in my Ludacris CD and turned the volume up to twenty. No matter how old that CD is, I still bump it like I just peeled the plastic off. By the end of "What's Your Fantasy," I was done with my hair and starting my makeup. Alexis was ironing her outfit and dancing to the music in the hallway.

"Leave the iron on when you done," I yelled.

By the time I made it to the ironing board, she was already dressed. She had on a red dress that fit like a girdle, but she looked cute in it. Her red stilettos matched it perfectly, and her silver accessories sparkled in the light.

"You look cute," I said.

"Thanks," she said, posing in the mirror. "I'm turnin' some heads tonight."

"I hear that! You will with that dress fittin' like that."

"Girl, don't be jealous of the booty," she said as she smacked her butt. "Just ask Mama why she didn't give you none."

"Whatever. I got enough to make a difference, baby girl," I replied.

We left the house at about eleven and met Tielle and her sister, Kaelin, in the parking lot across from the club. Kaelin and I were cordial, but we didn't really get along. Of course, she was cool with my sister, Miss Personality, though. Nina was there, too. Her and Tielle used to go to the same church. She was kinda quiet but was one of those girls whose bad side you wouldn't wanna be on.

Tielle had her hand on her hip, and she looked pissed. As we walked toward them, I knew she was gonna have something to say.

"I thought you said 11:15," she said.

Alexis pointed at me. "Talk to this one. I was ready at 10:30."

"Let's go," Tielle said, quickly walking to the door. "I'm tryin' to drink for free and y'all playin'."

We could hear the bass bumping as soon as we got to the sidewalk. The line was fairly long, but it was moving. We all showed our ID's, paid ten dollars, and sauntered in. The place was packed already. We weaved through the crowd, passing the little hot girls who arched their backs and rubbed their asses against the guys who were leaning against the wall, and successfully avoided the country-ass niggas with played out No Limit Records medallions and dull gold teeth. We took a table near the dance floor, and I immediately

17

ordered a cranberry and vodka. I rarely hit the dance floor without a little something in me. Kaelin stayed at the table with me because she was waiting for her and Tielle's Hennessy and Cokes to arrive. Everybody else made their way to the dance floor.

I sank into the velvety cushions of our booth and leaned back to casually scope the place. The clouds of cigarette smoke accented by the strobe lights made it a little difficult to see clearly, but I managed to make out a few familiar faces. I was impressed by the club's class. Each table had an oblong glass bowl with three ivory floating candles, glass ashtrays, and menus that weren't covered with sticky alcohol residue and peanut grease.

The wait staff wore black bottoms and matching vests with white button-down shirts and crimson ties. Although the majority of them seemed to be courteous, there was one overweight girl standing three tables away who repeated everyone's order so loudly that I thought she was trying to yell it to the bartender way across the club. I guess her high-water pants and suffocating shirt weren't enough to draw attention to herself.

Kaelin and I made small talk while we sipped our drinks.

"So how's Chris doin'?" I asked, referring to her son.

"He's okay. He's been cranky lately, though, 'cause his dad is out of town."

"Oh? Where did Gary go?"

"He's in Virginia on business. He'll be back Monday."

"That's cool."

Just then, a sweaty Nina and breathless Tielle came back to the table.

"Woo! Girl, it's hot out there," Tielle said.

"Where's the waitress?" Nina asked. "I need a drink."

"Did you see Dap and Carmen, Kaelin?" Tielle asked.

"Naw. Where they at?" Kaelin asked as she looked around.

"Over there by the bar."

"I'll be back."

She went to the bar and sat on a stool next to Carmen. Carmen is one of Dap's younger sisters. She talks a lotta shit. She's about 5'4" with a six-foot wide mouth. She's willing to back it up, but not that many people get into it with her because they're intimidated. Was I? Hell no. The only thing that kept me from fighting her was maturity. As with her sister, our hatred for each other went way back to waiting by the lockers after the last bell. Funny thing is we never fought because the teachers always broke us up.

18

I ordered another drink, and Nina ordered hers. Tielle's song, "Work It" by Missy Elliott came on, and she hopped up from the table to go do just what the song implied. Toward the middle of the song, Carmen came over to our table. I ignored her and kept watching the people on the dance floor.

"What's up, people?" she said as she helped herself to a seat.

"Hey girl," Nina answered.

"Why ain't y'all out there with them?"

"Girl, we waitin' on our drinks." Nina paused once she spotted the waitress. "And here they come now."

"Tameka, I'll watch your drink. I know this song brings back some memories. Why don't you go on out there and work it like you used to in the strip club?" Carmen taunted.

"Carmen, don't start tonight." I sipped my drink and kept looking ahead.

"Naw, I'm sayin' why not show 'em how to really do it. You a pro. Hell, we can clear the table if you wanna make a lil' extra change."

"You know what," I said, grabbing my drink. "I'm not doin' this tonight. Nina, I'll be over there."

I walked to the bar and sat down. Once I finished my drink, I went out to move a little something. On my way to the floor, I was swooped up by Jesse, one of TJ's friends. We grooved to Nelly, and I sang along with Kelly Rowland as we two-stepped in the crowded space. Out the corner of my eye, I noticed that Tielle was dancing with Maurice. She looked a little uncomfortable, but gave me the thumbs up when I mouthed, "Are you okay?"

The song ended, and Prince's "Adore" came on. Romeo went up to Tielle and asked if he could dance with her. Maurice was pissed, but what could he say? I didn't dance to that song because it made me think of TJ. I knew there was probably another slow song coming, so I sat back down at the bar. I hadn't warmed the stool five minutes before I heard a male voice say, "Why are you sittin' here by yourself?" It was Tyrone.

"I'm chillin'," I answered dryly.

"Why ain't you out there dancin'?" he asked.

"I could ask you the same question."

"Dap's in the bathroom. You know how y'all women take forever."

"Yeah, I guess."

"You in a bad mood or somethin'?"

19

"I'm cool, Tyrone." He was irritating me, and I was hoping he'd catch a clue.

"Okay, I'll back off. You must be PMS'n or you need some lovin'."

"And you can't do nothin' about either one."

"I could help you out with one thing."

"What? You got some Midol on you?" I asked.

"Naw," he laughed. "But remember that thing I used to do for you in high school? I do it even better now."

"Is that right?" He brought a smile to my face.

"Yeah, it is." He moved closer to me.

"You better back up. Here comes your girl."

Dap marched over to us with her attitude three feet in front of her. Tyrone backed up and tried to act like everything was cool. "Hey baby," he said, hugging her.

"Get off of me," Dap replied, pushing him away. "What the fuck is this, Tameka? Didn't I just tell you the other day to stay away from him?"

"Time out," I said as I stood up. "Look at who was sittin' down when you got over here and who was standin' up. Your man came over to talk to me."

"Baby, let's just go dance," Tyrone said.

"Fuck that. Look ho, I'm tired of lookin' up and seein' you around him every damn time y'all in the same room. Give it up. That was high school. He don't want you no more."

"First of all, you can back up outta my face. Second of all, I don't want Tyrone. You need to remind his ass that this ain't high school, and that I don't wanna know how much better he can eat pussy now. Trust and believe that if I want Tyrone, I can have his ass, 'cause I already got him here," I said, pointing to the area just below my waist. "And since you're so aware of how old we are now, grow up and stop actin' like you still 17."

Carmen, Nina, Tielle, Alexis, and a host of strangers gathered around. When Carmen stepped in my face, Lexis got in it.

She grabbed Carmen. "Look. Y'all ain't gon' gang up on my sister. Back up! If they got somethin' they need to settle, let them settle it. You don't see me jumpin' all up in Dap's face!"

"I ain't scared of her, Lexis. You ain't gotta hold her back. Let 'em show everybody how petty they are," I said.

"You ain't gotta be scared to get fucked up!" Carmen replied.

"That's real cute, Carmen," I said. "Too bad that little slogan went out ten years ago."

TJ busted through everybody and grabbed me just when we were about to go to blows. I didn't even know he was there. "Get your purse," he demanded. I grabbed my purse from the stool and turned back around. Dap was still bumpin' her gums.

"Ain't nobody gon' do shit!" TJ yelled. "Now back the fuck up and let us through."

"Yeah, somebody saved yo ass again. Go on home, bitch," Dap said.

"Whatever, Dap. If you wanna see me, you know where I live. Ask Tyrone if you don't remember," I yelled, as TJ dragged me outside. By then, the bouncers had realized that something was up, but TJ reassured them I was going home and everything was cool.

While we were outside, Tielle and Alexis came out to check on me. TJ still had me hemmed up, standing behind me with his arms wrapped tightly around my torso.

"Are you alright?" Tielle asked.

"What the hell happened in there?" Alexis asked.

"Same ol' shit. She was pissed because Tyrone was all in my face. I told her to check his ass because he's still tryin' to get in my panties," I replied. "I'm not worried about them. I'm goin' home."

"Don't let Dap and Carmen ruin your night," Tielle said.

"They already have. I don't even feel like partyin' now. I lost my buzz."

"I'ma take her home," TJ said. "We'll probably stop somewhere and get some drinks first, though. I think Miss Tameka needs somethin' to relax her."

"Alright, then," Lexis said. "You be careful with my sister."

"C'mon, Lexis. You know I will," he said as he kissed me on the cheek.

"Well, if you're sure you'll be alright..." Tielle said.

"I'll be fine, Tielle. Y'all go on back in there and have a good time. I know Romeo's probably waitin' on you."

"I'll call you tomorrow," she said.

"I'll see you at home," Alexis said as we hugged.

"Alright, y'all. Have fun!"

TJ and I got in his car and drove off.

When Tielle and Alexis went back in the club, Romeo was waiting. "Is everything alright?" he asked.

"Yeah, Tameka's cool. She's goin' home," she replied.

21

"So, you wanna sit down and talk?"

"Yeah, that's fine."

He was 25, graduated from Clark Atlanta University with a bachelor's degree in art and a head buyer at a major gallery. She was glad to hear that he didn't have any kids and that he owned a two-bedroom condo.

She told him she had a communications degree from the University of Michigan and was a disc jockey at WTIZ, a local radio station.

"Oh, so that's you I hear in the mornings? Are you LT?"

"Yeah."

"What made you come and talk to me earlier at the mall?" Tielle inquired.

"I can't just stand around and not say anything when I see a fine woman."

"You are a trip," she said as she laughed. "No wonder why your mama named you Romeo. She must've known how you were gonna turn out."

"I'm serious. I'm not tryin' to spit game or nothin' like that."

"Well, you're definitely charismatic. I've never met anybody like you."

Chapter 2

They stayed until three, when the club was shutting down. Tielle, Romeo, Nina, and Kaelin went to the IHOP, and Alexis and Robert went to our place. TJ and I wound up at Nick's, a small bar and lounge near the IHOP.

TJ was a sweetheart. We sat in Nick's and reminisced until about four. He kept the drinks and the laughs going to keep my mind off of kicking Dap in her throat. After we left, we sat in the alley and talked in his car for another half hour or so. He parked back there so those clowns who were after him wouldn't see it.

His plans didn't work, because as we were debating about who approached who on the day we first met, a guy went up to TJ's window and pointed a gun at him through the glass. TJ pushed me onto the floor and grabbed his own gun. The guy ordered him to get out of the car, and TJ obliged, tackling him and holding him at gunpoint on the damp asphalt. He yelled for me to drive off.

I got up from my crouching position and slid into the driver's seat. As I started to bring my other leg over the hump, the passenger door opened and another man got in. He was dressed like the one attacking TJ, but he had on a hat and a bandana covering everything but his eyes. His counterpart only wore a bandana.

I tried my best to hurry and step on the gas, but the guy grabbed my leg and took the keys out of the ignition. "You ain't goin' nowhere," he growled.

"Let me go!" I yelled, kicking him in the chest and struggling to get free. "TJ!" I could hear him and the other guy fighting right outside the car.

"Leave her alone!" TJ yelled.

He didn't pay him any mind. Instead, he locked my leg under his and ran his fingers across my cheek. "Damn! My boy didn't tell me you look like this."

"Get off me!"

"Play nice," he said as he kissed just below my lips. "I want this to feel real good to you."

I suddenly noticed the muffled sound of the live band in Nick's and chirping crickets were the only noises I heard. I started crying. "What did he do with TJ? Why are you bothering me?" I asked.

"I'm just here to make you feel good while my boy handles that nigga, sweetheart." He kissed me on the cheek, then moved down to my neck.

I wiped my face and squirmed to get away. I tried to take the calm approach, praying that maybe he would listen to reason. "Please leave me alone. I won't tell anybody anything. I don't even know what you look like."

"I'm about to show you what I feel like," he said. He grabbed himself. "Look what you did."

His breath smelled like Jack Daniels and nachos, and his eyes were a piercing dark brown. All I could do was cry harder as he flung me into the back seat and ripped my pants open. It was the first time in my life that I'd ever felt helpless. Between the fear and the alcohol, any sense of coordination and ability to defend myself was out the window. I could feel his penis getting harder as he laid on top of me and pulled my shirt up. As he sucked on my breast, I tried my best to scream, but nothing came out. I thought of ways to escape, but there really weren't any. He was too big for me to push off, and he had my arms pinned above my head. He pulled his pants down with his free hand and shoved himself inside of me. My body slid across the cold leather seat and my head rammed against the door handle.

The suffocating smell of must, sex, and alcohol engulfed the car and fogged the windows, and I couldn't decide whether I wanted to hold my breath or try to scream again. I sobbed as I listened to him grunt and moan on top of me. Every time his body slammed against mine, huge drops of his sweat dripped onto my face. I felt violated with each thrust, and I thought I was gonna throw up each time he forced his tongue down my throat. If that wasn't enough to disgust me, I had to lay there and listen to him tell me that he was doing it because of TJ and to thank him the next time I saw him.

After about five minutes that seemed like five hours, the guy got up. Before he exited the car, he told me that he'd kill me if I ever told the cops. I laid there in the backseat, sore, battered, and scared. I couldn't believe TJ left me. I was paralyzed with shock and muted by terror. I heard police sirens, but evidently they weren't coming for me, because they faded away within seconds.

***

Tielle said goodbye to Romeo. They were standing outside of the IHOP, watching the three police cruisers speed by. "I'll give you a call tomorrow," Romeo said. "Maybe we can get together or somethin'."

"Okay," Tielle replied. They hugged, and Romeo got in his car and drove off.

Nina said goodbye to Kaelin and Tielle. "Hey, why don't y'all walk me to my car? I don't know where those police cars are going," she said.

"Come on, scaredy cat. You shouldn't have parked in the alley anyway," Kaelin teased.

The three of them walked behind the restaurant to Nina's car. After Nina drove off, Tielle and Kaelin started back down the alley. "What time is it?" Kaelin asked.

"Ten 'til five," Tielle answered.

"Damn! We've been in there forever."

"I know." Tielle stopped to fix her shoe while her sister casually looked around. "We need to hurry up and get home so I can get outta these things," she continued.

Kaelin was preoccupied. "Ain't that TJ's car?"

"Where?" Tielle stood up and looked down the alley. "Yeah, that's his car. It don't look like nobody's in it, though."

"I know, and he don't just leave his car parked in no alley."

They looked at each other and headed toward the vehicle. "I hope ain't nothin' wrong," Tielle said.

"I hope they ain't in there bonin'," Kaelin added. "I'm not tryin' to see that." They approached the car and looked through the tinted driver's side window. "I don't see nobody."

"Hold up," Tielle said with suspicion. "What's that in the back?"

"It looks like a person. I hope TJ didn't smoke somebody."

"He might have, but he ain't stupid enough to leave 'em in his car. That don't make sense. But Meka did say some dudes came to her house this mornin'."

She moved to the back window. All she could see was a body that was covered with a black jacket. As she pressed her forehead against the glass to see more clearly, she saw long hair hanging from one part of the jacket.

25

"Oh my goodness," she said. "That's Tameka. She probably fell asleep after they did it. You know they'll get down anywhere. Maybe TJ's in the IHOP and we just missed him." She knocked on the window.

***

I cried silently to myself, hoping the monster hadn't come back. Tielle knocked harder, yelling my name this time. As she tugged on the door handle, I raised up to a sitting position. I looked out to make sure that it was her and manually unlocked the door. Once she opened it and the interior light came on, she immediately looked concerned.

"What happened to your face? What's wrong, Meka? Why are you shakin' like that?"

"Tielle, I didn't ask for this."

"You didn't ask for what?" she asked.

"I'ma go get the car," Kaelin said. She ran down the alley.

"He said he wouldn't ever let anything happen to me," I continued. I clenched the jacket tightly and rocked back and forth. "I shoulda went home."

"Tameka, you gotta tell me what happened. Where's TJ? Did he beat you up?"

I shook my head, no. More tears welled up in my eyes. "He raped me," I blurted. As soon as I said it, I had another outburst of tears.

"TJ raped you?" Tielle asked, enraged. I shook my head again. When she asked who did it, I just shrugged my shoulders. "Oh my God," she said. I could see the tears in her eyes.

She helped me out of the car, into the back seat of Kaelin's car.

"So what happened?" Kaelin asked.

"Somebody raped her," Tielle answered. "We're goin' to her house."

"Shouldn't we be goin' to the hospital?"

"We're goin' to her house first. We need to get Lexis."

I was still shaking when we walked in the house. Kaelin and Tielle helped me to the couch where I curled my body tightly into a little ball. Tielle yelled up the steps for Alexis. Finally, she came dragging down the steps in her robe.

"What you come in here screamin' for? Some people *are* sleep," she said with an attitude. "Meka, you just gettin' here?"

26

"You need to get dressed," Tielle told her. "We gotta go to the hospital."

"For what?"

"Somebody raped Meka," Tielle replied, trying not to cry.

"They what?" Alexis asked. She walked over to the couch and sat down beside me. She pushed my hair away from my face and hugged me. "Meka, I'm so sorry." She wiped away her tears as more fell.

"We found her in TJ's car in the alley behind the IHOP," Tielle continued.

"I can call the hospital and tell them we comin'," Kaelin said.

"Yeah, that's a good idea," Alexis replied. In a comforting voice, she asked, "Did TJ do this to you?"

"No," I answered.

"Who did it?"

"I don't know. I don't wanna know. I don't wanna talk about it," I said, my voice cold and frightened. "I just wanna take a shower and lay down."

Kaelin came back into the living room. "They want you at the hospital," she said.

"I'm not going," I said, staring into space.

"Tameka, you have to," Alexis said.

"I'm not going."

Kaelin stepped in. "Tameka, you can't be stubborn about this. You have to get this done so they can find the guy who did it."

I knew they were right, but I didn't care. I just wanted to forget about the whole night. I wanted every trace of that man washed off of me, and I couldn't wait to burn the clothes I had on.

"I'ma go start the car," Tielle said. She went outside.

"Kaelin, can you get Meka a jacket out of the closet over there?" Alexis asked.

"I wanna change my clothes," I said.

"Baby, you can't do that yet. The police might find something— a hair, a piece of skin—anything that leads them to this guy," Alexis said.

I started crying again. Kaelin helped me put my jacket on, and she walked me to the car. Alexis ran upstairs, changed her clothes, and left Robert a note.

As we walked into the emergency room, I felt like all eyes were on me. There were two police officers waiting at the front desk, ready to hear all the details of my disgraceful encounter. The receptionist checked me in, and a nurse took me back to Room 5. Alexis joined me in the small space, and Tielle and Kaelin waited in the designated area.

I was told to undress and put on a backless gown. The nurse placed my panties in a special bag and put the rest of my clothing in another container. She drew blood for HIV and pregnancy tests and swabbed the inside of my mouth with an oversized Q-Tip. A female doctor entered the room and examined me, trying her best to make me feel comfortable. I felt nothing but humiliation, though, as she combed through my pubic hairs and dabbed blood and semen from my inner thigh with a wet gauze pad. After the exam, the nurse tended to the cuts, scrapes, and bruises on my face, arms, and legs.

The police took my clothes as evidence, and I was given hospital scrubs to wear home. The detectives asked me tons of questions, most of which I couldn't answer. I couldn't tell them anything about what the guy looked like, except that he had dark brown eyes and wore a black hoodie with tan Dickies. They were relying on the DNA tests that could be run on hairs or bodily fluids found on my clothes and hoping they could find the dude before he changed clothes.

Before I left the hospital, they let me take a shower. Even after I was done, I still felt grimy and nasty. The smell of his saliva lingered on my upper lip, and I felt like his greasy fingerprints were still on me. If I washed another time, though, I was afraid that I would remove skin.

As we were on our way out the door, something on the front desk caught my eye. It was one of those daily calendars that had the big number in the center and small words. It read, "Today is June 6" and served as a reminder of the worst day of my life.

I took off work for two weeks and spent the first two days cooped up in my room with the curtains and blinds closed. Mary J. Blige's *My Life*, Toni Braxton's *Secrets*, and Whitney Houston's *Greatest Hits: Disc 1* were on repeat in my CD player in that order, and every time the songs, "My Life," "How Could an Angel Break My Heart," and "All At Once" came on, I'd cry like it was the first time I'd ever heard them.

I only left my bed to go to the bathroom and take showers. Alexis brought my meals to me. It was killing her that she couldn't do anything else to help me. I didn't feel like talking, so the most I would say to her was, "Thanks" when she handed me the food, and I wouldn't accept any phone calls—not even from Tielle.

Alexis called our parents to let them know what happened. She couldn't reach our dad. His 28 year-old fiancé said he was in Vegas for a week with his boss and that she couldn't get in touch with him. Our mom was supposedly upset. I don't understand how she can be so upset but have to ask if her daughter really needs her because she has to work (even though she's been living off of my dad's alimony for years). Once Alexis told me her response, I remembered why I only talked to her every four or five months.

By the third day, the phone was ringing off the hook. The incident had been reported in the news, the paper, and on the streets. Before long, people knew I was the rape victim. We all know I don't have that many friends, so who was calling? Nosey-ass people. TJ hadn't even called, and that hurt me deeply. I guess he really didn't give a damn when it came down to it. If something happened to him that night, most likely it would've made the news, but Travis M. Jones' name wasn't reported at all.

At the end of the week, I migrated downstairs. I still didn't have much to say to anyone, which was beginning to piss Alexis off. I heard her on the phone with the doctor when she called to check on me. Lexis asked her why I was still so withdrawn and what she could do to help me. I felt bad, but I just didn't have any meaningful conversation, and the only thing everybody wanted to discuss was the rape.

The following Monday, Dr. Crenshaw called with the results of my STD tests. She said I didn't have anything, and I was totally relieved. She informed me that my HIV test results wouldn't be in for about another week, but I knew I didn't have to worry about that. I figured I'd get something small like chlamydia or gonorrhea before I got HIV.

Later that afternoon, Detective Nelson called. He was one of the men who initially questioned me. He told me that they had a possible suspect in custody.

"Who is it?" I asked.

"I really don't want to get into that over the phone," Detective Nelson answered.

"Well, why did you call me?" I asked with an attitude. The police had been pissing me off all week because they weren't doing their job. They kept feeding me bullshit about how things take time. They had plenty of time to catch the dude who did that to me, and he'd had plenty of time to skip town.

"We need to see if you can identify the man in a lineup," the detective continued.

"If he's gon' have on a hat and a bandana covering his face, I'll point him out with no problem."

I arrived at the police station at four. Detective Nelson and a fat white cop led me into a room like the one I always saw on *New York Undercover*, with glass on one side and a mirror on the other. They told me to let them know if I recognized any of the guys once they brought them in.

"Before we start, I have a question," I said. "How did y'all find this guy?"

"We were able to match a hair found on your shirt to this guy's DNA. There's also another guy who was just picked up for raping a young lady behind the corner store on the block where you were raped," the fat guy said.

"Alright. Bring 'em on," I said. Seven guys came out and stood against the wall. "Oh my God!"

"Do you see 'em?" Detective Nelson asked. His tone didn't hide his excitement.

"What the hell is TJ doin' here?"

"Who?"

"Number four."

"Do you identify him as the rapist?" the fat guy asked.

"No! He's my ex-boyfriend. He was with me that night. Shouldn't y'all have that in the report? I told y'all he was gettin' beat up by the other guy."

"Well, Ms. James," Detective Nelson said. "His hair was the one we found on your shirt."

"No shit! We were together all night and it probably got on me when we hugged. Damn my shirt! Y'all need to be checkin' my pants and my underwear. That's where the rapist was," I yelled. "Plus, I told y'all that I wouldn't know the dude if I saw him without a disguise. For all I know, I could've passed him on my way here. Do some real investigative work, then call me!"

I stormed out of the room. The entire lobby must've heard me because they were staring as I maneuvered past them. Fat boy waddled after me, and Detective Nelson stood in the doorway calling my name, but I kept it moving. They had wasted my time, giving me false hopes, and I had to leave before they locked me up for choking one of their incompetent asses.

When I got home, I told Alexis what happened. We must've sat there and bad-mouthed them for a good twenty minutes. It was cool because it was the first time we'd had a real conversation since the dreaded night.

"So do you think that's why TJ hasn't called? 'Cause he's been locked up?" she asked.

"Nope. The way the police were talkin', they just brought him in today."

"Damn. I can't believe him."

"You find out who your real friends are when you hit rock bottom."

"Do you really think he'd leave you out there by yourself?"

"He did, didn't he?"

"I guess," Alexis said. "I just don't understand. There's got to be more to it."

"Whatever," I said. "The facts are the facts."

Alexis was quiet for a few seconds. "Do you still have those nightmares?" Her voice was soft, with a hint of caution.

"Sometimes," I answered. We sat silently again. I'd never told her about my nightmares, but she said she knew because she would hear me scream. Many nights, she made a pile-it at the foot of my bed, hoping that in some way her presence would fight away the demons that haunted my sleep. I never knew she was around because she'd leave the room before I woke up. After she revealed her little secret, I realized how much she cared, and for the first time in four years, I felt close to my sister again.

Minutes later, I told her how the rapist's voice still rang in my ears and his scent lingered in my pores. I told her I was scared to have sex again—almost disgusted by the thought of a man kissing or touching me. It was something I was determined to overcome because I didn't want that sick stranger to ruin the rest of my life. How was I supposed to move on if I allowed my encounter with him to affect my future relationships? Nevertheless, I had to take it one day at a time and trust that the day I wouldn't feel violated would come sooner than later.

We ate dinner and talked about regular stuff. She caught me up on everything that went on while I was in seclusion. Tielle and Romeo were going out on the regular. Lexis said they were meeting for lunch quite frequently and had gone to the movies twice the previous weekend. I knew I had to talk to Tielle, because he had to be something special—it wasn't her character to have a dude up under her all the time.

Lexis also told me how nosey people are. She said three girls at her job asked who raped me, what was I gon' do about it, was I leaving town, and every other question imaginable. Every deacon, deaconess, minister, and choir member from my church and a few other churches had called to see how I was doing. I'm sure some of them were actually sincere, but most of them had never said a mumbling word to me because they were too busy judging me as the girl who used to work down at the devil's playground, stripping. Half of them wouldn't have known about my previous occupation if their husbands weren't tucking dollar bills in my g-string and asking if I could "just touch it one time" every Friday and Saturday night.

I looked at the mantle lined with flowers from my coworkers and my mom. Out of all the names on the flower arrangements and cards, still no TJ. No concern from the man I put my life in danger for (many times)—the same man who claimed he'd die for me.

Chapter 3

It was seven o'clock. Alexis and I were watching Jeopardy when the phone rang.

"You want me to get it?" she asked, looking at the caller ID. "It's unavailable."

"Yeah," I replied.

She answered the phone. "Un unh, she don't wanna talk to you."

"Who is that?" I asked.

She mouthed TJ's name. I don't know where I got the strength from, but I told her to give me the phone. I wanted to see what kind of excuse he could come up with for leaving me by myself in a dark ass alley.

She covered the phone. "Are you sure?"

"Yeah," I said. As soon as she handed it to me, I started snapping. "What do you want?"

"Damn! I can't get a 'Hi. How you doin'? Sorry to hear that you got pistol-whipped, dragged into the woods and left there, and that you had to hide out at your grandmother's house, only to have the police find you there and bring you in over some bitch who's sayin' she got raped?'" TJ snapped back.

I thought I was gonna lose it. "You heartless son of a bitch! I'm sorry that you got pistol-whipped. I didn't know that. Maybe if you didn't do all of the crooked shit you do, you wouldn't have been in that situation. And maybe it's my muthafuckin' fault that I still chose to deal with your ass after knowin' what you do for a living. I mean, after all, I wouldn't be the bitch goin' around sayin' she was raped if I wasn't hangin' around you," I yelled as tears streamed down my face.

"So I'm sorry if I can't engulf you in apologies. I'm goin' through some pretty rough shit myself," I continued. I threw the

33

phone down and ran into the bathroom. When I get upset, it's what I usually do.

Alexis grabbed the phone. "What the fuck did you say to her?"

"She got raped?" TJ asked.

"Yeah, TJ. She's the reason you were in the lineup today. The police found your hair on her shirt."

"Oh shit. Hold up. Who raped her?"

"One of your thug buddies—the other dude who was in the car with her."

"I'ma kill them niggas," TJ yelled before he hung up.

When I came out of the bathroom, Alexis kept her eye on me, but tried not to be obvious. I could tell she didn't know what to say.

"I can't believe he didn't know," she said after a while.

"Please. TJ knew what went on. It was all over the news. Don't fall for that shit."

"But Meka, he was hidin' out at his grandma's. You know she don't believe in watchin' TV, and TJ's ghetto ass don't read the paper."

"Whatever. TJ can kiss my ass. You can believe him, but I don't."

"Was his face messed up when you saw him earlier?"

"It looked like he was in a fight or somethin', but I don't believe that pistol-whip story either. It don't take more than a week to call and check on somebody. He wasn't in no coma."

"I think he's goin' after those dudes tonight. At least that's what it sounded like."

"He should've already been tryin' to find them if they hurt him so bad."

The phone rang again. I prayed that it wasn't TJ calling back. Alexis looked at the caller ID and answered it.

"What's up, cuz?" she said.

"Hey, what's goin' on?" It was our cousin, Jermaine. Last I knew, he was living in Florida, working as an intern at some record company. I was really proud of him because he used to be involved with gangs and drugs, but he moved away and got his life together.

"Are you still at the record company?" Alexis continued.

"Yeah, I just got promoted two months ago. They hired me on permanently."

"That's cool. You know you gon' have to hook me up with one of those fine ass rappers, right?" They laughed and made small talk

34

for a few minutes. "Hey, I don't mean to be rude, but what made you call us all of a sudden?" Alexis asked.

"Aunt Gina called me earlier today to see if I was gonna come over for dinner. We was talkin' a lil' bit, and she told me what happened to Meka. How's she doin'?" he asked.

Alexis went into the kitchen. "She doin' as good as could be expected," she whispered. "She's just takin' it one day at a time."

"I'm comin' up there."

"For what?"

"Aunt Gina said she's comin' up there in a couple weeks, so I told her I'd come too."

"Come on, Jermaine. Why you really comin'?"

"Look," he said with a sigh. "Aunt Gina said the police didn't find the dude who did this to Meka. I figure I'll come do a little detective work of my own."

"That's what I'm talkin' 'bout!" I heard Alexis yell. I didn't know what they were discussing, but I figured he was gonna bring her some good weed the next time he visited or he told her he'd introduce her to somebody at the record company.

"Listen. Don't say nothin' to Meka about me comin'. You know how she is. She'll think I'ma get caught up or somethin'. You know she's Miss Goody Two Shoes now," Jermaine continued.

"I got you," Alexis agreed.

Shortly after that, they hung up. When I asked Lexis what Jermaine wanted, she just said he wanted to see how I was doing and that he'd call back later because he had to get back to work. I didn't ask too many questions about their conversation, because I knew she'd probably tell me something that I didn't want or need to hear.

Sunday, Tielle came over after church. She'd asked me to go with her, but I wasn't ready to be around all those people. There ain't nobody worse than church folk sometimes. They'll talk about you the worst, right after they put holy water on your head and pray over you. She told me I was on the prayer list and that a lot of people were asking about me. Oh well. Like I said, I don't trust them.

I told her about TJ's ignorant ass and my equally ignorant mother. Tielle didn't understand why my mother would act like that because I'd never told her why my mom and I didn't get along. My parents rarely came up in discussions, but when they did, I would get off the subject quickly. The only person besides Alexis who knows where my hatred for my mother stems from is Nicole, my other best friend. We go way back, back to third grade, before I moved to Texas.

She still lives in Ohio, and we try to visit each other at least three times a year. She's a freelance photographer, so she can still work while she's on vacation, too. After I was raped, she was so upset that she couldn't come console me. Alexis reached her on her cell phone while she was on a shoot in Montana for *National Geographic*, but she couldn't leave. At my last count, she had sent two bouquets of flowers, three inspirational cards, eight emails, and a care package with our favorite penny candy and other reminders of our childhood. Her instructions were to accept those tokens of love until she could come visit at the end of the month.

Tielle and I ate dinner, and she told me she was really digging Romeo. I asked her if they'd kissed yet.

"Yeah, but girl, I try not to kiss him too much, 'cause he gon' mess around and make me drop the panties," she said.

"Is it like that?" I asked. "Never would he make super-glue coochie Tielle give it up before the three month trial period!"

"Kiss my ass, Tameka."

On the 19th, I woke up at eight o'clock. My appointment wasn't until eleven, so I had time to fix breakfast before I left. I don't know how I kept anything down because I was so nervous about getting my HIV test results. That was my first time being tested…ever. You can't even prepare yourself to hear that you have HIV. How are you supposed to react? What are you supposed to do if the results come back positive?

As I walked through the hospital entrance, I had a flashback of the night I was there. I stared at the calendar at the nurse's station, blinking to erase the image of "June 6" from my eyes.

I sat in the waiting room for a half hour. My nerves were shot. I had skimmed through every article in *People* magazine, and I was about to grab the *Newsweek* when I heard a nurse call my name. As I walked into Dr. Crenshaw's office, I took a deep breath.

"Look," I said quickly. "I just wanna know my results, so can we cut the small talk?"

"Well," she said, shocked by my straightforwardness. "Okay, I guess I can do that. Can I ask how you're doing mentally, though?"

"What you mean? I ain't crazy or nothin'."

"Rape can be a huge mental strain, Tameka. Dealing with this can affect your job as well as your relationships with those close to you."

"I'm maintaining. The only mental strain I'm under right now is the one you puttin' me under. Can you please tell me the results?"

After she explained the logistics of how the tests were done, she said, "Your tests came back negative, Tameka."

I swear I could've grabbed her and hugged her. I felt like a huge weight had been lifted off of my shoulders. I had to get retested every six months to make sure the virus hadn't entered my system and just not shown up. So before I left, I thanked her and went to the receptionist to schedule my appointment for December.

When I got home, I called Nicole and told her the good news. Then I told Alexis. I explained to her that I wasn't totally in the clear because I'd have to get tested every six months for the next few years.

"Girl, whatever," she said. "You ain't got AIDS. Now all they gotta do is find the nigga who did this, and everything'll be cool."

"Yeah, I guess."

"Girl, don't tell me you still depressed. I mean, I know you upset and everything, but you need to get over it. Go out and start doin' some shit. Get your mind off of it," Alexis said as she walked in circles, looking for her keys.

I didn't entertain her comment. The look on my face spoke for me. The old, insensitive Alexis was back.

"You can look at me crazy if you want to, but you ain't sayin' nothin' 'cause you know I'm tellin' the truth." She found her keys and headed toward the door. "I'll be out kinda late, so you don't have to cook for me." Just as she stepped out the door, she said, "Call Tielle or somethin'. Maybe she can think of a way to get yo ass out the house."

When she left, I threw the May issue of *Essence* at the door. "Bitch!"

I was too mad to cry, so I paced around the house, mumbling to myself. Yeah, maybe I should've tried to get out and take my mind off my troubles, but what about when I went to sleep and had the recurring nightmare of the rapist coming to my house and attacking me again? What about the random times throughout the day when I smelled his stench and dry-heaved at the memory of his body on mine? Or how about the fact that I didn't know what he looked like, so he could sit right beside me at the movie theater and I'd have no clue? How was I supposed to escape that? Was leaving the house gonna change those things?

***

Alexis knocked on Tiffany's door. It was her first time visiting her at her new place. She'd been there for about three months, but she and Alexis had fallen out about five months prior.

Tiffany and I were pretty cool, despite her connection to Dap. She's Marlon's babymama, and Marlon is Dap's brother. From my understanding, she tolerated the ignorant cow, but didn't really fancy hanging around her too much.

Tiffany answered the door with her youngest son, Tony, in her arms.

"Come on in," Tiffany said. "These kids 'bout to drive me crazy."

Tiffany handed Tony to Alexis. "So what took you so long to get over here? You said two o'clock."

"I would've been here if I wasn't arguin' with Meka."

"What was y'all arguin' about this time?"

"I don't even remember. That's how stupid it was. She always has an attitude about somethin'."

"Maybe you should give her a little space. You know, be a little more sensitive to her situation. I remember this chick on *Oprah* was talkin' about how messed up in the head she was after she had been raped, and I think it had been like two years. Her family said she had all kinds of mood swings and she was depressed. It's kinda like that child molestation stuff," Tiffany continued. "Some people never get over that."

"Man, whatever," Alexis said. "I'm tired of everybody tellin' me to be sensitive to her needs. Fuck that. Everybody caters to Tameka, whether it's her dude, her job, her friends…I try my best to be cool with that chick, and every time, she manages to piss me off."

"That sounds like a personal problem," Tiffany suggested. "Maybe you need some counselin' or somethin'," she joked. "You talkin' like this goes back to y'alls childhood."

"Go to hell, Tiffany. Just 'cause you goin' to school for psychology don't mean you need to go around makin' up shit like you really know what you talkin' about."

"Don't be mad at me," Tiffany said. "Y'all the crazy ones. It sounds like you jealous to me. I'ma keep it real with you. You know that." She walked into the kitchen. "Now c'mon, the food is ready."

After they ate, Tiffany put the kids to bed, and she and Alexis sat on the back porch with their Black & Milds.

"Did Tameka go back to work yet?"

"Hell naw. I told you they let her do what she wants around there. She's off for two weeks."

"Two? Well, I guess that's not too bad considering what she went through."

"She's livin' the life at that job. But of course when I applied, the bastards didn't hire me."

"What'd you apply for? I mean, what position?"

"Entry-level, girl! And still didn't get hired. All I wanted to do was some data entry or somethin'. Hell, start me in the mailroom!"

"Tameka couldn't help you?"

"Tameka wouldn't help me. I asked her to talk to the people, but she kept hollerin' about me bein' irresponsible. All I wanted was a chance, you know? Maybe I'd stay at a job if I actually liked it."

"That's shady. She could've at least given you a chance."

"Exactly. But I bet if Tielle wanted to work there, she'd be the first one singin' her praises to Human Resources."

"You just gon' have to be the bigger person," Tiffany said. "Just try to deal with her until this whole rape thing blows over. Either that, or move in with Robert."

"I thought about that, but all bullshit aside, I really don't know how to survive without Tameka. I mean, she's been the only constant in my life since Mom and Dad moved away." Tears welled up in her eyes, but she refused to let them fall. "Even after all the fucked up shit I've done and said to her, she still hasn't kicked me out or nothin'. She don't need me at that place. Meka had already planned on getting a two bedroom by herself, but she said I could move in."

"Maybe y'all just need to sit down and talk about all this stuff you tellin' me."

"I can't. It's like, whenever I want to talk to her, she's either busy or in one of her fucked up moods. Then the times when she's in a good mood, I forget about the bad shit because I just wanna enjoy her company…It's a shame I gotta come over here and vent to you."

They sat in silence. All kinds of thoughts ran through Alexis' head as she played with her fingers and nibbled at the inside surface of her jaw.

"I've never told my sister that I love her," Alexis said softly. "Not since I was like 11 or 12."

"Well, do you?" Tiffany asked.

"More than anything in the world. I'm just not into that mushy shit. I can never get the words out. I think I resent her at the same time, you know? I mean, don't get me wrong, I'm proud of her for

39

bein' successful, but I don't understand how we're so much alike, but I can't have what she has. And I'm tryin' not to feel like that, but it's like she throws the shit in my face everyday, just by me living there with her."

"Does she say it to you?"

"Yeah, she don't have a problem sayin' it." A tear trickled down her face. "Do you know how much it hurts when you can't tell your own sister you love her too?"

Chapter 4

Tielle came to the house at five. She convinced me to go to Ponderosa with her so we could catch up. We'd talked on the phone almost every day of the past week, but she thought I should get out of the house. Since she was one of the many who'd suggested that, I figured I'd finally give it a try.

Once we got our first plates, we sat in a booth by the front window.

"I need national recognition for gettin' you out the house," Tielle said.

"Shut up," I laughed. "It feels good, though. I get to see some folks besides Lexis."

"Right. Now, my next challenge is to find you a man." Tielle became visibly uncomfortable after she realized what she said. "I mean, whenever you're ready," she corrected herself.

"I know what you mean."

It wasn't like I hated the entire male species. I just couldn't picture myself in a relationship any time soon. I could tell that Tielle was still a little uncomfortable so I changed the subject.

"So what's up with you and Mr. Romeo?"

"Girl," she said with a huge grin. "He is so sweet."

"So are y'all still meetin' for lunch every day?" I asked.

"No, not every day. We still see each other a lot, though."

"You haven't found out that he has any kids or no crazy shit like that, have you?"

"Nope. No kids, no crazy ex-girlfriends in town, no nosey mother…"

"Hold up," I interrupted. "How do you know what his mother is like?"

"She was at his house the other day, and he invited me over."

"Okay, you scarin' me, now. I know for a fact that you don't go around meetin' a nigga's parents after a few weeks. Talk to me, now. What's the deal?"

"Naw girl, it wasn't even like that. He told me that he was cookin' dinner and invited me over. When I got there, his mom was there. He set me up."

By our second plate, Tielle and I had discussed the infamous TJ. I told her how he had been calling every day, all day, only to speak to the answering machine.

"So you ain't gon' talk to him again?"

"Probably not—not after what he said on the phone that day. I don't even wanna hear his voice."

"Maybe it's for the best. He'll just be a constant reminder of what happened."

"Yeah, you're right." I started to feel a little uneasy again. "But let's talk about somethin' else."

"Cool," Tielle agreed.

"What are y'all doin' next week for the Fourth?"

"We'll probably have a barbeque out at Cedar's Run again. I think my mom reserved it last month."

"That's cool."

"You know you welcomed to come if you ain't doin' nothin' else."

"Is it gonna be a big family thing?"

"And friends. But I think we'll have a few more family members comin' this year. I talked to my cousin, Craig, yesterday and he said he'll probably be here."

"Craig," I recited in an effort to remember him. "Do I know him?"

"Un unh," Tielle replied. "You met his brother, Chauncey, last Thanksgiving, though."

"Oh yeah! I remember Chauncey. He's a big dude, right?"

"Yeah. Craig ain't as big as Chauncey, though."

"How old is Craig?"

"I think Chauncey's 28, so that'll make Craig like 25."

We finished eating and rode around to see who was out. The basketball courts were full, so we stopped. Gary, Kaelin's boyfriend, saw us and ran over to the car.

"What y'all up to?" he asked.

"Nothin'," we said in unison.

"You talk to Kaelin today?" Tielle asked him.

"Yeah, she should be here in a little bit. My game starts in 20 minutes."

I swear Gary was the finest white boy I had ever seen. To hear him tell it, he's Italian and black because his dad is half black and half white, and his mama's Italian. I try to say as little as possible to him because I know that after I say 'Hi', anything else I'd say would be laced with flirtation.

While we were talking to Gary, a car pulled up beside us with tinted windows. The music was blaring, and the bass thumped so hard that you could barely hear the melody of the song, let alone the words. The driver rolled his window down and asked if we knew Kendall King. Gary went around to the car and tried to explain where the guy lived. Tielle and I glanced over at the raggedy group. We figured they were just some teenagers with a new stereo system who just wanted to show off.

Suddenly, I heard a familiar voice. "Hey, dawg, where da hoes at?" the passenger asked. Gary laughed and continued to give the driver directions.

Tielle looked at me and rolled her eyes. "Did you hear that?" A cold chill ran through me as my jaw dropped. "What's wrong?" she asked. "Who do you see?" She looked in the direction that I was staring but saw nothing.

I was just looking that way because I was scared to turn my head. That voice was the same one that came from the guy who raped me. My heart pounded and I could feel my stomach turning. I slowly turned my head to get a good look at the dude, but Gary was in the way. Tielle was still asking me what was wrong, but I couldn't answer her. I leaned forward in my seat to get a better view. He took a drink of his beer, then turned towards the driver. Immediately, I recognized his eyes and quickly turned my head. Seconds later, I was hyperventilating.

Both the driver and the passenger looked over at me. I faintly heard Tielle ask me if I was okay, but I gave no response. The passenger must've recognized me, because his friend drove off without getting the rest of the directions.

After about a minute, I pulled myself together. I told Tielle why I reacted the way I did, and she immediately drove in the direction the guys went. We were on a mission to get a license plate number, a better description of the car…something. We rode around for about fifteen minutes with no luck.

Tielle grabbed her cell phone and started dialing a number.

"Who are you calling?" I asked.

"The police."

"Girl, there ain't no use in callin' them. What are we gon' say? Hey, we saw the guy, but we don't know where he went?"

"We have a description of the car," Tielle said as she pushed the send button.

She was always optimistic, even when it came to the sorry ass police department. She spoke to Detective Nelson and gave him the information about the car. By the time she hung up with him, we had pulled into my complex.

We went inside, and Alexis and Robert were sitting in the living room.

"What's up, y'all?" Robert asked.

"Drama," Tielle answered.

"What's that supposed to mean?" Alexis asked.

"I just saw the guy who raped me," I said.

"What?" Alexis said, jumping up. "Where was he? Did he try to come after you?"

I told her the story.

"Dammit!" Alexis yelled, frustrated that we didn't catch up with the bastard.

"I called the police and gave them a description of the car, though," Tielle said.

"That's all you could do," Robert responded.

"What's that smell?" I asked. I was tired of discussing my depressing life.

"Robert cooked shrimp," Alexis answered.

"Aw, how sweet," Tielle said. "I didn't know you had it in you, Rob."

"Yeah, you know. I can do a lil' somethin'."

"Well it smells good," I said. "Enjoy."

I headed upstairs to my room. Tielle stayed downstairs for a little while. Robert went into the kitchen to put some final touches on the food.

Alexis motioned for Tielle to join her on the couch.

"What's up?" Tielle asked.

"We need to find somebody for my sister. I think she needs to meet a nice guy—soon. You know…get back in the mix."

"I don't think she's ready right now."

"Do you see how depressed she is, though? She hides it well, but I still see it."

"I think a man is the last thing she needs."

"It could be the best thing to happen to her, though. If somebody shows her attention, maybe she'll get her confidence back and stop thinking that nobody wants her now that she's been raped."

"You got somebody in mind?" Tielle asked. It was obvious that Alexis' mind was made up.

"Not really. I figured you might know somebody—maybe one of Romeo's friends or somebody from the radio station."

"I can check with Romeo, but I don't know nobody at the station who's Tameka's speed," Tielle said. "Where is all this coming from?"

"TJ called earlier, and I started thinkin'. He's the only one who calls. How's she supposed to move on when he keeps cryin' about how sorry he is every day? I mean, don't get me wrong, he used to treat Meka right, but she ain't feelin' him right now. Plus, I blame him for the situation she's in right now."

"Meka doesn't need help findin' a man. How many dudes approach her every day?"

"And how many have their shit together?" Alexis asked. "You know she likes those college graduate, briefcase totin', clean cut niggas. The only one who slipped past her standards was TJ."

"And he's gon' keep slippin' past. They're connected, like it or not."

"Not if I can help it. If it wasn't for him, she wouldn't even be goin' through this."

Tielle shrugged helplessly. "I'll keep my eyes open."

Tielle left, and Robert and Alexis had dinner. I know how much Alexis appreciated it because I was awakened at two o'clock by Robert's moans of pleasure. I was mad that they woke me up, but amused by Alexis' pleas for him to be quiet before he woke me.

Since I was up, I went to the bathroom and ran downstairs to get a glass of orange juice. As I walked out of the kitchen, the phone rang.

"Who in the hell?" I said as I looked at the clock.

"Hello?" I answered, unable to hide my attitude.

"Meka, don't hang up," TJ said on the other end.

"What do you want?"

"I'm callin' to apologize for what I said the last time we talked. I didn't know that happened to you."

"Okay. Mission accomplished."

"Don't hang up!" he yelled in desperation.

"TJ, it is two in the mornin'."

"I know, baby. I'm sorry. I'm just glad you finally answered. I know you've seen all my calls. When I call any other time of the day, either nobody answers or Lexis picks up. I called this afternoon, as a matter of fact. All I wanted to do was apologize."

"You didn't call here today."

"Yes, I did. I told Lexis to tell you to page me."

"Well it's not on the caller ID and she didn't tell me, so as far as I'm concerned, you didn't call."

"Evidently she didn't tell you. Right now, I don't care about that. I was callin' to see how you doin' and to tell you that I'm still lookin' for them niggas."

"I'm fine," I answered. He was breaking me down, but I was trying to resist the charm of his concern.

"I'm so sorry I put you in the middle of this, baby. I know you sick of hearin' me say that, but I'm tellin' you…as soon as I see them niggas, it's over."

"Haven't you learned your lesson? Leave it alone, TJ. Just stop all this shit!"

"I can't. Look. I love you, and if you need anything, you know how to get in touch with me. I'ma let you go."

"Wait!" The words slipped out before I could stop them.

"What's up?" he asked.

"I love you, too," I said, then chastised myself with a hit to my forehead.

"I know. I'ma give you time, though. We both need it. I won't be ready for you until I settle this shit anyway."

"So you know who raped me?"

"Naw. Ol' boy in the car with you was too tall to be the other nigga that got beef wit' me. I know who got me, though, so it won't take long to find out who he is."

After we hung up, I went back upstairs and went to sleep. I was startled when my alarm went off at 5:45. I stole another 15 minutes, then got up and took a shower. By 7:15, I was scarfing down a bowl of Frosted Flakes, and when 7:30 rolled around, I was off to work.

When I arrived at my office, I was greeted by a colorful banner that read, "Welcome Back Tameka…We missed you!" along with an oversized card that everyone in my department signed, a half dozen of white roses, and balloons and streamers everywhere.

I sat down at my desk and started sorting through the stacks of paperwork and mail that had come while I was gone. Periodically, people would stop in and say hello. Everyone was very cautious about what they said when they asked me how I was doing. It was often awkward, but kinda funny listening to them struggle to say any word except "rape".

At lunchtime, the head manager took me to The Day Grille, an upscale café near our building. We talked a little about how I was handling the rape, and he asked me if I felt comfortable being back at work.

I lied, telling him how strong I was and how I wasn't going to let one night dictate my future…that unbreakable black woman façade.

"That's good. So have you started counseling yet?"

"No. I still have the option, but I really think I'll be fine."

"Well Tameka, I have to disagree with you on that one. One of my cousins was raped three years ago, and I feel that one of the best things she could've done was to go to counseling."

"Peter, I really don't see the point. I told you, I'm fine."

"You don't think about it at all anymore?"

"Yeah, but that's a given."

Just then, I thought about the nightmares. The experienced had changed my life, and as much as I tried to front, Peter could see the sleep deprivation through my Visine-drowned eyes and hear the fear in my quivering voice. I knew he meant well, but I always thought of counseling as something that white people did. And lo and behold, a white man was sitting across from me, recommending that I attend counseling in between bites of his grilled chicken salad. It didn't take him long to realize that he wasn't getting anywhere.

"I'll tell you what, Tameka," Peter continued. "I'll make a deal with you. If you go to counseling for a month, I'll pay for it."

"I don't need your money, Peter," I said, cutting him off.

"I wasn't finished. I'll pay for your counseling and take you to lunch every day for that month also."

He knew food would get me. I often amused my coworkers by telling them I'm the skinniest fat girl they'll ever know. I could eat with the best of them. Still, I looked at him like he was crazy.

"I mean it, Tameka. You're an invaluable asset to this company, and I care about your well-being. We can't afford to lose someone like you, especially if this thing gets out of hand and starts to get the best of you."

"How's Mrs. Bradshaw gonna feel about you spending all that money on another woman?"

He smiled. "Does that mean you accept my offer?"

"Yes," I said, reluctantly.

"Great! Just let me know the name of the doctor the hospital referred you to, and I'll take care of everything else."

I couldn't believe he'd talked me into getting therapy. I thought about reneging on his offer throughout the rest of the afternoon but decided not to. As soon as I got home, I told Alexis about Peter's offer.

"That's crazy! What's he gettin' out of it? You fuckin' your boss?"

"He said he wants his employees to be of sound mind and all that. He probably thinks I'll snap if I don't get help. I don't mind eatin' free for 30 days."

"And gettin' your head shrunk."

"Whatever," I said. "And I'm not bonin' Peter, thank you very much. This cat is worth much more than a sandwich and a doctor visit."

"I don't know. I gotta watch you."

When I checked the caller ID, I remembered I had a bone to pick with Alexis.

"Did anybody else call me?" I asked.

"Ain't you lookin' at the box?"

"Yeah, and I looked at the box yesterday too, but TJ's number was somehow erased. You know how that happened?"

"Oh, here you go." Alexis rolled her eyes.

"You didn't think I'd find out?"

"I didn't think you'd care. Any other time, you don't want nothin' to do with him. Does it blow your head up to see how many times he called on the caller ID? Is that what it is?"

"All I ask is that you give me my messages—all of my messages—when I get in the house. Is that so hard?"

"No it's not, but it's hard to figure you out. One day you love the nigga and want him to come over so y'all can work things out, then the next day you hate his ass and tell me to tell him that you don't wanna deal with the man who got you raped." She stood up. "I'm sick of this shit! I try my best to protect you and help you however I can, but every time I look up, you sayin' some old unappreciative shit. You ain't gotta worry about me no more, Miss Tameka. Believe that!" She grabbed her purse and headed toward the stairs.

I opened my mouth to speak, but she continued. "The next time you need somebody to talk to about them damn nightmares and shit, call Peter or Tielle. I bet you don't treat them like shit when they try to help you. You can even call Nicole long distance. Just don't call my ass!" She walked up the steps.

"That tantrum was real cute, Lexis," I yelled. "Grow up!"

Alexis and I didn't talk for two days. I needed time to get over her throwing the nightmares in my face, and she needed time to rationalize her anger toward me. She finally broke the silence one evening after our mother called and said she'd be in town in two weeks.

Chapter 5

July 4th finally came, and Alexis and I were getting ready for Tielle's family cookout. I must admit that I was looking too cute in my orange and yellow halter top and matching shorts. I'd done my toes the night before, so I wore my orange sandals to show 'em off. As I stood in front of the mirror, I adjusted a few wayward strands of hair and shook my head to make sure my oversized silver hoop earrings were secure. Just as I was putting on my lip gloss, Alexis came to my bathroom door.

"Which ones?" she asked, holding up two different black sandals.

She was wearing tiny blue jean shorts and a black halter that said "Sexy" in rhinestones.

"You look cute," Alexis said. "When did you get that shirt?"

"Yesterday, girl. Ten dollars on sale."

"Aw shit! Look out! Tameka James is back in effect."

"Somebody better let 'em know," I said as I flung my hair and admired myself in the mirror.

She had given my confidence a serious boost. I couldn't wait to get to the park. I was hoping to run into one of Tielle's fine ass family members, because the local niggas were tired. I had my eye on one of her cousins last year, so I was hoping to run into him again.

"Is Robert comin'?" I asked.

"Hell naw, girl! Didn't you say there was gon' be some niggas there?"

We pulled into the parking lot around two o'clock. There were already a lot of people under the shelter dancing, and everybody else was eating at the picnic tables. I spotted Tielle and Romeo hugged up in one corner of the shelter. Naturally, Alexis' buddies, Dap and Carmen, were there, so she ditched me for them within a matter of seconds.

There I was in the middle of the grass, looking like a lost puppy. I had to make a move before I drew more attention to myself and my bright-ass outfit. Miss Rosie, Tielle's mother, was standing nearby, so I went over to speak.

"Hey, baby! How you been?" she asked.

"Pretty good, and you?"

"Oh I can't complain, child. I'm just blessed to see another day." I nodded in agreement as she pulled me aside and spoke softly. "I've been prayin' for you, baby. You know Tielle told me about your situation, and you just need to put it in God's hands and leave it there," she continued.

"That's what I'm doin', Miss Rosie," I replied.

"Good. Now, I'ma tell you somethin' that you've probably been hearin' a lot, but you know I mean it. If you ever need anything— and I mean anything, you call me. And don't let me hear months down the road that you needed somethin' and didn't ask me, 'cause I mean what I'm tellin' you."

"Thanks, Miss Rosie." We hugged. "I'll remember that."

Tielle ran over to us. "When did you get here?" she asked.

"A few minutes ago," I responded.

"You would've seen her if you wasn't all wrapped up in that boy," Miss Rosie, said.

Tielle rolled her eyes. "Girl, let's go over here so you can get somethin' to eat," she said.

I fixed a plate with a hot dog, a hamburger, and some chips, and we sat at an empty picnic table.

I gazed around, looking for cute guys. A lot of the men were older—like in their late thirties, early forties. I did spot a couple of guys my age, but none of them really caught my eye.

"What ever happened to Lionel? He's not coming this year?" I casually inquired.

"Naw, girl. I meant to tell you he got married last weekend. They're on their honeymoon in Jamaica right now."

So much for him, I thought. As I was taking the last few bites of my burger, some guy came over to our table. He must've been a family member or something because Tielle's face lit up as soon as she saw him.

"What's up, girl?" he asked.

"Oh my goodness!" She jumped up and hugged him.

I really wasn't paying attention to them. I was having too much fun watching the old folks do the electric slide, thinking they were

51

jamming. I heard Tielle call my name after a couple minutes. As I turned around, I got a good look at the dude she was talking to. His skin was a deep chocolate color, he had the cutest lips, and his dark eyes sparkled every time he blinked. His goatee was well-trimmed, and his hair was cut low with waves I wouldn't mind riding all night. I snapped out of my trance and answered her.

"What?"

"This is my cousin, Craig," she said.

"How you doin', Miss Tameka?" Craig asked with a big smile.

Oh my Lord. He has pretty teeth, too. I'd never seen a man with a smile so beautiful.

"I'm fine," I answered. "So you're Craig, huh? Tielle told me a little bit about you."

"Oh yeah?" He turned to Tielle. "Why didn't you ever mention her to me?"

"I'm her best friend," I said, pushing Tielle playfully.

"Well, it's nice to meet you," he said.

"Same here."

I watched his fine ass walk halfway across the park, then snatched Tielle by her arm.

"Why didn't you tell me he looked like that?" I asked.

"Girl, I don't be lookin' at my cousin like that."

"Whatever. You know when a nigga's cute or not. I don't care who he is. I'll tell anybody that my daddy is a nice-lookin' man."

"Well, that's you."

"He is too cute," I continued.

"Say somethin' to 'em!"

"Naw. That long distance shit don't work," I said.

"You never know."

Cameo got the party jumping when "Candy" blasted through the speakers, and I headed to the dancing area. I wound up near Alexis. We clowned together, dropping it like it was hot on unsuspecting dudes. In the middle of the song, I felt somebody behind me. I didn't want to turn around, so I signaled for Lexis to tell me whether he was cute or not. Once she gave me the okay, I started really working it. I turned around after a few seconds and saw Craig's smiling face.

"You happy with what you see?"

"I'm still dancin', right?"

Aaliyah's "One In A Million" was the next song. I instinctively stopped dancing as the intro faded in for two reasons. One, I didn't know if I was ready to be that close to a male I didn't know. And two, I always felt a wave of sadness whenever I heard an Aaliyah cut. It was a constant reminder of her death, which also reminded me of how short life can be.

"Un unh. Where you goin'?" Craig asked as he gently took my hand. "I think you owe me a full dance."

"I didn't know I owed you anything," I said.

"Well let's just consider this dance an advance payment."

"Payment for what?"

"For the dinner we're havin' tomorrow."

He pulled me close, and we swayed to the music. The aroma from his cologne mesmerized me as I cozied my head on his shoulder. Something about his embrace seemed calming, protective…familiar even, and my reluctance to be in the arms of a stranger disappeared. I felt like Whitney Houston in *Waiting to Exhale*, when she let out a sigh of relief while she was dancing with that one dude.

There were only three other couples dancing, so we didn't blend into the crowd. I could see Dap and Carmen pointing and whispering, Tielle grinning, and Tyrone staring at us, but none of them mattered. All I could focus on was the tickle of Craig's breath against my neck as he softly sang the lyrics and the hardness between his legs. Suddenly, my thoughts ran wild. Was he actually serious when he said we were going to dinner? What if he was? What was I gonna wear? Where were we going? Why was I getting so excited when I didn't even know the man?

When the song ended, Craig asked if we could go somewhere and talk. We walked past the co-recipients of the Hater of the Year Award, Dap and Carmen, and I flashed them the biggest smile my mouth would allow. *Bitches*, I thought to myself. *Your number one enemy is on your cousin's arm.*

We sat at a table behind the shelter where not many people could bother us. He told me a little about his background in Chicago and said he was supposed to move in with Tielle's mother in two weeks. He was in town until Tuesday, which only gave him Monday to look for an apartment of his own.

"You can always look once you get here," I said.

"Yeah, I know. And Aunt Rosie's cool, too. It's just that I'm a grown man, and I wanna have my own place and do as I please without worryin' about disrespectin' anybody."

"I feel you."

53

We talked about his basketball career extensively. He told me that he was Mr. Basketball in Illinois, and he played college ball for Georgetown. I asked him why he never went pro, but he really didn't wanna talk about it. He said that he'd made some bad choices and he'd leave it at that.

Once we got into my information, I became a little uncomfortable. He wanted to know about my family, but the only person I mentioned was Alexis. When he asked about my parents, I told him that was my sore spot and that it was something I'd rather not discuss. He respected my privacy, and we moved on to other things. I told him that I was a stripper while I attended college, but that I left the pole and became part of corporate America after graduation. I watched his eyes for any signs of disgust when I revealed my skeletons, but didn't see any. He actually seemed to sympathize with me.

I was impressed to learn that he didn't have any kids. A 25 year-old athlete, fine as hell with no kids? That was unheard of! I assured him that I didn't have any either, so we were free of babymama/babydaddy drama.

"Can I ask you somethin' a little off the subject?"

"Go ahead," I said.

"Do Dap and Carmen have beef with you?"

"Beef ain't even the word."

"Why? Over some dude?"

"Partly, but there's a lot of females around here who don't like me. I used to call it the New Girl Syndrome. They catch it as soon as a new girl comes to town. If she's pretty, smart, and well-liked by the fellas, they hate on her from the time she arrives 'til the time she leaves. Dap and Carmen have severe cases of it."

We talked a little while longer, and before I knew it, it was 6:30. We exchanged numbers, then walked back to the shelter where everyone else was.

"I'm about to go over there with my brother, so I'll talk to you later, sexy," Craig said, smiling.

"That's cool," I said.

"Don't forget about our date tomorrow," he said as he walked away.

"Alright," I replied, struggling to keep my smile under control.

No sooner than he got a few feet away, Dap was in my face.

"What?" I asked as she approached me.

"Why you all up in my cousin's face?"

"Let's get this clear," I said. "I'm a grown-ass woman, and what I do is my business. Your cousin approached me, and he's grown as well. Be glad that somebody was around me so Tyrone wouldn't be tryin' to crawl up my ass."

"Whatever, bitch. We've been through this already."

"Exactly. So why is it that every time you see me, you gotta say somethin'? Does it bother you that much that your man can't get over me?" I walked toward her, backing her against the wall. "Or does it bother you that I don't let you get to me? Is that what it is? You want me to get mad?"

By that time, her body was flush with the wall, and people were crowding around.

"What's goin' on over here?" Miss Rosie yelled.

"Nothin', Miss Rosie," I replied. "Me and Dap were just gettin' a few things straight."

"Daphne, when are you gonna grow up?" Dap's mother asked. "You'd think you was still in grade school."

"Why y'all trippin' on me? She the one that got me against the wall!"

"I'm just givin' you what you want," I said through my clenched teeth. "Evidently you wanted some special attention 'cause you made it a point to come fuck with me again. Ever since that night at the club, I vowed that if you ever started with me again, I'd pretend like I was a hood rat bitch and beat the shit outta you. The night at the club wasn't enough?" I felt myself go into the zone. I grabbed her by her neck. "I left there because of your ass, and look what happened to me. That didn't give you enough satisfaction?" I squeezed harder and felt an eerie sense of pleasure. The deeper my nails dug into her skin, the more her arms flailed, never touching me. I looked her dead in her eyes, waiting for her air supply to run out.

It took Alexis, Tielle, and Chauncey, Craig's brother, to pull me off of her. Chauncey carried me to the parking lot. I stood with my arms folded, watching Miss Rosie and Miss Tina, Dap's mother, help her to a picnic table. I knew I was gonna have to do some serious apologizing to Miss Rosie for the scene Dap started and I finished.

Tielle stood in front of me with her back to everyone at the shelter. Her shaking head and smirking face said everything that her mouth didn't. It would've been inappropriate to run over and cheer for me with all her family around, but I could tell that she was glad that I'd put her smart-mouthed cousin in her place. Once Chauncey saw that I was calm, he trekked through the grass and joined Dap,

55

Carmen, and some of their other family members. Carmen was still over there talking shit, and so was Dap.

Craig looked astonished. What a way to make a first impression on a dude—choke his cousin at their family picnic. Still, he handled the situation far better than I expected. He had me face him as he held me around my waist and cracked corny jokes, hoping I wasn't about to run over and clock Carmen or finish Dap off. Every time I looked in their direction, he'd block my view and divert my attention to his sexy face.

Alexis looked at me and shook her head. "I told her to stop fuckin' wit' you," she said. "I told her you crazy, but she didn't wanna listen."

"Did you see her face?" Tielle added. "She was in shock. She could barely move."

"I just thought she couldn't breathe," Alexis said.

"I see what you was talkin' about now," Craig said. "She didn't have to come at you like that. Look at you fighting over me already." He smiled and ran his index finger under my chin.

"You better get over there before your family disowns you," I said. I was a little embarrassed and just wanted him to go away.

"Are you gonna be alright?"

"I'm cool. We 'bout to go home anyway."

"I got her," Alexis confirmed. "She ain't gon' choke nobody else."

Craig laughed. "I'll call you tomorrow afternoon, Miss Tameka."

On the ride home, Alexis described the look on Dap's face when I mentioned the rape. She told me how horrified and guilty she looked. Before the argument, I never thought about Dap's involvement, but I guess your true feelings come out in the heat of a confrontation.

"Just tell that bitch to stay away from me. Her and Carmen," I said.

"I been told her to leave you alone."

"Well, you reiterate that shit to her before I wind up in jail."

We got in the house, sat down in the living room, and started watching TV. Lexis asked me what was up with Craig, and I told her that we were going out the next day.

"Are you sure?" she asked. "I mean, you did just choke the shit outta his cousin."

"You heard him," I said. "He saw that I didn't start with her stupid ass."

"Well he is cute with his chocolate self. You need to jump on that."

"I intend to," I said. "Now who was you dancin' with all night? Don't think I didn't see that."

"Who? Marcus? Girl, he ain't nobody."

"I couldn't tell," I teased.

"We was just dancin'."

"You didn't get his number?"

"Girl, what's my name?"

We busted out laughing. Alexis thought she was slick. She was able to fool Robert, but she for damn sure couldn't fool me. I knew her operation. Since Marcus was worthy enough to get the number, he definitely had the potential to be placed on her Back-up Nigga List for the times when Robert was getting on her nerves.

The next day, Craig called at two. He'd just gotten home from church and changed his clothes. I was glad to hear that he was a God-fearing man. I, on the other hand, had been home from church for about 45 minutes and was watching a Lifetime movie. We talked about how each other's services went for a while, then he asked what my agenda was for the day.

"Nothin'," I said.

"Wrong," he replied. "Unless you've decided to refuse my offer."

"What? Dinner?"

"Yeah."

"I thought you meant what else was on my agenda."

We made plans for him to pick me up at 4:30. As soon as we got off the phone, I ran into Lexis' room and told her that the date was on for sure. She helped me pick out an outfit and curl my hair. I was ready 20 minutes early, so I had time to sit downstairs and pretend like I wasn't nervous.

The phone rang at 4:15—it was Tielle calling to see if I was ready. She told me she saw Craig at her mother's house and he was excited.

"I'm so nervous," I said. "You should see my hand shakin'."

"Why? It's just a regular date."

"I don't know. I just am. I gotta make up for that shit that went down at the barbeque. I don't want him thinkin' I'm a hood rat."

"Girl, whatever. Craig ain't worried about Dap. His dad and her mom fell out a long time ago, so him and Chauncey ain't never really been close to Dap, Marlon, and Carmen. Don't sweat that. He

57

wouldn't be takin' you out if he thought you were like that. And furthermore, I don't hang out with hood rats!"

We talked for a few more minutes, then there was a knock at the door. I got off the phone, jumped up, and fixed my clothes. "Do I look okay?" I asked Alexis.

"Girl, yeah. Answer the door."

When I opened the door, Craig was standing with a single red rose in his hand. He had on black slacks and a gray silk shirt with white and black designs. We almost matched perfectly because I had on a fitted, but sophisticated, black dress accented with a black and white scarf.

He handed me the rose and gave me a hug. "You look nice," he said.

"So do you." I inhaled his cologne and tried not to hold him too long. "Thanks for the rose."

"No problem."

Alexis came to the door to be nosey. "How you doin', Craig? We didn't get formally introduced at the cookout, but I'm Alexis, Tameka's sister."

"Nice to meet you," he said, shaking her hand.

"Don't have my sister out late," she continued. "I'm 'bout to take down your license plate number so I can find you if I have to." She pulled out her yellow legal pad and purple gel pen and stepped outside.

"Ignore her," I said as we headed out the door.

"Call me if you need me," Alexis leaned over and whispered.

"Okay, Mama," I teased.

Craig took me to Claude's, a classy restaurant on the other side of town. When I say classy, I mean valet parking, linen napkins, and menu items the Average Joe can't pronounce. We sat at a candle-lit table in a corner with bay windows overlooking the beautiful downtown skyline. Craig ordered some wine as we checked out what was on the menu. I didn't see anything on there cheaper than twenty dollars besides the appetizers, and they weren't less than ten. I placed my elbows on the vanilla table cloth and pondered over what I would order as Craig sipped water from the crystal glass that I was too afraid to touch.

Once the waitress returned, I ordered a fancy steak that was covered in some kind of sauce I'd never heard of, and Craig ordered the shrimp. He poured us both a glass of wine, and we started our conversation on an awkward note.

"I hope you don't mind me askin' this, but I just wanna get this out the way."

What could he possibly have to ask me? I sat up straight and gave him my full attention.

"Go ahead." I gulped my wine and held my breath.

"Okay. I heard somethin' yesterday at the picnic, and it's been botherin' me," he continued.

"What?"

"Somebody said you were..Well, I heard a few people mention that you were...raped. Is that true?"

"What you mean 'Is that true?'"

"No, no. I didn't mean it like that. I meant, did I hear you correctly?"

"Yeah."

"Was this recently?" he asked, taking a sip of his wine.

"Last month," I replied. My tone was uninviting.

"Wow," he said sympathetically. "Did the police catch the guy?"

"No," I said and took another sip of my wine. "It's complicated. I'd rather not get into it."

"That's understandable. So is this your first date since then?"

"What makes you think that?"

"It was just a question."

"Yeah, this is my first date since then, but I don't date that much anyway."

Slowly but surely, we moved away from the rape topic. Craig was truly a gentleman. He told me that he didn't mean any harm and apologized for prying.

When our food came, we talked about his dreams and why he was moving from Chicago. He told me he was hoping to coach a high school team and eventually a Division I college team. He'd already applied to two of the big high schools in town and was supposed to interview with one of them a few days after his arrival.

Thank you, Jesus. Finally a man with real goals. I tried not to get excited over him, but I couldn't help it. He was a triple threat—sexy, intelligent, and childless. To make things even better, he came with a referral. His cousin was my best friend. I knew I'd be a fool to pass him up.

We pulled up to my place at eight o'clock. He opened the car door for me, and I headed to the house. He took a little while to catch up with me because he was rummaging through his backseat. When he caught up with me, something didn't seem right.

"What you got behind your back?" I asked.

"Nothin'," he replied.

"Umm hmm," I said suspiciously. I unlocked the door, and as I turned around to invite him in, I saw a bunch of roses in my face.

"What is this?" I asked.

"The rest of your roses."

"What?"

He handed me eleven roses. "I gave you one at the beginning, and I'm givin' you eleven more since the date went so well."

"So what were you gonna do with 'em if it didn't go well?"

"I've got aunties that I could've given 'em to, but I knew you were guaranteed at least six."

"How'd you figure that?" I asked.

"Because each rose represents the twelve things I look for in a woman. I saw six of those qualities when I first met you."

I invited him in so we could continue the conversation. "So what are those twelve qualities?" I asked, intrigued by the whole idea.

"Alright. The first rose was a courtesy one, just because you agreed to the date."

I laughed, and so did he.

"What?" he asked. "I'm bein' serious." He continued. "Okay. You got five more roses 'cause you have a pretty smile, you're beautiful, sexy, employed, and your body is on point."

"And how many of those were physical?" I teased.

"Hold on, now. I could only go by physical stuff when we first met. I learned the real stuff during our date," he said.

"Oh, well enlighten me."

"I intend to. For instance, you looked good at the picnic, but that didn't mean you were gonna dress right for the date. You had no idea what kind of restaurant we were goin' to. I could've taken you to Friday's for all you knew, right? But when I came to the door, you were dressed elegantly, and I could tell that you dress for the occasion. It's always better to be overdressed instead of underdressed. That was your seventh rose."

I couldn't stop smiling. He was saying all the right things.

"You're on your own and you ain't dependin' on nobody—not even Alexis, even though she stays here. Rose number eight. When I talked to you on the phone, you said you'd been to church today, and when you talked about the sermon touching on the problems you've been dealin' with, I knew you weren't just lyin' to impress me. That entitled you to rose number nine."

"You swear you have this all figured out. Do you do this with all of your dates?"

"Honestly? Yeah. But the most I've ever given away was nine." He flashed that heartbreaking smile.

"So what are the other three for?" I asked.

"Intelligence, good conversation, and being real."

"What's your definition of real?"

"You're a lady, but you ain't gon' front like some females do when a dude is around. Like at the picnic, you kept it real about your relationship with Dap. So when that stuff went down, I already knew what was up. You told me you were a stripper…You didn't have to come out with that."

He was right. I still wasn't sure why I'd spilled my guts to him.

"And little things count, too. I hate when I take a female out and she picks at her food 'cause she don't wanna look greedy. You weren't shovelin' food in your mouth, but you ate. You know what I'm sayin'?"

I was flattered by his method of evaluation. Even if it was all bullshit, his game was tight and he did something that no other man had ever done. He made me feel like I was the most superior woman in the world—like he had never met anyone like me.

Chapter 6

The next week was a good one. I had started counseling and it actually seemed to be working. It was a good outlet for me to express things that I didn't feel comfortable talking to anybody else about. And contrary to my apprehension about her, Dr. Rogers was a cool lady.

It was Friday and I was expecting Nicole to arrive in town any minute. As I waited at the security checkpoint near the flight information monitors, my mind drifted. I started thinking about my conversation with Craig the previous day and anticipated seeing him again. We had talked every day and engaged in some very stimulating conversations, none of which I could get out of my head. My daydream was interrupted when Nicole playfully smacked me on the back of my head.

"Wake up!" she said.

I jumped up and gave her a hug. It was refreshing to see her smiling face. She had a carefree spirit that was contagious and sincerity that echoed through every word she spoke. Her visit was sure to be therapy at its best.

As I expected, she hadn't changed a bit. Her hair was still light chestnut brown with copper red highlights and cut short. The only difference was that she was wearing the oh-so-popular flips instead of the stacked style she'd sported for two years. Her trendy outfit was cute, but something that I'd never be bold enough to try. Fitted capris with a short denim jacket, a vintage t-shirt, and heels. It had to be a style she'd picked up during one of her photo shoots in New York. She looked like she'd stepped out of an Abercrombie magazine (but in a cute black girl way).

"You alright?" she asked.

"Yeah, girl."

"You look good as long as I ignore them bags under your eyes," she joked.

"I'm just tired as hell…stressed."

"Well let's go to your place so you can lay down. You need to rest up 'cause we goin' out tonight. I probably need a nap, too."

I told her that my stress was mostly because my mother was coming to town. She agreed it would be a very interesting visit and the ultimate test of my patience and self-control. Nicole couldn't have come at a better time. Hanging out with her would definitely be my excuse to stay as far away as possible from that lady.

Later that night, Nicole and I went to Smoothies, a fairly new poetry and jazz club with a laid back vibe. The majority of the performers' creative sparks were ignited by Newports and Virginia Slims, but they always managed to finish a set without coughing. As much as I attended, I was destined to get lung cancer via secondhand smoke.

As soon as we walked in, I saw Judge, a spoken word artist who wooed me with an impromptu poem about my lips the first time we met. With his neatly twisted locks and skin the color and texture of maple syrup, he was the most gorgeous Jamaican man to walk the Earth. I was all set to give him my number after our first encounter until Tielle informed me he had five kids, no job, and a problem with domestic violence. From my understanding, he made ends meet by doing yard work for anybody who'd let him while he pursued his dream to be on Def Poetry Jam. A dollar and a dream was not what I built my relationships on, so I simply gained pleasure from him being my eye candy and sucked on his sweetness from afar. I introduced him to Nicole and convinced him to add her to the list for open mic.

She read one of her poems at the end of the first set and captured the audience with every word. I had never heard her perform, so I was just as attentive and impressed as everyone else. When she came back to the table, she told me that Judge wanted her to meet two of his partners and join their little spoken word group. She graciously declined, but promised to return to the club whenever she came to town again.

I sipped on my cranberry and vodka as we listened to the live band. When I looked over the rim of my glass, I saw Dap coming.

"This is ri-got-damn-diculous," I said, slamming my glass down. "This bitch is everywhere I go!"

"Who?" Nicole asked as she looked around.

"Dap. That's her right there in the red."

"That's her?" Nicole asked. "I thought she was bigger than that for some reason. Is she comin' to the table?"

Before I could answer, Dap was in our presence. Immediately, she put her hands up and said, "I'm comin' in peace, Tameka. Me and Craig had a long talk the other day, and he made me realize some things about the way I've been actin'. I just came over here to tell you that I'm through. You don't bother me; I won't bother you."

I gave her a blank look, unimpressed and emotionless. I didn't have anything to say to her. She still didn't apologize, and I wasn't gonna thank her for leaving me alone.

"Is that it?" I asked, wondering why she was still standing there.

"Yeah," she replied. After a moment of awkward silence, she walked away.

"What the hell?" Nicole said, laughing.

"Was I supposed to say something, 'cause I wasn't feeling it? I wanna know what Craig said to her."

We were forced to change topics when we started jiving on the drunk guitarist who would only strum one string every couple minutes. When our mozzarella sticks arrived, we put a hurtin' on 'em and washed them down with more alcohol.

When we got in, I pulled out the sofa bed for Nicole. It took a little longer than usual since I was drunk as hell. I couldn't muster up the strength to pull it out by myself. After five attempts and five minutes of laughter, Nicole helped me yank it out.

"You know what I just thought about?" I said. "You could've just slept in Lexis' bed tonight 'cause she's at Robert's."

"Too late now," Nicole said, slurring her words.

"That might not have been such a good idea anyway," I said. "I don't think she changed her sheets, and you know how she is."

We laughed until we didn't have any more energy. It felt so good to be around my other best friend again. I didn't realize how much I'd missed her.

The next morning, Alexis came home and cooked breakfast. When I woke up and went downstairs, she and Nicole were already at the table eating pancakes, sausage, and eggs. I joined them in mid-conversation. Alexis was talking about our mother.

"She's comin' tomorrow," she said.

"I thought she wasn't comin' 'til Monday," I said.

"She changed her mind, I guess."

"You excited?" Nicole asked.

"I really don't care," Alexis said. "She's only comin' up here to see Meka anyway."

"Bull…shit," I replied. "If she wanted to be here for me, she would've been here last month."

"You take that up with her," Alexis said.

"Where's she stayin'?" I asked.

"I guess here."

"You givin' her your bed?"

"Damn, Meka! If it's that big of a deal, yeah, she can sleep in my bed. Don't worry. You don't have to give her yours."

"I'll just get a room, and she can have the sofa bed," Nicole intervened.

"Don't even think about it," I said.

We ate in silence for the next few minutes. Nicole finally broke it by telling Alexis about Dap's speech at Smoothies the night before.

"Well that's cool that she apologized," Alexis replied.

"She didn't apologize," I said.

"Well Meka, just be glad that she ain't gonna mess with you no more."

Nicole cut me off right before I was gonna snap. "Time out," she said. "You're friends with this chick, right?"

"Yeah, we cool."

"Why?"

"What you mean, 'Why?' Me and Dap been cool since my freshman year in high school. I can't help it that her and Meka don't get along."

"I understand that, but how can you let your friend constantly disrespect your sister in front of you and everybody else?"

I got up from the table and went to the kitchen to wash my dishes.

"I can't help it that Tameka ain't got no friends around here. People like me, and I'm not gon' stop bein' cool with somebody over her. That shit between her and Dap is stupid anyway. They both need to let it go."

"Don't get defensive," Nicole said. "I was just wonderin' why you haven't tried to at least keep things civil between them."

While they continued their conversation, I went upstairs to take a shower.

***

Nicole asked Alexis if she met Craig. She described his appearance from his freshly cut Caesar to his Gucci shoes, leaving no detail unexplained. When speaking about his character, she could only go by Tameka's account since she hadn't had a real conversation with him.

"She told me about the roses. I thought that was sweet."

"Yeah, it was original," Alexis replied.

"You think she really likes him, or is he just a distraction from TJ?"

"A little bit of both," Alexis answered. "But she needs somebody right now. Craig seems alright so far, I guess. How long you stayin'? You might get to meet him."

"I'm leavin' Monday or Tuesday," Nicole said.

"Oh. I don't think he's comin' 'til Friday."

***

That night, we all went to the club. I was a little uneasy at first, but I loosened up after my second drink. It was on then. We had a blast. Nicole hollered at every guy that crossed her path and collected numbers from the ones with potential while Alexis shook her ass all night. I was doing the same thing they were until a bug-a-boo had me hemmed up on the dance floor for the last five songs of the night.

Alexis drove home because I was drunk off my ass. Nicole is a big drinker, and my lightweight ass always tried to keep up with her. She was fine, so she helped Lexis carry me in the house.

I staggered to the downstairs bathroom once my feet hit the floor. I heard them laughing at me, but I was too busy hurling to cuss them out. By the time I was done, Nicole was sprawled out on the sofa bed, and Lexis was upstairs in her room. I made my way up the stairs, crawling to get up the last three, and went to bed.

At 8:15, somebody was ringing the doorbell like I owed them money. Over and over, I heard the annoying doorbell chime in a relentless effort to be answered. I tried my best to ignore it and covered my head with a pillow, hoping to drown it out. Suddenly, it stopped. *Good*, I thought. I could go back to sleep in peace…Wrong. A few minutes later, I heard a very familiar voice.

"You never could wake up at a decent hour."

I lifted the pillow from my head and turned towards my bedroom door. I forgot my mother was coming.

"Please don't start with me, Ma. It's only eight o'clock," I grumbled.

"Umm hmm, and you probably didn't go to bed until three."

"4:30. Give me until ten," I said and rolled back over.

My mother mumbled something under her breath and walked across the hall to Alexis' room.

"Lexi," she said in her sweetest voice. "Wake up, Boo Boo."

Alexis struggled to open her eyes as she stretched and yawned. Regina went over to the bed and hugged her.

"When did you get here?" Alexis asked.

"About 15 minutes ago. Nicole let me in."

"Oh."

"You didn't tell me she was gonna be here."

"Okay, and?"

"I feel like I'm intruding now. Tameka already has company. That's probably why she was so brief with me a second ago."

"You know that's not why, Mama. Let's not go there."

"Well…" She paused. "I intend to have a long talk with you and Tameka about that."

"Mama, just let it go. You just gon' open up a whole new can of worms—especially with Meka. Just leave her alone."

"I can't. That's what I've done for almost 25 years."

I held true to my word and didn't lift an eyelid until ten. My head felt like somebody had kicked me with steel-toed boots until their leg got tired, and my stomach was bubbling and cramping. I assumed the position from the night before in front of the toilet and flushed down the remains of alcohol and potato chips from my body.

Feeling relieved, I brushed my teeth and went downstairs. Nicole and Alexis were watching TV with my mom. She was fussing about the disgusting fat man who sat next to her on the plane and ate peanuts until they gave him gas. Her complaints instantly irritated me, so I walked directly to the kitchen to get some Tylenol. After I popped the second pill, she acknowledged my presence.

"Well look who decided to join us," she said.

I shot her an evil glance and drank the rest of my orange juice.

"You should probably drink water," Nicole said. "That orange juice will probably make you throw up again."

"Anything will probably make me throw up again," I replied. "This shit ain't no joke. I ain't never drinkin' that much again."

Mom grunted in disapproval, but I didn't comment. Instead, I joined everyone in the living room and pretended like I was interested in the crap she was talking about. Once I couldn't take it anymore, I went upstairs and soaked in the tub. I sang along to Joe's "Treat Her Like A Lady" while I dried off and as I put on my robe, somebody turned my music off. I walked out of the bathroom, eyebrows lowered, wondering who the hell touched my radio. To my dismay, it was my mother.

"We need to talk," she said.

"About what?"

"Our relationship."

"I've got company right now. I'm not tryin' to hear that heavy shit."

"How long can we keep avoiding it?"

"You haven't been concerned for years."

"Just listen to me. I know you have you reasons for despising me..."

You're damn right! I thought. She put on a front for the whole town when we moved to Texas. From everyone else's point of view, she was a perfect mother—always at school functions, member of the school board, head of the church youth group. At home, our points of view were very different.

My dad adored my mom and treated her like she was a precious diamond until he found out that she was fucking around on him with Darryl, a guy from her job. After he found that out, life at the house was hell. They constantly argued about each other's whereabouts, and they were unhappy for the remaining five years of their marriage.

I remember hearing parts of one particular argument while Lexis was at camp. My mom made a comment that led me to believe that somebody else was Lexis' father. I don't know if she said it in the heat of the moment to hurt my dad's feelings, but when I asked her about it later, she told me to stay outta grown folks' business. When I asked my dad, he told me that we were both his babies and that he couldn't love us more. He made me swear that I wouldn't tell Lexis what I'd heard because she would only get upset for no reason.

Ever since then, I felt the need to protect Lexis and help her whenever I could. If she knew the secrets between our parents she'd never speak to them again. She never could understand why I hated our mom so much, but that's because she only knew half of the story...the half that only involves me.

My mother always told me that if I got good grades and graduated high school without getting pregnant, she'd put me through college. I graduated with a 3.5 and still don't have any kids, so why did I strip to pay for my classes?

It wasn't because she didn't have the money. My mother is a corporate lawyer and to supplement that, my dad is a top-notch accountant.

I took off my clothes in front of drooling nerds, working-class men, and thugs because she listened to all her jealous-ass friends. They told her that she spoiled me and Lexis and that we'd never learn how to live on our own if she continued to baby us. Instead of telling them to mind their business, she told me to talk to her "friend," Darryl, because he owned his own business in addition to working at the firm with her. I figured it was worth a shot. I was gonna need a job anyway for miscellaneous expenses and small bills, but I trusted that my mom was still gonna help me with tuition.

When I met Darryl at his bar, I felt uncomfortable. He was cool, but something about the place didn't seem right. It wasn't the stale smell in the air that was unsuccessfully masked by Glade air freshener or the red and blue bulbs in every light fixture. It was more of an aura that wasn't based on physical reservations. We talked in his office about what kind of hours I needed to work and what days would be best. According to the times I gave him, he concluded that I should probably work the special shift. I didn't understand how I could work any shift since I didn't have any bartending skills and refused to work as a waitress.

When I asked him what the special shift was, he led me down a flight of stairs and flipped the light switch. Once my eyes adjusted to the brightness I saw a big-ass stage with a pole in the center. The glossy black platform was so shiny that I could see my reflection in it. Coffee brown leather stools surrounded the stage, and red oak tables and chairs filled the space on the floor. I already knew what was up so I told Darryl that I couldn't accept his offer.

I rushed in the house that evening and told my mom what happened. I explained to her that it wasn't just a bar and that Darryl wanted me to be a stripper. The look in her eyes told me everything she was thinking. She already knew damned well what was going on at Darryl's "business."

"You're gonna have to make your money fast so you can make those tuition payments, right? That's what you said the other day when I suggested you work at the mall. You said you want quick money."

"How could you even feel comfortable about your daughter showin' off her body to strangers?" I felt a knot form in my stomach and tears well up in my eyes.

"I don't feel comfortable with you giving your body to these little horny boys around here, but you do that anyway, don't you? At least you can make some money doing this, and it's so low key that no one will really know."

She was actually serious! Her face was emotionless and heartless, and I couldn't believe she put me out there like that. My whole body shook with anger, and my stomach tightened until it cramped. I busted out crying and ran into my room. I remember Alexis coming to check on me and asking what happened. I couldn't talk clearly because I was crying so hard. After I finally got it out, I threw up all night. The pain in my stomach couldn't compete with the pain in my heart, though. My mom had basically told me that she didn't give a damn about me.

Toward the end of the summer, I ran into Darryl at the grocery store. He told me that he understood where I was coming from before, but that the offer still stood if I ever needed a job. He promised that he'd make sure I wasn't harassed or anything like that. I just thanked him and went on my way. In mid-August just before school started, though, I broke down and called him. I was working at the club within three days.

My dad never knew why I worked at U-Turn, and he for damn sure didn't know who owned it. He just knew that I got naked in front of a bunch of horny men and he didn't like it. He would even give me money that would last for a months at a time, just so I wouldn't strip. The bad thing was that the money went to paying rent and I still had to work for some of my tuition. I don't know why I didn't tell him the truth. I guess I just didn't want things to get any worse in the house for him and my mom, not to mention that I was good and I was the main attraction at the club.

I replayed the whole story in my mind as I listened to my mother babble on.

"…Honey, I've changed. I just got saved again, and I've really stepped back and looked at the mistakes I've made with you girls and with your father. I was at a completely different place in my life, and we both know it wasn't the right one. I know my apologies won't erase what I did and how I acted toward you. All I can say is that I'm sorry and I want to move on from here," she continued.

70

"Honestly, I don't believe you. If you wanted to make some changes, you should've been here right after I got raped. You always a day late and a dollar short. You may feel bad about what you did to me, but you ain't sorry. If you were truly sorry, that weight should've been unbearable on your heart for all these years," I replied.

"Regardless of what you think, I truly am sorry. And as far as the rape goes, I couldn't get off work. I had clients that I couldn't push to the side."

"But you could push your daughter aside without blinkin', right? Do you have any paperwork on you? What do I need to do to become one of your clients?" I asked. "Maybe I'll be a priority then."

"I called you every day after that happened, Tameka. That's all I could do at the time."

"No, you could've been a real mother and came up here to raise hell until they found out who did this to me!" All the emotion I'd held in from years before came out. "You know what? I hate to bust your bubble, but you can save the rest of this sentimental, regretful shit. The truth is, you hurt me more than I can even begin to tell you when you left me in the cold with my only feasible option to strip. You had the money to help me, but you didn't, and I'll never forget that. You hear me? Never. There's nothin' you can say that'll make me change my mind, 'cause I can't go back. I can't erase the images of my body in the minds of hundreds of men in this city. I can't erase the fact that I upped my status, getting a college degree by degrading myself night after night onstage. I can't take all of the nice stuff I bought with that money back to the store and forget I had it. It's too late. If I can't go back, neither can you."

At that point, I was crying and so was she.

"Well, you've made your point clear," she said, standing up. "Just know that I'm still your mother and if you need me, I'll be here."

She left my room, and I sat on my bed for a while and thought about our conversation. I felt kinda bad because I was so blunt, but at the same time I felt good 'cause I said what I wanted to say—what I'd needed to say—for six years. She didn't give a fuck when she basically called me a ho, so what would make me bite my tongue?

Chapter 7

Nicole left the next day. I hated to see her go. She and Alexis heard the majority of me and Mom's conversation through the vent, so we had a long talk about it during our drive to the airport. We concluded that me and my mom would never have a good relationship because there's some shit I just couldn't let go.

After I dropped Nicole off, I met Tielle for lunch at Applebee's.

"I missed all that?" she asked after I recapped the weekend's events. "It sounds like y'all had more action here than me and Romeo."

"Y'all didn't have fun at Six Flags?"

"Girl, it rained all Friday and most of Saturday, so we stayed in the hotel room damn near the whole weekend."

"You make that sound like a bad thing," I said. "There wasn't no action in the room?"

"We fooled around," Tielle said with a smile. "No penetration, though."

"What the hell is that? Was y'all grindin' and dry humpin' like the early high school days?" I asked, laughing.

"No, heffa. Let's just say that he was hungry, and I fed him."

We laughed so loud that people were turning around and staring at us. We asked for our check and got outta there. She had to go back to work, and I had to go in for a half day.

When I got off, I still couldn't go home. I was off to another therapy session. This time I was anxious to go because I wanted to get the stuff about my mom off my chest. Dr. Rogers and I talked about my parents, my home life when I was a child, and how all those factors relate to how I dealt with traumatizing issues such as the rape. I learned that my "We shall overcome" attitude was derived from my past of coping with difficult circumstances. She told me that I feel I can pick up the pieces and move beyond any embarrassment and pain on my own terms because it's what I did before. However, she cautioned that my way most likely wouldn't work in this instance.

I mentioned that I'd gone out with Craig, and she was glad to hear that. She said it was a big step to take and was glad that I was continuing on with my life. She encouraged me to take it slow and told me to keep her posted on any progress we made.

I dreaded going home because I felt like I was walking on eggshells with my mom. I walked in and was surprised by the pleasant aroma of a roast baking. While I checked the caller ID, I heard Mom telling Lexis that she hoped I would at least enjoy the food. I couldn't deny that her roast beef had always been my favorite, so I didn't let my dislike for her interfere with my growling stomach.

The three of us made it through dinner in a civil manner, mostly engaging in small talk. Alexis mentioned that she'd talked to Jermaine and that he'd be in town by the weekend. He was originally supposed to come with our mother, but had to handle some last minute business with a new artist they'd signed at his job. Mom threw in her two cents, boasting about the girl she hooked him up with and how she was the sweetest thing that ever lived.

Right when I was finishing the last of my carrots, the phone rang. I was glad because I would've thrown up if I had to listen to another second of my mother's voice. I answered the phone, surprised to hear Craig's voice on the other end.

"I thought I'd give you a few days, since you were havin' company all weekend," he said. "Did you have fun kickin' it with your girl?"

"Yeah, it was cool. I just took her to the airport this morning."

"When's your mom comin'?"

"She's here already," I answered.

"Damn, girl. You pretty popular this week, huh? All these people comin' to see you."

"I wanna know when I'ma get to see you," I said. *Oh shit! I didn't mean to say that out loud.* I held my breath as my stomach dropped.

"You'll see me this Friday," he said. "You just make sure you look as good as you did before I left."

"As long as you promise to do the same," I said.

"Then it's a deal."

We said our goodbyes and hung up. I looked up to find the peanut gallery grinning at me.

"What?" I asked.

"That was Craig, right?" Alexis asked.

"Yeah, and?"

"I heard you talkin' all sweet to him," she said, smiling. "You really dig him, huh?"

I waved her off.

"Is this a new guy?" my mom asked.

"Yeah," I replied, dryly.

Lexis immediately spit out the whole story of how we met and what our first date was like. I was shitty that she was telling our mom about it. That was something I normally shared with someone I was close to, and Regina James wasn't in that category.

"When's he coming?" Mom asked.

"Friday."

"Maybe I'll get to meet him before I leave. What time will he be here?"

"I don't know, but don't worry about it. You don't have to meet my dates anymore. I'm grown."

I retreated to my room to escape the third degree. Alexis and Mom stayed downstairs.

"I just wanted to know what was going on with her love life," Regina said. "I'll be glad when she finds somebody who cares for her. Anybody would be better than that thug, TJ. Does she still talk to him?"

"Sometimes," Alexis answered.

"He's the one who got her into all this mess in the first place, isn't he?"

"Somethin' like that. I could sit here and name at least three other people who we could blame, but the ultimate blame falls on the dude who did it. And Mama, TJ ain't the worst guy on the planet."

"I can't tell. All I hear is drama every time y'all mention his name."

"That's all you wanna hear."

Alexis stared at her, wondering why she was such a bitch sometimes. Moms are supposed to be loving, caring, and understanding—not evil, judgmental, and close-minded. Regina eventually broke the silence.

"When's the last time you talked to your father?"

"Sometime in May."

"Tameka didn't call and tell him what happened?"

74

"I called, but his little girlfriend said he was outta town with his boss on business and she didn't have a number where she could reach him. I told her to tell him to call us when he got back…and now it's July."

"That figures. That young tramp probably has him in bed all day. He ain't got time for nothin' but sex and work."

"I just think somethin' ain't right. Daddy usually calls us at least once a month."

"He's a man—a dog—just like all these fools y'all run into. They ain't from shit, and when it comes down to it, your father isn't either."

***

The end of the week couldn't come fast enough. I was excited because my mom was leaving and Craig was coming, but I still didn't know why Jermaine was coming. If I went with my first instinct, his visit had "illegal" written all over it.

I ran around the house Friday morning, cleaning up and making sure everyone's schedule was going as planned. Craig called from the road to tell me that his trip was going well. Jermaine wasn't supposed to arrive until Saturday, but I called anyway to make sure he was still coming. I wanted to make sure we had enough food.

Mom packed her Fendi luggage in Alexis' room. Her flight wasn't leaving until five, but she was going to visit her friend, Christine, before she left. Alexis and I had called off work to take her to the airport, so we were pissed when we learned that Miss Christine had that covered. She picked Mom up at one o'clock. We said quick goodbyes, and she was on her way.

No sooner than we shut the door, there was a knock on it. *That can't be Craig already*, I thought. Just in case it was, though, I ran into the bathroom, checked my lipstick, adjusted my clothes, and finger-combed my hair. I walked out of the bathroom, as if I wasn't primping, only to see Robert standing in the living room with Lexis. I felt like an ass for doing all that. Why was I trippin' when Craig already told me that I was beautiful? I just needed to relax. I spoke to Robert and went upstairs to watch TV in my room.

By six o' clock, I was becoming restless. Craig estimated he'd get in around six or seven, but I hadn't heard from him since early in the afternoon. I hadn't eaten anything but some Froot Loops and a banana all day, trying to save my appetite in case we went out to eat. Lexis and Robert had ordered pizza, so I went downstairs and snatched two pieces before I passed out from starvation. I must've looked as pitiful as I felt because Robert asked me if I was okay.

"Yeah, I'm cool," I replied.

"You heard from Craig?" Alexis asked.

"Not yet."

"That's why you mopin' around," she joked.

"Fuck you," I said with a fake smile.

"There you go misplacin' your anger."

"Girl, ain't nobody mad."

"Whatever."

Shortly after that, they went upstairs to start their sex marathon. They barely saw each other the whole time our mom was visiting, so I already knew I was in for a noisy night. I wiped the dust off of my *Sugar Hill* tape and popped it in the VCR. I guess my night had turned into a movie night. I grabbed a blanket out of the hall closet, curled up on the couch, and turned the volume up so I couldn't hear Robert smacking my sister's ass.

Right when Wesley was about to tell his brother that he wanted to make a new life for himself, somebody knocked on the door. I looked at my watch.

Anybody who came to see me usually called first, so I figured it was one of Alexis' ignorant friends or TJ's ass. I had a strong attitude when I walked to the door, and I couldn't tell who it was through the peephole because the person had their back to the door.

"Who is it?" I yelled.

"Craig."

I didn't even have time to check myself. I knew I looked rough because I was dressed in my bedtime sweats and my faded high school track t-shirt.

I opened the door and stood there, not knowing if I would look desperate if I hugged him. I felt like hugs were only for family, first dates, and boyfriends, and he was neither. I opted to go with a simple hello.

"What's up, beautiful?" he said, giving me the warmest hug ever.

"Excuse my appearance," I said. "I wasn't sure if you were still comin'."

"You chillin' at the crib, right? You're supposed to be comfortable."

We sat on the couch and he finished watching the movie with me. We talked about his trip, and he told me about the crazy hillbillies he ran into at a gas station in Arkansas. I could barely concentrate on what he was saying because I was staring at his lips the whole time.

We decided not to go anywhere since he was tired and I was already in my nightclothes. Instead, we laughed and joked with each other. He jived on my big teddy bear slippers, and I talked about his thick-ass herringbone chain that had been played out since '96. I told him not to let me see him with it on again if he didn't want to get talked about.

He playfully tackled me. "You got jokes, huh?" he asked.

"Yep," I replied, still laughing.

The next thing I knew, I was kissing those soft lips of his. I normally didn't allow tongue action with the first kiss, but that rule went out the window. He was a hell of a kisser, and he could've done just about anything to me at that moment. I felt his blood rush to that special place as he slowly grinded on top of me. My hips found the rhythm of his as I squeezed him tightly and moaned softly with pleasure. As he reached for his belt buckle, he pulled my arms above my head and kissed my neck. All I could think of was that nasty-ass rapist who pinned me down the same way. I opened my eyes and focused on Craig's face. I concentrated on his features and assured myself that he was nothing like that monster.

As he pulled his pants down, I pushed him off of me and jumped up.

"Whoa!" he said, pulling his pants up. "What'd I do?"

I was embarrassed as hell, and my eyes were filled with tears. "I'm so sorry. I wasn't tryin' to tease you or anything," I said. "It's just that you had my arms pinned down, and the guy…I got flashbacks of when…the night when—"

He put his finger up to my lips and hugged me. "You don't have to be sorry, sweetie. I'm the one who's sorry. I shouldn't have even come at you like that. I should've known you wouldn't be ready for this. I wasn't tryin' to be disrespectful or nothin'." He struggled to find the right words.

"Listen," I said, pulling away from him and wiping my eyes. "I'm not blaming you for anything." I laughed uncomfortably. "Damn, I didn't even know I was gonna feel like this."

"It's cool, sweetheart."

He held me again as I cried some more. I felt like a big baby. I'd never cried so much in my life. It was then that I realized how much the rape had messed me up.

After a few minutes, Craig let me go. "If you think you gon' be alright, I'ma go on and get outta here. I know you probably need some space," he said.

Great. I ran him away.

"You got any plans tomorrow?"

I told him about the fair that Robert, Alexis, and I were going to. He asked if he could come along.

"I mean, I don't wanna cramp your style or nothin', but if you go with them you won't have anybody to ride with." He smiled.

"So you wanna go with me?" I asked with a hesitant smile.

"Just let me know what time."

"Call me around three, 'cause I think we're leavin' at five."

"Alright, beautiful," he said and kissed me on the forehead. "I'll talk to you tomorrow."

***

The next morning, I told Alexis about the previous night's events.

"So he wasn't trippin'?" she asked.

"He didn't show it. I felt stupid as hell, though," I said.

"Why?"

"Girl, you shoulda seen the way I jumped up off that couch! It was like some shit you see in the movies."

"Fuck that. I probably wouldn't have no niggas touchin' me for a year or two without screamin' and shit. You a good one."

"No, he's a good one. Girl, that man can work wonders with his lips. I just couldn't get through the arm pinnin'."

"Well I hope he ain't too freaky, wantin' to tie a bitch up and shit. Did you ask him if he's into that dominatrix stuff? You can't handle all that," she said, rolling a blunt.

"Shut up," I laughed.

When she grabbed the lighter off the table, I couldn't hold my comments. "You 'bout to smoke at 11:30 in the mornin'?"

"Is there a smoking start and stop time?"

"Lexis, you need to slow that shit down."

"Kiss my ass, Tameka," she said, taking her first pull.

"I'm serious. That shit ain't cute."

"But I am, and that's all that matters. Now back to Craig. Did you feel anything?"

"Feel what?"

"Damn, you want me to say it? His dick! Was it big?"

"I'm not gon' get into this with you right now."

"Why? You was 'bout to tell me everything a few minutes ago. Now that I got a blunt in my hand, you don't wanna tell me shit?"

"I don't like talkin' to you when you're high, point blank."

"Well point blank yo ass outta here then, and holla at me tomorrow. I'ma be high all day."

I got up and headed upstairs. "What time are we goin' to the fair so I can tell Craig?"

"Oh, I didn't know he was comin'. When did you invite him?"

"Last night."

"That's the part of the story I didn't get to hear yet, I guess."

"What time, Lexis?"

"Ask Robert. He's still up in the room."

Robert confirmed that we'd be leaving at five, so when Craig called at three, I told him the plan and he agreed to meet us at the house by 4:30. While I had him on the phone, I brought up the incident from the night before.

"…I just don't want you to think that you can't touch me or kiss me anymore," I said. It flowed off my tongue so freely that I didn't realize how pathetic I sounded until I finished my sentence. "I mean, if you…You know, like if you ever wanted to show me affection or somethin', I—"

"I understand," he interrupted. I was glad he cut me off. "Don't worry, beautiful. You didn't scare me away."

Thank you, Jesus! Where was this man from? He couldn't have been from this planet 'cause I didn't think there were any guys like him left. Wherever he came from, I just hoped he never went back.

When we hung up, I called Tielle. I already knew she was going to the fair with Romeo, but I was calling to see what time they would be there.

"Did you and Craig go out last night?" she asked.

"Girl, naw," I said. I told her the whole story.

"Whoa," she said.

"That's what he said when I jumped up," I said. "Girl, it was a nightmare."

I went back downstairs after we got off the phone. Lexis and Robert were watching TV.

"Have you heard from Jermaine?" I asked.

"Nope." She was high as a kite.

"He didn't tell you what time he was comin' when he called earlier?"

"No, Meka. Damn! He'll be here. Relax."

"You and that damn weed, Lexis. You better calm the attitude down."

Robert laughed. "I ain't never seen nothin' like y'all."

Chapter 8

We arrived at the fair at a quarter after five. We had the couple thing going on...Tielle and Romeo, me and Craig, and Lexis and Robert. I was apprehensive as hell and on the defense because I already knew what to expect. True enough, our city was big, but people recognize new faces—especially gangstas and hoodrats. The gangstas wanna make sure the new nigga ain't beefin', and the hoodrats wanna throw ass to the new nigga. And there I was, the most hated female in town, walking with a fine man that hardly anybody knew...Drama.

As soon as we walked through the gates, all eyes were on us. I'd warned Craig that it was gonna happen, but he thought I was over-exaggerating until he saw everybody staring like he was the main attraction.

"Keep your eyes straight ahead. That's what I have to do. Otherwise, it's liable to be an altercation."

"No more fightin'. Don't mess up that pretty face."

"Whatever. You don't know these broads like I do."

"Man, ain't nobody payin' attention to you," Alexis chimed in.

"Once again, Alexis, I'ma tell you to stop talkin' to me. You high, and I will knock you down if you keep talkin' to me."

"C'mon, y'all. Cool out," Tielle said. "I don't wanna have to split y'all up."

We all got on the ferris wheel so we could get a bird's eye view of the fairgrounds. While we were riding, I spotted TJ and his boys shooting air rifles at paper targets. My worse nightmare would come true if we ran into each other. He had the potential to clown if he saw me with another dude, even though we weren't together. Craig started talking to me, so I tried to pay attention to him instead of worrying about my ex.

We got off the ride and stopped at the elephant ear stand.

"I wonder if Dap and Carmen are here," Alexis said.

"They should be around here somewhere," Tielle replied.

That reminded me…I pulled Craig off to the side. "Hey, I wanna ask you somethin'."

"What's up?"

"I saw Dap about a week or so ago, and she said you had a talk with her."

"I just told her that she needs to act her age and be more considerate of your situation."

"My situation doesn't make me helpless or handicapped. I can handle my own problems."

"I wasn't tryin' to cause problems or speak on your behalf. I just told her how I felt. Evidently what I said sunk in 'cause she said somethin' to you. I didn't tell her to say anything."

I could tell he was getting heated, and I didn't care. I felt like he was trying to control shit and be a hero when he didn't even know the whole story.

"Well for future reference, I can take care of myself. I don't need you talkin' to nobody for me."

He just looked at me. "I'm here to have a good time, so do you wanna join the rest of the group, or do you wanna stand over here and argue?"

We rejoined everyone, though I held on to my attitude for a while. After a few rides, we all split up. Craig and I sat on a bench behind the gaming area to rest our feet.

We got on a couple more rides and decided to leave before all the youngins arrived. Of course, we talked some more in the car. I liked the fact that Craig was so talkative. A man who can express himself and hold a decent conversation is a man I could keep around. Quiet men always seem to have something to hide.

When we pulled up to the house, I saw that Alexis and Robert were already home. I also saw a royal blue Chevy Caprice with glistening rims, tinted windows, and a Florida license plate, so I figured it was Jermaine's. Craig and I walked in the house. Beer bottles were all over the kitchen counter, and incense was lit to try to cover the weed smell. Alexis, Robert, and Jermaine were in the dining room. There were cards on the table, but I couldn't figure out what game they were playing with only three people.

I sat the giant stuffed dog (that Craig won for me) on the couch and walked toward the dining room table. Alexis just looked at me and took a swig of her beer.

"Why you lookin' at me like that?" she asked.

"'Cause you ain't gotta have the damn house tore up like this. This don't make no sense, Lexis!" I went in the kitchen and threw the empty bottles away. In the midst of my frustration, I realized that I didn't speak to Jermaine.

"Hey, Jermaine. How you doin'?"

"I'm cool, cuz. Sorry about the mess," he said.

"This is Craig. Craig, this is my cousin, Jermaine."

They exchanged the universal black man head nod.

Two seconds later, I heard a voice say, "What…I don't get no introduction?"

Oh my God. It was TJ. He strolled out of the bathroom. I wanted to crawl into the sink and slide down the drain. Why in the hell was he at my house while I wasn't there and why did Alexis let him in knowing that Craig was with me? Yeah, Craig knew all about TJ, but TJ didn't know shit about Craig until that moment, nor did he have the right to know.

I gathered myself, but not in enough time. TJ had already continued talking.

"What's up? I'm TJ."

Craig spoke, but I could tell he wasn't feeling the whole vibe.

"I'm Meka's man," TJ continued, then came into the kitchen, hugging on me. I pushed him away.

"Is that right?" Craig responded.

"Stop! You drunk," I said as I batted TJ's hands away.

He finally gave up and stepped back into the dining area. "Yeah, you know. We been on the outs for a while, but me and my boo tryin' to make it work and shit, you know?"

Craig stood with his arms folded.

"Sit your drunk ass down, TJ," I said.

I grabbed Craig by his arm and led him to the stairs. "Nobody comes to my room," I said, looking directly at TJ. On my way up the stairs, I eyeballed Alexis, committing her guilty facial expression to my memory. Once we were in my room, I closed the door and faced Craig.

"Look. Before you even get started, you ain't gotta explain shit," he said. "I ain't trippin'. I ain't your man."

"And TJ ain't either," I said. "Craig, I know I ain't gotta explain nothin' to you. I just feel like we're better than that. I'm not just gonna blow off what just happened. That's like havin' a big ass elephant standin' here in the room and pretending like it ain't here.

So *you* look. I already told you the deal with me and TJ. Yes, I still have feelings for him, and he has feelings for me. No, we are not together, nor do I have any intentions of bein' with him now or any time in the future."

His face didn't break.

"He's drunk, and he's talkin' shit. He knew damn well that I was out with you, so he pushed your buttons. And even though you actin' like you ain't pissed, I know you are." I paused to see if he had anything to say. "I don't even know what he's doin' here, 'cause he normally ain't here unless I've invited him. My sister had somethin' to do with it 'cause I saw the look on her face. What I do know is that we've spent a lot of time talkin' on the phone, gettin' to know each other. And during the little time that we've spent together, I've enjoyed every minute of it."

I grabbed his chin and turned his face toward mine. "Look at me. Craig, I haven't even known you that long, but I can honestly say that I'm diggin' you. I care about what you think, and I care about how you feel. I've never felt this way before so soon and I feel crazy; standin' here, pouring my heart out to you. I don't explain myself to anybody. Now you may not feel the same way, but I felt like I owed you this much—to come up here and talk to you alone."

Still, he stood in front of me, speechless and stone-faced. I've never been one to beg, so I headed for the door. Just when I unlocked it, he grabbed my arm. "Wait," he said. He didn't have to say anything else because I read his soul through his eyes. He tucked my hair behind my ear. "I know that took a lot. You didn't have to explain yourself." He held me tighter. "I'm sorry I acted like that. I just didn't know what to think." His strong arms embraced my body.

We pulled away from each other slightly, then he planted the sweetest kiss on my welcoming lips. I was ready to continue, but he stopped abruptly.

"My fault. I forgot," he said.

I'd really scared him away. After my little freak-out episode, how was he supposed to know what I was comfortable with and what wasn't allowed? I was determined not to let thoughts of the rape interrupt my (sex) life again.

"Don't stop," I whispered.

I pulled his head towards me, and we kissed again. That time with pure passion. I felt like I was gonna explode inside. We made our way to the bed where he laid me down and slipped his hand under my shirt. With one hand, he unhooked my red lace bra and

84

softly massaged my sensitive breasts. Soon, his face replaced his hands, and he was drawing perfect circles around my nipples with his tongue. I stopped him, but only to lock the door. It was definitely going down. I was determined to fight the demons in my mind that kept chanting, "I can at least let you know what I feel like," in the rapist's chilling voice.

I got back in the bed, and an anxious Craig continued to explore my body. Once he reached my belly button, he said, "I just wanna be gentle with you."

His words were sweet and sincere. I thought I was gonna just throw the coochie at him after he said that. He licked around the area for a while, then returned to my lips. *Tease*, I thought.

I felt his manhood grow as his tongue slid gently around mine. He pulled off my capris and made his way to my thighs. His lips touched every area possible, and I quivered each time his breath tickled my skin. He tugged on my Vicki's with his teeth…a true sign that I had a freak on my hands. And within seconds, I was completely naked. I clenched the sheets as he buried his face in my forest of fornication and licked all over my forbidden fruit. *Jesus, I know I shouldn't be calling your name, but I can't find no other words. Forgive me.*

"Damn, you taste good," he said between laps. He had to hold my legs down so I wouldn't squirm off the bed, and I bit my pillow so nobody would hear me downstairs.

After I climaxed, he took off his pants. He stood next to the bed in his boxer-briefs at full attention, ready to give me the business. While he put the condom on, I grabbed my stereo remote and pushed play. Luckily, I had R. Kelly in there because I was listening to it earlier.

We made love from "TP2," to "Feelin' on Yo Booty," following the rhythms, and at times, making up our own. Out of all the men I'd had sex with, Craig was definitely a shoe-in for number one, with TJ close at number two. He was so sensual, and he knew when to work me slow and when to beat it up.

After we were done, we didn't say a word. We were so exhausted that we fell asleep butt-naked, holding each other. In his arms, I felt more secure than I'd felt in years.

***

Meanwhile, Alexis, Jermaine, and TJ had a secret plan in motion. Alexis had TJ come to the apartment so she could introduce him to Jermaine. They had a common interest: finding the guy who raped Tameka and killing him. TJ explained the beef between him and the dudes, and they discussed the possibilities of their whereabouts.

Jermaine planned to stay in town as long as he needed. Getting justice for Tameka was his top priority. He would do anything to protect his family, and he knew he wouldn't sleep at night knowing that Tameka was in danger.

Alexis couldn't tell her sister what was really going on because she knew Tameka wouldn't approve. She wouldn't want any of them going to jail or getting hurt. Unfortunately, that meant that Tameka would think she had TJ at the house out of spite, and she would have to take the heat for a misconception.

After they finished scheming, TJ headed to the staircase. Jermaine stopped him. "Go home, dawg."

They argued about it for a little while, but TJ finally left. There was no use in making another enemy.

***

The next morning, Craig woke up early. I heard him in my bathroom. When he came back in the room, I greeted him with a smile.

"What's up, beautiful?" He grinned from ear to ear.

I looked down. "Looks like you are."

"So what you gon' do about that?" he asked as he climbed back in the bed with me. He went to kiss me, but I stopped him in his tracks, blocking his mouth with my hand.

"Hold up." I reached into my nightstand drawer and pulled out two pieces of gum.

"I don't do the mornin' breath thing."

He laughed.

Seconds later, we began part two of our sex-a-thon. I concluded that he had to have Viagra flowing naturally through his system for him to stay hard so long. As with the previous night, we did it in every position, from me riding him like a wild boar, to clenching his broad shoulders, holding on for dear life. Afterwards, we didn't fall asleep. We laid there and talked instead.

"You know your sister's gon' wanna know what happened up here."

"I know," I said. "And so will TJ. That don't mean I'm tellin' them."

We took a shower together, and he left. I went right back upstairs after I walked him to the door. When I returned my room, I dove onto the bed. My pillows smelled like Craig's cologne, so I sniffed the hell out of them until somebody knocked on my door.

"What?" I asked with an attitude.

"Let me in," Alexis called from the other side of the door after unsuccessfully turning the knob.

"What do you want?"

"I gotta ask you somethin'."

I opened the door and stood with my hand on my hip.

"Damn, I can't come in?" she asked.

"Nope."

"You trippin'. Well anyway, what happened last night? Mr. Craig didn't leave 'til this mornin'." She grinned, waiting for details.

"I should knock your teeth down your monkey-ass throat."

"Hold up now. I ain't comin' at you all crazy, so you ain't got no reason to come at me crazy."

"Back up out my room."

"Or what?"

"Or you gon' hear some shit you ain't ready for."

"Try me. What? You mad about last night?"

"Why was he here, Lexis?"

"Who?"

"You know damned well who."

"Look. TJ wanted to kick it, so I told him to come hang out."

"When you knew Craig was bringin' me home."

"Whatever, Meka. You ain't with neither of them. And I didn't even know Craig was comin' back to the house."

I had to catch myself before I choked the shit out of her. I clasped my hands together and took a deep breath.

"You did that shit to be funny. You ain't slick. I don't know what I've done to you to make you wanna start some shit, but you did this on purpose."

"I don't know what you talkin' 'bout," she said. "I just came over here to see what happened with you and ol' boy 'cause I know he didn't leave last night. I'll leave you alone since you in a bad mood." She headed across the hall.

"Your best bet is to stay over there. I ain't got shit nice to say to you, Alexis. I don't know how your mind works. I thought that you

87

actually wanted to see me happy, not set me up for some drama. And since you wanna know what happened in my room last night so bad, let me tell you. I realized that my sister ain't shit."

I slammed my door and locked it. I knew I'd hurt her feelings because she hated when I shut her out of my life, but I didn't care. I meant every word of what I said.

Alexis went in her room and plopped on the bed. Robert rubbed her back.

"She hates me for this."

"That's because she doesn't know what's really going on," Robert replied. "You gon' be able to do this? She's gonna keep lashing out on you."

Alexis shrugged. "She'll understand when it's all over."

Chapter 9

Tielle called to see how my night went. I told her about Alexis' antics and hinted that Craig had stayed over. She asked if there were any fireworks.

"I don't kiss and tell," I said.

"Naw, you screw and tell," she responded. "Now stop playin'."

"Okay…We did it," I said.

"Oh my goodness. No details, please. Remember, he's my cousin."

"I wish he wasn't, 'cause there's so much to tell."

"I guess you'll have to save that for Nicole."

She had called to tell me that she and Romeo were officially a couple. Her excitement was so apparent I could see all her teeth through the phone.

I was happy that Romeo worked out for her. Tielle deserved someone nice, and it didn't hurt that he was a cutie, either.

I had to end our conversation earlier than I would've liked because I had another call come in. It was TJ's punk ass.

"What do you want?" I asked.

"I just called to see how your night was since we both know you didn't get much sleep," TJ said.

"You don't know a damn thing about how much sleep I got. You didn't even have no business at my house in the first place. Then, your drunk ass sat up and told my date that you were my boyfriend. What kinda shit is that?"

"Man, I was just bullshittin'."

"That's your problem. You always bullshittin'. You were at my house like them niggas ain't still lookin' for you. You don't respect me worth shit. You want them to kill me or somethin'?"

"My car was parked two blocks down the street."

"And?" I asked.

"Man, look. Lexis called and said y'all cousin was in town and they was gon' be drinkin' and shit, so I told her I'd stop through."

"Since when has Alexis been your welcome wagon? Y'all fuckin' or somethin'?"

"You really trippin' now. I saw her at the fair and we talked for a second. I told her to hit me up if she knew of anybody throwin' a set or somethin'."

I could tell he was lying because his voice went up an octave.

"Save it, TJ. Just don't fuckin' call here for me no more."

"You in love with that nigga or somethin'?"

"Don't worry about it."

"Lexis already told me about dude. You ain't even known him that long."

"Well evidently she didn't tell you the whole deal, 'cause if she did, she woulda told you that I'm really feelin' him."

"It's cool. You can go through yo little actin' out stage if you want, but we both know who you love and who you'll always love. I'll holla at you," he said and hung up.

I needed something to do to get my mind off the whole TJ-Alexis ordeal, but since it was Sunday, my options were limited. My only alternative was to ride around town, stopping at small shops on the avenue. I picked up some cocoa scented candles for my bedroom and a box of Magnum condoms during my shopping spree. My rubber supply had been depleted for a while because TJ and I rarely used them. Whenever we did, he brought his own.

I had a feeling that Craig and I were gonna need them since we had taken our relationship to that level. Even though he seemed like a nice, clean guy, I never had sex without a condom unless I was in love. That said, TJ was the only one who had ever experienced the true feeling of my walls.

***

I invited Craig over for dinner, and afterward we went to the park. I felt awkward because I didn't know how to act anymore. Before we had sex, we just kicked it. It was like we were good friends who were also attracted to each other. Since sex had entered the equation, I felt like we needed to discuss what was next. I didn't expect him to ask me to be his girlfriend or anything, but I wanted to know where his head was. I needed to know where to cut my "like" for him off before it turned into love.

90

We walked hand in hand on the Lovers Trail. It led to a gazebo with a swing inside.

"You wanna sit down?" Craig asked.

"Yeah," I answered. "I wanna talk to you about somethin' anyway."

We sat down, and Craig leaned forward. "What's up?" he asked.

"That's what I wanna ask you," I said in a shaky voice. "I feel like so much is up in the air since last night."

"What you mean?" he asked.

"I just wanna know what you're thinkin' right now."

"Do you wanna know if I still respect you or somethin'?"

"Whatever's in your head. I'm not askin' if you wanna be with me or anything like that. I know you're new in town and I'm not the only female here. I just wanna know what's next."

Craig looked shocked. He took a deep breath before he replied. "I'ma put it to you like this. I don't put time and effort into somethin' that I'm just gon' give up. And after what happened last night, you definitely ain't gotta worry about me cuttin' out no time soon."

How comforting. Basically all he said was, *You gave up the booty and it was good, so I'll be back to hit it.* All that other crap he threw in was padding to fill in the blanks. He talked his way around the question, then told his true feelings in one sentence. The disgust I was feeling must've shown on my face.

"What's wrong?" he asked.

"Nothin'," I said, trying to lower my eyebrows back to their neutral position and uncurl my upper lip. "Can we leave?" I asked.

"Already?"

"Yeah. I'm gettin' sleepy."

We walked back to the apartment and said our goodbyes. I think he could tell that something was bothering me, but he chose not to say anything.

***

When Craig got to his Aunt Rosie's house, Tielle and Kaelin were there, playing with Chris. He walked over to his nephew, picked him up, and started bouncing him up and down.

"Where you comin' from?" Tielle asked with a smile.

"Tameka's," Craig answered. "But I'm sure you already knew that."

"So you like her?" Kaelin asked, frowning.

91

"She's cool. Why?"

"To each his own, I guess."

"She don't really like her," Tielle said.

"Damn, man. She's got a lot of haters," Craig said.

"It ain't like she's done anything to anybody. People just don't take the time to get to know her. Hell, I didn't know she was so cool 'til we had to work together in high school," Tielle said. She motioned for him to follow her into the kitchen.

Craig handed Chris back to Kaelin and joined Tielle at the kitchen table.

"Talk to me. What do you think about my girl?" she asked.

"You don't waste time, do you?" he asked.

"I just wanna know."

"Why? So you can go back and tell her?"

"If you tell me not to say anything, I won't."

Craig looked into his cousin's eyes, wondering if he should open up to her. He had a lot on his mind about Tameka, and he knew he couldn't tell his boys without sounding soft.

"I guess I'll go ahead and tell you since you're my favorite cousin," he said.

"And because I'm the best friend who can give you the inside scoop, right?"

"Yeah, right. I know how y'all females are. Y'all stick together. I'm sure she's probably told you stuff that you can't tell me, and I respect that. You just gotta do the same for me. Don't tell her what I'm about to tell you."

"Alright. So do you like her?"

He admitted that Tameka was girlfriend material. He just wanted to take it slow and make sure he got to know her better.

"Well make sure you don't wait too long, 'cause if you haven't noticed, she's a hot commodity around here."

Chapter 10

By the beginning of October, things were going well. I decided to continue with counseling until the end of the year as long as I still felt like I was getting something out of it. Alexis and I had mended our fences with Scotch tape. We got along for the most part, but I still didn't feel like I could trust her the way I should trust my sister.

On the relationship side of things, Tielle and Romeo were the cutest couple. She finally gave him some, holding strong to her three-month rule. From what she told me, the waiting period only made things better. She said he was so ready he worked her like his life depended on it.

Robert and Alexis were "taking a break." He had gotten fed up with all of her weed smoking, drinking, and partying, so he told her to give him a call when she slowed down. I couldn't believe he was actually sticking to his decision. Usually, Lexis would look at him with glassy eyes to make him feel bad, then throw the booty at him. After that, they'd be in love again.

Don't think she didn't try, though. He just wasn't going for it that time. The result: Alexis was wilder than ever. She was spending the majority of her time with Marcus, the dude she met at Tielle's Fourth of July picnic. They'd kept in touch periodically while she was still with Robert, but she never did anything with him. That had definitely changed, and whatever they were doing, she hardly came home anymore.

As for my love life, a lot had changed. Craig and I still went out a lot, but I felt like it was only a matter of time before he started dating someone else. I didn't want to become too invested in him, so I slowed myself down. I was beginning to like him too much—more than he liked me, so I buried myself in my work to have an excuse not to kick it with him at times.

TJ hadn't called in a while. The last time I'd heard from him was sometime at the beginning of September. He told me that our attackers had skipped town. One of his boys heard through the grapevine that they went to New York because the police were getting more leads on my case. They were supposedly getting closer to finding out the rapist's identity. I thanked him for telling me, and we hadn't talked since.

It was a relief to know that I wouldn't have to continue walking around scared. I would've been more satisfied if the police would've caught those idiots, but New York was good enough for me. As long as they stayed away from Texas, I was fine.

Jermaine left shortly after TJ told me the news, finally admitting that the two of them were plotting to find the guys and kill them. I told him to stay out of it because I didn't want him living the life that he used to. He agreed to leave but told me that he'd be back if he heard anything about the guys returning.

I still hadn't heard from my dad, but I tried not to let it bother me. Deep down, it crushed me that Dad hadn't called to see how we were doing. It wasn't like him. He still didn't know about the rape because we never got to tell him, and when we called again, his numbers were changed. My mom, on the other hand, called us once a week like clockwork. And even though my ill feelings for her hadn't changed, it was still comforting to know that she cared about what was going on with us.

***

It was a Thursday night, and I was bored as hell. I called Tielle to see if she wanted to go to Smoothies because I didn't have to work on Fridays anymore. We decided to meet there at nine. I pulled into the parking lot at ten of and waited in my car. As I grooved to Alicia Keys, there was a tap on my window. It was TJ, and he looked a hot mess. I rolled down my window and frowned.

"What?" I asked.

"Damn! You ain't gotta be like that," he said. "Why you just sittin' here?"

"Why are you standin' here?"

"I'm about to go inside!" He hated my attitude. "I just saw your car, so I came over here to speak. Plus, I need a favor."

"I knew it!" I said. "I knew somethin' was up."

"For real, boo. I need my hair braided. You see this shit. You know I don't walk around lookin' like this."

He was right. His hair was all over his head from when he had taken his braids out. Even though he picked it out, it looked raggedy, and I never found TJ attractive with an afro.

"Where's the girl who usually braids it?" I asked.

"Her grandmother died, so she left to go to Alabama yesterday."

I could braid hair, but I didn't make a practice of it anymore. It was my other little hustle when times got hard at school, but that was it. My fingers had been retired for almost two years.

"C'mon, Meka," he whined.

"Twenty dollars," I said.

"Oh, you wanna charge a nigga now that you ain't wit' 'em."

"You damned straight."

Tielle pulled up and I got out of the car. She gave me a questioning look when she saw TJ.

"LT!" TJ yelled. "What's good?"

"Nothin'. What's up with you?"

"I'm just tryin' to get my hair braided. Your girl over here trippin', tryin' to charge a nigga."

"It ain't like you ain't got the money," Tielle replied.

TJ agreed to pay me twenty dollars, and I told him to be at my house the next day at two. We all walked in Smoothies together, but once inside, we split up. I had my usual cranberry and vodka, and Tielle started her night with a screwdriver. I was done with my drink within ten minutes, so I grabbed the next waiter I saw walking by.

"Excuse me," I yelled, motioning for the guy to come to our table. "I'm gonna need another drink." I was immediately distracted by Judge's sexy voice and thick accent as he recited a poem titled, "Hey You." Tielle nudged me and asked what I wanted. I looked up at the waiter and noticed that he was fine as hell. He was chocolate with a curly, baby fro. He had a goatee, a nice little build, and long eyelashes that enhanced his ebony eyes.

"I'm sorry," I said, smiling flirtatiously. "I want another cranberry and vodka and your number."

Tielle cracked up. He smiled, took Tielle's order, and walked away. When he got back, he handed Tielle her drink, then sat mine in front of me.

"Thank you…" I read his nametag. "…Isaac."

"No problem," he said, handing me an extra napkin.

"Oh, I'm cool. I don't need another napkin," I said.

"Keep it," he said. "It's what you requested." He winked at me and walked away.

"What?" Tielle asked.

I shrugged and laid the napkin on the table. When I looked down to grab my glass, I saw Isaac's number scribbled on it in blue ink.

"No, he didn't!"

Tielle turned to see what I was talking about. She laughed when she saw the number. "Girl, you are too much," she said.

"I didn't know he was really gon' give it to me."

Nevertheless, I put the napkin in my purse. I waved goodbye to Isaac on our way out of the club and flashed another flirtatious smile. He was too cute to ignore, so I made sure I put his number in my panty drawer when I got home. I didn't really plan on using it, but I figured it could stay there until my next spring cleaning.

When I checked my messages, I found that Craig had left two. It was already one in the morning and I knew he had to go to work, so I decided to call him the next afternoon.

I didn't wake up until 12:30 the next day. I remembered I had to do TJ's hair, so that meant I needed to hurry up so I'd have time to eat, take a shower, and put on some fresh clothes. As soon as I got dressed, TJ rang the doorbell. I ran downstairs and let him in.

"What's up?" he said. He brushed past me, went straight into the kitchen, opened up the refrigerator, and pulled out a Pepsi.

"Your price just went up to twenty-five dollars," I said.

"'Cause I got a soda?"

"Yep."

"I can get a case of these for five dollars."

"Then put my can down and go get you a case."

"How 'bout I pay you another way?" he said, coming up behind me and wrapping his arms around my waist.

"Go on now," I said, freeing myself from his hold. "Let's go. I already don't wanna do this nappy shit." I grabbed his hair and led him into the living room.

We walked over to the couch and he sat on the floor between my legs. I grabbed the comb and parted his hair.

"I remember this position," he said. "I used to face the other way, though."

I smacked his head with the comb and laughed. "Behave."

"So where's your boy?"

"Who?"

"Your boyfriend."

"Craig is not my boyfriend," I said, pulling his braid tighter.

"Ow!" TJ yelled. "I'm just sayin'. I thought y'all was in love. You can't call a nigga no more."

"I won't call you no more. There's a difference. And you know why I don't wanna call you or be with you no more."

"Man, I ain't even out there like that no more."

"But you're still out there," I said. "Leave it alone, TJ. I don't wanna get into this."

"So you would be with me if I straightened up?"

"I didn't say that."

"It's cool. You ain't gotta admit it. I know what I gotta do to get you back."

"Whatever."

I was almost done at 4:30. He wanted a bunch of crazy designs in his head, so it took me longer than usual. When I was in the middle of the last braid, Alexis walked in. She spoke and sat down in the recliner.

"What made you start braidin' hair again? I know a whole bunch of niggas who'll pay you to do their hair," she said.

"This was an emergency situation," I replied. "He was lookin' a mess."

In the middle of our laughter, somebody rang the doorbell. Alexis got up and answered the door. TJ and I were still joking around. He brought up a time when I was looking crazy with my hair all over the place.

I was almost in tears from laughing so hard. I grabbed his head and put mine next to it, giving him a slight hug.

Wouldn't you know that Craig walked his ass around the corner right at that moment? TJ and I both stopped laughing and turned toward the living room entrance. I pushed him forward and swung my left leg over his head so I could get up. Craig looked furious.

"What's up, baby," I said and gave him a hug. He didn't hug me back.

"You tell me," Craig replied.

"I just got done braidin' TJ's hair."

"Is that right?" he said sarcastically as he glared at TJ.

"Yeah, that's right," TJ said with an attitude and stood up.

I felt a confrontation arising. Alexis stood behind Craig with her hands in the air, mouthing, "I tried not to let him in."

"Alright, y'all. That's enough," I said. "TJ was just about to leave."

"No, I wasn't. Don't front on me just 'cause this nigga's here," TJ said.

"Ain't nobody frontin'," I said. "I'm done with your hair, so all that's left for you to do is pay me and leave."

"Why don't I leave? It seems like y'all was havin' a good time before I came," Craig said.

"No, Craig. Just stay—"

"Yeah, why don't you leave?" TJ said, walking toward Craig.

Craig stepped closer to him. Alexis tried to pull him back by his shirt, but it didn't work. I jumped in between them, hoping I wouldn't catch a stray punch.

"Hold up!" I yelled. "Y'all ain't gon' do this in my house. TJ, you need to step outside. And—"

TJ pushed me out of the way and swung on Craig. He clocked him in the jaw. Craig immediately reacted, hitting TJ in his left eye. Alexis and I yelled for them to stop, and we tried to separate them. She jumped on Craig's back, trying to get him on the ground, and I rushed TJ, pushing him all the way out the door.

"Keep him in here," I ordered Alexis.

I closed the door and started in on TJ.

"What's your problem?" I asked. "Don't disrespect me or my house like that."

"Fuck that nigga," he said. "I'ma kill his ass. That nigga hit me in my fuckin' eye," he continued, holding the side of his face. "I'ma fuck him up."

"That's your problem…always wantin' to retaliate. Take it like a man. You hit him first! Did you think he wasn't gon' hit you back?"

He pulled two twenties out of his pocket and threw them at me. "There's your fuckin' money," he said as he walked to his car. "You ain't worth all this shit." He got in his car and drove off.

I picked up the money and walked back inside. Alexis met me at the door. "Girl, he's shitty," she whispered. "I'd leave him alone for a minute if I was you."

"Where's he at?" I asked.

"In your room. You shoulda seen the look on his face when you went outside with TJ."

"I needed to get his hot-tempered ass outta here."

"Well, that's not how Craig saw it," Alexis said. "I'm about to go up here and get outta these work clothes. I'll stay in my room on alert, so scream if he starts trippin'."

When I opened my door, Craig was sitting on my bed holding a bag of ice on his face.   "You alright?" I asked timidly.

"That's all you can say?"

"What do you want me to say?"

"You can start off by tellin' me why I walked in and saw you all hugged up with that nigga between your legs."

"First off, you're makin' it more than it was. I was braidin' his hair."

"It looked done to me."

"I'd just gotten done, Craig."

"So is that why you didn't call me back last night? He was here then, too?"

"I didn't call you back because I got in late. TJ wasn't over here. We haven't even talked in weeks."

"Man, whatever. You tryin' to play me for a fool. I shoulda known to stop dealin' with you a long time ago when he was over here after the fair."

"It wasn't even like—" I stopped myself. "Hold up. I don't even know why I'm explainin' myself to you. True enough, I care about you and you claim you care about me, but that don't make us shit but two people who happen to care about each other. You came up in my place, clickin' on me 'cause a nigga was sittin' between my legs. I ain't never clicked on you when I see them lil' hoes all up on you at the clubs, now do I?"

"Well maybe you don't give a fuck," he said, standing up. "But I got a problem when my girl's ex is always in her face. That nigga always finds a way to be around you."

He kept talking, but I didn't hear anything after he referred to me as his "girl." What was that all about? I let him finish going off, then I asked him.

"Time out," I said. "What did you just call me?"

I could tell he was embarrassed, but he still tried to play hard. "My girl," he said, looking me dead in my eyes.

"You mean your 'girl' as in, your homegirl? Or..."

"You know damn well what I mean."

"I just need some clarification, 'cause I've learned to never assume anything."

"My girl as in, I love you," he blurted.

My heart fell to the ground, and I was hoping that my legs didn't look as shaky as they felt. The sincerity in his eyes was absolutely beautiful, but something suddenly came to mind.

"When did these feelings pop up?" I asked.

"They've been there. I just never said anything 'cause I wasn't sure."

"So were you ever gonna let me know you considered us a couple?"

"Eventually, yeah."

He looked so pitiful, sitting there with the ice on his face and a helpless look in his eyes. There was no more doubt about my feelings for him. I'd been fighting them all along, trying to avoid him in any way I could, but it was finally safe to let my guard down. I loved him, and he felt the same way about me. I walked over to him, sat the bag of ice on my bed, and pulled his face towards mine.

"Come here," I said. We gave each other a soft peck. "I love you, too."

Chapter 11

Things were going great with me and Craig. I'd been spending a lot more nights at his place, where we had the whole apartment to ourselves. I didn't know if that was a good or a bad thing. I was trying to get back into church like I knew I should've been, and having sex with my man almost every day wasn't blazing my trail to heaven. I talked to him about slowing down, but he didn't think I could do it. My simple request turned into a fifty-dollar bet that I couldn't go two weeks without sex. He told me his loving was so good that I wouldn't be able to stay away from it. I took the bet for two reasons: One, I wanted the extra money; and two, I was hoping that if I held off that long, we might not do it as often and I could at least be halfway right with God.

During the two-week period, I stayed at my house. I knew that if I went to his place, it was all over. I didn't even see Alexis for the whole first week. She was either at work or at Marcus' house. I was beginning to wonder if Robert had lost his place in her life.

When I came home from work the next Thursday, she and Tiffany were there. Her face looked scratched up, and her shirt was torn.

Before I could ask what happened, Lexis jumped up from the couch. "Look at this shit!" she said, pointing to her face.

"What happened?"

"I got into it with Adrienne."

Adrienne was one of Dap's friends. She and Lexis had never gotten along because she had a huge crush on Robert. Whenever Alexis hung out with Dap, she usually made sure Adrienne wouldn't be there.

"Where at?" I asked.

"At Dap's."

"What were you doin' over there while she was there?"

"She wasn't there at first. She stopped by to give Dap some money for liquor for the party this weekend," Alexis said.

Tiffany came out of the bathroom with a wet washcloth and two bandages. She handed the stuff to Alexis.

"Were you there?" I asked her.

"For every minute of it," Tiffany replied.

She told me the story, saying how Adrienne had come by to drop off the money, but hung around after she saw Lexis.

"She walked all up in the kitchen, got somethin' to drink, sat down in the den with us...everything. Then, the broad starts makin' small talk with Dap about stupid shit. Mind you, she still ain't spoke to me or Lexis. So, next thing I know, she asked me about me and my babies, and if Marlon still took care of them like he's supposed to," Tiffany continued.

"Why was she all in your business?" I asked. "And why didn't Dap check her then for bein' in her brother's business?"

"Keep listenin'," Alexis said.

"So, I told her that Marlon was doin' what he was supposed to do 'cause I wasn't settlin' for less. Now, I guess she was hopin' I'd say somethin' like that, 'cause here she go: 'Girl, that's what I'm talkin' about. I already have my eye on somebody. He just became available, too!' So I asked her if he was from here, and she said he was. Then Dap asked who she was talkin' about, and she was like, 'Ask Alexis,'" Tiffany said.

"And that's when I got up and punched her in her fuckin' mouth," Alexis said, dabbing her cheek with the wet rag.

"So she was talkin' about Robert?" I asked to be sure.

"Yeah and little did she know, Robert had already told me he saw her a couple weeks ago at the gas station. He told me about their whole conversation."

"Evidently he ain't too available if he's still reportin' to you," I said. "See, that's why I told you to stay away from Dap and her little buddies. They're all the same. They always wanna start some mess over a nigga. You think I just get mad 'cause you smoke with them and stuff, but it's deeper than that. And what'd she do while y'all was fightin'?"

"Not a damned thing!" Tiffany chirped in. "I had to break 'em up by myself."

"I ain't gon' keep sayin' I told you so, 'cause I know that's the last thing you wanna hear, but you already know how I feel about that broad."

Lexis kept her distance from Dap for the next three days. That may not seem like much, but that was unheard of for her. Marcus became her time-filler, so he was at the house a lot. He was cool, but he got on my nerves sometimes—I had to listen to him crack corny jokes and be loud and obnoxious.

When Saturday came, all bets were off. Marcus' loud ass was still at my house, the two weeks were up, and I was horny as hell. I called Craig at ten o'clock that morning and told him I was on my way. I gave him orders to have my favorite Silk CD playing and to answer the door naked.

My baby didn't take me for a joke. He had the remote to his stereo system in his hand and nothing on his sexy body when he opened the door. I immediately took control once I walked in.

We made our way to the couch, and I straddled him. I didn't want him to waste time with foreplay. I pulled down my panties, and we kept kissing as he ran his fingers down the small of my back. Once my underwear were off, he went to put it in. I stopped him.

"Where's the rubber?" I was irritated because he wasn't prepared.

"Come on," he said in a whiny voice. "Stop playin'." He tried again.

"You need to quit playin' and go get a condom."

"I ain't got no more. I didn't have time to get any before you came. It's cool. You know I ain't been with nobody but you all this time. Let's just do this. I know you wanna feel me." His lips brushed against my neck.

I was hesitant because I'd never had unprotected sex with anybody but TJ. Craig was determined to break me down, though, gently licking all the right spots. As he saw me melting, he eased himself inside. My body shivered with raw pleasure. I opened my mouth to tell him to stop, but the only thing that came out was a soft moan. I actually felt like screaming in the name of orgasm, and a few strokes later, that's exactly what I did.

From then on, Craig and I didn't use protection. We agreed to use the pull-out method and be extra careful. Plus, we'd both been tested for STD's and we were both clean.

***

103

One evening, me, Craig, and Alexis were eating dinner at the house when the phone rang. I told Craig to answer it since he was closer. After he answered, he turned to us and said, "It's your dad."

Alexis took the phone to ask why he was calling all of a sudden, and he didn't understand why she asked that.

"I thought you knew I was outta town," he said.

"Daddy, you ain't been outta town for six months straight," Alexis replied.

"'Six months straight?"

She told him about her conversation with his fiancé. Evidently there was a mix up because Dad didn't get the message when Lexis called.

"Well you need to take that up with your little girlfriend," Alexis told him.

"She's not here right now," he said. "There has to be some mistake. I can't believe that she wouldn't tell me you called—especially if you said it was important," Dad said. "Plus, she had the number where she could reach me."

"Well somebody's lyin', and it ain't me."

"We'll get to the bottom of that once she gets here. So I take it she didn't call you with our new numbers either?"

"Nope. The operator let us know that your numbers had changed."

"In the meantime, what's goin' on there? What was so important when you called, or is it too late?"

Alexis hesitated. "Why don't I let you talk to Meka about that?" She handed me the phone. I got up from the table and went upstairs for some privacy.

"So I hear you didn't get the message," I said with an attitude.

"No, I didn't," Dad said. "How've you been, Punkin?"

"I don't think you really wanna know."

"What's wrong, baby?"

I couldn't speak. I sobbed for a couple minutes before I pulled myself together.

"I'm sorry," I said as I wiped my eyes and cleared my throat. I didn't expect to feel the same emotions—not to that extent. I thought I had made progress, especially after going to therapy and starting a relationship with Craig.

"Don't apologize. Just talk to me."

I told him I was raped, but didn't go into too many details.

He cleared his throat, something he does to keep his composure. "I can't believe I didn't know anything about this. You know I would've left my business trip and been right there with you, baby," he said.

"Shit happens, I guess." I still wasn't sure whether I believed his story.

"No, messages don't get delivered. Don't shut me out, Tameka. I know you're hurting. You've been hurting for all this time, and I should've been there. You better believe April's gonna hear my mouth when she comes home."

Once we got past all the rape stuff, I asked him why it took him so long to call us.

He didn't offer up excuses. "I could sit here and tell you how many business conferences and trips I've had to attend, but that never stopped me before. I guess I just figured y'all would call me if you wanted to talk. I thought maybe y'all were still mad about me being with April."

I really didn't have anything else to talk about and I wasn't satisfied with our exchange up to that point, so I said goodbye and took the phone back to Alexis.

The next day was December 7th. Craig had spent the night, and he left for work from my house that morning. I wasn't going to work until noon because I had my six-month retest with Dr. Crenshaw at 9:15.

When I got to her office, the routine was pretty much the same as the first time. She asked me if I'd had any problems or noticed anything unusual happening with my body. Of course, my answer was 'no'. Next, she asked the million-dollar question…Did I have sex with anyone since the last time she'd seen me?

"Yes," I replied. I hated when doctors asked personal questions.

"At any time, have you had unprotected sex with this man or these men?"

"Yeah, me and *the guy* have had unprotected sex."

I could tell that she was judging me by her facial expression.

"In that case, we'll be giving you a pregnancy test also."

My pregnancy test came back negative, but I had to wait two weeks for the other results.

When the 21st rolled around, I was in great spirits. Christmas was coming soon, there were great sales all over town, and Dad called to say he'd be in town the day after Christmas. He was coming to my rescue, and that's all I really wanted from him.

I didn't wake up until 10:15, and my appointment was at 11. I broke every traffic law on the way there, but I walked into her office at eleven o'clock on the dot. It seemed like I waited forever, but the nurse called me back 15 minutes later.

Dr. Crenshaw finally arrived. She had my file in her hand, and she didn't have the normal smug look on her face. She spoke to me and sat behind the desk.

"Give me the good news. Merry Christmas to me!" I laughed at my corny giddiness.

"Okay, Tameka. Slow down. You know the drill."

"Alright," I said. "Go ahead and give me your little speech about how the tests are done and all that jazz."

"Did anybody else come with you?" she asked, peering over the brim of her glasses.

"No. Why?"

She took a deep breath.

"I didn't have nobody here last time, and I don't need nobody here today." I looked at my watch. "Now let's get this show on the road, please. I gotta finish up some shopping."

Dr. Crenshaw opened the file and flipped through the papers. "First things first. Your routine STD testing was fine. Everything was negative."

"Cool."

"As for your HIV tests..." Dr. Crenshaw stalled.

"Will you stop playin'?" I said, laughing. "You're not supposed to torture me like this. Just go on and tell me the test was negative so I can leave." I grabbed my purse and stood up.

"Tameka, I had no intention on telling you this while you were by yourself." She paused, and I held my breath. "You're HIV-positive."

"Oh my God," I said. My eyes lost focus and my head became heavy. Dr. Crenshaw's face was soon a brown blur that moved with the spinning room. The next thing I knew, I woke up in a hospital bed and saw Dr. Crenshaw and Dr. Rogers standing over me. I broke into tears.

"I guess I wasn't dreaming," I said. "This shit is real."

"I paged Dr. Rogers so you'd have some support," Dr. Crenshaw said.

"I know this is hard to swallow, Tameka, but we discussed this possibility in our sessions, right?"

I just laid there. What had I done in a past life to deserve the punishment of living with HIV?

Dr. Crenshaw took over. "Before you leave today, we'll discuss some things we can do to help control any symptoms that may arise in the future. Of course, you'll be spending a lot of time here at the hospital…"

I tuned her out from that point on and let the tears roll down my face. She stopped talking when she realized that I was in a daze. All I could think about was, *I have AIDS*. I never asked to get raped. All I ever wanted in life was to be happy, and just when I'd finally achieved my goal, the walls were crashing in.

Chapter 12

Dr. Crenshaw must've called Alexis to come get me because she rushed into the hospital room a frantic mess. She ran over to the chair I was sitting in.

"What's wrong?" she asked.

"Let's just go home," I said, staring out the window at the swaying trees.

"Meka, what did the doctor say?" she asked.

I got up and started walking toward the door. I felt like a zombie. I couldn't cry anymore, and I couldn't think straight.

"What do you think she said?" I turned to face her but could barely see through my swollen eyelids.

Her mouth dropped open, and her eyes opened wide enough to fit apples in them. "No," she said in disbelief. "You don't have—"

"AIDS?"

"I thought it was HIV," she said.

"AIDS, HIV—it's all the same. Whatever you wanna call it, I got it."

She ran over and hugged me. She had to have held me for at least ten minutes, crying and clenching the jacket to my velour track suit. Although I hugged her back, I didn't feel any emotion. I just wanted to get out of that hospital and go home, where I didn't have to face reality for a while.

We rode in silence the whole way. As soon as we got inside, I told Alexis I didn't want to talk to anybody, nor did I want company. She understood and told me that she'd call my job and fill Peter in.

I went upstairs and fell face down on my bed. I cried until I threw up, then laid on the cold tile of my bathroom floor until Alexis knocked on my door and asked if I wanted something to eat.

I told her that I didn't have an appetite and I probably wouldn't be able to keep food down anyway. From that point on, she kept her distance, knowing I needed time to absorb the shock.

Later that night, reality hit me. I had HIV—something I had to discuss with my boyfriend (or soon-to-be-ex). How in the hell was I supposed to tell Craig that I may have given it to him? We weren't a Hollywood couple like Magic Johnson and Cookie, so that happy ending garbage wasn't even a thought. And what about me? What happens when people find out and push me away? There was no way I could have a social life and return to my routine at work and church without being shunned, ridiculed, and judged.

I also had to get in touch with TJ and tell him to get tested. After all, we'd had unprotected sex before, too. And since I'd never been tested before the rape, he could've given it to me for all I knew. *How embarrassing.* I tried to comfort myself with the thought that the rapist might've given it to me and that I wasn't the initial carrier, but whether or not I was the initial or final one, the fact still remained that I had the virus. *Guess there was really no comfort at all.*

I picked up the phone and called Nicole. When her answering machine picked up, I remembered she was at a photo shoot in New York. I hung up and debated whether I was gonna call Tielle. I decided not to because she would've wanted me to tell Craig that night, and I wasn't ready to deal with that.

Although I didn't have many friends, I sure had a lot of people to share the news with—or at least people I was supposed to tell. I tried to imagine how everyone would react. My mom wouldn't know how to take it. My dad would be in denial. Alexis was already looking for answers and wanting to talk about it. TJ was destined to flip out. Craig was gonna be scared to death that he might have it and kicking himself in the ass for ever talking to me. Nicole was gonna cry, but find something positive to say. Tielle would cry, too, but not on the phone with me. She'd try to be my rock and save her tears until after the dial tone. In the midst of all the emotions, I wondered who would take the time to ask how *I* was feeling.

I heard Alexis come upstairs at midnight. I called her into my room so we could talk. I couldn't live with myself if I vented to someone else before I shared my fears with my own sister.

"You want some food now?" she asked.

"No," I answered. "I need to talk to somebody before I explode."

Alexis sat on the corner of my bed as I leaned against the headboard.

"I don't know what I'm gon' do. This shit couldn't have happened at a worse time. What am I supposed to tell Craig?"

"Are you serious? You're mad for all the wrong reasons. You ain't even mad 'cause you have to live with HIV. You mad 'cause you gotta tell Craig. I mean, I know he's important to you, but you've gotta come to grips with this. How do you expect him to react if you go to him actin' like your whole life depends on whether or not he stays with you? He's gon' feed off that and eat you alive before the damn disease does. You stronger than that. You just got knocked down for a second."

I buried my head in my hands. She didn't understand how much Craig meant to me and I didn't know how to express it. He had become my happiness.

"Right now, you should be thinkin' about other stuff, like whether your insurance will pay for the medication, how often you have to go to the hospital, what you have to do to stay healthy…stuff like that."

"But how can I not think about him?" I asked. "Over the past five months, he's become a major part of me. I care that I've put him at risk and that he might have it, too."

Alexis lowered her head, trying not to show how frustrated and disgusted she was. She took a deep breath. "How do you know he didn't give it to you if he tests positive? And what about TJ? What if it was him? You can't sit up here and blame yourself for this shit, Meka!" Tears rolled down her cheeks. After seeing her tears, mine fell ten times faster. "Let me know what I can do to help, 'cause I don't know! If you need me to sit here and watch you cry every night, that's what I'll do. If you wanna throw shit all over the room, I'll pick it up. I just wanna see you let your feelings out. Feel for yourself—not anybody else. It's okay to be selfish now."

We talked until three o'clock. From the way Lexis talked, she sounded more scared than me. She told me to call the police station in the morning and tell them about my test results. She was hoping that the news would light a fire under their cold asses and get them to pursue my case more seriously.

Against my wishes, she also said she called both of us off work for the rest of the week. Honestly, I think she was on suicide watch. She had to know that I had a lot of crazy thoughts running through my head. That wasn't one of them, but I'd seriously considered skipping town and going somewhere random like Kansas to start over.

I paged TJ at one o'clock the next afternoon. For the first time, I hoped he wouldn't return my page, but to my dismay, he called right back. I answered the phone, only to hear his cockiest tone ever.

"It was only a matter of time," he said. "Did you and Loverboy break up, or are you callin' me 'cause you want a Christmas gift?"

"TJ," I said impatiently. "Don't make this harder than it has to be, please. I didn't call for either of those reasons."

"Damn, girl. I was just playin'."

"Listen. I have to tell you somethin', but I'd rather do it in person."

"Well, you gon' have to wait 'til next Tuesday. I'm in Arkansas right now."

There was no way I could wait that long. If I didn't tell him right then, I probably wouldn't tell him later.

"Well I guess I have to tell you now."

"What's wrong? You sound sad."

"'Sad' doesn't even begin to describe how I'm feelin'."

"What's wrong?" he asked again.

"TJ," I said, tears falling already. "I was diagnosed with HIV yesterday."

He sat silently on the phone for a few seconds. "Oh shit," he finally said. "I'm sorry, baby. I—I don't even know what to say."

"I just thought I'd let you know so you can get tested," I continued, hurriedly forcing the words out through my sobs.

He was still quiet, then I heard him sniff. Finally he said, "It was that muthafucka who raped you, right?" I realized he was crying, although he tried his best to hide it.

"I don't know," I said. "But you need to get tested to make sure you don't have it."

"We haven't done anything since you got raped," he said. I didn't say anything. "Wait. You sayin' I gave the shit to you?"

"No, TJ. I'm saying that my doctor told me to inform everybody I've slept with—especially the guys I've had unprotected sex with. That's only you, the guy who raped me, and Craig."

He cut the conversation short and told me he'd try to get back by Monday and let me know when he got his results.

My next call to the police station wasn't very productive. I told Detective Nelson my results and asked if he'd heard anything from the authorities in New York. In so many words, he said he was sorry about my "condition" but that I had no priority over anyone else. Before I slammed the phone in his ear, I told him to throw my file out if they were going to keep pushing it to the side. I was frustrated because they could never tell me anything. There were never any new developments. I was always calling them with word from the "street."

The phone rang seconds after I hung up. "I'ma scream if it's him callin'," I said to Alexis. I answered the phone without looking at the caller ID. "What?"

"What's wrong, baby?" Craig asked on the other end.

My eyes bucked, and my heart raced so fast that it could've qualified for the Olympics. "Oh, I thought you were one of the officers at the station," I said.

"Did they find the dude?"

"No, I had to call and give them an update." I tried to hold my voice steady.

"Oh," Craig said. "Why ain't you at work today? I was callin' all day, but I kept gettin' your voicemail. Then, when I asked the operator if you were there, she said you weren't gon' be in 'til next Wednesday. You alright?"

"Not really," I said. "

"What's wrong?"

"We'll talk about it when you get off. Just come over after work."

"Do you need me to come over now? I can get off early and have Dave cover practice."

I was about to start crying, so I rushed off the phone. "I'm fine, Craig. We'll just talk when you get here later. Don't take off early."

"You cryin'?"

"No." I bit my lip so it would stop quivering. "Bye, Craig. I gotta go."

***

When Craig knocked on the door, I was scared to death. "Do you want me to leave for a while so y'all can have some privacy?" Alexis asked.

"Naw, that's okay. We'll go up to my room."

"Alright. Stay strong. Once you tell him, you'll feel better."

I answered the door and Craig greeted me with a half dozen yellow roses. He was making it even harder for me to reveal my devastating news.

112

"What's up, beautiful?" he said, hugging me. He handed me the flowers. "I decided to bring a little sunshine to your day. You sounded depressed on the phone."

I looked back at Alexis, who simply shook her head and closed her eyes. She was probably thinking the same thing I was.

"What's up, Lexis?" Craig said. "Damn! You look sad, too. Maybe your sister will share a rose with you if you ask her nicely."

I grabbed his arm. "Let's go upstairs. We need to talk."

He followed me up to my room. "Do I get to find out what's botherin' you now?" he asked.

"Yeah. Listen, Craig. I have some news that's gonna change both of our lives."

"Are you pregnant?"

I shook my head, no.

"Is this your way of breakin' up with me?"

"No. Believe me. I don't want anything more than to be with you." I took a deep breath. "Remember I told you I had a doctor's appointment yesterday?"

"Yeah. I tried to call you last night to see how it went, but Lexis said you were sleep."

I looked up at him, teary-eyed and ashamed.

"She was lyin'?" he asked.

"Yeah. Craig, please don't get mad at me, and no matter what, please don't tell anybody what I'm about to tell you."

"Alright." He wiped my eyes and looked deep into them. I hung my head because I couldn't face him.

After counting to three, four times in my head, I finally blurted, "I—I—I have HIV." I didn't look up to see his initial reaction, but when I did, his mouth was wide open. He grabbed me and hugged me tightly. I could feel his warm tears drip onto my shoulder as he clenched my shirt.

"I'm so sorry," I said. "I'm so sorry."

I must've repeated myself at least ten times. I couldn't say anything else. Craig said nothing. He just kept holding me. When he let me go, I didn't know what to expect.

"Did the rapist give it to you?"

"We don't know for sure."

"Why not?"

"All the guys I've had unprotected sex with need to be tested."

"I thought the only other dude was TJ."

"Yeah…You, TJ, and the rapist."

113

"Ain't this a bitch?" he said. I knew he was disgusted.

"You don't have to stay here. I don't want you to feel obligated." I pulled another tissue out of the box and dabbed my eyes.

"So I gotta get tested now?" he asked.

"They don't know how long I've had it, so yeah."

"Fuck!" He took out his anger on my mattress, pushing it clear off the box spring and onto the floor.

"I'm sorry," I said again as I shook in the corner by my dresser. I was crying so hard that I gagged and ran to the bathroom.

Craig came in to check on me while I was between hurls. He wet a washcloth and put it on the back of my neck. When he saw that I wasn't done, he knelt beside me and rubbed my back. "It's alright, baby. Let it out," he said.

It amazed me how sweet he was. He stayed on the bathroom floor with me until I was done, then helped me up. I brushed my teeth, and he walked me back into the bedroom. Since the mattress was already on the floor, I crawled onto it and covered my head with my comforter, wishing I would die. Craig uncovered it.

"You want somethin' to drink?" he asked.

"No. You can go home now. I'll be okay."

Alexis knocked on the door. "You okay, Meka?" she yelled. She probably heard the thud from the mattress.

"She's cool," Craig answered.

"I was talkin' to Tameka. You straight, girl?"

"Don't worry. I got her. She'll be fine," he answered again.

She cracked the door open and peeked in to make sure the thud wasn't from my body hitting the floor. Once that was confirmed, she discretely closed it back and returned downstairs.

Craig shuffled around the room, making all kinds of noise, so I peeked from under the covers. He was taking off his clothes. Even though it was only seven in the evening, he laid beside me and held me through the night. We didn't say a word the whole time.

Chapter 13

The next morning, I woke up and Craig was gone. There was a note on the pillow next to me that read:

Good Morning Beautiful,
Sorry I had to leave so early, but you know I had to go to work and get the rugrats ready for the Christmas tournament. I'll call you when I get home, 'cause we still need to talk about what you told me last night. Until then, no more throwing up, and no more crying.

Love you!
-Craig

I didn't know how to take the note. I knew we had a lot more to discuss, but I was afraid his actions the previous night were done out of some false sense of obligation and sympathy, and that once we discussed the situation in depth, his true feelings would be revealed.

The phone rang at noon. It was Tielle calling from her cell phone. "What's goin' on, girl?" she asked. By her tone, I could tell she wasn't just calling to say hi.

"Not too much," I replied.

"The truth, Meka," Tielle said.

"What you mean?" I asked. She must've talked to Craig. I was gonna be pissed if he told her my news after I specifically asked him not to tell anybody.

"I talked to Craig a little bit ago, and he told me that I needed to call you."

"What else did he say?"

"That's it," she said. "Did y'all break up or somethin'?"

"No."

"Then why do you sound so sad?" She paused. "Wait a minute. You went to the doctor Tuesday, didn't you?" I didn't say anything.

"And when I called, Alexis said you was sleep, but it was only six o'clock…And Craig didn't sound good when I talked to him…"

She'd figured it out on her own. "Oh my God, Meka. Don't tell me…Oh shit! Do you have—? What did the doctor say?"

The next thing I knew, her phone clicked off. I figured she lost her signal. As I dialed her number to see what happened, somebody knocked on the door. Actually, they banged on the door. I put the phone down and answered it. Tielle stood on the doorstep with tears in her eyes. Turns out, she was just a block down the street at the pizza place she likes to go to for lunch. She didn't speak. Instead, she hugged me and cried harder.

"I'm sorry, girl," she said.

"Tielle, don't do this. You gon' make me cry again."

We sat in the living room and I told her the specifics of what Dr. Crenshaw said, and she held my hand through the whole story.

"When do you back to see her?" she asked.

"Well I go to the hospital tomorrow, but not to see her. I'm seein' some guy named Dr. Owens."

"What time?"

"Ten."

"Maybe I can take off—"

"No. I'll be fine. Go to work. You don't have to deal with this. I do."

"I'm goin' with her," Alexis said. "I took off the rest of the week."

"Good," Tielle replied. "'Cause this stubborn chick is gon' be a piece of work."

The conversation shifted to Craig. I asked her for the details of their conversation. She saw that I wasn't happy with her answer. "I told him not to mention it to nobody. I guess he thought that excluded you."

"Well when were you gonna tell me?" Tielle asked.

"Tonight or tomorrow. I was just tryin' to have a little period of time when I could think about somethin' other than this. It's like I'm goin' on a confession spree or somethin'. And don't feel bad. I haven't even told my parents yet."

"Well Craig is worried as hell. You should've heard the way he sounded," she said.

"Did he stay last night?" Alexis asked.

"Yeah," I answered.

"So, he's cool with it?"

"Yeah right. We didn't even discuss it. You know me and my sensitive stomach. By the time I told him what was up, I was runnin' to the bathroom. I think he stayed because I was so pitiful."

"That's not the impression I got," Tielle said. "He seemed genuinely concerned about you. And when we talked, I didn't even know what was wrong."

She turned out to be right. Craig called when he got home from work and asked me to come over. We had a long talk about the new direction my life was moving in, and he wanted to make sure I was keeping my spirits up. He asked if he could come to the hospital the next day, but I didn't feel like he should be there.

"Craig, I don't expect anything from you anymore. You're a good man, and you've proven that to me over the past five months, but you're not a superhero. I don't expect you to stay with me. This has to bother you almost as much as it bothers me. You can't be with a woman who has HIV. How could we build a future together? We can't have sex the way we want, and we can't have kids."

"Slow down," Craig said. "First off, we were friends before we were anything else, and I'ma be here for you regardless. Baby, this is just as new to me as it is to you. I don't know how to react. I just know that I love you, and since love is all I can go by right now, I'ma listen to my heart and be here for you whether you like it or not."

"And what happens when your tests come back negative?"

"If they come back negative, I'm still gonna love you."

"And when people find out and clown you for bein' around me?"

"I'll still love you, and I'll tell them that. Get it through your thick skull, Meka. You're stuck with me. And tomorrow, I'm goin' to the hospital with you and your sister. I already called to schedule an appointment for my test, so I'll do that while I'm waiting for you."

What a man…Sure enough, Craig went to the hospital with me and Lexis. The visit was basically a consultation to let me know how things would work since I'd been diagnosed. The doctor explained the different types of medications that were available, and when I'd need to take them.

For the most part, he said I wouldn't be on a lot of medicine until I experienced symptoms, but he would put me on a couple medications to help keep my immune system strong. Alexis had more questions than I did, and Dr. Owens took the time to answer hers as thoroughly as he answered mine. I left his office feeling somewhat relieved.

We met Craig in the lobby and went out to lunch. I briefed him on the consultation with Dr. Owens.

"I really like him," Alexis said. "He's straightforward."

"So when will you get your results?" I asked Craig, trying my best to sound casual.

"I'll know in two weeks just like you did."

And those next two weeks were quite interesting. I finally got in touch with Nicole and told her the news. She wanted to hop on the next plane out of Columbus and come see me, but I convinced her that she needed to stay put unless she was flying down with a cure securely packaged in a carry-on cooler.

Things went much differently when I told my mother. She couldn't strum up any encouraging words, so she resorted to asking, "Do you have enough money for medicine?" and "Why haven't they found that bastard who did this to you?" Since my dad was coming to town soon, I decided to tell him in person.

In an unexpected turn for the worst, Craig became very distant. His phone calls slowed up drastically a week after he went for his HIV test. I wasn't too surprised because I thought he would act like that from day one. Even though it wasn't much of a shock, it still hurt.

On Wednesday of the second week, he came by to tell me that his test came back negative. "I'm glad to hear that," I replied. There was an uncomfortable silence. "So, how have you been?"

"I'm alright."

"I haven't heard from you in a while. I guess reality finally settled in with you, huh?"

He sat in the chair with his arms folded and an uninterested, unemotional, unconcerned look on his face. "I don't know what you want me to say."

My body shook with anger. I couldn't believe that the man sitting in front of me was the same man I fell in love with. "You don't know what to say?" I repeated. "Well you know what, Craig? You didn't have to say anything. You should've never told me that you wouldn't abandon me and all that crap. You didn't even have to come over here today. You haven't been sayin' shit or droppin' by for damn near two weeks so why start now?"

"I just wanted you to know my results and I decided to tell you in person." He stood up to leave, and I followed him into the foyer

118

near the door. He wasn't getting off that easy after giving me a false sense of security.

"So can you tell me in person that you can't back up all that 'I love you no matter what' shit you talked before? Can you do that? Is that why you actin' like a asshole, so I'll get pissed off and end it first? What the fuck do you want me to do? Apologize again? I can't help what happened to me. Nobody wants to get raped, and you knew my story from the start. I didn't keep no secrets from you. I've never opened up like that to anybody until you came along. Now, you standin' here with a attitude when I'm the one who has to suffer for the rest of my life. Oh, it's too bad for Craig that his girlfriend has AIDS, but fuck her. Poor Craig. Boo fuckin' hoo. You poutin' like you have the shit."

He tried to walk away, but I stood in his path. "I'd be more than happy to trade places with you. I've gone through hell the past three weeks, dealin' with this and wonderin' who'll be the next person to find out that I have this shit. And on top of that, the man who swore up and down that he'd be my fuckin' support system is standin' right in my face, showin' his true colors—showin' me that he's just a shit talker who'll say anything to make himself look good. Fuck you, Craig."

Alexis walked into the apartment. "What's goin' on? I heard you all the way outside."

I ignored her and waited for Craig's response.

"My intentions weren't ever to hurt you," he said.

"Fuck your intentions, Craig, 'cause guess what? I'm hurt. You hurt me every time you opened your mouth, harpin' about how much this disease didn't matter. You hurt me every time I got my hopes up, thinking that you may be the one guy on earth who isn't a asshole. Don't say shit to me from now on, 'cause all your words do is hurt me. And the only way I'll let you address me is if you come and tell me that you have HIV and that you understand what I'm goin' through."

"Tameka…"

"Un unh," I said, putting my hand over his mouth. "Do you have HIV now?" He didn't say anything. "Well, don't say shit to me." I went upstairs.

Alexis turned to Craig. "I think it's time for you to leave. Let yourself out." He obliged but didn't leave without slamming the door hard enough for the walls to shake.

119

When Lexis came upstairs to check on me, I was walking in circles in my room. "What was he doin' here?" she asked. I couldn't answer her because I was still heated. "Meka, you need to calm down before you make yourself sick. You can't be gettin' all fired up like this. Stress ain't gon' help your condition."

She persuaded me to sit on the bed, and I told her about my argument with Craig. "Don't sweat him," she said. "We knew he was gonna act like this eventually."

"I know, girl. This is a shame. Just when I thought I was handlin' everything pretty well…."

***

Craig walked into his apartment and threw his keys on the kitchen counter. "What just happened?" he said to himself as he sat down and sunk into his leather couch. After lengthy contemplation, he picked up the phone. Before he could dial a number, it rang. "Tameka?"

"Naw, nigga!" It was Malik, one of his buddies from college. "You sittin' up there longin' for that broad, dawg?"

"Shut up, nigga," Craig replied. "What's up?"

"You tell me! What's up with the results?"

"Aw, I'm straight. They came back negative."

"Did you tell ol' girl?"

"Yeah, I just told her."

"What she say?"

"Nothin'. She was just glad that I don't have it."

"I bet she was. That broad need to be kissin' your ass for the rest of your life for puttin' you out there like that."

"You trippin, man."

"Naw, you trippin', answerin' the phone, thinkin' it's that girl. Man I know it's a whole bunch of fine hoes down there. Find you somebody that ain't got AIDS, dawg."

Craig didn't respond. He was actually trying to tune out Malik's words because it was his opinionated advice that had Craig on bad terms with Tameka. Their conversation was interrupted when Craig's line beeped. When he clicked over, Tielle was on the line.

"What's wrong with you?" she snapped.

"Hold on," Craig said. He told Malik he'd call him back, then clicked back over to Tielle. "Now what you say?"

"I just talked to Meka a few minutes ago," Tielle replied. "I didn't know you had it in you to act like that."

120

"Act like what? Man, look. I hadn't even talked to Meka all last week, and we barely talked the week before that. She figured out where I stood on her own," Craig snapped back. "Is she on the phone right now? Y'all got me on three-way or some shit, 'cause I ain't got time to play games?" he continued.

"Slow up," Tielle said. "I've been outta town for the past week and a half so I don't know what's been goin' on with y'all. I didn't know nothin' until I called Meka to tell her about my trip."

"So if you don't know that much, why you callin' me, trippin'?"

"I'm tryin' to remain objective about a relationship that involves my best friend and my first cousin. That's hard as hell, and I don't try to take sides. Maybe I came at you wrong at the beginning of the conversation and I apologize for that, but I had to listen to the pain in Meka's voice when she told me how you've been for the past couple weeks."

Craig let his guard down and his tone of voice became one of concern. "Was she still cryin'?" he asked.

"Does it matter?"

"Hell yeah it matters, Tielle! I still care about her feelings." He had mixed emotions. He wanted to stand by his choice to break up with Tameka, but he also wanted to be there for her.

"Tell her I'm sorry," he finally said, breaking the silence.

"You tell her. I didn't tell her you didn't wanna be with her anymore. You started it. Finish it."

"I gotta go," he said, and hung up.

The day before Christmas Eve, Craig called Alexis on her cell phone. He had Tameka's Christmas gifts and wanted to know if he could drop them off. She told him she didn't see a problem with it and they might bring a smile to her sister's face.

"You need to drop 'em off and make a quick exit, though," Alexis warned. "She still can't stand to hear anybody mention your name, so she probably don't wanna see you. I mean, I can't guarantee you anything. If you get over here and she gives you a hug, good for you. If you get over here and she cusses you out, you know you deserve it. It's on you if you wanna take the risk."

***

Alexis and I got home at six. We'd been out all day doing some last minute Christmas shopping. I was dead tired, so my plan was to go upstairs and go to sleep. We sat our bags down by the stairs and took off our coats. I noticed that Alexis kept looking at her watch.

121

"You expectin' somebody to call or somethin'?" I asked.

"Huh?"

"Why were you lookin' at your watch?"

"Oh. I wanted to order some pizza, but I know that some of the restaurants close early tonight."

"Well if you hurry up and call now, Pizza Hut should still be open," I said. "Order some breadsticks, too." I headed upstairs.

"Where you goin'?"

"I need to take a nap. I'm tired," I said.

***

She called and ordered the pizza. Once she hung up, she called Craig to reschedule the drop-off. The last thing she needed was her tired, crabby sister to be awakened by the man who broke her heart. The phone rang, but there was no answer. She looked through Tameka's purse to see if she could find Craig's cell phone number, but to her surprise, Tameka had erased it from her phone's memory.

The doorbell rang at a 6:45. Alexis figured it was the pizza man, so she grabbed her money and answered the door. Instead, Craig stood before her, holding a huge box. "Where have you been?" she asked as she yanked him inside. "I've been tryin' to call you."

"My cell phone was on," he said.

"That ain't no good to me if I ain't got the number. And damn! What you got in that big ol' box? The statue of liberty?"

"You know this box ain't that big," Craig said, laughing.

"Shh! You gotta be quiet 'cause she's sleep. That's all she's been doin' lately. I never told her you were comin'. "

"Has she been taking her medicine?"

"Yeah, she says she has."

The doorbell rang again. Alexis paid for the pizza and sat it on the kitchen counter. She offered Craig a slice and as he walked over to the counter to get one, Tameka walked downstairs, rubbing her eyes.

***

"That pizza smells good. Where are my breadsticks?" I asked. When I looked up, Alexis and Craig were standing near the kitchen entrance, frozen in place. "What are you doin' here?" I asked Craig.

"I brought your Christmas gifts over," he said after he finally swallowed.

122

I walked past him and got a slice of pizza. "Did you bring me the cure to AIDS or somethin'?" I was being rude to hide the excitement I felt just from seeing his face. Even though he'd done me wrong, I hadn't gotten over my feelings for him. Still, I couldn't let him think everything was cool just because he bought me a couple Christmas presents.

"You'll have to wait 'til tomorrow for your stuff. I haven't wrapped nothin'," I said as I exited the kitchen.

"'Cause you were about to return everything, right?" He smiled.

Why did he do that? I felt that all too familiar twinge travel down my spine. "Somethin' like that," I said, displaying a fake smile. I was feeling uneasy.

He turned to Lexis. "Can you give us a little privacy?"

"Craig, I'm about to go back to sleep," I said, turning to walk away. He grabbed my arm and tugged just enough to pull me toward him.

"Meka, please," he pleaded. "I just wanna talk to you."

Alexis looked at me, and I gave her the go-ahead. She was well upstairs before Craig let my arm go. I snatched away from him and stood with my hand on my hip. "Talk," I said.

"Can we sit down? I feel awkward standin' here."

"Probably because you left what I thought was a relationship—a friendship—in a awkward way." I sat on the couch.

"Meka, I'm sorry," he said as he leaned on a nearby chair.

"It doesn't matter anymore. We're not together. You decided that. You even took it to the point where I don't even wanna be friends with you. You know I don't have that many friends, but when I care about somebody enough to befriend them, I hold them close. There's nothin' in the world I wouldn't do for my friends, and I expect the same from them. If you were in my position, I'm not gonna say that I wouldn't be shocked and scared, but I can say that I wouldn't abandon you. As your friend, I couldn't do that after I've told you how much I love you for the past two months. But you did that to me, and I won't forget that."

The whole time I was talking, I barely looked into his eyes. When I finished my last sentence, though, I looked up at him and saw how hurt he looked. I quickly turned my head to avoid feeling sorry for him.

"Meka, I know I was wrong." He was getting frustrated. I could damn near see his temple throbbing, and the vein in his neck was protruding. "People handle situations differently. I handled this one wrong, but I don't know what you want me to do. I can't change the past, and you won't accept my apologies. What do you want me to do?"

"I want you to leave me alone. Stop doin' this. You haven't made up your mind about what you want, and every time you feel a different way, you can't come to me with confusion and empty promises."

"I can't. Do you know how bad I wanted to call you yesterday?"

"Not that bad, 'cause my phone didn't ring."

"You said you didn't even want me to speak to you if we saw each other on the street. I wasn't about to call you and get hung up on."

I guess that was the part where I was supposed to be like, 'Oh, I didn't really mean it, baby,' but I didn't stick to the script. I just stared off into space, nibbled on my bottom lip, and swayed my crossed legs back and forth.

"So when I ran across your presents, I figured I could talk to you when I dropped them off. Look. I'm only gonna say this once. I wanna be with you. I've had a lot of time to think about how I acted, and I had a long talk with Tielle. She opened my eyes to some things. I don't know what steps we need to take to get back on the right track or whether or not it'll work out in the long run, but I know I wanna try. I love you, girl, and I wanna see you through this."

I wasn't buying that change of heart mess. I knew how mushy people got around the holidays, and Craig's wishy-washy ass wasn't any different. I wasn't trying to relive my relationship with TJ, where we were with each other, but not really. I didn't feel like Craig was really ready for the issues that could arise in our relationship. He may have meant what he said, but I wasn't convinced that he could back it up when it really mattered.

"Talk to me, beautiful," he said, placing his index finger under my chin and turning my face towards his.

I told him I wanted like hell to be with him, but didn't want to be his charity case. I believed when you made a decision about something, your first instinct was the one you should stick with—not all the other choices that run through your mind after you've had time to think about it. I was always told to go with my gut, and I passed that advice on to Craig. But he said he was always told to go with his heart.

"So have you figured out that I'm not willing to let you go?" he asked.

I was tired of feeling like a big baby all the time. My life was dealing me cards that made me extremely emotional. As I'm sure you figured, I started crying. This time, it wasn't because my feelings were hurt; I was just confused.

"Hey, hey. Why you cryin'?" Craig asked softly.

I tried to gather myself before I answered him. Just when I opened my mouth to speak, he leaned over and kissed me softly.

I didn't know how to answer him. I was totally confused about my feelings toward him. I prided myself on being a strong woman, but it seemed like when it came to Craig I was weak as hell.

Sensing my hesitance, he lightened the mood and asked me if I wanted to open one of my gifts. After a short pause and a shrug, he got up and handed me one of the wrapped packages from the box. "You gotta start off small," he said.

I ripped the red and silver paper decorated with angels and bells. When I opened the box, a lacy red negligee with a matching thong was folded neatly inside the white tissue paper. I couldn't believe he had the nerve to give it to me after all that happened between us. Maybe he thought he'd persuade me to model it for him or something…cocky bastard.

"O…kay," I said as I examined the skimpy ensemble that rested effortlessly on my index finger. "It's nice, but…"

"I know it's kinda weird, but I've had it for over a month and didn't see the point in taking it back. Just don't let another nigga see it."

We talked a little while longer, but I started falling asleep mid-conversation. At 11:30, Craig excused himself so I could to go to bed. He said he'd be over the next day to spend some time with me. As I laid in my bed, I anxiously awaited the next morning. I desperately needed to talk to Alexis about Craig's latest profession of love because I knew she'd tell me if I was stupid for falling for his shit again.

Portia A. Cosby

Chapter 14

Christmas morning was pretty cool. Alexis banged on my door at eight o'clock. She was so excited about giving me my gift.

"Open yours first," she said.

I opened the package and was immediately impressed. She'd gotten me a Palm Pilot to organize my hectic life and she tucked a fifty-dollar bill into a Shoebox card that joked about sisterly relationships. It was the first Christmas since our childhood that she had actually put some thought into what she gave me. I can't tell you how many candles and smell-good sets from Bath & Body Works she'd given me in recent years. I thanked her, gave her a big hug, and handed her a large gold package from me.

I nervously awaited her reaction. I'd put a lot of thought into her gift because I wanted her to remember it forever.

She pulled out the note that sat on top of the items inside. "When you pull out each item, I'll tell you why I gave it to you," she read. "You always tryin' to be creative," she teased.

The first thing she pulled out was a box of Kleenex.

"Okay, let me explain. That's to replace the ones you used when you cried with me through all the drama that's been goin' on this year."

"Aw, shit! Here you go bein' all sentimental. Meka, don't have me in here usin' up the Kleenex already."

I laughed. "I just appreciate you bein' there."

Next, she pulled out the Jay-Z boxed set. "Thank you!" she squealed.

She'd been complaining about losing three CDs from her Jay-Z collection for over a month, so I figured I'd buy all of his CDs before she had a conniption. She removed the next layer of green tissue paper, which revealed a tan suit with a matching blouse.

126

"Ooh, this is hot!" She stood up and held the jacket against her torso. "Girl, you are too good to me."

I sighed, relieved that she liked the suit. Business suits weren't her usual choice of dress, so I took a chance when I bought her that.

"I don't know where I'ma wear it, though" she said. I pointed to an envelope that was still in the box. She reached down and pulled it out. "Is this gonna make me cry?" She slowly opened the envelope containing a list of job openings at Baker & Phillips, a sister company to my employer. Alexis' eyes widened as she smiled with childlike joy.

"It was posted on our bulletin board before I went on vacation. I figured I'd bring it home and see if you'd be interested. You asked me a long time ago if I would help you, but I was waiting for you to prove yourself," I explained. "They're starting interviews right after New Year's, so if you pursue it, you can wear the suit to the interview. I'm not gonna get into your weed smokin' because it's Christmas and I'm not tryin' to argue with you. All I'ma say is, you know what you gotta do. Merry Christmas."

She leaned over and hugged me. She said nothing, only because she was overcome with emotion. I prayed that the new year would bring her a new attitude and a new perspective on life.

While we cleaned up the boxes, ribbons, and tissue paper, I asked Lexis' opinion about my conversation with Craig. I told her about his tear-jerking speech and how I didn't stop him from assuming we were back together.

"You really love that dude," she said. "That's all it could be, because you don't let no nigga sit up and tell you that he's gonna be with you whether you like it or not. TJ didn't even have a hold on you like that."

"You think I was stupid for lettin' him lure me in again?"

"Not really. Technically, you lured him in again. He's the one who came crawlin' back to you, bringin' Christmas presents and shit. When you cut niggas off, that's when they wanna act right. Just don't take everything he says to heart. Once you start leanin' on his every word again, you'll be more vulnerable to gettin' your heart broken again. Just play that nigga off."

We talked a little longer, then Alexis got dressed and went to Robert's house. They'd been talking more often and I guess they were trying to work things out. While she was gone, I called Tielle to wish her a Merry Christmas. She said she'd be stopping by later to hang out. Shortly after we hung up, the phone rang again, and the caller ID showed the same number—Tielle's mother's house.

"What did you forget, punk?" I asked with a slight chuckle.

"Huh?" Craig asked on the other line.

"Oh! I thought you were Tielle."

"Okay. Let's try this again. Merry Christmas, beautiful!" He sounded overexcited. "You didn't open up the gifts yet, did you?"

"No."

"And did you wrap my present?"

"Yes," I lied. Actually, I'd forgotten, so I walked over to the hall closet and pulled out his gifts and some wrapping paper. He told me all about Christmas with his family. I listened and tried to act like I was interested, but the TV kept distracting me. I still loved him, but he hardened most of my heart when he treated me the way he did. I was no longer okay with holding the phone, listening to him ramble about how his day went and stuff like that…but at the same time, I couldn't tell him to leave me alone.

He finally finished his sappy story and ended our conversation, saying he'd be over in about an hour. After we hung up, I finished wrapping his stuff and turned on the radio to hear some holiday music. I sang along to TLC's "Sleigh Ride" and danced into the kitchen. Just as I was about to dig into the sugar cookies, the phone rang again.

"I'll be damned!" I said as I shuffled back into the living room. I figured the phone interruption was God's way of telling me to stop eating them damn cookies before I became the fattest AIDS patient ever. I didn't have a chance to check the caller ID because I had to answer before the answering machine picked up.

"Hello?"

"Ain't you supposed to say Merry Christmas?"

It was TJ. I hadn't heard from him since I dropped the HIV bomb, so I was completely shocked that he called.

"Yeah, I guess so," I replied.

He told me he didn't wanna call again until he got his results. He talked about how scared he was, thinking that he had it and could've given it to me. I assumed from his tone that he was negative, then he eventually confirmed my assumptions. It was weird because he was very apologetic. It was like he felt bad that he didn't have it, too. He didn't think it was fair that I was the only one punished when the whole ordeal happened because of his grimy past. I could only tell him not to worry about me because I'd be okay. I wasn't fully convinced of that, but I figured if I talked a good game and played the part of a hopeful optimist, I could become one in time.

"I've been through a lotta shit, you know? I just look at this as somethin' else I have to go through," I said.

"But you actin' like this ain't nothin' big," TJ replied. "You can only go through so much, baby girl. I know you better than anybody. You can't sit up here and tell me that you just chillin'."

"Yeah, it's a big deal, but life goes on. I went and talked to Pastor Johnson last week, and I'm feelin' a lot better about life. I'm about to get back into church and start fresh."

The conversation suddenly turned to me and Craig. TJ asked if I was still with "that nigga." I told him we still talked, but I didn't see a bright future for the two of us. I didn't go into details because it wasn't his business. Plus, TJ fed off of negativity. He would've loved it if I told him how ignorant Craig had been acting.

"So why are you bein' bothered?" TJ inquired.

"Why do I still bother with you?"

"I'm different."

"How?"

"We're supposed to be together. He's just somethin' to occupy your time."

"Whatever you say."

He made plans to come over the next day, but I told him to call first because my dad would be in town. Daddy couldn't stand TJ when he first met him, and he still didn't like him. I didn't want them in the same vicinity.

I heard a knock at the door and went to answer it. Before I could speak, Craig kissed me sweetly on my forehead, then passionately on my lips. Now I said my feelings for him had changed in my heart, but those feelings had nothing to do with the ones my little friend below still had for his little…well, big friend. That was all nature's doing.

The kiss became a little heated, so I pulled back and wiped the corners of my mouth. "Where did that come from?"

He pulled my hips toward his. He was hard as a rock. I already knew what was up. I'd tasted a hint of Michelob when he kissed me. He was drunk. Mind you, it was only 4:30 in the afternoon.

"You know where it came from," he said, looking deep into my eyes.

"Whatever," I said, laughing him off. He didn't crack a smile. "Craig, you're drunk in the middle of the afternoon. What's your problem?"

"I've been drinking, but I'm not drunk."

He kissed my neck. My brain shut down and my body did its own thing. I felt my neck turn to give him a better angle to reach "the spots." After a few pecks, my mind joined the party again, and I realized I was giving him what he wanted too easily and too spontaneously for us to not be on the best terms.

"Un unh," I said. I pulled away again, then walked over to the Christmas tree and grabbed his gifts. "Ain't this what you came for?"

He didn't say anything. Instead, he walked over to the couch and sat down.

"Don't pout now, nigga!" I said and threw his boxes at him. He caught them and laughed reluctantly.

We opened our gifts, and I believe it's safe to say we were both satisfied with what we got. From the Coach purse and knee boots to the Baby Phat ensemble, I was sure to be super fly the next time I stepped out. He wasn't gonna look bad in his dress slacks and shirts at his basketball games or the new Iverson's he'd been begging me for either.

I rested my head on his lap and exhaled. Slowly, I was starting to recognize the man I fell in love with. I ran my fingers along the threads of his jeans, and he ran his through my hair and down my arm. After a few strokes, his hand traveled all the way down my arm and he grabbed my hand.

"Can I ask you somethin'?"

I turned and faced him. "What's up?"

"Were you afraid to make love to me earlier, or did you just not want to?"

I wasn't ready for that question. I swallowed every bit of saliva that was in my mouth and answered him with a question.

"Why would I be afraid?"

"There could be a lot of reasons. I ain't sayin' I'm irresistible or anything, but you haven't turned me down since the first night I ever tried to get some."

"Okay. If you really wanna know, I'll tell you. I don't understand how you can be so attracted to me, knowing I have HIV. I mean, I know I still look the same and my personality hasn't changed, but it's just weird," I replied.

"Even if it *is* weird, it's still the truth. You're still the same sexy-ass Tameka that I've wanted since day one. It threw me at first 'cause I was like, 'Damn! We can't have sex no more,' but that ain't the case. We just can't do it like we used to," Craig said.

"What if the condom falls off?"

"What if it doesn't? Meka, I know you too well. You can't go the rest of your life without sex. You'd die after like six months."

"Fuck you," I said, chuckling. "Forgive me for lookin' out for you. I'm tryin' to be cautious, and you wanna make jokes."

"It's cool. If you're uncomfortable, I'll wait...but not too long." He grinned.

"You horny bastard," I said.

Craig stayed the night. We were awakened the next morning by the doorbell. I looked over my shoulder at the clock. Who was at my house at 9:15? I wiped the sleep from my eyes and rolled to the edge of the bed. After staring at my slippers for a good thirty seconds, I got out of bed and made my way downstairs. Craig was still sound asleep.

As I neared the door, I closed my robe and looked through the peephole. It was my dad. I had totally forgotten that he was coming. "Hold on," I said, clumsily tying my robe. If my leg was long enough, I would've kicked myself in the ass for having my boyfriend stay the night the day before my father came to town.

I unlocked the deadbolt and took the chain off the door. When I opened it, Daddy was waiting with one huge suitcase and a garment bag. "Hey, baby!" He kissed me on the cheek and walked inside.

"Hi, Daddy," I said, smiling. He looked better than ever.

"I was able to catch an earlier flight, so I decided to just take a cab over here instead of waiting around at the airport for y'all to come get me."

We sat in the living room, and he immediately opened his suitcase.

"You know I brought gifts," he said.

When he pulled them out, I noticed that they were poorly wrapped. I could see parts of the boxes where he must've run out of paper or underestimated the length.

"Can you tell I wrapped them myself?" he asked, laughing.

"I wasn't gon' say anything," I said, laughing just as hard.

"The mall gift-wrapping line was too long, so I really didn't have a choice."

131

"What about your girl?" I asked. It wouldn't have been right if I didn't say something sarcastic about his little lying-ass fiancé. "Doesn't she usually wrap our stuff?"

"We're not together right now." I tried to hold back the smile that was forming on my face as he continued. "I told her it'd be best if we spent some time apart."

It turns out that the bitch didn't tell my dad that Alexis called because she was "tired of (us) calling and not speaking" to her. Hell, she never spoke to us either! Anyway, she and my dad got into a big argument, and he told her to get out.

"…But enough about that," he continued. "It's early, and I know you probably wanna get back to sleep. I think I might crash on the couch for a while myself."

And we did just that. Dad stretched out on the couch, and I went back upstairs and joined Craig in my bed.

Alexis came home at noon with Robert. Dad was still asleep. By that time, Craig and I were awake and I had briefed him on what to say to my dad. We decided to say that he had car trouble and had to stay overnight. I felt like I was 16 or something, making up such a bogus story. I knew I didn't owe him any answers, but I felt like I was being disrespectful having Craig there while he was in town.

When we went downstairs, Dad was flipping through the latest *Jet*. I tried to ignore the inquisitive glance he gave us as he peered over the brim of the magazine. Our explanation went over pretty smoothly. I'm sure my dad knew the real deal, but he couldn't knock me for trying to save face. From what I could tell, he seemed to like Craig. He, Craig, and Robert talked a lot about basketball and all that other guy crap while Alexis and I talked about her and Robert.

In the middle of our conversation, I remembered I hadn't taken my medicine. I went upstairs and swallowed the pills with a handful of water. No sooner than I returned to the table, I felt a sharp, cramping pain in my stomach. I leaned forward in the chair to relieve the pain and took short breaths.

"What's wrong?" Alexis asked.

The pain was so terrible that I couldn't answer her right away. When I was able to sit up, my mouth started watering. I knew what was next, so I went into the bathroom. That had been happening quite frequently, and it was beginning to get on my nerves. My doctor told me that the medicine was probably causing my stomach discomfort and it would take some time for my body to get used to it.

132

With that in mind, I just took the sick spells as they came, knowing one day they would pass.

After Craig and Robert left that evening, Dad sat down to have an important talk with me and Lexis. He told me he had contacted his police buddy in New York, and he was gonna call his two local friends on the force the next day.

I segued into my HIV diagnosis, briefly explaining the medications I was taking and reassuring him I wasn't expected to advance to full-blown AIDS any time soon.

Dad's eyebrows rose to his hairline, and his jaw dropped to his shoelaces. "What?"

"Yeah, I know. But can we just leave it at that? No tears, no questions…Not right now."

He obliged, knowing he could just ask Alexis for the details.

I could tell she felt a little overshadowed. She didn't have any big news, except for the fact that she and Robert were a couple again. That really wasn't something you'd expect your father to get excited about, though, especially when he never knew that you had broken up in the first place. Recognizing her need for attention from Daddy, I excused myself, claiming that I was tired and heading to bed. That gave them time to talk alone, even if they just chatted about the weather.

Dad's four-day visit went by quickly. He spoke to the police officers he knew, just like he said he would, and gave me their direct numbers. When I dropped him off at the airport, he hugged me tightly and said, "Remember what I said, baby. Everything's gonna be alright. If the authorities don't handle it, I will."

An indescribable calmness fell over me. "I love you, Daddy."

Chapter 15

It was the 10th of February, and I was still getting sick from those stupid pills. Tielle suggested I call my family doctor and ask him if I had a stomach virus or something. I took her advice and went to the doctor's a few days later.

After the normal questions and protocol, the doctor asked when the last time I had unprotected sex was.

That was the last thing I expected to hear. "Like sometime in November or early December. Why?" Before he could answer, I continued. "You must think I'm pregnant, huh?"

"Those *are* symptoms of pregnancy you've been describing."

"I've had my periods, though. I mean, I know you can still have 'em, but I haven't noticed any changes in body or anything."

"Well let's do a test to make sure before we investigate a virus. Okay?"

"I guess, but…" I just stopped talking. I peed in the cup Sandy handed me and waited for the results.

Pregnancy and HIV do not belong in the same equation. I sat on the exam table, praying that I wasn't with child. Now they say prayer changes things, but it didn't in my case. Dr. Martinez walked his ass right through the door with a little white cardboard wheel in his hand and calculated that I was three months pregnant and due in August.

"You have got to be kidding me," I said. I fell straight back onto the table and wondered when I was going to leave the twilight zone. The shock was so strong that I couldn't cry. I simply regained my composure as I put my clothes back on and exited the office with a list of obstetricians tucked in my purse and a gift bag full of parenting magazines, formula samples, and diaper coupons hanging on my wrist.

Craig and I weren't in a good place. Ever since we'd gotten back together, he'd been fluctuating between loving me like crazy and acting like an asshole. There had been times when we hadn't talked for three or four days at a time, and his generic excuse was that he was just busy. He was busy being on some bullshit, though, because when I would call him at any point in the day, he wouldn't answer the phone. Then after four days of no communication, he'd show up at my job to take me to lunch, or I would come home from work and find him in my kitchen, cooking dinner. I found myself becoming stressed out because of our relationship, and I was starting to realize that he wasn't worth all the drama.

During the ride home, I coached myself on different ways to tell Craig we were having a baby. I thought of the straightforward approach: *Craig, I'm pregnant. Are you gonna act right or what?* Or would the *Baby, I need to talk to you* approach work better? It wouldn't be right to just not tell him, so my final decision was to simply go for it. Whenever he called, I'd just ask him to come over and tell him straight up.

When I got home, Alexis told me Craig called and needed to talk to me ASAP; Mama called and said to call her; TJ called from New York, and Jermaine called 'cause he had some news for me. I went upstairs to relax and make my return calls.

I popped in India.Arie and hummed along to her soulful lyrics. I closed my eyes and felt myself sink deeper into the mattress, and for a brief moment, my troubles were non-existent. I didn't have a hoodrat for a sister; I didn't have two men in my life who were driving me crazy; I didn't have HIV; and I didn't have a life growing inside of me.

My escape from reality ended when the phone rang. Craig was on the other end. "Why didn't you call me back?"

"Hey, I'm fine, and you?" I said sarcastically. The bastard could've said hello.

"Man, whatever. Where you been?"

"What's with the attitude?" I asked.

"We need to talk."

"Yeah, I know."

"So are you comin' over here, or do you want me to come over there?"

"I don't feel like leavin' the house," I said.

"I'll be over there in a hour." We hung up. Minutes later, Alexis yelled for me to get the phone again.

She must've been on the other line because I didn't hear it ring. I figured it was Craig calling back to tell me he wasn't coming. It turned out to be Jermaine. He kept the small talk to a minimum and cut right to the chase.

"You haven't had any problems, have you?"

"What kind of problems?"

"Threats…anybody followin' you."

"No..."

He sighed. "Ol' boy is back in town, baby girl."

Instantly, I was scared to death. "What do you mean? He's *here*? How did you find out?"

I'd grown used to the fact that the guy was still running the streets. I was okay with it because he was running the streets of New York. He was out of Texas and out of my life, and I could accept that. If what Jermaine said was true, he was back in my life and possibly back in my city.

Jermaine told me he contacted his friend, Christian, while he was in New York on business and told him my situation. He promised to keep his eyes open and his ear to the street. While Christian was shooting pool at a bar one night, he met a dude from Texas. In general conversation, he learned that the guy was in town visiting his cousin and laying low because "a bitch was crying rape back home." It's amazing what people say when they're drunk. During the course of the conversation, he also mentioned that he was "goin' back to Texas in a couple days."

"Did he find out his name?" I asked.

"He goes by Smoke," Jermaine replied.

"Well how can you be so sure he's here?"

"Trust me, Meka. He's there and I'm pretty sure he's not there to visit family. He already knows the cops are lookin' for him, so he could only be there for one thing—to shut you up. I'm tryin' to work somethin' out with my boss right now so I can get there. I already talked to TJ this mornin', and he said he's already on it. Between the two of us, we'll find that nigga."

Ten thousand thoughts ran through my mind. First of all, why didn't TJ let me know? Then I remembered Alexis said he called from New York. *Damn*, I thought. He didn't need to be up there getting into trouble. I knew I had to page him as soon as I hung up with Jermaine.

Questions and confusion commanded all my brain's attention as I tried to continue my conversation with Jermaine. He could tell that I was spooked, so he suggested I go out and get a gun permit first thing Monday morning. That was when it really hit me. This was a serious matter and if I wasn't careful, I could be a victim of more than just a rape.

I sat on the side of my bed and rummaged through my nightstand drawer, looking for TJ's new pager number. (I never saved it in my phone out of respect for Craig.) Ever since Christmas, we'd kept in touch often. TJ would call at least once a week to make sure I was okay.

"What you doin'?" a deep voice asked.

I jumped so high off that bed, I thought I was gon' hit the ceiling. It was Craig. "What happened to knocking?" I held my hand over my heart, assuring that it didn't fall out of my chest.

"What's wrong with you? You act like you've seen the Boogieman or somethin'."

"I haven't seen 'em yet," I said under my breath. I tucked TJ's number back under my phone book in the nightstand and closed the drawer.

"You trippin'," Craig said as he sat on the bed.

I was so irritated by his presence that I didn't even want to say anything to him—not about the pregnancy, not about Smoke. I just wanted him to get out of my room. We sat in silence for a few seconds.

"So what did you want to talk to me about?" I asked.

He shifted so he wasn't facing me directly. "Look. The past few months have been real stressful for us. It just seems like the relationship has either been at a standstill or it's been goin' backwards."

"I agree."

"We need to do somethin' about that."

Was he trying to pull the breaking up shit again? I prepared myself as much as possible for the words that were about to follow.

"I still wanna be with you, but maybe we should give each other some space or consider having an open relationship."

I chuckled to myself. "It's cool, Craig."

"What you mean, it's cool?"

"Just what I said! Do you expect me to sit up here and beg you to reconsider? It seems like your mind is made up."

"But I can tell you're mad. Speak up."

"I don't have a problem with it. I'm glad you came at me like this instead of bein' your usual wishy-washy self. I'm sick of you canceling our plans and arguing with you over petty shit. I'm not gonna keep feeling inferior to you or like you're only stayin' with me out of pity. The truth is, you wanna fuck with other people but you don't wanna lose me. It's cool. Do what you do. Just remember an open relationship works both ways."

"It ain't even like that, Meka. I think that ultimately, this'll be best for us."

"Okay," I said with confidence.

I decided not to tell him about the baby that night. He would have seen it as my tactic to keep him close in case he strayed too far. I had to do some serious thinking about when I would break the news to him since our status had changed.

I figured I'd call Nicole to get her input. It would be more ideal and a hell of a lot cheaper to call Tielle, but she had a personal stake in the dilemma. Craig is her cousin, and the baby would be, too. There was no way I could tell her the news right away.

After he left, I paged TJ, and while I waited for him to call back, I dialed Nicole. First, I told her about Craig's decision, and then I eased in the news of my pregnancy and Smoke.

She suggested I leave town for a while to be safe, but I argued that I couldn't run scared for the rest of my life. If he really wanted to find me, I was sure he could, no matter what city or state I moved to. And where would I go? I wasn't gonna stay with my dad because he'd be super overprotective. My mom? Yeah right.

We were interrupted when my line beeped. When I said hello the first time, no one said anything. I impatiently repeated myself.

"Tameka?" a guy asked.

"Yeah, who's this?"

"You don't recognize my voice?" he asked.

"TJ?" I guessed, even though it didn't sound like him.

"Close."

"I'm about to hang up, whoever you are."

"I wouldn't do that. You already in trouble 'cause you didn't follow my last directions. Didn't I tell you I'd kill yo ass if you went to the cops?"

It was the muthafuckin' rapist. I swear the devil was having a field day because all the stuff that was happening to me in one day was unreal. How did he get my number? *Duh, Tameka. You're listed in the phone book. But how would he know my last name?* Before I thought about it, I clicked back over to Nicole.

"It took you long enough, heffa," she said. "Was that TJ?"

"I'm comin' to stay with you for a while," I said.

138

"O…kay," Nicole said. "Where did this change of heart come from? I mean, it's cool, but just a couple minutes ago, you were adamant about not leavin'."

"That was Smoke on the other line." My voice was shaking.

I didn't have to say much more. Nicole wanted me to leave on the next plane out to Columbus, but we both knew that wasn't too feasible. I told her that I'd get back with her as soon as I made preparations to leave.

When we hung up, I called the police and urged them to do their job. They were supposed to protect and serve, but in eight months, I'd received all my pertinent information from TJ and Jermaine. Detective Nelson arranged for an officer watch our townhouse 24 hours a day for a week.

I paged TJ again—this time, 911. It had been an hour and a half since I'd paged him the first time. He called back within five minutes. I was scared to even look at the phone, so I let it ring until Lexis picked it up.

When she yelled for me, I answered cautiously.

"What's up?" TJ responded.

"What took you so long to call back?"

"I was tied up, baby girl. Chill."

"Chill?" I repeated. "I'm sorry. I can't do that right now."

"You must've talked to Jermaine, huh?"

"And Smoke!" I snapped.

"What?"

"You heard me," I said. "The muthafucka called here, talkin' 'bout how he told me he'd kill me if I went to the cops."

"Did you get a number?"

"No. He blocked it."

"Damn. He must be there already."

"Why didn't you tell me that you knew somethin'? You and Jermaine got me walkin' around here dumbfounded and shit, like everything's cool. Y'all knew his plan all along. Does my sister know? I know she's the one who brought y'all two together."

Alexis appeared in my doorway with a bag of Cool Ranch Doritos in her hand. "Know what?" she asked, still chewing on the last handful she'd stuffed in her mouth. I ignored her and kept questioning TJ.

"Now what am I supposed to do?" I asked.

"Calm down, first."

"Oh I'm sorry, TJ, but I'm not used to niggas callin' my house, threatening to kill me." I was frantic and yelling, frustrated that he wasn't showing enough concern.

"Who gon' kill you?" Alexis asked, stepping into the room.

"Look. I'll be there tomorrow afternoon. Lay low until then. If you don't have to, don't leave the house."

"You say all that and expect me to be calm? And where's the dude who pistol-whipped you? Is he after me, too?"

"You ain't gotta worry about him," TJ said. I didn't like his tone.

"What do you mean?" I asked.

"Look. I'll holla at you when I get there. Just stay in the house and have Lexis answer the phone when it rings. Tell her not to leave you there by yourself, either."

He hung up. I hated when he rushed me off the phone. I fell backwards on my bed and screamed. *How did all this happen? All I wanted to do was get a ride home after the argument at the club.* Years ago when we first got together, TJ was deep in the drug game, and his rivals never used me as a pawn. But fast-forward to a time when his bad boy lifestyle was no longer exciting and we weren't a couple anymore, and there I was in the middle of it all. I had become the stereotypical girlfriend of a thug.

"Are you gon' tell me what the hell is goin' on?" Alexis asked.

I told her what happened, including my plans to leave town.

"So now what? How do we know he won't show up here?"

Alexis called Robert, and he insisted on staying at our place until things blew over or Smoke was captured. She knew having a man in the house wouldn't hurt anything, but she was alright with me, her, and "Blaze" being there alone. "Blaze" was her gun, and she was very skilled with it. During the day it was in her purse, and at night it was under her pillow. Although she hadn't used it on anybody, I'd seen her at the range and that alone gave me a little security. I knew if she had to shoot somebody, she wouldn't miss.

I tossed and turned all night, struggling to go to sleep. I tried drinking hot chocolate, burying my head under the pillow, listening to music, counting sheep, deer, cows—you name it. Nothing worked. I was glad when morning came because I at least had an excuse to be awake.

It was only 9, but I felt like I was going stir crazy. I couldn't sleep, keep food down, or leave the house. If I watched another DVD, I was gonna kill myself, so I pulled out my journal and wrote until the phone interrupted me. I picked it up without thinking.

"Mornin', chick! I knew you'd be awake," Tielle said on the other end.

"Hey," I said, breathing a sigh of relief.

"Girl, who are you trying to dodge?"

"Hmph," I grunted.

"You and Craig into it again? I'm so sick of y'all. One minute y'all in love, the next minute—"

"He called."

"Huh? Who called?"

I explained. "And before you ask, I don't know how he got my number; I don't know where he called from; Yes, I think he's back in town; Yes, I've called the police; No, I haven't told Craig; and I didn't call and tell you last night because I wanted to go to sleep so the day would end."

"Okay. One more question. What are you gonna do?"

"I'm leavin'."

"Moving?"

"What else am I supposed to do? Take a police escort everywhere I go? Take nerve pills until they find him? I'm not stayin' forever. Just 'til this mess settles."

"Where you goin'? Back to Ohio?"

"Most likely. I'll probably just stay with Nicole. I would stay with my cousin, Yari, but I think her fiancé lives with her. I don't wanna intrude."

Before we hung up, I told her not to mention any of our conversation to Craig. I trusted that she would keep her word, but I didn't trust *myself* to tell him my plans. I was trying to create more distance between us to make it a lot easier for me to leave. I would probably be criticized for not immediately telling him about the baby or that I would be moving, but only I could determine what was best for me.

If I had shared the information with Craig the previous night or even waited until the next week, his attitude would change for the best, but for the wrong reasons. Neither his guilt nor his unborn child should be the reasons why he would start acting like my man again.

Chapter 16

A week passed and the police had stopped their surveillance. Smoke had stopped calling, but I felt like I was being tortured anyhow. When he called those few times, we knew his so-called plans. We knew he was getting a sick thrill out of threatening me. Once the calls stopped, I worried more for my safety. What if he was done playing games and ready to make a move?

I was able to leave the house, but I was a nervous wreck until I'd return. Making random trips to department stores and movie theaters was no longer on my agenda. Every outing had a purpose—if I wasn't at work, I was preparing for my move.

I put in my notice at work, confirming that my last day would be March 5th. That gave me time to celebrate my birthday, pack my stuff, and leave by the 18th. I had already bought my plane ticket, Nicole arranged for me to see her OB/GYN a week after my arrival to continue my prenatal care, and my doctor referred me to an AIDS/HIV specialist. I was taken off of my medicine because of the baby, but I had consultations and check-ups to make sure no symptoms were trying to sneak up on me.

Craig and I had made no progress. After I told him about Smoke, he made a point to call everyday, but it meant nothing. He never stopped by, using the excuse that Chauncey was in town.

***

Craig and Chauncey lounged in the living room Sunday morning. After a long night at the bar, Craig was debating on whether he was going to church. Chauncey had decided he was staying home, but he urged Craig to go.

"How you gon' tell me to go, but you stayin' your lazy ass here?" Craig said, throwing a pillow at his brother.

"You need Jesus, nigga. All the stuff you been tellin' me about you and Tameka…"

"Whatever." Craig thought about how much he missed her.

142

"Whatever? Man, you better get outta that mentality before you lose her. Or is that what you want?"

Chauncey was happily married, so he knew how to make a relationship work. For months, he'd listened to Craig spill his guts about the problems he and Tameka were having and it was obvious how much Craig cared about her.

"I don't know what it is, man," Craig said. "I feel like I'm bein' pressured to make a decision about us. It's like, 'I'm HIV-positive. You say you love me, so what's the problem?'"

"Have y'all…?" Chauncey pointed below his waist.

"A few times. It's hard, though, 'cause I get paranoid about the rubber slidin' down or somethin'. And I know she thinks I'm fuckin' somebody else, but I'm not. I could be almost worry-free hittin' somebody else, but I don't want to."

"And that's scarin' you," Chauncey interrupted. "In your heart, you're ready to take the next step, but you're lettin' your mind take over. You thinkin' too much. And one day, right in the middle of one of your thoughts, she's gon' throw you them two fingers and be like, 'I'm out.' Then what you gon' do? Be a lonely nigga who fucked up. Then on top of that, you done already messed up other booty 'cause you was steady turnin' it down when y'all was together. It'll just be you, your lotion, and a stack of flicks."

Craig laughed. "This love shit is crazy, man. I feel like I gotta be around her all the time to protect her, especially with that nigga harrassin' her. I don't know what I'd do if somethin' happened to her."

"You'd lose your damned mind," Chauncey replied. "And you know what? You gotta drop that shit about her havin' HIV if y'all gon' be together. You takin' on a big responsibility by stayin' with her. Most niggas would've been gone before she could finish sayin' the three letters. It's all or nothin', though. Either you gon' deal with it, drop it, and do whatever you can to help her, or you gon' leave her alone. Make sure you ready for all that comes with a relationship with her now. You gotta know the risks before you tell her you tryin' to be with her." He paused. "I may sound like I'm soft, but I'm givin' it to you real. I'm your brother, not one of your boys."

"I feel you," Craig finally said after a short interval of silence. "It's just that when I start thinkin' long-term, I can't see us together. I want kids one day, but we can't do nothin' without a condom, so how is that supposed to happen?"

"Have you talked to her about that?"

"It never came up. Well I guess it kinda did once, but I told her not to worry about all that."

"Well you need to figure it out. She's fine as hell and she must be doin' somethin' else right for you to still be with her through all this. I take my hat off to you for that, lil' bruh. I don't know if I could do it."

"Maybe I'll ask her to go to church with me," Craig said getting up.

"A couple that prays together, stays together," Chauncey joked.

***

"Hello?" I answered after Robert handed me the phone.

"What's up?" Craig said.

"Oh," I replied dryly.

"You goin' to church this mornin'?"

"Yeah, why?"

"'Cause I think we should go together. I guess that's a step toward us bein' on better terms. If you don't want to, I understand."

I accepted his invitation, but told him he had to join me at my church. I was still bitter and angry about how he'd been treating me, but I remembered all the praying I'd done—asking the Lord to step in and guide me through our failing relationship. I needed to know if it was time to let go of my former Prince Charming or if I needed to hang in there a little longer. Maybe my answer was on its way. Maybe God would touch us while we were in the same place and give us some direction.

I broke down during service. Craig and I went to the altar together, and it seemed like the more the pastor prayed, the more Craig squeezed my hand and the more I began to think. I felt like Craig was really trying to reach out to me, but it was too late. I thought about the plane ticket that was tucked in the right side of my sock drawer and the baby that was growing in my stomach. I knew that Craig deserved to know about at least one of those things, but I still couldn't tell him—not yet.

While I was thinking all of those thoughts, call me crazy, but I heard a voice say, "Tameka, do the right thing." I opened my eyes and looked around, but no one else's eyes were open except for a few of the kids who didn't want to be at altar call in the first place. Deep down I knew that the Lord was speaking to me, but I fought with all my might to ignore His words.

After a few short sniffles and taps of my foot, it all came out. I cried my eyes out. You don't understand. My knees buckled, and I was on the floor, bawling. All I remember is Craig and Alexis lifting me to my feet and taking me to the back of the church. I wouldn't tell either of them what was wrong. They both knew not to pressure me then, but the full fledged interrogation began when we got home.

Craig went upstairs with me and sat on the bed as I changed clothes. He'd been quiet the whole way home, so I knew I'd hear his mouth soon.

"So how long is Chauncey stayin'?" I asked, trying to make small talk.

"Three more days. So what was up with you in church?"

"I told you...nothin'."

"You full of it."

"You don't have to believe me." I hung up my dress.

"I know, 'cause you're lyin'."

"Like I said, I got a lotta stuff on my mind. I don't wanna discuss it with you right now, but I'll let you know what you need to know in a couple days."

He got up to leave and accused me of playing games.

"This is far from a game, Craig. Trust that. So, you can get up and storm out like a big baby if you want, but there's a lotta shit goin' on with me that you have no clue about."

"I know, 'cause you won't fuckin' tell me!" Craig yelled before he walked out. I could understand his frustration, but he wasn't gonna bully me into talking when I wasn't ready.

After I found my fuzzy blue slippers, I walked downstairs and went into the kitchen. Alexis was at the table studying the phone bill.

"Where are all these Ohio numbers comin' from? I don't recognize none of 'em except Nicole's."

"They're mine."

"To who?"

"Employers."

"Huh?" Alexis asked.

"I'm leavin', remember?"

"I thought you were just goin' for a month or two. I didn't know you planned on startin' a new life!"

"The sooner they find that idiot, the sooner I'll be home; but ain't no tellin' how long these stupid detectives will take," I replied. "I don't mind having a break. There's too much goin' on here. I got people comin' up to me, sayin' they heard I have AIDS; me and

145

Craig don't get along; I just found out I'm pregnant; and if Smoke calls here again, I'ma lose my mind."

"So you just gon' run?"

"I'm not runnin'," I said.

Alexis put the bill down and looked up at me. "Wait. Did you say you're pregnant?"

I nodded and rested my head in my hands.

"By Craig?"

"Who else?" I was offended.

"When did you find out?"

"Last week."

"And you just now tellin' me?"

Alexis was insulted. She assumed I had already told Tielle and Nicole the news and that she was the last to know. I explained that only she and Nicole knew and I wanted to keep it that way. Somehow, my words fell upon her deaf ears because our casual chat quickly turned into one of our infamous arguments.

"Man, you shady as hell. You waited a whole week to tell me?" She waited for my answer but didn't get one. "We supposed to be sisters, and you kept that from me?"

"Lexis, quit exaggerating. It's been a week. Now you know. So what, you got any advice on how I should handle this latest complication?"

"Exaggerating?" She leaned back in her chair and looked at me like I was crazy. "Last time I checked, I was the one you asked about your so-called relationship with Craig. And if you weren't worried about that, you were talkin' to me about your nightmares or how you thought somebody was followin' you home from work. Now you can't talk to me? I thought we were in this together, but you runnin' off for Lord knows how long. We could've figured somethin' out—somethin' that ain't so extreme."

"This is so much bigger than me and you. This is the rest of my life. This is my safety and my peace of mind. Do you get that? Get over yourself and stop takin' everything personal."

Alexis blinked away a tear. "Yeah, I get it. Hope you get your little fairytale ending in Columbus." She exited the kitchen as the doorbell rang, answered it, and went to her room.

Tielle entered the foyer and looked around. I yelled for her to join me at the kitchen table.

"What took you so long to get here? I thought you were comin' right after church."

146

"Girl, me and Romeo had to go get Aunt Tina from Dap's house and take her to my mom's. They've had me runnin' around town all day."

"What's he been up to? You haven't really mentioned him lately."

"We've been goin' at it because he don't like Maurice callin'."

"Oh, so he's still blowin' you up?"

"Not really. I guess Romeo's gettin' Craig's syndrome about TJ callin' you."

I laughed, then told her about the spat Craig and I had earlier. She advised me to hurry up and tell him I was leaving town.

"He'll know by the end of the week."

"Oh yeah!" she suddenly remembered. "Dap said some dude's been askin' about you."

"Who? Tyrone?" I joked.

"No, stupid. He's got a ghetto nickname. Umm…." She struggled to recall the information. "It was somethin' like, Smokey, Smoke…somethin'. I don't know. Maybe Gunsmoke."

"Smoke?" I repeated. She had to be mistaken. "Did she say when this was?"

"Like a week or two ago. I guess he knows Marlon or one of his boys and they were at the same party. She overheard him askin' people if they knew you, and when she told him she did, he asked if you were comin' to the party. He told her he'd been tryin' to get back in touch with you 'cause he lost your number."

"What?" My heart was pumping faster than my blood could move. I felt dizzy with anger.

"I guess he said he tried to holla at you before. You remember anybody like that? He's probably one of those dudes from the music festival last summer. They all had corny nicknames. Remember the one guy had on…"

As she rambled on, I realized I'd never mentioned Smoke's name to her. He was always "that muthafucka." She had no idea that she'd just told me that Dap was chatting with the rapist about me.

"…Meka!" Tielle said loudly. She'd been calling my name, but I was dazed.

"Huh?"

"You alright?"

"Did she give him my number?" I asked.

"Yeah. She said he was kinda cute."

147

"Who told that bitch that she could go around, givin' out my number?"

"Well the way she put it to me was that she was tryin' to make amends and show that she doesn't have no hard feelings towards you any more. Or maybe she did it to keep you away from Tyrone," she teased.

"She's a damn lie. She knows I'm still dealin' with Craig. And like I said, we ain't on that level for her to spit off my number to anybody who asks. I don't give a fuck who they say they are. If my mama went up to her and asked for my number, she ain't got no business givin' it to her."

"Don't kill the messenger," Tielle replied.

"Do you know who Smoke is, Tielle? Have you ever heard me mention a nigga with that name? No, 'cause I just found out who he is."

"Who is he?"

"The dude who raped me!"

"Are you kiddin' me? Oh my God. So that's how he got your number? From Dap?"

"I'm whoopin' her ass when I see her." I paced around the room.

"Cool out, Meka. She didn't know."

"Please. Me and her ain't even cool, Tielle, so why—"

"I know. Why would she give him your number?"

"Exactly. I know that's your cousin and everything, but when I see the bitch, I'm clockin' her right in her mouth."

"Don't go over her house, startin' shit, Meka." Tielle hated confrontation.

"I'm not gon' chase her down. I'ma let her come to me so she can walk right into my fist. We're bound to be in the same place at the same time within these next few weeks. If you don't want nothin' to go down, you better tell her to stay as far away from me as possible. If she even thinks I'll be somewhere that she's goin', tell her not to go."

"I'm stayin' out of it," Tielle said.

"Okay. Just make sure you stay out of it when I beat her ass, too," I replied.

True, Dap may not have known who Smoke was, but I was ready beat her ass for all the things she'd put me through over the past eight or nine years. All that grown stuff that held me back before was out the window.

Chapter 17

I went to Craig's apartment Tuesday after work. I was ready to tell him the news I'd promised. Hell, I was even ready to tell him that I was pregnant. With my timing and nonrefundable ticket, there was no way he could say anything to keep me around.

He'd cooked dinner, so we sat at his kitchen table and talked over sirloin steaks and baked potatoes. Our conversation was going well. He was excited that his team was going to be in a championship game, and he was the first coach in ten years to get them to that level. I was genuinely proud of him because I knew how hard he'd worked for that.

"You gon' come see us, right?" Craig asked.

"When is the game?"

"On the 17th."

I took a deep breath before I spoke. "Okay Craig, I'm not gon' beat around the bush. I'm leavin' town on the 18th. I need to get away for a while." I paused to give him a chance to say something, but he just looked like he was waiting for me to say "Psych" or something. "Once this stuff with Smoke is resolved, I'll be back."

I could tell he wasn't pleased. "So, what am I supposed to say? You lookin' at me like I actually have some say-so in your plans. It sounds like you already have your mind made up."

"Craig, can you please kill the attitude? I don't want any bad blood between us."

"You can't expect me to be excited. You're tellin' me we're about to break up now that you've decided—without talkin' to me—that you're movin'."

"We're not *really* together right now. Remember the open relationship thing? You made that call. But right now, that's not even the issue. There's a lot more to my decision. I have to think about my safety and the safety of everybody around me."

149

Craig stood up. "I was gonna keep you safe."

"How?"

"Do you know me and Chauncey sat here the other day and talked about my plans with you? I was lookin' for a way to stop that nigga from messin' with you. I was gon' do whatever I could to make sure our future wouldn't be ruined. If that meant we had to pick up and leave, then that's what I would've been willin' to do."

"When, Craig? 'Cause in the past few weeks you haven't acted too concerned. It's funny how you could sit up and talk to your brother about our relationship, but you couldn't fill me in until now. You act like you wanna keep your distance from me, so my move should be right up your alley."

"Well, it's not. And like I said, I might as well plan on bein' by myself now. I don't see a future for us no more, even if you do come back."

"How can you say that?" I asked.

"When you make a decision as big as this without tellin' the person you supposedly love so much, there's a problem. Who's to say you won't do the same shit later on? I need some stability in my life, and I'm just glad you showed me your true colors before it was too late."

He had his nerve. He wouldn't know stability if he lived in a group home on a military base, with his wishy-washy ass. I bit my tongue to keep from hurting his feelings.

"Okay," I said as I grabbed my jacket and walked to the door. "I see that we can't talk about this like adults. I guess this is goodbye."

"Take care," Craig replied dryly, playing the nonchalant role to a tee. He was treating me like an acquaintance—like we never had a connection. On my way out, I looked back at the man I no longer recognized, desperately hoping he would stop me once I took my first step. It didn't happen, so I walked into the hallway and out of his life.

I was too pissed to cry. I hopped in my car and peeled off, driving aimlessly down the expressway. Within minutes, I pulled into Smoothies' parking lot. I found a table in a secluded corner and sat down. I had my head down when I heard a familiar voice.

"Can I take your order?"

I looked up and saw Isaac. I'd forgotten all about him. I forced a smile, hoping it didn't look as fake as it actually was.

"Hey," I said, trying to sound friendly.

"I haven't seen you around lately."

150

"Yeah, I know." The conversation fell dead.

"Cranberry and vodka?" he asked.

"How did you remember?"

"How could I forget? I've never had an order like the one you put in last time." He winked and walked away.

Tielle called my cell. She had me on three-way, with Craig holding on the other line. Evidently he called her, ranting about how selfish I was and how I was throwing our relationship away. She figured I must've told him I was leaving, but she wanted to make sure before she made any references to that. Before we hung up, she told me she'd call back after she got off the phone with him. I told her to just meet me at Smoothies instead.

Then I remembered I didn't have any business up in Smoothies, ordering a drink. I figured my baby probably wouldn't appreciate having fetal alcohol syndrome, so it was time for me to leave. I hadn't hit the "End" button yet, so I quickly raised the phone to my ear again, hoping Tielle hadn't hung up either. She hadn't—and Craig was on the line, too. I pushed "Mute" so they couldn't hear all the background noise.

Boy, did I get an earful. Craig told Tielle the same crap about us not having a future anymore, and she was trying to understand why he felt that way. He fed her the same bull that he told me, with an added twist.

"...I was mad at first, but the more I keep talkin' about it, the more I realize that this had to happen. Somethin' would've stood in our way eventually. I was having weird vibes for a while, but everybody said I was just scared of commitment."

"So, you're not?" Tielle asked.

"Naw. This has to be God's way of releasin' me from that girl. I've been prayin' about it, and all this time I thought I wasn't gettin' a response."

"Okay, Craig, you takin' it too far now," Tielle said, laughing.

"I'm serious. Think about it. I want to get married and have kids. We couldn't have had that."

"Y'all could've adopted and you *would've* adopted in order to adapt to the circumstances if you really wanted to be with her. Maybe that's just it. You've realized that you don't wanna be with her, and it feels better to lash out at her than to own up to that."

"Man, whatever. I'm not lashin' out. I'm bein' real. And forget adoption. I wouldn't do that for anybody. I want my own seed, and I'm perfectly capable of bringing a life into this world. The only child I'd be able to get outta her is one with a fuckin' disease. Who wants that?"

I dropped my cell phone and sat in shock. That was probably the most hurtful and hateful thing I'd ever heard anyone say about me. That even topped the situation with my mother.

Isaac came back with my drink, and he could tell I was flustered.

"Are you okay?" he asked.

"No," I said, picking my phone up and turning it off. I threw it into my purse and got up from the table. "I'm sorry, Isaac. I have to go."

I bolted into the parking lot and sat in my car until my head stopped spinning. My tears blended with the rain that poured onto my windshield, making it impossible to see clearly. I was overwhelmed with emotions—enraged, disappointed, helpless...damaged. His words didn't just hurt; they destroyed my spirit, cutting to the bone.

I eventually made it home, but didn't go further than the couch. Craig's words ran through my mind like a broken record as I buried my face in the round throw pillow. After a while, the doorbell rang, but I didn't move. I wasn't in the mood to see anybody. The dinging continued until Lexis came downstairs to see who it was. We still weren't talking, so she gave me a dirty look when she saw me sprawled out facedown on the couch.

"Is Meka here?" Tielle asked Alexis. "We were supposed to meet at Smoothies but she wasn't there."

"Her lazy ass is right in there," Alexis said, pointing to the living room.

Tielle walked over and playfully smacked me on my back. "How you just gon' stand me up?" she asked. "I was walkin' all through that place lookin' for you. Isaac was the one who told me you'd left already. You coulda called a sista."

I wanted to explain, but my body had shut down.

"Why do you even bother with her?" Alexis asked as she walked into the kitchen.

I laid motionless and sick to my stomach, debating on whether to cuss Lexis out or answer Tielle's question. I chose the latter. I sat up and ran my fingers through my hair.

"You been cryin'?" Tielle asked. "What's wrong?"

Without looking at her, I responded, "I heard what he said."

"Huh?"

I told her about my unplanned eavesdropping.

Her face showed it all. "So what did you hear?" she asked.

"I heard I can only give him babies with a disease," I sobbed. "He acts like this is my fault!"

Tielle hugged me and sighed. "Meka, I'm sorry. I can't apologize for Craig, and I can't tell you he didn't mean it. All I can say is brush it off and thank God y'all ain't even on that level to be talkin' about gettin' married and havin' kids."

"But I'm pregnant, Tielle," I blurted.

All activity stopped. Alexis was on the phone in the kitchen, but she quit talking in the middle of her sentence. Tielle's grasp loosened, and she kinda pushed me away from her so she could see my face.

"Are you serious?" she asked. I didn't answer. "You are," she said. "Oh my God, Meka. You're pregnant?"

I heard Alexis in the kitchen. "Girl, I'll call you back," she said to the person on the other end. She walked cautiously into the living room, and stood near the entryway.

"How far along are you?"

"Almost four months."

"How long have you known?"

"Since last month. I found out the same day that Smoke first called." Tielle sat in disbelief. I still didn't look her in the eyes. I twisted my fingers and continued talking. "I wanted to tell you, but I was afraid you'd tell Craig before I did."

"I don't know what to say," Tielle said. "I mean, I understand you didn't want me to tell him, but all you would've had to do was say that." She wanted to go on, but she decided not to. "So is everything cool? Did the doctors say that everything should be normal?"

"As normal as possible. I'm supposed to keep my stress levels down, as you can see I'm doin' so well about."

"Did you know about this?" Tielle asked Alexis.

"Yeah," she said, entering the room. "So what's the story?"

I didn't say anything because we hadn't been talking before then, and I wasn't gonna act like we were cool just because I was in the middle of another crisis. Tielle told her the full story.

"Aw, hell naw!" Lexis snapped. "So who does he think he is? My sister was good enough to fuck, but she can't have his kid? He wasn't screamin' out 'HIV' when he was over here beatin' it up."

Her reaction was kinda shocking because it came out of pure instinct. She had forgotten that we were just at each other's throats.

153

"So are you gonna tell him now?" she asked me. "You should call his ass right now and say, 'Congratulations! You have a baby with a disease on the way!'"

"I'm not tellin' him nothin' until I'm ready. Right now, it wouldn't do me or the baby any good if I called him, goin' off. And now that you know, Tielle, I don't want you sayin' nothin', either."

***

It was March 7th, my birthday. Tielle was throwing me a birthday/going-away party that evening, and I was looking forward to having a good time. She made sure to tell all the attendees that I was going to Arizona on business when they asked. Since Smoke and I were linked through mutual associates, we came up with the phony destination and elaborate details that almost made *me* believe the lie.

I spent most of the day running around, searching for a cute outfit because most of the clothes in my closet didn't accommodate my thickening thighs and slightly round stomach. Although my new figure wasn't noticeable until I was looking at my naked profile in the mirror, I felt more comfortable in loose-fitting shirts in public in case somebody had a good eye for pregnant folks. I didn't need anymore of my business out in the streets.

When I got home at four, I noticed that TJ and Craig had called. Craig left a message as usual. It had been a week and a half since the drama between us went down, and he was driving me nuts. Everyday there was a new message—a new way of saying, "Please call me. We need to talk." I refused to return any of his calls.

Instead, I called TJ back. Our call frequency had increased to daily chats about a bunch of nothing—much like the good ol' days—and I enjoyed every minute of them. Despite our romantic history, we were friends. I could talk to him about almost anything, and I could be myself with him. There were no games between us—only cold, hard facts that weren't always pleasing. As much as I wanted to hate him for his involvement in the whirlwind that turned my life around, I couldn't. I knew he was only trying to help that night at the club. It was a night he'd never forget and would definitely not forgive himself for.

He wished me a happy birthday and asked what time the party started. We figured it would be safer to see each other at the clubhouse given the circumstances. Before we hung up, he told me I'd find my gift to the right of my doorstep, behind the small bush.

His friend hid it there since TJ was being careful not to come near my house.

When I opened the small box, I found a two-way pager. I had been drooling over that little device for the longest. I couldn't wait to clip it on my belt and pull it out occasionally to look important. Since I only knew two other people with one, that's about the only thing mine would be good for: decoration.

"You happy now? But I don't pay attention to anything you say, remember?" he said.

"I know. I guess I was wrong," I replied.

"I have my selfish reasons, too. I gotta have some way to holla at you since you goin' up north, right?"

I thanked him, then rushed off the phone to take a nap. When I woke up, I ironed my clothes, got in the shower, and went downstairs to get something to munch on.

"I need to talk to you," Alexis said.

"About what?"

"Look. I didn't mean to come at you like that the other day. I just didn't know how to take it when you said you weren't comin' back right away. I've had some time to cool off, and when I talked to Tiffany's psychological ass, she put some things in perspective. I guess what I'm tryin' to do is apologize. You only have a week or so left, and you don't need to leave here with us bein' on bad terms."

"I still don't understand why you were so shitty. It ain't even like you to be all emotional."

"It's always been me and you. No matter how much we don't get along or whatever, we've always looked out for each other. So when you told me you were leavin', I didn't think about your safety. I took it as you leavin' me. And I ain't gon' lie and say I don't still feel that way 'cause I do, but I also see your side of things now. I was emotional 'cause I took it personal."

I accepted her apology and we called a truce.

***

I arrived at my own party late. The security officers Tielle hired were standing on the sidewalk near the entrance and patrolling the parking lot on-foot. Their presence didn't guarantee my safety, but their large builds, stern faces, and shiny guns were sure to make Smoke think twice before crashing my little gathering.

"Is it the cool thing for the guest of honor to be late for her own party?" Tielle asked when I entered the building.

155

"Fashionably late," I corrected.

"Happy birthday, girl," she said, hugging me. "I would lead you to the alcohol, but you know," she whispered jokingly in my ear.

"Your rock-head cousin ain't here, is he?"

"Not yet," Tielle said, looking around the room. "But you know he's gon' show up. He's trippin' 'cause you keep ignoring his calls. He keeps askin' if you've said anything about him."

"I got some words for his ass alright." I scanned the room, looking for Dap.

"I know who you lookin' for," Tielle said. "I told her not to come."

Romeo approached us and asked why we weren't dancing. "Especially you, Miss Birthday Girl," he said.

"I just got here. I gotta warm up."

He grabbed my hand. "Let's go warm up, then." He turned to Tielle and gave her a kiss. "We'll be back, baby."

Romeo and I danced to Jay-Z's "Give It To Me." He had me all over the clubhouse floor, dancing silly. He definitely made me feel more comfortable. I didn't leave the floor for at least a good half hour because Tielle's coworker was jammin' on the turntables. When I'd get ready to leave the floor to sit down, he'd mix in one of my songs, and I'd find myself in the same spot, shaking my ass.

I took a break and mingled with the people I knew. While I was standing near the entrance talking to Lynn, my ex-coworker, Craig walked in. I looked up, and our eyes met briefly.

Lynn recognized him from the company gatherings and called him over. "Do you remember me?" she asked as I rolled my eyes. "I used to work with Tameka."

"Yeah, I remember you," he replied, glancing at me. "You're Lynn, right?"

"Good memory," she said, laughing.

Lynn's talkative ass was driving me crazy! I didn't know if I could be in the same vicinity as Craig any longer. Just when I was easing away from them, he said, "Happy birthday, Meka."

I ignored him and kept walking. During my journey, I spotted Tielle by the deejay booth, so I went over and stood by her.

"I already saw it," she said.

"I can't believe that fool even fixed his lips to say somethin' to me," I said.

"Just cool out. You're supposed to be havin' a good time."

TJ and his buddies walked in around midnight. I was out on the floor dancing when I saw them. I kept grooving, and when I looked around to find them again, I saw everybody but TJ. All I could think was, *I hope he ain't somewhere arguin' with Craig.* I weaved through the crowd, determined to find him. I didn't get to the middle of the floor before somebody grabbed my arm.

"You ain't leavin' this floor. I came all the way over here just for you. You gotta move somethin'," TJ said with his trademark grin.

I smiled and rocked my hips to the beat. Soon, he was spinning me, dipping me, and being goofy. It reminded me of our first date, when we went to an old school Stepper's Ball—an event I never would've imagined he'd attend.

Every time I looked up, Craig was staring at us. He was near the gift table standing with Tielle.

"Why don't you stop starin' at them?" Tielle asked him.

"She's just tryin' to make me jealous, dancin' with that nigga."

"Well, it looks like it's workin'!" Tielle said, stepping in front of Craig to block his view.

"Naw, I'm cool." He pushed her to the side. "It's all good. We ain't together no more."

I was hot and sweaty, so I went to the bathroom to get some paper towels. While I was in there, I figured I'd touch up my lipstick and finger-comb my hair.

I stepped out of the bathroom and there was a line of females waiting. I recognized one of them, so I stood beside her and shot the breeze. In mid-conversation, I spotted the one and only Daphne Thomas entering the room with Tyrone. I paused our conversation and pushed through the crowd until I ended up in Dap's face.

"Happy birthday, Meka," Tyrone said, face beaming.

I put my hand in his face, signaling for him to shut up.

"Don't even start, Tameka," Dap said. "I ain't here to bother you."

I put my head down and laughed. As I raised my head again, I also raised my fist and clocked her in her mouth. My hand hurt like hell, but my adrenaline allowed me to ignore the pain.

"I told Tielle to keep you away 'cause I'm done playin' with you; and I promised myself that I wouldn't let you walk by me without punchin' you in your fuckin' mouth. You always seem to be the root of my fuckin' problems, and I'm not lettin' that shit slide no more. Stay outta my business."

Dap laid near the entrance, dabbing her lip in disbelief, as I shook my aching hand and sashayed back to the dance floor. I felt so good. That hit was six years in the making—long overdue. By the time Tyrone helped her up, security was helping them out of the clubhouse. The big white guy made it clear to Dap that she was not to return as she yelled profanities and threats at me through the window. She didn't deserve a response, so rapped along with Cam'ron and two-stepped with Kyle, a guy I went to high school with. I played it so smoothly, most of my guests didn't even know about the commotion.

The party ended at 3:30. I sat down for the last hour because I was tired and my feet were killing me. TJ called my cell and stayed on the phone with me while Alexis and I drove home to "make sure nobody was waiting" at my place...namely, Dap. I told him I wasn't afraid of her, but it didn't matter. He was used to being my protector, so I didn't make a fuss.

We rode in silence for a little while. "So you and ol' dude really ain't together no more, huh?" he suddenly blurted.

"Where did that come from?"

"I didn't see y'all talkin' or dancin' all night."

"'Cause we're not together. I told you that before."

"I know, but I thought you was bullshittin'."

"What were you doin'? Watchin' me all night?"

"You know I was," he replied, sounding so sexy.

When we pulled up to my place, I noticed that Craig's car was parked nearby.

"Shit!" I said as I put the car in park.

"What's wrong? You see her?"

"No."

Alexis and I exited the car and started up the walkway. Craig was standing on our doorstep. I told TJ I would call him back and hung up before he could respond.

"Why are you here, Craig?" I asked.

"We need to talk."

"You had all the time in the world to talk to me earlier."

"I want to talk to you in private."

"Ain't no privacy here," Alexis chimed in.

"I don't wanna listen to anything you have to say. I've heard enough," I added.

Suddenly, we heard tires screech, and I turned to see TJ jumping out of Carlos' black Impala. He quickly made his way to the porch as Carlos pulled off.

"Awwww shit!" Alexis said excitedly. She turned to Craig. "Bet you 'bout to leave now." She unlocked the door and stepped inside.

"Is this why you got off the phone so quick?" TJ asked me. "I thought that nigga, Smoke, was here or somethin'."

"What's this all about? Oh, you can't talk 'cause you back with this nigga?" Craig followed, pointing at TJ.

I covered TJ's mouth before he could say a word. "It's none of your business whether we're back together," I said, stepping in front of TJ to hold him back. "And you don't have the privilege to stop by my house unannounced anymore, so you can leave."

"I have to ask you somethin' first," Craig said.

"Goodbye, Craig."

"Yeah, nigga," TJ cosigned. "Get yo punk ass outta here."

I pushed him inside and followed close behind. My hand was throbbing and swelling again, so I iced it while TJ and I talked in the living room. He said he would come visit me in Columbus once he made sure Smoke and his people weren't watching him.

"I just want this stuff to be over," I said.

"I know, baby," TJ replied. He took the ice off of my hand and laid the bag on the table. "Come here."

I was nervous about having him in my house, but when he hugged me tightly and kissed me on the cheek, I felt like nothing or no one could harm me. From the day he made me his woman, TJ had been my rock. If I had a problem, he'd solve it. If I needed to talk, he was on the other end of the phone. If anybody hurt me, he was ready to make them pay. He'd shown me what strength was. And during a time when I felt weaker than ever, he was right by my side, holding me—teaching me to be strong again. I sunk into his chest, wishing he could take all my troubles away like before.

Portia A. Cosby

Chapter 18

March 18th came quickly. I'd endured 11 days of hell to get to it, though. Craig kept calling and leaving messages. I wasn't sure how much longer I could avoid him. Dap also called a few times to make empty threats. Alexis intercepted a couple of the calls and made a few threats of her own. Ever since their relationship had soured months before, she was starting to see what kind of person her former best friend was.

Tielle and I hung out almost every day, making trips to the mall, going out to eat, and going to see old movies at the two-dollar movie theater. I was really gonna miss her, and it hit me the last day we hung out at the mall. We were sitting in the food court, reminiscing about the day she met Romeo.

"...I'm so happy for you, LT," I said. "You've finally found true love, and you didn't have to go to the church revival to find him."

I tried to joke around to keep myself from crying. Pregnancy and my already sensitive emotions didn't work well together. Thinking about that day at the mall reminded me of how much fun we always had, and it reminded me of the days when I was HIV-negative and not with child. My major problems were so minute compared to my new reality.

The day had finally come for me to leave and I was having second thoughts. Smoke had stopped calling, so I wondered if it was even necessary to go. My logic kicked in, and I realized that I still needed to get away, maybe not even because of him. I needed time to get my mind right. A lot of shit had been thrown at me, and I had to figure out how I was gonna handle all of it.

As Alexis and I waited for Tielle to take us to the airport, the phone rang. Miss Rosie's number appeared on the caller ID.

"This heffa is still at her mama's house," I said.

"She ain't left yet?" Alexis asked.

"Hello?" I answered.

"Meka, don't hang up." It was Craig.

160

"Ten seconds."

"Huh?"

"That's how long you have before I hang up," I said.

"I'm just callin' to say goodbye. I was gonna follow Tielle to the airport, but she told me not to. I figured I'd call instead."

"Either way it goes, we have nothin' to say to each other."

"You sure about that?" he asked. "I feel like you're hidin' somethin' from me 'cause you keep avoidin' me."

"I'm not hidin' shit from you."

"C'mon, Meka. I called you about a hundred times over the past week and you wouldn't even pick up the phone to cuss me out about whatever's got you so hostile. You didn't even pick up and tell me to stop callin'. That's not like you. You only stay to yourself when there's somethin' you don't wanna slip up and say."

"When I wanted to talk, you dismissed me. Now I'm about to go. Your time's been up." I hung up.

Tielle pulled up and blew the horn. Lexis and I grabbed my luggage and went out to the car. Tielle looked over at me and shook her head.

"I can't believe you leavin'," she said.

"Tielle, don't start," I replied.

"Right," Alexis agreed. "Save the mushy stuff for when we at the gate."

"Wait. Wasn't TJ supposed to come?" Tielle asked.

"Yeah, but I'm not surprised that he didn't show. He's not good with goodbyes," I said.

"He probably didn't wake up on time," Lexis added.

We arrived at the airport in a half hour, and I was all checked in by 7:45. We thought we'd have to say our farewells in the lobby, but Alexis knew one of the TSA agents, so he let them walk to the gate with me.

None of us said a word. Instead, we fumbled through our purses, picked dirt from under our fingernails, and played games on our cell phones.

Tielle broke the silence. "Can I please say somethin' now?" she asked.

Alexis and I laughed. "What?" I asked.

"I'm gon' miss you, girl. It's just now hittin' me that we're not gon' see each other for months."

"I'ma miss you, too." I pulled some tissue out of my pocket.

161

Alexis continued to stare at the planes in an effort to ignore our crying.

"I won't be gone long," I said. There was a long pause. "Okay, that's enough," I said as I took out my compact mirror to check my face. "No more cryin'."

"Thank you!" Alexis said. "I told y'all to stop all that sappy stuff."

I put on my best poker face, but I was overwhelmingly nervous. In 25 minutes, I'd be on my way to start another life for an undetermined amount of time. Unfortunately, whenever I could return to town safely, my life would never be back to normal. A voice came over the loudspeaker. "Flight 491 leaving for Columbus will be boarding in ten minutes. Once again, Flight 491 leaving for Columbus…"

Alexis looked over at me, and I smiled uncomfortably. Tielle was staring in the direction of the hallway. She squinted and cocked her head to the side as if she was trying to get a closer look at something.

"Is that TJ?"

"Where?" I asked, suddenly feeling a flutter in my chest.

She pointed. "Right there."

"In the gray shirt?" Alexis asked.

"Yeah," Tielle replied. "Standin' at the information desk."

Before I knew it, Alexis screamed, "TJ, we over here!"

I put my head down, embarrassed as hell because everyone in our area was staring at my ghetto sibling. Unashamed, Lexis continued to wave her arms to make sure he saw her.

TJ made his way over to us and I stood up to give him a hug. "I didn't think you were comin'."

"Man, I woke up late as hell. Then, when I got here, they made me buy a fuckin' ticket so I could come to the gate," he said. "What's up, y'all," he continued, acknowledging Tielle and Alexis. "This is your big day, baby girl!" He winked and held my hand.

"Yeah, I know." My voice didn't have the same level of excitement as his.

"We'll be back, y'all," TJ said. He led me to a nearby corner. "You cool?"

"I'm okay."

"You know you won't be gone long, right? I'ma have this shit handled by the end of the month."

I stared at the floor. He lifted my chin and looked me in the eyes.

162

"I'm serious. I'ma find that nigga and bring you home. You hear me?"

I nodded. I felt the tears coming, so I didn't wanna talk. TJ kissed my forehead. "You know I still care. Just hang on a little bit longer. I'ma come through for you."

"I know."

"C'mon, baby girl. You ain't gotta do all that cryin'." He held me as Tielle and Alexis watched from afar.

"We will now begin pre-boarding for Flight 491. All first class passengers, those with small children..."

I pulled away from TJ. "That's my flight. They'll be callin' my seat in a second."

He planted a tender kiss on my lips, then said, "Guess that means we don't have time to sneak off to the bathroom so I can give you your goin' away present, huh?" His hands lingered on my hips.

I punched him playfully in the chest. I was so glad he added some humor to our goodbye. We walked back over to Tielle and Alexis.

"Okay. I'm gon' say bye right now, real quick, so we don't do the cryin' thing again," Tielle said. We hugged, then she turned to Lexis. "I'll be over by McDonald's."

"Okay," Alexis said as Tielle walked away. She walked over and gave me a quick squeeze. "Take care of yourself."

"I will," I replied. When we let go, I saw that she was about to cry, which made my tears come right back. "I'll call you when I get settled in," I said.

The lady called my seat number.

"I love you," I said as I walked to the gate.

"Call me as soon as you get there," Alexis said as she wiped her tears.

After I handed my ticket to the man at the gate, there was no turning back. I was on my way to Columbus.

***

When Tielle arrived at her mother's house to pick up her nephew, Dap, Craig, and Carmen were there.

"What's this? A family reunion?" she asked as she sat her keys on the coffee table.

"I came over here to find you before you took that bitch to the airport," Dap said.

"How did you know I was over here?" Tielle asked.

"Romeo told me when I called earlier."

"So what did you want?"

"I was gonna go over there with you. Don't think I forgot about our little altercation."

"Ooh, she's lucky I wasn't at that party," Carmen said, scowling.

"Y'all need to get over it," Tielle said.

"Man, whatever. I'm tired of you always takin' up for that skank instead of your own family. You wouldn't like it if some bitch came up and snuck you, would you?" Dap ranted.

"Hold up. I told you to stay away from her, and I made a special point to tell you not to come to the party. Why would you wanna go to your enemy's party anyway? She's such a bitch, remember? It ain't my fault you underestimated her." Tielle was fired up.

"Calm down, y'all," Craig said after Dap stood up. He tried to get an understanding as to why Tameka wanted to fight Dap so badly, and Tielle told him that Dap gave Smoke Tameka's number. Craig agreed with Tielle and told Dap she was wrong for doing that, even though she didn't know who he was.

"Now that I think about it, you can help Meka's case," Tielle said. "You saw what he looked like, right? I mean, he didn't have on a disguise or nothin', right?"

"No," Dap replied. "He was wearin' regular clothes."

"Man, don't tell the cops shit. How you gon' help her after she embarrassed you in front of half the town?" Carmen interrupted.

"That's so ignorant," Tielle said with disgust. "This is the one way she can redeem herself for this mess that's happened with Smoke."

"What if I don't wanna redeem myself?" Dap asked.

Tielle stared at Dap in disbelief. After a couple seconds, she went upstairs to get Chris. When she came back downstairs, she turned to Dap. "You remember all that evil shit comes back to you. The same dude you protectin' could find you and do the same thing he did to Meka. Don't go to the cops then, either."

"Okay, Minister Thomas," Carmen said. Dap simply looked away.

"Y'all need to grow up," Tielle said as she walked out.

***

My plane landed in Columbus on time. As its wheels hit the runway, a feeling of relief came over me, and I knew I had made the right decision. I walked through the tunnel, rode the transit, and stepped into the lobby, searching for a familiar face. Nicole had a big photo shoot, so she couldn't pick me up. Instead, my cousin, Yari, was supposed to come get me. I hadn't seen her in years, so I was hoping she'd recognize me.

I watched as other passengers' families snapped pictures and videotaped their arrivals. I maneuvered through the crowd, and just when I was about to sit down, I heard someone call my name. I looked around and spotted Yari and her daughter running toward me.

"Sorry I'm late," Yari said, giving me a quick hug and trying to catch her breath.

"It's cool. I just got off the plane," I said. I looked down at the little girl. "So, who is this cute lil' thing?"

"This is Paradise," Yari said.

"Hi," Paradise said softly.

"Her daddy named her," Yari said.

"I got you," I replied.

Yari was absolutely beautiful. I didn't know what to expect because I hadn't seen her since we were a lot younger. She had a coconut-caramel complexion and her hair fell a few inches past her shoulders. She was a slim 5'9 and didn't look like she had a 3-year-old child.

"Man, it's been a long time," I said as we walked toward the baggage carousel.

"I know," Yari replied. "Like ten years or so, huh?"

"Yeah."

"It's cool, though. We've got all the time in the world to catch up."

She didn't live that far from the airport, so we got to her house in about 20 minutes. When we pulled up to her place, I was confused. I saw the huge house and figured she had to make a quick stop there before we went to her apartment. Like a dummy, I sat in the passenger seat while Yari got out and took Paradise out of her seat.

"You comin'?" she asked.

"Oh, this is your place?"

"Yeah, girl. C'mon."

I remembered that my uncle had a lot of money, and figured that was how she could afford the lavish living quarters. When he was killed and the will was read, she found out that he left almost all of his money to her and not my aunt. I was amazed that she was responsible with the large sum at such a young age. Most people would've bought everything except a house.

We grabbed a few of my bags and carried them inside.

"Baby!" Yari yelled. "Can you help us with the rest of these bags?"

A few seconds later, a fine-ass human being walked down the stairs.

"Daddy!" Paradise yelled and ran over to him.

"Hey, baby girl!" He lifted her into his arms and swung her around.

It was so sweet to see a man show so much affection to his child. I felt my eyes get a little misty as I thought about the baby growing in my stomach who would never experience that type of love and affection.

"Tameka, this is my fiancé, Dallas," Yari said, putting her arm around him.

"Nice to meet you," I said.

"Same here. All I've been hearin' for the past two weeks is, 'My big cousin's comin' to town.' Now, maybe she can shut up," Dallas joked.

I tried my best not to stare at his perfectly straight teeth, but when he talked, his top lip curled slightly, and I couldn't help myself. After seeing him, I realized why Paradise was so gorgeous. She couldn't have gone wrong with her mom's features combined with her dad's wavy hair and Hershey brown eyes.

After we finished our small talk, Dallas and I went out to the car and got the rest of my luggage.

"That's it," he said when we got back inside.

"Thank you."

"I'm 'bout to get outta here, boo," he said to Yari.

"Where you goin'?" she asked.

"To play ball with Mike and them. I'll be back in about two hours." He headed for the door.

"I wanna go, Daddy," Paradise said, running over to him and grabbing his leg.

"Daddy's gonna be busy, baby. You can't go this time," Yari said.

She immediately started crying.

"C'mon," Dallas said, picking her up.

"How are you gonna watch her if you playin' ball?"

166

"Trina and them'll be there," he said, referring to his sister and her friends.

"Whatever," Yari replied.

Dallas and Paradise left, and Yari and I sat in the den to relax.

"So what's up, cuz?" What's been goin' on with you?"

"I don't even know where to start," I said.

"I know. It's been so long."

"It's not even that," I said. "I don't think you're ready to hear everything."

Yari sat up in her chair, intrigued. "I know somethin' big has to be goin' on for you to come back to this place. I didn't wanna ask you why you were comin' over the phone, though."

I ran down the story from the rape to the stalking. "...And on top of all that, I'm pregnant," I said.

Yari's jaw dropped. "By this Craig dude?"

"Yep. Funny how life goes, huh?"

"Meka, this is crazy. I am so outta the loop. I feel so bad. I mean, I know we haven't seen each other or talked in a long time, but..."

"It's okay. I just assumed my mom had told Aunt Kathy and that she told you. Guess since it didn't fit into her perfect, glamorous lifestyle, she decided to leave that out of their conversations. It's a lot easier to talk about the latest pay raise you received."

"Y'all still don't get along, huh?"

"Nope."

"Well, tell me a little more about Craig."

"There's not much to say. When we first met, everything was cool. We became a couple, and everything was still cool. Even after my diagnosis, he said we would work through that. Then all of a sudden, he started showin' his true colors. The phone calls slowed down, the attitudes showed up, and I just became less and less attracted to him. And after he said he didn't want kids with me, that was it. He didn't have to be cruel like that."

"So you're not gonna tell him about the baby?"

"I haven't decided. Now that we're sittin' here talkin' about it, I have the mindset to call and tell him that he's about to have a baby with a disease—just what he didn't want—but that's ignorant. I'm not that spiteful. And who's to say that my baby will have HIV? I do believe in miracles, and Lord knows that I'm overdue for one. So right now, I'ma wait it out. I'll tell him when I'm ready."

We sat and talked for hours. There was an immediate bond between the two of us. We vowed to keep in contact even after my return to Texas because there was no reason for us not to be in touch anymore.

Nicole pulled up at about five. I gave Yari my contact numbers, grabbed my bags, and was on my way.

"It's not gon' hit me that you stayin' here until like next week," Nicole said as we got settled in her apartment. "I'm so used to you comin' for a few days, then leavin'."

"Well get used to me. I'm here for a while."

"Did you call Lexis?"

"Yeah. She said Craig had already called, askin' if I made it safely."

"That dude is so lame, girl," Nicole said as she turned on the TV. "You betta not ever deal with him again."

Chapter 19

I'd been in Columbus for a month and pretty much had things squared away. I got in touch with one of Tielle's contacts, and he found me a job at a local modeling agency, managing the agents and their clientele. I loved my job. I came into contact with so many different people throughout the course of my day. My schedule was always different, depending on which clients I was meeting with. Most of my time was spent giving presentations and having business lunches, though. I was definitely loving the free lunches. I'd eat six times a day if somebody let me.

I talked to Tielle and Alexis regularly. Tielle told me that Craig was on a mission to get my number from her or Lexis. He was also on a mission to get with Jacqueline, a 30-year-old mother of two, who taught at his job.

TJ and I two-wayed each other almost every day. He'd been trying his best to come see me, but I'd been putting him off. He had no luck finding Smoke, but he'd gotten word that he was somewhere in Florida. He still promised to find him, but I'd given up on that dream two weeks after I left Texas. I was perfectly comfortable with Smoke simply staying away from me. I didn't care what state he was in, as long as it wasn't Ohio.

During our last messaging spree, I'd run out of excuses to give TJ. We decided that he would come on the 25th, which was only a week away. I was kinda glad he was coming because he was bringing my car to me and flying back to Texas. There was one problem, though. He still didn't know I was pregnant. I knew he was gonna have a heart attack once he saw me because I was definitely showing.

Speaking of which, the pregnancy was going well. My doctors were very optimistic and determined to keep me HIV symptom-free. I found out I was having a little boy. The news was exciting, but bittersweet. I had always said if my child's father had a decent name and I had a boy, I would name the baby after him. It was a shame I couldn't do that, because I didn't want my son to be named after Craig's simple ass.

On another medical note, I had my first appointment with the HIV specialist, Dr. Burns. The majority of our time was spent talking about how I'd been feeling and what medications I was on. While we were talking, he asked why I wasn't on medication that would control any symptoms that could occur.

"The doctor in Texas told me that I didn't have to be on them because they could hurt the baby," I said.

"That's not exactly true. It's not proven that the medications will affect your baby, and in my past experiences, my other pregnant patients didn't experience any complications with the drugs," Dr. Burns replied.

"So, are you gonna put me on some medicine now?"

"I'd feel a lot better if I did. The main drug that I'm shocked you're not on is ZDV. Basically, it's an antiviral drug that you'll take while you're pregnant. It'll be in your system during your labor, and we'll most likely use it after the baby is born to protect him from acquiring the virus. It's not a sure-fire guarantee, but it has lowered the risk for infant acquisition."

"And this won't mess me up, either?"

"No, it won't," the doctor assured me. "The only thing that you may consider messing you up may be the scar left after we do the cesarean section."

"So, they were right when they said I'd have to deliver like that?"

"Yes. That'll also decrease the chances of the baby getting the virus because it won't have to go through the birth canal."

"When will we know if the baby has it?"

"Not until he's between three and six months, usually."

I liked Dr. Burns. He was a black doctor, and he looked like he was only thirty-something. I could relate to him better than some old white man in his late fifties who thinks everyone with HIV is promiscuous. I found myself asking more questions and taking a more active role in my health issues. Before I left, he gave me tips on managing my diet and handed me a list of multivitamins and supplements that I needed to get. He also gave me a prescription for ZDV.

I couldn't wait to tell Nicole everything once I got home. Dr. Burns had really opened my eyes, and I learned a lot more about my condition.

"…Do you know that there's an increased risk of gettin' HIV if you're sexually assaulted or forced into havin' sex?" I asked Nicole.

"That's what the doctor told you?" Nicole asked. I nodded. "Did he say why?"

"I was too tripped out to ask, but it's probably because the dudes normally don't use condoms in those situations."

"That's true."

"And on top of that, everything is dry down there because a stranger cussin' at you and rammin' himself inside of you isn't a turn-on. That means you get cuts and stuff, and the virus can just seep right in."

Nicole gave me a puzzled look. "I can't believe you're talking— damn near joking—about this like you haven't been through the exact same thing."

"I can't walk around here, frownin' all the time, right?" I replied. "This is my personal therapy. I gotta smile, Nikki. I don't care how bad things are. When I'm at work or just hangin' out around town, nobody looks at me and thinks, *Man she's unhappy.*"

"But that's frontin', Meka."

"It's coping. Smiling is my way of dealin' with this. Blockin' it out right now is my mechanism. I just wanna live life until this shit catches up with me. I'm about to have a baby. I'm about to have a *blessing*—the only thing good that's come out of these ten months of hell. You can't understand that?"

"I can't say I do. I haven't been through what you have, though. I just don't want you to walk around hiding your true feelings. Keeping all that bottled up ain't good for you."

***

It was Friday, April 25th. The previous night I'd planned out my day. I was going to sleep until noon, then wake up and straighten the house. After that, I was free to do nothing until dinnertime, when I would prepare lasagna, TJ's favorite. I stuck to my schedule religiously and found myself lounging in my baggy gray sweats and red Adidas t-shirt for hours, watching MTV and BET's special coverage of the one-year anniversary of Left Eye's death. My eyes stayed glued to the screen as I sang along with TLC's videos and did the "Waterfalls" dance in my seat. I thought back to the days of wearing Cross Colours outfits and slicked-back ponytails at age fifteen and sweating my hair out from dancing so hard at the local rec center. Life was so simple then.

When "Red Light Special" came on, I thought about the night I met TJ. That song was still hot when I first started working at U-Turn, and I did my first pole dance to it. TJ was intrigued enough to approach me—I normally didn't give customers the time of day, but something about him was genuine. From that night on, we were connected.

I swayed to the melody and smiled at the memory of the good ol' days. My groove was interrupted by a knock on the door. I was slightly nervous all day, but all the butterflies rushed in when I opened the door and saw TJ standing before me, looking finer than ever. His freshly braided hair had grown, overlapping the hood of his velour Roc-A-Wear jacket, and his oversized t-shirt hid the top of his black boxer-briefs, still slightly uncovered by his sagging pants.

"What's up, baby?" He hugged me—the very thing I didn't want him to do. I gave him a half-hearted hug in return and pulled away.

"Damn, girl!" TJ said as we sat down at the kitchen table. "You moved to Ohio and started lettin' yourself go, huh?"

I excused his insult and tried to change the subject. That didn't work.

"You lookin' rough as hell! Why you got on them baggy clothes?" he continued.

"'Cause I'm grown, and I can dress how I want. I'm at home, relaxin'."

"You look like you gained some weight."

"I'm glad I don't have low self-esteem," I said.

"It really ain't that bad, though." He looked me up and down. "Your titties look bigger. That's always a plus." He cracked up laughing, and I sat quietly, not amused.

"You know I'm just fuckin' wit' you, girl!"

"Whatever, TJ."

"Where's Nicole?"

"Out on a date," I said.

"Oh. So what we doin' tonight?" he asked.

"We chillin' in the house tonight. We'll go out tomorrow."

"What if I wanna go out tonight, too?"

"You'll be goin' out by your damned self."

The lasagna was baking in the oven, so when it was done, we ate dinner. After two pieces and a couple glasses of Cherry Kool-Aid, we wound up on the couch, watching movies. We talked about my new job and his search for a legitimate career. He said he wanted to have a job secured before he found Smoke and killed him.

"What's the point of that?" I asked.

"'Cause at least I won't have a felony to put down before I get the job."

"So you'll just commit the felony once you have the job?" I asked, giving him time to realize that he wasn't making any sense.

He laughed. "Damn. I guess that plan won't work, huh?"

Before I got up to put another movie in, he asked when Nicole would be back. I told him I didn't expect her until sometime after three.

"So we have time," he said as he leaned over and kissed me.

"Hello…" I said, pulling back. "Somebody here has HIV. Eenie, meenie, minie, me!" I stood up. I was extremely agitated by TJ's advances and didn't want my pregnant body to be touched.

"That's why they make condoms. You know damn well I wasn't tryin' to go up in you raw. If you don't wanna get down, just say that shit. Don't make up excuses. I know what you got, and I know why you got it," he continued.

I was uncomfortable with the idea of sex and HIV. TJ (and Craig) didn't seem to have a problem with it and that tripped me out. I knew I had that fire between my legs, but come on. I wasn't the only girl in the world with a pretty face, a banging body, and some good coochie.

"An excuse is, 'I got a headache.' HIV is a fact. I'm pregnant. That's a fact." I didn't mean for it to come out like that, but I continued anyway. "You wanna know why I have on these big clothes? That's why. I'm five months pregnant."

TJ's eyes opened almost as wide as his mouth, and he didn't say a word.

"I wasn't gonna tell you until right before you left, but there you go," I said.

"You havin' that nigga's baby?" he asked, referring to Craig.

"Yeah."

"I can't believe this shit."

"He doesn't know," I said.

"So when you gon' tell him?"

"I don't know. I'm not in a rush because he doesn't want it anyway."

I could tell TJ was pissed off, hurt, and concerned, all at the same time. After he got past the disbelief, he asked me what the risks were for me and the baby. Once I was done explaining everything, the conversation fell dead. He just wanted to go to sleep, so I led him to my room. I slept out in the living room because I knew he needed space.

The next day was extremely awkward. TJ did more talking with Nicole than with me. We didn't even go out like I had planned. Needless to say, his trip was a waste.

We didn't talk or page each other much after he left. I tried leaving messages, but he only returned a select few. I felt like there was a huge void in my life. Every other time we had stopped talking, I was the one who made the decision. That time, he was the one shutting me out of his life, and it didn't feel good at all. Even though we weren't together and hadn't been for almost two years, I still wanted him to be a part of my life, even if it was a only small part.

***

It was true that TJ was hurt—not necessarily by the news that Tameka was pregnant, but because he realized that he wouldn't be able to father her first child. When he first saw Tameka at 20-years-old, he was instantly attracted to her. Why wouldn't he have been? She was a beautiful, half-naked woman, moving seductively on stage. It wasn't until he met her a week later that he became love-struck. This girl actually had a brain—and a smart mouth—which showed she was street-smart, too.

He knew instantly that he needed to make Tameka his lady. After about a month, he achieved his goal, and he knew he could be with her forever. His boys accused him of being soft because they'd never seen him fall that hard for any woman.

The blow of the pregnancy was an extremely hard one because he remembered the many conversations he and Tameka had about starting a family. Two years prior, they were actually going to start one. They were at the peak of their relationship, and TJ was on the verge of proposing. Tameka had stopped taking the pill, and they were actively trying to have a baby. They stopped when she found out he killed someone after a deal went bad. She no longer felt safe around him and didn't want to bring a child into that situation.

Since TJ's lifestyle was turning toward the straight and narrow path, he'd had high hopes of getting back with Tameka and eventually marrying her and having kids. The news of her having HIV posed as an obstacle, but his hopes were crushed when she told him she was pregnant by Craig.

He didn't know how to handle his feelings. He didn't want to abandon her because Craig had already done that, but he also didn't feel like it was his duty to be by her side. So what did he do? He spent all of his time searching for Smoke and the guy who hired him. It kept him busy enough to avoid contact with Tameka. At the same time, though, he was busy working for her cause.

***

The first week in June was very stressful for me. I had meetings with clients every day and sometimes had to meet with two or three clients in one day. That Thursday when I got home, Nicole had baked some chicken and cooked mashed potatoes, corn, and dinner rolls. I trudged through the living room, threw my briefcase on the loveseat, and made my way into the kitchen.

"Damn, girl," Nicole said as she took the rolls out of the oven. "You look like you need a hug, a nap, a long bath, *and* a drink! You alright?"

"I'm so tired," I said. "I think I'm gettin' sick."

"You might be. A few of my coworkers had colds last week."

I sat at the table and laid my head on my folded arms.

"Tielle and Yari called you," Nicole continued. "Tielle said she'll call back later, and Yari said to call her."

"Alright." I still hadn't lifted my head.

"Maybe you need to make a doctor's appointment," she suggested.

"I already have one tomorrow. I have to meet with Dr. Burns so he can see how this medicine is working."

I got up to fix my plate and returned to the table with one chicken wing, maybe five teaspoons of mashed potatoes, a small bowl of corn, and one roll.

"What the hell is that? Are you eatin' for the baby first, then fixin' your plate?" Nicole asked.

"I don't have an appetite," I said after I finished laughing.

"Yeah, something's definitely wrong. Make sure you tell the doctor this stuff. What time is your appointment tomorrow?"

"3:15."

"Oh. You're lucky I have a shoot, 'cause I was gon' be all up in the exam room with you like, 'Yeah, Dr. Burns, you need to fix her little cold or whatever, 'cause she's up in my house wasting food!' You're seven months pregnant, eatin' like you're anorexic."

I ate my tiny portions and called Yari. She was in the middle of telling me about her argument with Dallas when the line beeped.

"Hello?"

175

"What's up, trick?" Tielle responded. I clicked over and told Yari I'd call her back since Tielle was calling long distance. I slouched in Nicole's comfy leather chair as I returned to Tielle.

"So, how you doin'?" she asked.

"I'm livin'," I replied.

"Still haven't heard from TJ?"

"Not recently. The last two-way message I got from him was about a week or so ago, and he was just returnin' my page from a few days before that. It's cool. I mean, it hurts, but I can understand why it's hard for him to swallow."

"Still, though. He don't have to be shady like that."

"It's cool. So what's goin' on with you?" I asked, desperate to change the subject.

"Well, I just got back from Smoothies."

"You and Mr. Romeo went, I'm assuming."

"Yeah, and Craig and Jacqueline," she said cautiously.

It was interesting to know that Craig was dating already, especially after he was supposed to be so concerned about what and how I was doing. I had to admit I was a little jealous.

"Oh?" I tried my best to sound unaffected.

"If you don't wanna hear no more, I won't tell you the rest."

"No, go ahead," I said, anxious to hear how their date went.

"Alright. First off, the broad was way overdressed. She had on a evening gown, fully accessorized with the rhinestone earrings and everything. Can we say, 'This is not the prom'?"

I laughed.

"Then, we went inside and she claimed that she didn't know it was gonna be so informal. And she said it with her nose turned up, so I'm sure 'informal' was a nice version of the word she really wanted to use."

"She's saditty like that?" I asked.

"Yes," Tielle said. "I can't stand her. Anyway, we sat down at one of the tables near the stage, and guess who our waiter was?"

"Isaac?"

"Yep! And he was lookin' so good, girl!"

I thought about Isaac occasionally. I had wanted to call him and apologize for leaving abruptly the last night we saw each other, but when I searched for his number, I quickly remembered I had already thrown it away.

"Did he recognize you?"

"Not at first. He took our orders and when he came back, he asked me if I knew you."

"You better shut up." We'd never had a real conversation, so I couldn't believe he asked about me. "What did you say?"

"Naw, let's talk about Craig's facial expression," Tielle said. "That vein in his forehead popped out so far, you could see the blood pumpin' through it! He was eyeballin' Isaac like you were still his woman."

"He probably thought I was messin' around with him while we were together."

"I don't know, but that shit was funny. Okay, so anyway, he said he hadn't seen you in a while and he was wonderin' where you were."

"Did you tell him I moved?"

"Yeah, and get this...He's movin' out there sometime this month. He said he just got a job out there."

"Okay, that's weird." It sounded like a soap opera plot.

"I know. But it turns out that he's from Columbus, too. He's just here in Texas for grad school or somethin' like that. He asked if you had a man, 'cause he was surprised you never called him."

She told him that I was single, and he asked her for my number. She didn't know if I'd want her to give it to him, so she asked for his instead. "...But he said he was leavin' in a few days and his phone is gettin' cut off tomorrow."

"Shit. Did he say when his last day at Smoothies is?"

"Un unh. Why? You want me to go back?"

"Please," I said in a child-like voice.

"I can run down there after work tomorrow."

"Don't act like you don't wanna do it," I teased.

She told me how Craig grilled her about Isaac and how he got mad when she told him it was none of his business. I guess Jacqueline was irritated by the end of the date because he was more worried about me than he was about her.

The next day, I left work early to go to the doctor. I felt worse than the day before and was running a fever early in the day. When Dr. Burns walked into the examination room, it was obvious that I looked as terrible as I felt. I told him about my body aches, runny nose, sneezing, and shortness of breath. He told me there was a bug going around and gave me a prescription for an herbal drug. The other medicine he had me taking seemed to be working, so he decided to keep me on it until delivery and continue to check the progress.

"We'll monitor your symptoms through the next week to see if this bug will run its course. Like I said, this could just be the virus that's going around, but we also wanna make sure it's not anything related to the HIV," Dr. Burns said.

Before I pulled out of the parking garage, my pager went off. For a brief moment I was excited, thinking it was TJ, but that moment ended when I flipped up the screen and saw a message from Tielle.

It read: *Hey girl. Got bad news. I went to Smoothies, but no Isaac. His last day was yesterday. Hit me back later. –LT*

That wasn't much of a surprise. Whenever something seemed like it could work to my advantage, the Ghost of Tameka's Bad Luck always showed up to remind me that things couldn't go my way.

***

A week after I saw Dr. Burns, my symptoms got worse. I would wake up in the middle of the night drenched in sweat, and even after I changed clothes I'd be drenched again by morning. I ran a fever of at least 101 degrees almost every night, and my sneezing, body aches, and shortness of breath still hadn't gone away.

One night, Yari came over to bring me some chicken noodle soup. Nicole was in Cincinnati on a photo shoot, so I was home alone. I couldn't thank her enough for coming to my rescue because I was absolutely helpless.

"It's cool," she said, touching my forehead. "You don't need to be here by yourself anyway. I'ma pack a bag for you so you can stay with us. Have you taken your temperature lately?"

"Like a hour ago," I said, sipping the broth. I could barely lift the spoon to my mouth because I was so weak. "It was only 99.6."

Yari grabbed the digital thermometer off of the nightstand. "Here. Take it again. You feel hot."

I swallowed the contents in my mouth, and she placed the tip of the thermometer under my tongue. When it beeped, she took it out and looked at the screen.

"What is it now?" I asked, rolling my head to the side. Just being awake was exhausting.

Yari didn't answer. I couldn't see her because I didn't have the strength to lift my head, but I heard her dialing numbers on the telephone. "Yes, my name is Yari Davis, and I need to get in contact with Dr. Burns."

Why is she calling him? I wanted to tell her to hang up the phone, but I felt myself drifting to sleep.

"My cousin is seven months pregnant, she has HIV, she's been sick for over two weeks now, and she has a fever of 103. I need Dr. Burns to meet us at the emergency room, please. We're about to leave the house now, so we'll be there in like ten minutes." She hung up.

"Okay Meka, we gotta get you to the hospital," Yari said as she rummaged through my closet.

I heard everything she was saying but couldn't respond. My eyes wouldn't open, my body wouldn't move, and I was scared to death. All I could think about was my baby. I couldn't let anything happen to him.

Yari found a pair of my sneakers and put them on my feet. "Okay now. You gon' have to work with me," she said as she tried to get me out of the bed. "Just try to walk. I'ma help you."

My body was completely limp, and she realized this once she pulled me to a standing position. "Oh shit!" she said, looking at my face. "She done passed out on me."

She sprinted out of the apartment and banged on the door across the hall. A man who looked to be in his early thirties answered.

"Sir, I really need your help."

"What's wrong?"

"I need to get my cousin out to the car. She's sick, and she just passed out."

The guy ran into his apartment and threw on some shoes. "C'mon," he said as he and Yari entered Nicole's apartment. "Does she have a pulse?" he asked as they lifted me off the bed.

"Yeah. I checked before I came over to your place," she replied.

"She's pregnant, too? Why didn't you call the ambulance?"

They laid me in the back seat of Yari's Maxima. "I don't have time to wait for them to get here." She ran over to the driver's side and thanked the man again. In what seemed to be one motion, she slammed the door, plopped into the leather seat and started the car. Stunned, the neighbor watched as she sped away.

She drove down the highway like she was in the Indy 500. When we arrived at the hospital, she jumped out of the car and ran inside the sliding doors. She told the receptionist what was going on, and within seconds, emergency personnel were rushing to the car with a gurney.

I remember hearing unfamiliar voices surrounding me and being poked with needles. I figured I was in the hospital, but wasn't sure why. The whole incident felt like a dream. When Yari walked into my room, I was awake but still felt like hell. I was relieved to see a familiar face, though, after seeing the blurred faces of doctors and nurses hovering over me.

"You came to," she said with a sigh of relief. "How are you feelin'?"

"Terrible," I whimpered.

"Well, just take it easy. Don't waste your energy talking," she said as she stroked my arm. "You scared me half to death! This is a lot to put on somebody you ain't seen in years. Were you tryin' to test my loyalty?" she joked. "I hope I passed."

I barely cracked a smile, but inside, I was dying of laughter.

"I'm about to go out here and talk to one of these doctors. I have your two-way, so I was just gon' get Alexis' number outta there. Is there anybody else you want me to call?"

"Tielle and Nicole," I said.

***

Alexis was out with friends when she received Yari's call. "Is it the HIV?" she whispered.

"It could be. They're just speculating until the test results come back."

"What about the baby?" she whispered again.

"That's the main reason they're keeping her here. One of the doctors told me that he's gonna check the baby's heart again in a couple hours, and if it sounds the way it did when she first got here, they're gonna have to do an emergency c-section."

"Have you called Tielle?"

"She's next. I just wanted to let you know first."

"I'll call her. Just take care of my sister."

After they hung up, Yari called Nicole. She arranged to leave Cincinnati early the next morning. There was one more call to make before she returned to Tameka's room. She called Dallas to let him know where she was.

"…It's not lookin' good, baby," she told him. "I don't know when I'll be home."

Chapter 20

Tielle immediately started crying when Alexis told her that Tameka was in the hospital. She had a feeling that her condition was a lot more serious than Alexis was making it out to be.

"So when are you leavin'?" she asked Alexis once she calmed down.

"What you mean?"

"When are you goin' to Columbus? Tonight or tomorrow?"

Alexis didn't have any intentions of going to Ohio. She was content with getting phone calls from Yari about her sister's status.

"I was just gonna see what Yari says tomorrow instead of rushin' up there for nothin'. What if she goes home tomorrow?" Alexis said.

"She's not goin' home tomorrow," Tielle replied. "Look. You do whatever you wanna do. Just give me Yari's number, and I'll get all the information I need from her."

"You drivin'?"

"Naw. I was gon' ride with you if you were drivin', but I'll just fly up there."

"I mean, I know I got the money, but…"

"Look, Lexis. I'm about to go," Tielle said, cutting her off. "I'ma call these airlines to see who has the cheapest ticket, and I'll call you back for that number."

"Wait! Don't you get a discount through the radio station?"

"Yeah, why?"

"Get two tickets, and I'll write you a check. Call me back and let me know what time we leave," Alexis said, sighing.

"Don't sound so excited." Tielle hung up.

The next day, Tielle and Alexis flew to Columbus. While they were on the plane, Tielle expressed how guilty she felt for not telling Craig what was going on.

"There ain't nothin' for him to know right now," Alexis said.

"The possibility that his baby is danger ain't nothin'?"

"Nope. The fact that his baby is in danger is somethin'."

181

"You don't realize how serious Tameka's situation is, do you?"

"Yari said the doctors are waitin' for the tests, and when I talked to her earlier this mornin', she said they wouldn't tell her anything yet. If somethin' big was happenin', they woulda said somethin'."

Tielle just rolled her eyes and opted to be quiet before she strangled Alexis in the heat of frustration.

Nicole picked them up from the airport, figuring the three of them could offer each other support in case Tameka had taken a turn for the worse. Meanwhile, Yari and Paradise were already at the hospital. Yari talked with Dr. Burns outside of Tameka's room. "...We ran a lot of blood tests to determine whether Tameka's experiencing symptoms relating to her HIV."

"So what's the verdict?"

"Her counts were lower than we'd like them to be."

"So this is an HIV reaction or somethin'?"

"Yes. It's similar to what we call acute HIV infection, but that normally occurs closer to acquisition. However, everyone is different. She's just now experiencing what many experience within their first month of being diagnosed."

"Has she gotten better or worse since last night?"

"Neither. She's stayed about the same, which is somewhat promising."

"What's the baby's status?"

"It looks like we're gonna have to deliver him this afternoon. Dr. Schultz scheduled her for a cesarean at five o' clock."

"Can he survive?"

Dr. Burns told Yari that the baby had a pretty good chance. He explained that he would be tiny, but would be able to hold his own for the most part. "All of his organs are already developed and everything," he said. "That's about all I can tell you. Dr. Schultz would be able to answer that more in depth."

Their discussion ended when Dr. Burns was paged. While Yari and Paradise headed to the cafeteria, Tameka's pager went off. It startled Yari because she forgot that she had it.

Yari read the message on the screen: *Hit me back. I'm in Chicago visiting my folks. –TJ*

***

Bright rays of sunshine forced their way through the openings of the blinds. That was the closest I was gonna get to a bright moment in my day. Dr. Burns and Dr. Schultz told me my son would be delivered at five, and the anticipation was driving me crazy. I didn't realize I'd grown so attached.

My little boy was gonna be expected to fight for his life from the moment it began. How fair was that? And his daddy couldn't even be around to see him and urge him to keep fighting. Was I to blame for that? Yeah. Did it bother me that I still hadn't told Craig the news? Hell yeah, it did. I wanted to tell him before the delivery, but that was when I thought I had a couple more months.

I stared at the dots on the ceiling, wishing I would wake up at any moment and find that the entire ordeal was a nightmare. There were so many decisions I would've changed; so many things I wouldn't have taken for granted; so much respect I would've given to the importance of timing. I was drifting off to sleep when the nurse came in to recheck my temperature and my blood pressure. My fever was still lingering around 102.

***

Nicole, Alexis, and Tielle talked to Yari in the hallway. She briefed them on the most recent information.

"Have you seen her yet?" Nicole asked.

"No," Yari said. "I don't think I'm ready."

"She has to be trippin'. She hasn't even told Craig about the baby," Alexis said.

"Well there's no gettin' around that now," Nicole said, taking a deep breath. "I can't believe this is happening."

"So they said this ain't no sign of AIDS, right?" Alexis asked, peeking through Tameka's room window.

"They said it's something like an acute HIV infection. I guess this is kinda normal for HIV patients. It's just a case of them gettin' all these crazy symptoms at once. It's a lot worse for Meka because she's pregnant," Yari said as she tied Paradise's shoe.

Alexis turned to Tielle. "You alright?"

"No."

"You thinkin' about Craig?"

"What if his baby dies? Worst case scenario, what if the baby and Tameka die? How do you explain not tellin' somebody important stuff like that?" Tielle said, on the verge of tears.

Yari handed Tameka's pager to Alexis with TJ's message displayed. "Would she want him to know about this?"

183

"He doesn't know?" Alexis asked as she looked through all of the messages in the pager.

"The only people she told me to tell besides you were Tielle and Nicole. I don't even know how to get in touch with your mom and dad."

"She wouldn't have given you Mom's information anyway. I'll call her and Daddy. It's just like Meka to be spiteful from the damn hospital bed," Alexis replied, pulling out her cell phone.

"You gotta go outside to use that," Nicole said.

"I forgot," Alexis said. "I'll be back. Y'all go ahead. This should only take like 15 minutes."

She headed down the hallway toward the elevator while Tielle, Nicole, Yari, and Paradise went in the room.

"She looks bad," Nicole whispered to Tielle, who just nodded in agreement.

"Cousin Meka," Paradise yelled.

"Shh!" Yari said. "She's sleep, baby. Don't yell."

I opened my eyes and looked to my right. I couldn't believe Tielle was there. I figured Yari and Nicole would be around since they lived in town, but Tielle came up from Texas. You never know who your real friends are until you're at your lowest point.

One face I didn't see was Alexis'. That didn't really surprise me, though. I smiled. "Hey, y'all," I whispered.

"She speaks!" Yari exclaimed.

"How you feelin'?" Tielle asked.

"Worse than I look," I said. My words came out hoarse and choppy.

"See? I told you to eat that first day you got sick, but you wouldn't listen. Now look at you," Nicole said. "If you woulda had that extra piece of chicken and a couple more spoonfuls of mashed potatoes, you wouldn't be in here."

I laughed. I was glad that no one came in crying, because that would've brought me down even more. I motioned for them to come closer so I wouldn't have to strain when I talked. "What you doin' here?" I asked Tielle.

"You think I'ma sit at home knowin' you're in the hospital?"

"Did you tell Craig?" I asked.

"I'm gonna tell him, but I wanted to let you know first. I didn't want it to be a surprise when he calls you."

"I don't even care anymore, Tielle. I don't have the strength to argue with you about it, and honestly, I know he needs to know," I said.

"I'll be back," Tielle said.

Once she was outside, she pulled out her cell phone and dialed Craig's number.

"What's up? Where you at?" he asked. "I've been callin' your house all day. I lost your new cell number."

"What did you want?" Tielle asked.

"Jackie's sister gave her four tickets to the Maxwell concert tomorrow, and I was tryin' to see if you and Romeo wanted to go with us."

"I can't. I'm in Columbus."

"You visitin' Meka?"

"Yeah, somethin' like that."

"Why didn't you tell nobody? Your mom doesn't even know where you are."

"This wasn't a planned trip." She sighed. "Craig, Meka's in the hospital. Her cousin called Lexis last night and told her. We flew out here this mornin'."

"So what's wrong?"

"She's havin' complications from the HIV, and on top of that..." She stalled. "Are you sittin' down?"

"Yeah, why? They think she's gon' die?" His voice rose an octave.

"No, but she's pregnant, and they're delivering the baby tonight in order to save him."

Craig was quiet. Finally, he said, "How far along is she?"

"Seven months."

"I fuckin' knew it!" he yelled. "I asked you over and over if she was gainin' weight, and you kept playin' me off. You knew the whole time, didn't you? You didn't think I deserved to know?"

"Take it down a couple notches, Craig," Tielle said. "I thought you deserved to know ever since she told me, but I promised I wouldn't say anything. I was in a messed up position, okay? I don't feel good about this. I've wanted to tell you for the longest. It wasn't my place, though."

"So now it is?" Craig was beside himself. "I'll finish talkin' to you when I get there. What hospital is it?"

***

185

Portia A. Cosby

Alexis and Tielle entered the room around 1:30 when I was watching reruns of *Family Matters* and sucking on ice chips. I almost choked when I spotted Lexis because I thought she was still in Texas.

She told me she sent TJ a message but was still waiting for his reply. She also contacted our mother, who said she'd come to Ohio the next week, after her conferences were over. Once again, business came before her own family. Dad told Lexis to call him as soon as the baby was delivered, but I knew he was on his way. He had a nagging habit of wanting to be in charge when things weren't going right, so he was sure to be on the first thing smoking.

I noticed Tielle was very quiet. She stood at the window with her hands in her pockets, staring into the distance.

"Did you talk to Craig?" I asked.

"Yep. He knows everything."

"And?"

"He's comin'," she said.

Almost immediately, a sharp pain shot through my stomach. It was so intense that my whole lower body rose up off the hospital bed. My mouth opened and I felt like screaming, but nothing came out. Hot tears streamed down my face as I prayed for relief.

Tielle called my name and begged for a response, but all I could do was look at her with fear in my eyes. Nicole woke up in the midst of the commotion, instantly in panic mode. She ran into the hallway to find a nurse or doctor.

"What's takin' them so fuckin' long?" Alexis yelled as she stroked my forehead.

"I don't know," Tielle answered, trying to ignore the pain from my nails digging into her hand.

About ten seconds later, a group of doctors, nurses, and technicians ran into my room. They moved Alexis and Tielle out of the way and started shooting me up with all kinds of drugs. One person threw an oxygen mask on me while another squirted cold gel on my stomach to do a quick ultrasound. I closed my eyes and silently prayed:

Lord, I know I haven't been living the way you would have me to, but I'm asking for your help 'cause you're always there for me when I need you. I'm not even praying for me. I'm praying for my little boy. Lord, please don't take my baby's life. He hasn't had a

186

chance to live yet. He shouldn't suffer because of everything that's going on with me. If somebody has to go, please let it be me. Please.

I don't remember anything that happened after that. All I know is that I woke up in a different room. I was groggy as hell, and it took me a while to wake up completely. The first person I saw was a skinny white nurse in turquoise scrubs.

"Somebody's waking up. Can you tell me your name?" she asked.

I managed to answer her, but my voice was hoarse and my throat was sore.

"Good," the nurse replied. "How ya feelin'?"

"What's goin' on?" I asked, turning my head to look around. I saw a few other people in beds on each side of me.

"You're in the recovery room, dear," she replied as she took my pulse.

I lifted my other hand and put it on my stomach. It was sore, and it wasn't as big as it was before I passed out. I lifted my head and strained to see it.

"What happened?" I asked.

"Dr. Schultz had to do an emergency c-section."

I shook all over. Anxiety and fear were getting the best of me. "Where's my baby?" I asked.

"Calm down, honey. We'll tell you all about the baby in a little bit."

"I wanna see my baby!" I tried to sit up, but I was dizzy.

My heart rate shot up, and I started hyperventilating. The nurse called someone else over to give me a sedative. I was put to sleep with the thought of my son not surviving the surgery.

Chapter 21

Craig stepped off the elevator and rushed to the receptionist's desk, but no one was there. Impatient and frustrated, he slammed his hand onto the bell. Nicole was sitting in a chair nearby and heard the loud, but short ding. Instinctively, she turned her head and looked in Craig's direction.

"Excuse me," he said. "Do you know where the receptionist is?"

"I'm not sure," Nicole replied. "She just got up a few minutes ago." She looked more closely at Craig. "Who are you lookin' for?" she asked.

"My ex-girlfriend. I might have the wrong floor, though, 'cause I think she's havin' surgery right now." He started walking off. "Thanks."

"Are you Craig?"

He stopped and turned back around. "Yeah. How do you—?"

"I'm Nicole." She extended her hand to him and stood up. "You look a little different from the pictures I've seen."

Craig took his hand out of his pocket and shook hers. "I thought you looked familiar. I've seen you in Meka's photo album, too. Nice to meet you."

Nicole tried her best to hold her tongue. She wanted to speak for Tameka and cuss him out for the comments he made about the baby, but she knew that would only aggravate the already tense situation. Still, she had to say something.

"So what brings you here now?" she asked in a phony, inquisitive tone.

"I just found out that I'm about to be a dad, but I'm sure you already know that."

"What I know isn't important."

The tension in the air was growing, so Nicole tried to move on. "Well, they had to do an emergency c-section. We're waitin' for them to bring her back to her room."

"So how's the baby?" Craig asked.

"There's no word yet. I'm sure they'll tell us when they bring her back. All I know is that she's in recovery, doin' fine." She corrected herself. "Well, she's still experiencing a few symptoms, but they should be able to get those under control now that they don't have to worry about the medicine affecting the baby."

"Where's everybody else?"

"Tielle and Lexis are downstairs in the cafeteria."

They talked a little more as they waited for an update. Ten minutes later, Dr. Schultz entered the waiting area.

"How did it go?" Nicole asked.

Craig stood up. "Yeah. How's my baby?"

Dr. Schultz told them that Tameka's condition was more stable and the nurses would be bringing her up in about five minutes.

"How much longer does she have to stay here?" Nicole asked.

"Well, she's definitely not going home for three days, maybe more. Her body has suffered a great deal of trauma from both the baby and the infection. We're gonna have to take it one day at a time," the doctor answered. "The baby will have to stay for at least four weeks. That young man has been through a lot."

Craig's eyes widened. "It's a boy? I've got a son?" he asked.

"He's three and a half pounds and 15 inches long. I wish I could say that he's completely healthy, but since he was born premature, we need to keep an eye on him."

"Can he survive? Three pounds is tiny," Craig asked.

"Yes, he can. I'm not saying it will be easy, though. He was living in an extremely hot environment, you know? Tameka's body temperature really did a number on him."

"What about the HIV? Does the baby have it?"

Dr. Schultz explained the specifics of when the baby could be diagnosed and answered the rest of Nicole and Craig's questions. Nicole almost couldn't take it. Craig's concern for his son's health didn't seem genuine. In her eyes, Craig was hoping his son didn't have the virus for selfish reasons. He wanted bragging rights but couldn't see himself bragging about an infected child.

***

When I woke up again, I was in my original hospital room. The first person I saw was Nicole. She was sitting in the chair directly in front of my bed. I cut my eyes to the left and saw Tielle and Yari talking by the window.

Before I could look to my right, I heard, "It looks like somebody's wakin' up." I turned my head slowly and saw Craig's face. I gave him a short, blank stare. Alexis walked over and held my hand.

"How you feelin'?" she asked.

"Like shit," I answered as my stomach cramped.

Everyone else gathered around the bed. They were quiet for the most part, and whenever they did talk, they were very reserved and guarded, not wanting to slip up and say the wrong thing. I figured they didn't know if I knew what was going on with my son, so they didn't want to bring him up.

Eventually, I grew tired of the awkward silence. "Did you go see the baby yet?" I asked everyone.

"We have to wait until the nurse comes back and tells us we can," Alexis replied. "I guess they still workin' with him."

"They say he has a good chance of makin' it, though," Nicole added.

"Did you name him yet?" Yari asked.

"Not officially, but I wanna name him Darius Michael," I said.

"Darius Michael Thomas," Craig rehearsed.

"Darius Michael *James*," I corrected.

He let out an angry chuckle, rubbed on his goatee, and looked away. Everyone else looked at me, shocked. Alexis turned to Craig. "Craig Thomas, can you please come to the lost and found to retrieve your pride?"

"You know what, Alexis? You ain't got shit to do with this."

"Whatever," she said, waving him off. "Seems like you ain't had shit to do with this either, huh?"

"Everybody calm down," Nicole said.

Craig stormed out of the room. Tielle said her goodbyes for the evening; she and Craig were gonna get a hotel room. One person was allowed to be in the room with me, so Alexis stayed. She decided to run to the cafeteria first and get a snack before it closed, though.

***

On their way out, Tielle, Yari, and Nicole ran into a nurse.

"Ooh, I'm sorry," Tielle said, grabbing his arm to maintain her balance. She looked up and noticed a familiar face. "Isaac?"

Isaac squinted. "Wait a minute. I'm tryin' to remember where I know you from."

"Smoothies in Texas," Tielle replied. "I'm Tameka's friend."

"Oh yeah!"

"We'll wait downstairs while y'all have this reunion," Nicole joked as she and Yari walked toward the elevator.

"So what are you doin' here?" Isaac asked.

Tielle searched for an easy explanation.

"Wait," Isaac continued. He looked at the chart in his hand. "This is the Tameka I met at Smoothies?"

"Yep," Tielle replied.

He peeked through the room window. "How weird is this?"

***

When Isaac walked in my room, I wasn't paying attention. My head was very comfortable hanging to the left, and I didn't plan on moving it. I was tired of being disturbed by nurses wanting to make small talk, so I figured I'd make myself as unapproachable as possible.

"Hello, Tameka," he said as he approached my bed. I didn't reply. "Either somebody's feelin' groggy, or she just doesn't wanna talk to me." He put the blood pressure cuff on my right arm.

Bingo! I thought.

He recorded the blood pressure reading on my chart. "Well just so you know, I'm Nurse Gray. I'm yours for the night, so if you need anything, just push the button."

I could tell he was very uncomfortable with the silence in the room, so he decided to speed up his vitals check.

"Now are you gonna turn your head this way so I can take your temperature, or are you gonna make me walk around to the other side of your bed?"

I slowly lifted my head, disgusted because he was trying too hard to be cool with me. "Look Nurse Gray. It's been a long day. The last thing I wanna do is lay here, wastin' my breath, shootin' the breeze. Forgive me if I'd rather hear how my little boy is doin', which no one has bothered to tell me yet." By that time, my eyes were open, and I cut them in his direction.

Oh my Lord, it was Isaac. Or was it? "I need some medicine," I said, staring at him.

"Why?"

"I'm hallucinating. I thought you were a guy I know from home."

Isaac smiled, and I knew for sure it was him. His nametag was further confirmation. He saw the questioning look on my face and

191

started explaining. He said he was in Texas for nursing school, and he'd had the job lined up at the hospital months before he graduated.

I wasn't sure why Isaac and I kept running into each other, but for some reason, he was around during some of my most significant struggles—I met him after I was raped, saw him the night I listened in on Craig and Tielle's conversation, and he ended up being my nurse in a different state. Either he was destined to be my man, or he was a spy for Smoke. I shivered at the thought of the latter.

"So have you heard anything about my baby?" I asked.

"Yeah," he said. "He's still in the NICU, but he's stable. Your little man is a fighter."

"When can I see him?"

"If you're up to it, you can go in the morning."

Alexis returned to the room with an armful of snacks and a mouthful of chips.

"Hey," she said to Isaac as she walked over and sat in the recliner.

"How you doin'?" Isaac said.

"That's my sister, Alexis," I said.

"I'm Isaac. Nice to meet you."

"You too," Alexis said, checking him out and taking a bite of another chip. "So you're the nurse?"

"Yep. I'll be in and outta here checkin' on Tameka all night, so I apologize in advance."

"Well if she's sleep and you don't wanna bother her, feel free to check up on me."

The next morning, Isaac came in a few minutes after I woke up. He refilled my water pitcher and took my breakfast order. I was so glad they were letting me eat regular stuff because that green Jell-O wasn't cutting it.

Dr. Schultz came to check on me after Isaac left. I told him I was feeling a little better.

"Great! That's what I like to hear." He walked closer to my bed. "I just wanna take a quick look at your belly to see how you're healing." He lifted the covers. "So far, so good," he said, returning my gown to its original position. "No signs of infection. Well I'm pretty sure you want to know about that baby boy of yours."

I nodded.

"He's still stable—"

"But is he still critical?"

"Yes. We believe he acquired an infection while he was still in the womb, so we're watching him carefully. We have him on antibiotics right now and he'll stay on those four to five days."

"Can I go see him?"

"It's up to you. If you have the energy to sit up in a wheelchair, you are definitely welcomed to go see your son. Have you decided on a name?"

"Darius Michael James," I said.

He recorded it on my chart and left the room. Alexis woke up and I told her I would be able to see the baby soon.

"For real?" She stood up and stretched. "I wanna go. Will they let me?"

"Probably."

"What time is it?" She grabbed my pager and flipped up the screen. "One missed message?" she said.

"From who?"

Alexis read the message aloud. "I'll be there by tomorrow. Let me know if things get worse before I get there...TJ."

Isaac walked in with a vacant wheelchair and told me that it was time to go see my son. When he wheeled me into the room, the sounds of beeping heart monitors, singing mothers, and crying babies created an unfamiliar ambience. I washed my hands with the green antibacterial soap, and a nurse wheeled him around the corner in an incubator.

"I think you might be looking for this little guy," she said with a big smile.

I almost broke my neck trying to get a look at him as the nurse parked the incubator next to my wheelchair.

"Look at my little nephew!" Alexis said with excitement. "He's so tiny."

I got a closer look. He was absolutely beautiful. His little toes were curled up and so were his fingers. He had a head full of jet black, wavy hair, and his skin was the color of hot chocolate. It was hard to tell who he looked like with all the tubes in his nose and mouth.

"Hey, little man," I said, sticking my hands through the holes and touching his little hand. Chills ran through my body and goosebumps lined my arms. When he wrapped his fingers around my pinky, everything negative in my life became irrelevant. The joy I felt was indescribable. I knew that Darius would be the best thing in

193

my life, and he would be the only thing that mattered to me from that point on.

Chapter 22

My door opened at 11:15. Alexis sucked her teeth as Craig walked in.

"Where's Tielle?" I asked.

"At the hotel. I came alone so we can talk...*alone*," he stressed, looking at Lexis.

"Nigga, whatever. I ain't goin' nowhere, so you can—"

I gave her the okay to go and assured her that I would be fine.

She got up from the chair and stared Craig down as she walked past him. "I'll be right outside."

I raised the head of my bed to a slightly upright position, and Craig pulled a chair over. "I'ma try to be as calm as possible so we can talk rationally," he started.

I'm not. I have shit built up from before Christmas, so you gon' feel me today, I thought.

"Can you do the same?" he asked. "I heard you were feeling better , so you might have the energy to yell now." His attempt to ease the tension with humor had failed. "I just came from seein' the baby. He has your eyes. I think he's gonna have my complexion, though."

"Umm hmm."

"Okay, I see you have a attitude with me, and Tielle told me why last night. You heard our conversation when I said...Well, you know what I said."

"Refresh my memory."

Beads of sweat appeared on his forehead and his heartbeat was so strong, I swear I heard it. He wouldn't repeat his words, but he admitted he was wrong and claimed he didn't mean it.

"Then why did you say it?"

"I was mad!"

195

"You were ignorant! So the next time you get mad like that, you gon' tell Darius you really don't want him 'cause he might have a disease?"

"Now you're bein' ridiculous."

"How is that?"

"There's no way I could feel like that about my son."

"Now," I emphasized, finishing his sentence.

"He wasn't a reality then, Meka. I didn't even know you were pregnant. What do you want me to do? Apologize? If I do, you ain't gon' accept it, so why bother?"

"If you didn't come to apologize, why are you here?"

"Because we need to figure out some arrangements for our son."

"The arrangement is that he's stayin' with me," I said.

"Here in Columbus?"

"Until I decide to go back to Texas."

"So how am I supposed to see him?"

"Once you get back home to Jacqueline, you won't be worried about that. I'm sure she'll keep you company until we move back."

"So that's what this attitude's about. You're jealous because I've moved on."

"Trust me. I'm not jealous. You can keep on movin' for all I care. All I'm sayin' is, you were just beggin' everybody for my number 'cause you were supposedly so concerned, but next thing I heard, you were awfully cozy with her. Jealous? No. But evidently she did somethin' to hold your attention, 'cause your concerned ass never called."

"I didn't know how to find you!" Craig yelled.

"Bullshit. You knew Nicole's full name and she's listed in the phone book. Directory assistance would've been glad to help you," I said.

"Man, whatever. I'm not gonna let you turn this around on me." He stood up and rested his hands on the side rails of my bed. "Regardless of what happened between us, you should've told me that I was gonna be a daddy. If you were so mad about what I said, you should've called and said somethin'."

"I wasn't mad. Do you know how much that hurt me? Yeah, I could've called you, but I didn't want anything to do with you, so I cut you out of my life," I replied.

"If you're not mad, why don't you wanna give him my last name? And better yet, why ain't he named after me?"

196

I leaned forward. "I don't want him to be named after no punk. If that's the case, I could've named him Punk Pussy Thomas. Then his nickname could've been Craig. It's all the same."

I could tell by the look on his face that he either wanted to punch me in the mouth or strangle me. I had crossed the line. I'd done what almost every black woman has done at least once in her life. I challenged his manhood right before his eyes. I did more than call him a bitch. I called him a pussy. But you know what? I meant it.

I wanted him to feel disrespected like I did. I wanted him to feel lower than low and feel helpless 'cause he couldn't do anything to change my feelings. My mission was accomplished, and I watched him intently, silently daring him to even think of raising his hand to me.

Craig stepped away from the bed. "I'll be damned," he said in disbelief and shoved his hands in his pockets. He looked up at the ceiling and breathed loudly through his nose. After about ten seconds, he cut his eyes at me. "I promised Tielle I wasn't gon' come in here, trippin', but fuck that. I knew you was gon' take me there 'cause you don't know when to grow up! We have a baby now, and you wanna harp on the past."

"I have a baby now," I said. "You don't want this kind of baby, remember? He may not have HIV now, but it's possible that it could show up later," I yelled back.

"Grow up, Meka. Damn!" He pushed my tray stand across the floor and into the wall.

"Kiss my ass!" I said calmly, readjusting my covers and returning to my reclined position.

Before he could respond, Alexis and Isaac busted in the room. Isaac had on street clothes, so I figured he was outside in the hallway, waiting to visit me. He said he'd come see me after he got off of work, but I didn't expect to see him that soon.

"What's goin' on in here," Isaac asked, pushing the tray stand back where it belonged.

"Nothin' man," Craig said, walking over to the window. He hadn't looked at Isaac yet.

"What happened, Meka? I know this nigga ain't in here, trippin'." She went to open her purse.

"Man, shut up, Alexis," Craig said, turning around.

As she cussed him out, Craig recognized Isaac. "Hold up," he said.

Alexis stopped in the middle of her sentence, and I smiled to myself.

"You from Texas?" Craig asked.

"If you're tryin' to figure out whether you know me, yeah, you do," Isaac said.

"So y'all got somethin' goin' on ?" Craig asked me.

"Does it matter?" I asked. "Is that any of your business?"

"Hell yeah, it's my business. I wanna know who my son is gon' be around."

"He's gon' be around a nurse," I said.

Craig looked confused.

"I'm her nurse. I came to check on her 'cause her spirits weren't too high earlier." He looked at me.

"I'm feelin' a little better now. Thanks for stopping by," I replied.

"What type of shit is this?" Craig asked. "I ain't never heard of no nurse comin' back to check on their patients when they're off-duty. Somethin's up."

"It's called caring. People take extra steps when they care," I said.

The argument continued for what seemed like forever. The only reason the commotion stopped was because my dad walked in the room. "What's going on in here?" All of our heads turned and faced him as he took four long strides to the middle of the room. "I heard you all clear down the hallway."

"Hey, Daddy," Alexis said. "We were just clearin' up a little misunderstandin'." She gave him a big hug. Dad glared at Craig and Isaac, still waiting for an explanation.

"How you doin', sir?" Isaac said, approaching him with his hand extended. He introduced himself and they shook hands.

Daddy and Craig spoke, and Craig made a quick exit into the hallway. He claimed he had to make a phone call. Isaac left a few minutes later and said he'd call to check on me that evening.

Me, Daddy, and Lexis talked business after saying brief hellos.

"When will Darius be able to go home?" Alexis asked.

"Probably not for another month at least," I replied. "The doctors want him to develop some more."

"So you'll stay here in the meantime," Dad asked, phrasing it more as a statement instead of a question.

"Yeah! I'm not gon' leave my baby and go to another state."

198

"I don't agree with you moving back at all. That son of a bitch is still running free," he said.

"So? He may run free for the rest of his life. The police haven't caught him yet, so who's to say they'll ever catch him?" I asked. "I can't live my life for him. There's only two men runnin' my life now-a-days…God and my son."

"But are you putting my grandson first by moving back to an area you know is unsafe?"

I took a deep breath and let it out slowly. "Look, Daddy. I'm movin' back to Texas. If Smoke wants to find me, he'll find me— even if I do stay here. And the last thing I need is you tellin' me that I won't be safe and that I'm makin' a bad decision."

"I'll be there, too, Daddy," Alexis interrupted. "It's not like she'll be alone."

"Yeah, but were you able to stop him from raping her? Did you stop his phone calls?" he asked.

We all sat in silence for a few seconds. "You do what you wanna do," he blurted. "I know you will anyway. Just remember what I said." He stood up and kissed me on the forehead, then kissed Lexis on her cheek. "I'll be back. I'm gonna find your doctors and hear what they have to say about when the two of you can leave." He walked out.

Lexis and I were watching our CBS soaps when door opened. A delivery man stood in the doorway holding a huge, brown teddy bear and some balloons. There were so many balloons, we couldn't see his face.

"You can come in," Alexis said. "Just sit everything over here on the window sill."

"No you don't. I wanna see who got me a teddy bear. You can bring that right over here, sir."

He approached the bed and stretched his arms out to hand me the gifts. Alexis' face lit up as his face was unveiled. I still couldn't see what he looked like. I just knew that he had to look good because Lexis' jaw was on the floor. Once he lowered the bear a little more, I saw it was TJ. My mouth stretched open to form the biggest smile ever.

"What's up, baby," he said, then kissed me on the cheek. "How you feelin'?"

"A lot better now. A couple days ago was a different story, though." I stroked the big, brown teddy bear.

"Hey, TJ," Lexis said, grinning.

"What's up?" he said half-heartedly, waiting to hear more about my condition. He turned to me. "So are you gonna be alright? What happened?"

I ran down everything from the high fever to the emergency c-section. The concern in his face was almost tear-jerking. When I finished telling him about my first time visiting Darius, he dropped his head. "I'm sorry."

I looked over at Alexis and nodded my head toward the door. I wanted some privacy with TJ so I could hear what he really had to say and how he really felt.

"I'll be back," she said, walking to the door. "You know it's about that time for me to hit up the cafeteria again."

When the door closed behind her, I asked TJ why he was sorry. He apologized for being so distant and admitted he was hurt after I told him I was pregnant.

"I didn't know how to handle it, so I decided not to really deal with you at all. Now I'm feelin' bad and shit 'cause I shoulda been here for you."

For some reason, my heart softened way too quickly when TJ was involved. I could hold my ground with anybody else and play the tough girl role, but whenever TJ cracked that smile of his, every muscle in my body went limp. Needless to say, I forgave him almost effortlessly. I was just happy to see him. I thanked him for the balloons and the bear, and he told me that as soon as Darius could understand, the bear was his.

"That means you'll have to get me one of my own then."

"It depends on how you act," he replied.

We both laughed, then he changed the subject, asking if I would ever go back to Texas. He was pleased to hear that I had every intention on regaining as much of my old life as possible, which included returning to my house, my friends, and a sister that I'd become much closer to.

"I should be back down there by the time you get there," he said.

"Where you gon' be in the meantime?" I asked.

"New York."

"For what?"

"You don't wanna know that."

"Oh Lord," I said, shaking my head. Whatever TJ was up to wasn't good, and he was right. It was best if I didn't know.

Later that evening, Tielle, Dallas, Yari, Paradise, and Nicole came to visit. Everyone else was still around, too. Craig spent most of his time in the NICU watching Darius and asking the nurses every question under the sun. Nicole told me he and TJ almost got into it when TJ went to see the baby, but my dad intervened and stopped the argument. Surprisingly, she said that TJ was behaving himself and Craig was the one with an attitude because he didn't want "that nigga" around his son.

I really didn't mind all the drama that was taking place. I was just happy that so many people truly cared about me and my son. Everybody had taken time out of their work schedules, and some even bought plane tickets to come see me. That was deep to me, and I thanked all of them repeatedly for being around.

My dad stayed the night in the room with me, so Alexis slept at Yari's place. Craig and Tielle left the hospital way before visiting hours were over because they had to get up early the next morning to catch their flight. Craig didn't say goodbye, but I was okay with that. There was no need for us to pretend like we were cordial just because we had an audience.

After everyone was gone, I reflected on the day's events and actually felt good. An enormous weight had been lifted off of me because I told Craig exactly how I felt, and he was able to see and feel the emotions I'd held inside for so long. I also felt a tremendous amount of love from my circle of friends and family. Everyone I held dear showed up at my bedside, and I knew who my true support system was.

Chapter 23

Craig and Tielle surprised me at 4:30 the next morning. They were on their way to the airport, but Tielle had made arrangements with Isaac to come see me before they left. She was her usual inspirational self, encouraging me to keep praying and promising she'd see me soon.

Craig kept it simple, but his words were subtly sweet. "I know you didn't expect me to say anything, but I can't leave without sayin' goodbye. A lot of things were said yesterday, and now is not the time to discuss them. We'll talk when you get back to Texas. In the meantime, take care of yourself. Darius needs you to be strong. I'll be in touch to find out how he's doin', and you got my number if you need anything."

When he touched my hand, we both felt an uncomfortable vibe. It was like two enemies reaching out to hug each other, then suddenly remembering they don't like each other. I felt the same tingles I used to get during our first months together and so did he. I saw it in his eyes. Our awkward moment was cut short when Isaac cracked my door open and told them they needed to get going before someone saw them.

***

My release day was spent talking to the doctors about activity and dietary precautions. I was also given three more prescriptions to control the HIV. I could visit my son every day as long as it was during the specified hours, and the doctors told me they would do whatever they could to speed up his release date, provided Darius kept fighting as hard as he had been.

They instructed me to rest for at least two weeks while I was home, but my first few days were total chaos. I had to make arrangements with my job to move up the date for my maternity leave. I agreed to have phone conferences from home with four of our top clients. I really didn't want to do that, but I needed to have some money rolling in to buy some of the odds and ends that I didn't have for Darius.

Alexis was a big help. She made some kind of deal with her boss that allowed her to stay at Nicole's with me for a week and a half. She kept busy, calling my creditors and other bill collectors, explaining my situation, and making payment arrangements. I loved her for that because those thirty-dollar late charges were no joke.

The next few weeks went smoothly. Lexis and I remained argument-free, Nicole helped me plan my move back to Texas, and Yari and I spent many long days running around town, buying clothes and other things for Darius. The girls at my job threw me a baby shower the day before I picked him up from the hospital, so I racked up on diapers, bottles, rattles, bibs, and all sorts of little things for him. They also gave *me* a few gifts as going-away presents.

By the time July 26th rolled around, I had everything I needed to care for my son. The doctor called at ten o'clock and said Darius was ready for his mommy to come get him. I think I was more nervous than excited because he was gonna be solely under my care, and I felt like he would need extra special attention that I didn't know how to give.

I hung up the phone and told Yari we could go pick him up. I had been staying with her so she could give me a few firsthand tips on motherhood. Plus, she said she would ride to Texas with me so she could help with the baby during the long trip. We had become so close during my stay in Columbus, and I was glad we would be able to continue our time together for at least a couple more days. All I'd ever had was Alexis, so it was nice to have another female relative to talk to.

She was overly excited. She had already installed the car seat, and her video camera hung on her shoulder, ready for action. "Let's go, girl!" she said as I checked my lipstick in the hallway mirror. "You excited?"

"Nervous," I replied. "I've only held him a few times. They take care of him day and night."

"You'll be alright," Yari said with confidence. "I'm tellin' you...You two are gonna have an instant bond. He's gonna make you feel comfortable, and you're gonna make him feel just as comfortable. Being nervous is one thing, but being worried is another. You over here checkin' your makeup like Darius is gon' say you got on too much eye shadow." I laughed. "Now calm down and get out the mirror so we can go get your little boy." She pulled my arm, and we headed to the hospital.

We walked down the hallway of the maternity wing and entered the nursery. Nurse Reynolds stood at Darius' crib, preparing to feed him. "Uh oh," she said. "Look who's here, Darius. It's Mommy!"

I smiled and walked over to them. "Hey, sweetie," I said as I gently rubbed his head.

"He's lookin' better and better every day," Yari said. "It looks like he's gained a little more weight."

"He's about five and a half pounds now," Nurse Reynolds said. "We've been trying our best to bulk him up for ya! He's doing great."

I smiled proudly. "That's my little angel."

"I was just about to feed him, but I think he might like it if you do the honors," the nurse said.

"Okay," I said, hesitantly.

I lifted Darius from the crib and sat in the rocking chair. Yari was right. I felt an immediate connection with him. He rested his head in the fold of my arm, and his warm body sank into my lap. As he opened his bright eyes and looked into mine, I almost lost it. I became overwhelmed with happiness, relief, love, and acceptance. Loving him was automatic, but it was a special kind of love—a protective love. I knew just by holding his helpless little body that I couldn't and wouldn't let any harm come his way. And to feel him snuggle up to me and clench the bottom of my shirt let me know he accepted me with all my flaws, and I gave him a gentle squeeze in return to thank him.

Two days later, we hit the road. After alternating drivers and stopping at a few rest areas, we made it to Texas by six o'clock Thursday morning. We tip-toed into my apartment, trying our best not to disturb Alexis and Robert. Everything was cool until Darius screamed at the top of his tiny lungs to inform me he had a surprise in his diaper. I picked him up and tried my best to quiet him down, but he wasn't having it. Even when Yari put the pacifier in his mouth, he spit it out.

"This boy ain't playin'," she said, digging in his diaper bag.

"I know," I replied, grabbing a towel and laying Darius on the couch.

Yari handed me all the materials, and I changed his diaper. I was securing the left side of it when Lexis walked downstairs.

"You lucky it's time for me to get up," she said, rubbing her eyes and walking over to the couch. "Y'all wanna come in makin' all this damn noise."

"Shut up," I said.

"Especially you," she said to Darius as she rubbed his stomach. "Look at how big you got boy!" She picked him up and kept him occupied while Yari and I finished unloading the car. By the time we were done, Robert had come downstairs and was holding the baby.

"He's a cute little guy, Meka," he said, handing him to me.

"Did you expect any less?" I asked.

He laughed. I introduced him to Yari, and they made small talk for a while. Darius had fallen back asleep, so I figured that was my cue to take a nap as well. I went upstairs, put Darius in his bassinet, and laid across my bed. I woke up at about noon, wondering why my sleep went uninterrupted. I knew that newborns typically didn't sleep that long, so instantly, I panicked. I jumped up from my bed and looked into the bassinet. He wasn't there.

I ran out of my room and headed downstairs. *Maybe Yari has him,* I thought. But to my dismay as I reached the second-to-last step, I saw Yari sleeping on the sofa bed with no baby in sight.

I knew Lexis and Robert were at work, so there was no one else who could've had my son. Just as I was about to go back upstairs to recheck the bassinet, I heard a noise in the kitchen. I picked up one of the iron tools near the fireplace and slowly walked through the living room toward the kitchen. Once I got to where I could see in the room, I saw TJ leaning against the counter, feeding Darius a bottle. A smile of relief came over my face, and I stood near the doorway, watching how natural he looked.

TJ looked up and caught me staring. "I came up there to talk to you, but you was sleep. Then lil' man started cryin', so I brought him down here so you could get your rest. I know you was tired as hell after that long ass trip."

"Thanks," I said. I walked over to the counter. "How's he been treatin' you?"

"Aw, we cool. He knows I'm cool people."

"How long you been here?"

"About a hour."

"Oh, so you came to put some of his stuff together?"

I had a lot of baby furniture that needed to be assembled, and I was hoping to recruit either Robert or Romeo to do the job. I figured since TJ was around, he'd be perfect.

"I like how you slipped that in." He laughed.

"I don't know what you talkin' 'bout," I replied, trying my best not to laugh. "I thought you came over to help out."

"Yeah, whatever," he said. "How much stuff you got?"

"The crib, the stroller, and the changing station."

"Changing station? Man, you better change his ass on the couch."

"My baby's gonna have the best of everything."

I convinced him to put the crib together. He said he didn't have time to put everything else together right then, but he had plenty of time to lure me to the bedroom while Yari watched Darius downstairs. We hadn't dealt like that in a year, so it was definitely a big event, and I was still surprised that he wasn't afraid of getting HIV. Condoms aren't a hundred percent.

During our after-sex talk, he finally admitted that he'd taken care of the dude who pistol-whipped him. That piece of news messed up the semi-romantic mood we had going. I was hoping we'd talk about us or at least how good the sex was. Death was the furthest subject from my mind. I think his whole reasoning for telling me was to let me know he hadn't forgotten about what happened the previous year. He was still determined to protect me by any means necessary, and for some deranged reason, I was still determined to keep his thug-ass around.

Chapter 24

The next day, I was exhausted. I used all my energy romping around the bed with TJ then entertained Tielle into the wee hours of the morning. My plan for the day was to sleep as much as possible.

Yari came up to my room to watch Darius while I took my shower. When I got out, I talked to her for a while, then went back to sleep. I was awakened three hours later by a knock on my bedroom door, which in turn woke Darius up (for the fifth time in an hour).

"Who is it?" I yelled with an attitude. I lifted my baby out of his crib and patted him on the back to calm him down.

"Craig."

I walked over to the door and opened it. Darius was still crying.

"My fault," Craig said. "I didn't mean to wake him up."

"You woke both of us up." I walked to the dresser and grabbed Darius' pacifier. "Why ain't you at work anyway?"

"I'm off today." He came closer and leaned toward Darius' face. "What's up, man? It's Daddy. You remember me?"

I could've thrown up right then, but instead, I looked into my angel's eyes and smiled.

"Can I hold him?" Craig asked.

I reluctantly handed Darius to him. "Watch his head," I said as he adjusted his arms to do so. I made my bed and straightened the clutter on my dresser.

"Did you bring that money?" I asked. We had discussed his lack of contribution to his son's well-being the night before, and I told him he needed to come up with some money.

"Yeah, I got it," he said. I froze in place and waited. "What? You want it now? I can't get it out my pocket while I'm holdin' him!"

I didn't respond. I just went back to what I was doing.

"Come get it out my pocket, Tameka," he said. "Since you seem to want it right now, come get it."

Without hesitation, I walked over to him. "Which one?" I asked, patting his pockets.

"The right one."

"You can have a attitude if you want," I said as I stuck my hand in his right pocket. "I just want my money. I need to put this shit in the bank to make up for all the hundreds I spent."

I snatched my hand out and looked at the wad of money. "How much am I supposed to take?" I asked.

"All of it," Craig replied.

I flipped through the bills and counted five hundred dollars. His new job at the scouting agency had to be paying a pretty penny because I had never known Craig to drop money like that. "You sure?" I asked.

"Yeah!" Craig said, raising his voice. "I told you yesterday I was gonna give you some money."

"I was just askin' 'cause…You know what? Never mind. Thank you," I said as I placed the money in my purse. "I'll just leave it at that. Don't nobody wanna sit up and listen to your smart-ass."

"Ain't nobody bein' smart."

"Whatever. Look, I'm about to go downstairs and eat. Since you're holdin' him, change his diaper."

I went to the kitchen and fixed me and Yari some ham sandwiches, and we sat at the table and talked. Craig walked downstairs while we were finishing up.

He told me that Darius was asleep and he was leaving. Without taking my eyes off my food, I nodded and said a half-hearted goodbye.

"I'll be back later," he said on his way to the door.

"Why?"

He kept walking. The next thing I knew, the door opened and closed, and Craig was gone.

"Did he just walk out without answerin' me?"

"Yeah, I believe so," Yari said.

"That's the shit I'm talkin' about right there. He's just ignorant for no reason. But I'd be wrong if I didn't open the door when he gets here."

Yari just shrugged her shoulders and smirked. It was a weird smirk, like she knew something I didn't. I was about to ask her why she was looking like that, but she started talking about her flight plans for the next day, and I soon forgot what the hell I had to say in the first place.

208

**

Alexis got in from work late. She busted in my room at 6:30, out of breath. "What's up?" she asked, leaning on my doorframe.

"Where you been?" I looked at my watch. "Didn't you get off at 4:30?"

"I was supposed to, but I worked a little overtime. Lord knows I need all the extra money I can get. I just came to see my nephew. She took Darius out of my arms. "Hey, boo boo," she said, rocking him back and forth. "It's Auntie Lexis."

I laughed as she continued to play with him, making crazy facial expressions and noises. "Did his daddy stop by yet?" she asked.

"You already know," I said with a sigh. "I ain't ready for this stoppin' by every day shit. I don't wanna see him that much."

"You sure about that?" Lexis asked.

"Hell yeah, I'm sure. Why wouldn't I be?"

"I'm just sayin'. You talk a lotta shit on him, but when it comes down to you tellin' him to his face, you soften up." I started to interrupt her, but she continued before I could. "I mean, I know you've cussed him out and called him some names, but he hasn't felt the wrath that me, Nicole, Yari, and Tielle have. You tell us everything that you need to be tellin' him."

"I'm just tryin' to keep things halfway peaceful. Babies pick up on bad vibes, and I don't want Darius feelin' the tension that's between me and his father."

"Personally, I think you still got it bad for that nigga. Don't she, boo boo," Alexis said, playing with Darius again. "She wants your daddy back. Yes, she does!"

I gave Alexis the finger. She may have been right, but I would never admit that I still had a little spark for Craig. I knew I still loved him, but not enough to be with him. It was a residual feeling from a once happy relationship, and I simply cared about his well-being and loved him for helping me create our beautiful baby boy.

I didn't wanna discuss the matter anymore, so I changed the topic. "Why don't you keep Darius company while I take a quick nap?"

"You probably been sleep all day. Get up," Lexis replied.

"No, I haven't. Come on, Lexis. Please?"

"No! Get up and put some real clothes on."

"Why? I ain't goin' nowhere."

"We goin' out to eat. Me and Yari are treatin'. You need to get out the house."

It took about five more minutes of convincing, but I got up and put on some jean shorts and a t-shirt. "Let's go," I said as I walked out of the bathroom, dragging my feet.

Alexis had already put a new outfit on Darius and was finger-combing his hair. "Lil' man's ready," she said, proud of the grooming job she'd done. She handed him to me and we walked downstairs. When we got to the bottom, she reached for him again.

"You need to figure it out," I said. "Either you gon' hold him or you ain't." Lexis didn't say anything. "Where's Yari?" I asked, looking around the dim room.

Alexis walked through the living room and into the dining room. "Oh no!" she said in a panicky voice.

"What's wrong?" I asked as I ran behind her.

As soon as I rounded the corner, the lights came on and I heard, "Surprise!"

About ten people jumped out, and they all had decorations that they put up after they came over to greet me. I couldn't believe it. Alexis and Yari threw me a surprise baby shower. I turned to my sister and smiled.

"You got me," I said. "You got me good."

She laughed. "That's why I took Darius back. I didn't want you to be too surprised and drop him."

I was blown away. Everything looked so nice. Blue streamers were draped along the entryways and balloons reading "It's a boy!" floated around the room. Yari came over and told me how she strategically hid the decorations and some of the food. She also admitted she knew why Craig was planning to come back later. She had invited him to my non-traditional gathering.

Everyone was there. Tielle and Romeo, of course; Robert came; TJ, two girls from my old job, two girls from my church, and Tiffany. I was happy to see everyone, but what was wrong with the picture? Where was the father of the child? Well, he wasn't at my house. That was for sure.

Tielle walked over and put her arm around me. "So are you surprised?"

"Yeah," I said. "I was wonderin' why I hadn't heard from you all day. Now I see you were in on this, too."

Tielle and Nicole were co-godmothers. I wasn't gonna be forced to choose which best friend got the honors, so I let both of them hold the title. They were satisfied with my decision, and that made my life a lot less stressful.

I mingled with the rest of my guests, then Alexis officially began the shower. She was in charge of the games, so my guests played everything from baby bingo to the clothespin game.

We took a break to snack on the food after about an hour. I was sitting at the table talking to Tiffany about my job in Columbus.

"Do they have any branches here that you can transfer to?" she asked.

"Yeah, but I'm still debatin' on whether I'ma do it. It's gon' be like a hour drive, and—"

Just then, the door opened and in walked Craig and another chick. My eyes never left because I was wondering who she was. She turned around, and the two of them walked toward the dining room.

That's not her. I know he ain't stupid enough to bring that bitch up in my house, I thought, immediately assuming it was Jacqueline. *Naw, he's not stupid. That ain't her. He wouldn't disrespect me like that.*

Once they reached the entryway, all activity stopped. Even Vicki, who was performing her version of "Proud Mary" on the karaoke machine, stopped in the middle of the song. All eyes were on Craig and the mystery woman. It was obvious he was extremely uncomfortable.

"Hey everybody," he said with an awkward smile. "This is Jacqueline."

Oh my Lord. The fool did lose his mind! He brought that bitch to my house—to my baby shower. I tried my best to breathe and stay remotely calm as everyone's eyes shifted to me.

"I'm his girlfriend," Jacqueline added with an uppity tone. Craig turned and looked as if he wanted to choke her.

"This is some straight disrespectful shit!" Alexis said. Robert got up from the table and walked over to her. He'd been with her long enough to know that if somebody didn't grab her soon, she would be introducing Jacqueline to her fists.

I sat shaking my head and biting my lower lip as I rocked Darius back and forth. Tears of anger were just about to fall, so I stood up and went into the kitchen. I made it a point to eyeball Craig until he was out of my sight.

TJ stood up. "If she's in there cryin', I swear to God, I'm fuckin' you up," he told Craig as he followed me into the kitchen.

211

"I'd like to see that," Craig said.

"Hey, hey!" Yari interrupted. "We don't need all that up in here."

"Oh my," Jacqueline said, holding her hand over her heart. "This is crazy." She leaned over to Craig and whispered, "I told you I didn't want you around these ghetto people."

He rolled his eyes and walked toward the kitchen. Yari stopped him at the entrance. "I think it's best that you stay out here," she said.

She tried to get everybody back into party mode while TJ stayed in the kitchen with me. "You alright, baby girl?" he asked as he wrapped his arms around me from behind.

"I can't believe him," I said.

"Just calm down. Lil' man don't need to hear all that."

"I know," I said, wiping my tears with my free hand.

"Don't worry 'bout that nigga. I got him handled." He massaged my shoulders, then took Darius from me. "Now fix your face so you can go out here and have a good time."

I wiped my eyes with a paper towel and took a few deep breaths. I didn't wanna face everybody. I was completely embarrassed, and I knew that all eyes would be on me again. Yari peeked into the kitchen and asked if I was ready to come back in.

"Yeah, I'm cool," I said as I walked back to my seat. "Sorry everybody. Let's keep the party goin'."

"You sure?" Lexis asked under her breath.

"Yeah. What's next?"

We played two more games, and then it was time to open the gifts. After I finished, the shower was over. I was proud of myself for not looking in Craig or Jacqueline's direction the whole evening, and I was even more proud of Alexis for keeping her composure during a time when she'd normally show her ass. The guys helped clean up as I stood at the door and thanked everyone for attending.

Before I left the dining area, Yari was holding Darius. When I returned, Craig had him and Jacqueline was standing beside him, tickling my baby's foot. I walked over to them, and Jacqueline just had to say something.

"We haven't formally met," she said, extending her hand to me. "I'm Jacqueline. It's good to finally meet you and Darius. He's such a doll."

I looked at her hand, then into her eyes. I gave her a mama look. You know, the one when the person you're looking at knows what

212

you wanna say just from your facial expression. She must not have had a mother who did that because she kept her hand out.

"You got five seconds to get your hand away from me," I said. She quickly heeded my warning. "Give me my son, please," I said to Craig.

"I ain't held him all night. Now all of a sudden you wanna come get him?" he replied.

"You damned right. I'm about to go put him down."

"He's been sleep almost the whole time! Why you wanna put him down now?"

"Craig, let's just go," Jacqueline said.

"Yeah," I agreed. "You need to listen to your girlfriend."

Tielle and Alexis came out of the kitchen.

"This is what I was telling you, honey. It's not worth it. Let's go," Jacqueline urged again.

"What ain't worth it?" I asked, stepping into her personal space.

"Meka," Tielle started.

"I'm not gon' touch her. I just wanna make sure I can hear all the shit she's sayin' under her breath more clearly," I replied.

She took Darius out of Craig's arms and walked to the stairwell, motioning for me to follow her. "Don't let her take you there," she said. "Let Craig play these games by himself."

She suggested I go upstairs with her to cool off and wait for the happy couple to leave, but I couldn't. I demand respect—especially in my own house—and I certainly wasn't getting it. I turned around, and saw Craig standing alone.

"Where'd she go?" I asked.

"I told her to wait outside," Craig said. "You got a problem? You tell me about it. She ain't got nothin' to do with this."

"I can't tell! As far as I'm concerned, she has everything to do with this. You know you didn't have no business bringin' that bitch to my house, but I let it go in front of the church folk and my coworkers. I held my cool the best I could and tried to ignore y'all. But you kept the prissy bitch around afterwards like she was welcomed, and you expect me to be okay with that? After all this time, I thought you knew me better than that." I paused to take a good look at him, wondering why I'd never seen that side of him during our relationship—thinking I must've been so caught up in the good that I overlooked the bad.

"Just know that you've fucked up all your visitin' rights. That stopping-by-anytime-you-want shit? It's a thing of the past. Call first. And if you have a problem with that, I suggest you consult a lawyer near you." I got bold and pointed my finger just centimeters away from his face. "You got me fucked up, and you know it."

"Get your finger out my face," Craig said.

"Or what?"

He grabbed my arm and squeezed it tightly as he lowered it. Something in me snapped. He'd never handled me like that before, so I thought he was going to take it a step further. Once he let my arm go, I backhanded him in the face, then let my fists fly. He tried his best to grab my arms to restrain me, but I was moving too wildly for him to get a good grip. Finally, he grabbed one of my wrists and pushed me away. He did it so forcefully that I wound up on my back on the living room floor.

Alexis ran over to see if I was okay. Everybody in the kitchen must've heard her screaming profanities at him over the loud music and clanging dishes, because they all ran into the room. Robert stopped her as she ran in Craig's direction, while Romeo and Yari helped me up. I was crying, but only because I was mad.

TJ saw my tears and stepped to Craig. They had a few words, but Romeo got between them and pushed Craig outside before any blows were thrown. Robert then let Lexis go and snatched up TJ before he ran outside after Craig. At that point, I just wanted everybody to leave. TJ was threatening to shoot Craig, Lexis still wanted to fight him, and neither one of them would shut up about it.

Robert convinced Craig to leave, then came back inside. I sat on the couch with my head between my legs, exhausted. All of the yelling and swinging I did wore me out.

"Meka, I'm tellin' you. I'm fuckin' him up," TJ said, pacing back and forth.

"Please just sit down and shut up." I grabbed the bottom of his t-shirt and pulled him toward the couch.

He sat down, but didn't stop fussing. When he took a break, he noticed I hadn't budged. He put his arm around me and asked what was wrong.

"I'm tired, and I just wanna go to sleep," I replied.

"Well go to bed."

I stood up and took a step. I was dizzy as hell. "Whoa," I said, leaning onto him as he stood behind me.

"I got you, baby girl. You sure you just tired? You need to go to the hospital?" he asked.

"Naw, I just need to take my medicine and go to sleep."

214

He carried me to my room and laid me in the bed. Once he tucked me in, he kissed me on the cheek and said goodbye.

"Where you goin'?" I asked.

"Home," TJ replied.

"Can you stay here, please?"

The last thing TJ wanted to do was stay the night. He had every intention of going to Craig's place to finish their ordeal, but when he saw that I wasn't in good shape, he didn't wanna leave me alone. "You always get your way," he said as he stripped down to his boxers and got in the bed.

"I gotta keep my eye on you somehow," I said.

"You always worryin' 'bout somebody gettin' in trouble." He rolled over and put his arm around me. "It's cool, though."

When I woke up the next morning, TJ was gone. Darius was still knocked out, so I hurried to the bathroom and took a ten-minute shower. As I stepped out, I heard the phone ringing. A few seconds later, Alexis yelled for me to pick it up. I wrapped the towel around my body and retrieved the phone from my nightstand.

"Hello?" I held the receiver away from my head as I wiped the water off of my ear.

It was Detective Andrews calling to share some information with me. Detective Nelson was taken off my case while I was in Columbus, and he was assigned to it. He told me they found out Smoke's real name and matched his DNA to a smudge of semen on my pants.

My emotions were all over the place. I was relieved but also scared for some reason. "So are y'all goin' after him?" I asked.

"Most definitely, but it's not as easy as it sounds. Mr. Carter has been moving around the country an awful lot, so he's giving us a hell of a chase."

"So that's his last name? Carter?"

"Yes," he replied. "Rashawn Carter."

I grabbed the notepad on my dresser and wrote the name down with my plum lip liner.

"I called to tell you this information because I want you to really be on the lookout. Keep your eyes and ears open. I have reason to believe he may be visiting town again within the next month. My contacts have given me a lot of useful information, and I just want you to be safe."

"Do you know what he looks like?" I asked.

"We really don't have any specifics that would distinguish him from any other black male you see, except for the description you gave us when you saw him in the parking lot last year."

"I didn't get a good look at him, though. I just saw a scruffy-lookin' beard. That could be gone now."

"Right. Just try to stay away from unfamiliar people and places. We're working on cross-referencing some records to see if we can get a picture of him. We know he's in the system somewhere—just not here."

He'd heard how disenchanted I was with their investigation up to that point and assured me that he wouldn't sleep until he found Rashawn "Smoke" Carter. He took pride in having a perfect record of cases solved and wanted to add mine to the list. I tried to be as optimistic as he was and not hold him responsible for Detective Nelson's shortcomings.

I hung up the phone and glanced at the purple writing on the notepad. "One step closer."

Chapter 25

Craig called at six o'clock, begging me not to hang up on him.

He instantly dished out the apologies and begged for my forgiveness. He swore up and down he didn't want Jacqueline to come to the shower, but said he gave in because she was persistent.

"So she out-muscled you and got in the car anyway? That's bullshit. You didn't have a problem pushin' *me* outta your face. You coulda left her at home. What was she gon' do? Come to my house by herself? You wanted to piss me off, and your plan worked."

"She didn't believe I was coming to a shower since men usually aren't invited. She thought I was sneakin' away to spend time with you. I don't know what you want me to say. You don't want me to say I'm sorry, so..."

"So...if that's all you have to say, I'm hanging up," I said.

"Well can I come see my son this evening?" he asked.

"What time?"

"Around eight."

"I guess."

He arrived with a shopping bag full of baby clothes, placed it by the stairs, and proceeded to the couch. I sat in the chair beside the bassinet.

I pretended I was engrossed in an old *Cosby Show* rerun, but I still felt Craig's eyes on me. Trying to fight the uncomfortable feeling, I kept shifting positions in the chair and laughing at jokes that weren't as funny as they were in 1987. Darius woke up just as Craig started to make small talk. I motioned for Craig to tend to him while I went to the kitchen to get a bottle. The phone rang as I tested the milk's temperature on my wrist.

When I answered, a familiar voice greeted me and changed my gloomy mood.

"Hey, lady," Isaac said.

I walked the bottle over to Craig and headed upstairs. I was shocked to hear from Isaac. We didn't have a chance to talk before I left Columbus, and I didn't give him my number. Fortunately, he disobeyed the hospital's code of ethics and retrieved the number from my file. "I hope you don't mind," he said cautiously.

"It's cool," I said. "It ain't like you could've found out anything you didn't already know. What's worse than the girl who tried to holla at you havin' HIV, right?" I joked.

"Sweetie, I told you I ain't trippin' off that," Isaac said. "You act like you were out there bein' a ho or somethin'. You got raped, Tameka. You ain't gotta laugh it off like it doesn't bother you. Don't forget. I was in your hospital room when you went through some of your toughest times."

I couldn't speak without choking up, so I just wiped the tear that was tickling my cheek and sat quietly. Isaac continued his pep talk, pointing out that I was no less beautiful than I was the night we met. He wanted me to stop letting the virus determine the extent of my happiness and abandon the mentality that the only men I'd have a minute chance of being with were TJ and Craig.

He was the only person I had revealed those feelings to because everyone else expected me to be the strong, confident person I was before Smoke violated me. Even though I'd only known him for a short period of time, I could be myself with Isaac, and that's what I treasured in our relationship. No, I wasn't trying to get with him, nor did he wanna be with me. We were friends, and I counted on him for advice.

Still, he always threw me off when he gave me the international nice guy response to my insecurities. There was no way I could be convinced that a man could seriously overlook a deadly virus—no matter how good I looked. Craig tried, but we know how that turned out.

The conversation ended with Isaac making plans to visit. We didn't set a date, but he promised to get back with me after he checked his work schedule. I told him I'd be sure to tell Alexis. She would be ecstatic to see his flawless, smiling face again. They seemed to develop a liking for each other while she was in Columbus and they kept in touch until her cell phone fell in the toilet one day. She lost his number and everyone else's. He wasn't able to call her because he never had her number. Like any smart, cheating woman, *she* controlled their contact and utilized the *67 feature to keep drama to a minimum.

Interestingly enough, though, Lexis was really digging Isaac before they lost touch. He wasn't her type and she wasn't his, but they had undeniable chemistry. It was the first time she didn't have to be physically involved with a man to feel connected to him. And although she never said it, I knew if Isaac still lived in town, Robert would be old news.

Craig was watching TV when I walked back downstairs.

"Did he go back to sleep okay?" I asked.

"Yeah," he said.

I looked at him with my eyebrows raised. "Did you need somethin' else?"

"What you mean?"

"Why are you still here?"

He got up and snatched his keys off the coffee table. "I'm out," he said as he stormed off. He slammed the door on his way out and woke Darius up. I wanted to run outside and beat his ass for being inconsiderate, but I tried to get Darius to go back to sleep instead.

No such luck. Since he was up, I decided to go to the grocery store as I had planned. I needed some seasoned salt and a few other odds and ends. I threw my wallet into the diaper bag, and we were off.

As I was in the bread aisle, I felt like somebody was watching me. I glanced over my right shoulder, but the old man in tight gray sweatpants wasn't paying any attention to me. I glanced over my left shoulder and saw Dap make a pathetic attempt to act like she wasn't staring.

I pulled a loaf of Home Pride off the shelf and threw it in the cart. As I searched for the cheapest hot dog buns, I saw a shadow nearing through my peripheral vision. Dap walked over and looked at Darius.

"Can you back up out my son's face, please?" I asked.

"Oh my goodness," Dap said, taking two steps backward. "This is your baby?"

"Last time I checked, he was," I replied.

"So you were pregnant before you left?"

"Yeah."

As I pushed the cart away, she followed. "He's Craig's?"

I shot her a "What do you think?" look. It was hard for me to believe that she didn't know I had Craig's child. After all, they were family.

"So he's my little cousin," she said, touching Darius' hand.

I was disgusted and confused all at once. This was the same broad I never got along with, cheesing and claiming my son as a part of her family. I figured our first confrontation after I moved back would be completely different.

Tyrone walked around the corner with two bags of cookies. "Hey baby, which one you think—" When he looked up and saw me, he assumed the worst. "Aw, man. Don't start this in here, y'all."

"It's not even like that," Dap said.

He didn't hear her because he was too busy staring at Darius. "Who's baby is this?" he asked.

I was then convinced that Tielle wasn't lying when she said she and Craig hadn't been in contact with Dap or Carmen. Tyrone's reaction was proof that Dap really didn't know about Darius.

"It's her baby, boo," Dap replied.

Her joy came from knowing that Tyrone wouldn't want to deal with me if I had a baby. It was her time to feel secure in her relationship, and it was obvious because she was clinging onto his arm and giggling like a little 4-year-old. With me being HIV-positive and a mother, her Tameka Threat Meter had gone from code red to nothing at all.

"*Your* baby?" Tyrone asked. "When were you pregnant?"

"Well, he's almost a month and a half, so you do the math," I replied.

I excused myself and walked off as Dap's face beamed with joy. Even though her demeanor was cocky, I was impressed that she didn't attack me with HIV insults and quirky quips about Craig and I not being together. I wouldn't dare go as far to say that she'd grown up, but there was progress.

Once we got home, Darius was ready for bed. After I laid him in his crib, I took my journal out of the nightstand drawer and climbed in my bed. As I was writing, I thought about Tielle. We hadn't talked since the baby shower, and quite frankly, I missed my friend. Before she left that evening, she'd told me how upset she was with the way I handled Jacqueline's presence. In her opinion, I'd opened up a new can of worms when I confronted Craig, ultimately dragging TJ into it. I snapped at her because I felt she was holding me responsible for a series of events that all began with him coming to my house with that chick on his arm. She should've been chastising him instead of blaming me for reacting.

The solution to us not talking seemed simple: Just pick up the phone and call her. But for some reason, I didn't know what to say.

The tension between us was strong, and I couldn't think of a good approach. The last thing I wanted to do was call like nothing was wrong.

I finished my journal entry and picked up the phone. Tielle sounded like her usual self when she answered. She asked about Darius right off the bat and I told her that he'd just met his cousin, Dap. She got a kick out of my impersonations of Tyrone and Dap as I told the story, and we laughed until my stomach hurt.

I still felt the awkwardness of our conversation, though, so I apologized for snapping at her. She understood why I did, though, and apologized for seeming one-sided. We agreed that she involuntarily ended up in the middle of our drama all the time, and I offered not to talk to her about him anymore. Being a loyal friend, she couldn't allow that. Instead she suggested that I share the same verbal thrashings with Craig, believing that if we told each other all the things we tell her, half of our problems wouldn't exist.

She was absolutely right, but we both knew there was no way that he and I would be totally candid with each other. Relationship politics left no room for complete honesty. You subconsciously account for the other person's feelings and hold your tongue a little instead of spilling the hateful words you just told all of your friends. Honesty equaled vulnerability, and I couldn't see myself ever giving Craig that power over me again.

Once we moved past that topic, Tielle told me Romeo had been acting funny. She was wondering if he was kicking it with somebody else. I told her to let me know if I needed to go on a late night ride with her to follow his ass.

"Don't act like we ain't done it before!" I said. "This time, Darius would have to tag along!"

Tielle laughed. "Girl, you crazy. I don't think it's that deep. But if it gets there, just make sure you have your all black hangin' in the front of your closet."

I hung up with her and leaned against my headboard. It had been another tiring day, and my nerves were shot. I thought about Craig's visit. It was a shame that we couldn't act like adults, no matter how hard we tried. I tried to evaluate myself to see if I was causing the problems between us because of my attitude, or if our lack of a healthy relationship was because I hadn't gotten over our issues from the past.

I knew I was stubborn as hell, and sometimes that got me in a world of trouble. My usual "fuck him" way of thinking wouldn't

221

work anymore because Darius was a part of the equation. I felt like I was going crazy or something, because one minute I wanted to call him and suggest that we sit down to talk about everything that went wrong in our relationship, then agree to move past it. Then a few minutes later, I'd feel the opposite way. I'd think about how much he hurt me and consider leaving town and never returning, just to keep Darius away from him. He didn't deserve to have something as precious as a baby in his life.

My contradicting thoughts made me want to return to my psychologist for help. Unfortunately, I couldn't afford to because there was no longer a such thing as extra money. My best bet was to carry my behind to church and pray for guidance—not only for my issues with Craig, but for everything else that clouded my mind. Like, who was I gonna end up with? Would any man ever accept me, HIV and all? How could I expect somebody else to accept the condition when I hadn't accepted it myself? How could somebody else love me when I barely loved myself?

TJ…Well, he seemed to be dealing with it alright. Even though he was free to live his sex life however he pleased, he continued to occupy my bed and adapted to using condoms. I tried not to become too emotionally involved with him again because I knew he'd soon get tired of dealing with the extra precautions and find someone who could satisfy him in ways I no longer could. On the other hand, we didn't have sex all the time and it wasn't the basis of our relationship. I knew how much I meant to him, and that was never gonna change. You can't erase history. But if he did accept my messed up situation, did I really want to be with him? I loved him to death, but could we actually build a life together? A violence-free life?

Chapter 26

My mother came to visit a week later. She was all over Darius the whole time she stayed. I was shocked that we got along the entire week, because she was infamous for telling me what I should do about every matter in my life. Not once did she say, "Tameka, you need to hold him like this," or "Don't feed him right now." I learned a lot just by watching her care for Darius, and in the back of my mind I wished things could be better between the two of us. She had so much love to give but didn't always know how to express it. And even though I was fully aware that deep down she had a decent heart, it still didn't make her a decent mother. Maybe having her first grandchild would give her a chance at redemption…for herself.

During her visit, she met Craig. Their encounter was anything but pleasant since Alexis had already filled her in on everything that had gone on between us. She gave Craig the third degree about everything from his parents' backgrounds to his shoe size while Lexis and I eavesdropped from dining room. He handled himself well until she questioned him about the bad stuff. He didn't have an explanation and couldn't even think of a good lie. Needless to say, she tore into his ass like he had beaten me blind. For that period of time, I felt like she was my mother again—the woman I once respected and loved with all my heart.

We had an intimate talk the day before she left, and I wound up telling her about my insecurity issues. She did the motherly thing and told me there was no one on earth who should feel more secure than me. She revealed that she had admired my strength and perseverance ever since I was in grade school and stressed that it wasn't time for me to give up. I could tell she meant what she said when I looked into her eyes, and for the first time in seven or eight years, I hugged my mother.

Surprisingly, I didn't want to let her go, and I didn't…not for a while, at least. I cried tears of joy, relief, and unreleased pain that soaked her shirt and stained her heart. Without me saying a word, she finally understood the degree of hurt she had caused and said her most sincere apology by simply stroking my hair and rocking me with her chin resting on my head.

When she got home the following morning, she called and told me to look in the bottom drawer of my nightstand. To my surprise, I found a check for $7,500 and a note attached that read:

"I know you want to go back to therapy, so here's some change in case your insurance won't cover it all. I know this won't make up for the things I've done, but I hope you'll accept this and know that I am truly trying to make things right. I love you with all of my heart. Stay strong. –Mom"

I realized she was actually listening when I casually joked about needing professional help again, and she stepped in to help out. It wasn't another empty attempt to gain my forgiveness with her money. It was my mother instinctively coming to my rescue. I guess she really didn't want to see me fall apart.

***

TJ showed up at my house a day after my mother left. He knew better than to come around while she was there, but I was surprised to see him at all. He was supposed to be somewhere in Detroit handling business once again.

"What you doin' here?" I asked as he walked in.

"I'm happy to see you, too, baby girl," he said, hugging me.

"I thought you were in Detroit."

"Naw. That fell through." He sat on the couch. "My fault for not callin'. I was just around the corner, so I stopped through on my way home."

"In hopes of findin' Craig here, right?" I asked. I knew he still hadn't gotten over their confrontation at the baby shower.

He laughed. "Man, I ain't trippin' off that dude."

I looked at him in disbelief, then changed the subject. We sat on the couch with my feet propped in his lap, and I told him about my phone call from Detective Andrews. TJ didn't have much to say. Whenever he seemed distant, I knew he was withholding information.

"If you knew Smoke was here lookin' for you, you'd tell me right?" I asked.

"Yeah. I wouldn't even be around you. You know I'm not gon' get you caught up again. I still don't sleep good 'cause of that night in the alley." He couldn't look me in my eyes. "I wish I could just erase that shit. Not just that night—my whole lifestyle. I'm trapped."

"There's always a way out."

"Yeah, the grave. I can't live a normal life. I can't even be with you like you want me to 'cause I still got unsettled business out there."

He studied my face as I smiled uncomfortably. Before I could ask why he was staring, he asked, "What is this? What are we doing?"

"Huh?"

"What is this? We ain't together, right? So what do you call this?"

I was at a loss for words. I honestly didn't know what we were or what I wanted us to be, but I needed to find a way to tell him that without hurting his feelings.

"Where did that come from?" I asked, hoping to buy some time.

TJ shrugged and faced me. "I'ma be honest with you. You keep tellin' me that you can't be with me right now and I understand why, but…"

"But what?"

"I still got broads tryin' to get at me, and…" He left the sentence hanging.

"And what? You wanna be with 'em?" I lifted my feet off his lap and lowered them to the floor. "Don't let me stop you!" I wasn't as pissed off as I sounded.

"Man, here you go," TJ said, rolling his eyes. "It ain't even like that."

Before he could continue, his cell phone rang and seconds later, my phone rang. He looked at his caller ID and turned to me again. "I'll just holla at you later. I gotta go." He answered his phone and walked out.

I stood in place, frozen with disbelief. The fourth ring helped me snap out of my stupor. I rushed over and answered the phone. It was Isaac calling to check on me and Darius. We talked for about fifteen minutes, ten of which he spent begging for Lexis' cell number. Not a chance. I wasn't trying to get her caught up with Robert.

I thought about TJ's quick exit after we got off the phone, and I became a little suspicious. Why did he have to leave in such a hurry? I felt like all my thoughts of him wanting to explore other options

225

were becoming a reality. I was slightly annoyed with him because of the bullshit excuse he was using. He knew full well before we became involved again that I wouldn't consider a future with him if he was still thuggin'. If he wanted to deal with other females, that was all he had to say. I didn't appreciate him acting like I was forcing him to look elsewhere. I worked myself up to the point of being really shitty and called him to ask why he left. He didn't answer his phone, so I expressed my irritation via his voicemail, then two-wayed him to reiterate the same points.

Wouldn't you know I didn't hear from him for like a week and a half? He wouldn't return any of my pages or messages, and I decided by the third day that I'd leave him alone. Evidently he didn't wanna be bothered. Plus, his avoidance tactics reminded me of my dysfunctional relationship with Craig, so I figured I'd stay as far away from that type of shit as possible.

While I was on the phone with my pastor confirming the date for Darius' christening one afternoon, TJ had the nerve to beep in. I finished my conversation with Pastor Johnson and clicked back over to see what that fool wanted. Before I could get a word out, he asked me when I wanted him to take me to get a gun.

"Okay...I don't hear from you for almost two weeks, then you call, don't say nothin' about why you haven't been in touch, and you wanna know when I wanna buy a gun? Can we back up so I can understand where all this is comin' from? As a matter of fact, let's back up to when you walked outta my house the other week. What was that all about?" I asked.

"I can't get into that over the phone," TJ replied. "I'm callin' 'cause I remember tellin' you I'd take you to get a weapon."

"When I got my permit," I said. "I don't have it yet, and you know that. Is that nigga after me? Do you know somethin' you ain't tellin' me?"

"It ain't like that. I'll put it to you like this. If we don't go today, I can't tell you when I'll be able to take you again. I got a lotta shit to take care of, and you won't be hearin' from me for a minute. I'ma be on the move. Now you know ol' boy been in and out of town. If he's in while I'm out, how you gon' protect yourself? Alexis ain't around you all the time," he said.

I got an uneasy feeling in my stomach, worried about what he was getting involved in. At that moment, I realized I'd fallen back in love with a thug—the same thug I'd been trying to shake for years.

226

The shit he was spitting was damn near verbatim compared to the things he used to tell me when we first got together.

I wanted to beg him to stay—find a way to keep him out of trouble—but there was no use. As much as I wanted to protect him, I couldn't—and he couldn't let me. The streets were his girlfriend, and I was the chick on the side. I couldn't see myself stressing over his whereabouts and his safety again. I couldn't go back to late night crying and jumping every time a car backfired, thinking it was a gunshot. I may not have gotten it right the first time, but it was clearly time for me to get him out of my head, out of my heart, and out of my life. I needed to let him go, and the first step was to stop being dependent on him.

"I'll just get one on my own," I said.

"Meka, I told you I would take you, so when do you wanna go?" TJ asked.

"I don't. It's cool."

"Let me explain somethin' to you," he said. "My boy works at a gun shop and he can hook you up, but you need to go in there with me. And you never know…I might decide to buy it for you."

Only a thug would offer to buy his lady a gun as a going away present, and only a fool in love with him would accept it. Since I knew it was best for my safety, I went along with the plan to buy the gun. After the purchase, though, it would be time to say goodbye.

During our hour or so together, he told me he'd be gone for three or four weeks, but he wouldn't tell me where he was going. I listened to his half-assed explanation for why he was leaving, concentrating more on keeping my heart rate down and my nerves under control. I knew TJ wouldn't like the goodbye speech I was preparing in my head. I kept waiting for an opportunity to speak my piece, but he rambled so much that I couldn't get a word in.

On the way back to my house, he had segued into "our" future and what "we" were going to do once he got back. My moment had arrived. "I think you should ask me if I'm tryin' to do all this stuff you're plannin' instead of assumin' I'll be down with it," I said.

"Damn! I just said we could check out a couple ball games and go to the movies," TJ replied.

"This 'we' stuff you keep talkin' is a thing of the past," I blurted. It was time to drop the bomb that I was letting him go. I knew I wouldn't be able to stick with my decision if I let him give me a rebuttal, so I talked continuously. "Just the other day you were talkin' about other broads you been lookin' at, but you want Old

Faithful here to be around in case somethin' doesn't work out with them. That's crazy. We're not 18 and 19 no more. I dealt with that mess before, but it's a new day. I love you to death, TJ, but I can't do this shit no more for fear that I'ma lose my mind. I've never been a fan of breakin' up and makin' up or bein' on and off again. I used to clown Lexis about that all the time, but now I'm the one doin' it. At first I thought we could just kick it and that would be it, but it's become more than that for me now. I'm fallin' in love with you again, and the shit is startin' to stress me out."

"What's wrong with bein' in love with me? You never had a problem with it before!" he interrupted. We pulled in front of my house and he put the car in park. I felt like his eyes were burning a hole through me.

"I didn't have HIV or a baby then, either," I said. "I think differently now. The shit that's goin' on with me has forced me to grow up—fast. I'm thinkin' about my future, and I don't see you in it. You still ain't left that dangerous lifestyle, and I don't know if you ever will. I can't have that shit around my son. It's not just about me now."

"So you not fuckin' wit' a nigga no more? It's that simple for you?"

"TJ, you know it's not simple. You just have too much goin' on. I still think there's more to you buyin' this gun today than what you're tellin' me. You probably know that Smoke is comin' after me, but for some reason you won't come right out and say it. I don't wanna shut you out of my life, and you know that. But I'm at a point where I can't do what I want to do. I'm doing what I have to do." The tears came rolling down.

TJ looked away in disgust, like he didn't believe me or something. That struck a chord with me. The energy in the car suddenly converted from neutral to negative as I raised my voice.

"You wanna know the truth?" I asked, jerking his head in my direction. "I wish that Darius was yours, I wish you weren't a thug, and I wish we could be together, but a wish ain't shit but the opposite of reality. Why should we hang on to each other and grow closer when there's nothin' at the end of the road? It's not healthy. I still wanna know what's goin' on with you, and I still wanna be able to talk to you. We just can't be together. You're not ready to do the things I need you to do or give up the things I want you to give up."

He shook his head and looked away.

"What? Do you have a better solution?" I asked.

228

"Naw, that's cool. You ain't gotta worry about me bein' around to fuck up your life no more."

"I don't wanna leave with you havin' this attitude," I said. "You're takin' this the wrong way."

"I'm takin' it my way," he replied.

I reached into my purse and took forty dollars out of my wallet. "Here," I said, handing him the money. "That's all I have right now."

He looked at the bills. "What's that for?"

"The gun. I don't want you to say I'm usin' you or anything," I replied, rolling my eyes. I snatched the black plastic bag from the backseat and sat it in my lap.

"I don't want your money. I told you I was gon' get that for you, and I did. I don't back out of my commitments like you."

"What commitment—" I was too mad to finish my sentence. Instead, I exited the car, threw the two twenties at him, and slammed the door.

TJ's emotional reaction and made me second guess my decision. I stayed strong while I was in his sight, but as soon as I walked in the house, I fell to my knees. I cried so hard that noises couldn't even come out, and the pressure in my chest was so intense that I was having trouble breathing.

Alexis walked down the steps with Darius in her arms. "That was quick," she said. "I thought you was gon' be gone at least a couple hours."

She couldn't see me until she reached the bottom of the steps. "Meka?" she called, still standing by the steps.

I couldn't answer her.

"Meka, what's wrong?" she asked as she ran over to me. She squatted beside me and used her free hand to rub my back. "What happened? Did you see Smoke?"

I shook my head, no.

"Come on. Get up." She grabbed my arm and lifted me to a standing position. She led me to the couch where I tried to gather myself. "Breathe," she said.

I wiped my eyes and took some deep breaths. Darius made a funny noise that sounded like a laugh, and I looked up at him. Seeing his face made me smile. A few minutes later, I asked Alexis to hand him to me, and I told her about my decision to break it off with TJ for good.

She was in total disbelief. From the look on her face, an outsider would think TJ was her brother and I'd just told her that he died. I explained my reasons to her, and she seemed to understand.

"I feel you, but that's just weird. You without TJ is like…Man, I don't even know. It's just not right."

"I know."

"You havin' second thoughts?"

"No—Well, yeah, but I know I did the right thing. It's killin' me, though," I said. "You're probably the only girl he's ever cared about."

"He can care about me all he wants, but there's no use if he doesn't care about himself. If he hasn't learned by now that his actions affect me, he's a lost cause. I didn't want it to turn out so ugly, but…"

She suggested that I call TJ to explain myself. I disagreed, knowing that calling would only do one of two things: aggravate him or make him feel like I'm weak.

"But you are weak, Meka," Lexis said. "You over there on the floor, broke down."

"I can't be weak forever." It sounded like the right thing to say, but I had a hard time convincing myself that it was true.

***

Fortunately, my therapist was able to convince me. After my first week back in therapy, she had me believing that I did what was best for me and my son, and that I'd stopped the cycle of negativity that was breaking my spirit. She already knew my history with TJ, so she was aware of the destructive path we could've gone down.

Friday when I left her office, my cell phone vibrated to alert me of a text message. When I looked the screen, I saw a message from Tielle saying that I was needed at the hospital ASAP. She didn't include any details, but immediately I thought something was wrong with Darius. I'd left him with Alexis, so I assumed there was an accident of some sort. I jogged to my car as I dialed Tielle's number. By the time she answered, I was paying the parking garage attendant.

"I got your message. What's wrong?" I asked.

"You need to get out here quick," she said.

"Why? What's wrong?"

"It's Craig."

"What happened?" I asked, exiting the garage and racing down the street.

"Just get here. I'll explain everything then."

We hung up and I called Alexis to let her know where I was. Two minutes later, I was rushing through the doors of the emergency room. I saw Tielle standing nearby.

"What the hell is goin' on?" I asked.

"How'd you get here so quick?"

"I was right down the street," I replied, then looked at her impatiently, waiting for an answer.

"Craig was in a fight," she said.

"Just now?" I asked. "With who? He really don't know nobody around here."

Using Tielle's facial expression as my guide, I already knew the answer. "TJ," I said, sighing and closing my eyes.

"Yep."

"How bad?"

"Pretty bad. They just did some x-rays and a CT scan to check for internal damage. I guess TJ kicked him in his chest and his ribs a lot."

"I shoulda known he'd do this," I said while we walked to the elevator. As we rode to the fifth floor, I remembered TJ and Craig's argument at my baby shower. "He said he was gon' get him," I said.

"What?" Tielle asked.

"TJ told me that he was gon' get Craig the next time he saw him." I paused. "Where did this happen?"

"At the gas station on MLK," Tielle replied.

We stepped off the elevator and walked down the hallway, dodging two unsupervised kids and an old man standing motionless with his IV pole. We stopped at Room 518. Before Tielle opened the door, she turned to me. "You ready to go in here?"

"Why wouldn't I be?" I asked. "Oh! Is the prissy bitch here?"

"Naw, not yet," Tielle said. "I just want you to be prepared for what you're about to see. He wasn't just punched in the face. He was thrown into the pump, and TJ banged his head all up against it."

"You were there?"

"I was inside payin' for the gas. When I came outside, TJ was kickin' the hell outta Craig, and some dudes were pullin' him away."

I felt somewhat responsible for Craig's beat-down because TJ did it to defend my honor. I also felt a wave of satisfaction because he got the ass whooping I'd been wanting to give him for the longest. When I walked into his hospital room, though, I was no longer overjoyed. He looked terrible. His head was bandaged up, and his face was swollen and still bleeding in places. He was barely recognizable.

"Is he sleep?" I whispered.

Tielle nodded.

I cautiously approached his bed and examined the damage more closely. He looked like he was in so much pain. "Did he get *any* licks in?"

"I don't know. I didn't see anything 'til the end."

"Meka?" Craig called softly. His eyes were still closed.

"Yeah," I replied, looking over at Tielle.

He moved his hand around, searching for me.

"I'm right here," I said, lightly touching his hand. Before I pulled away, he clenched my hand and stroked it with his thumb.

He opened his eyes and looked over at Tielle. "I told you she would come," he said.

I didn't know if that comment was made out of cockiness or relief. Regardless, I kept my mouth shut.

"Where's Darius?" he asked.

"At the house with Lexis," I replied.

I stood there a little longer, then motioned for Tielle to go out in the hallway with me. "What's up?" she asked as she closed the door.

"Where's TJ?"

"Probably still in jail. The attendant called the police."

"So Craig's pressin' charges?"

"I don't know." She paused. "You alright?"

"Not really."

"Meka, this ain't your fault," Tielle said.

"Craig told you to call me?" I asked.

"He just kept askin' for you," she said. "Then he was like, 'Call her. She has to come,' so I did."

The click-clacking of high-heeled shoes echoed down the hallway. The noise got progressively closer, so I turned around to see who it was. Jacqueline appeared, all decked out in her schoolteacher suit and Louis Vitton bag.

I rolled my eyes and walked in the opposite direction. She asked Tielle how Craig was doing, then adjusted her blouse, flung back her weave, and walked in his room. I told Tielle it was time for me to go and to let me know if anything changed. I couldn't stay around with that girlfriend of his falling all over him. I was afraid I would catch a flashback of her behavior at my shower and put her ass in the bed beside her boo.

I walked in my house and no sooner than I stepped foot in the door, Lexis was in my face, hounding me for answers abut TJ and Craig's altercation.

"Damn! He put him in the hospital. That's crazy."

Alexis lived for that type of stuff. She couldn't stop asking questions about how many times Craig got kicked; who all was there to see the fight; have I heard from TJ; did he get his fair share of scrapes and bruises; and every other question in between. Finally, she calmed down.

"So was he real messed up?" she asked. I nodded. "I can't believe you went to see him."

"He's Darius' father."

"Naw, it ain't that. I mean, you mighta thought about that, but you went out of instinct. You still care about him."

"How can I not care? We used to be together. I used to love him."

"And you still do," Alexis said with a smirk. "I heard it in your voice when you called me. I bet you'd still be there if that bitch didn't walk in. What's her name? Jacqueline?"

"Whatever, Lexis," I said.

The phone rang. Alexis answered, then handed it to me. It was Tielle calling to tell me that Craig's x-rays were fine and she was about to take him home.

"But there's one more thing," she said just as I was about to hang up. "He wants to stop by and see Darius."

"He's sleep right now, but he can stop by real quick, I guess. Maybe he'll wake up by the time y'all get here," I said.

I let Craig and Tielle in and went upstairs to check on Darius. Tielle joined Lexis in the kitchen while Craig sat in the living room. I came halfway down the steps and told him that Darius was still asleep.

"So, I can't see him?" he asked with an attitude.

"I didn't say that. You just gotta come up here 'cause I'm not movin' him and wakin' him up."

He got up slowly, wincing from pain, and made his way to my room. He walked over to the crib and stared at out little angel. I watched from the doorway as he smiled at Darius and gently touched his hand.

"Hey, little man," Craig said softly. "It's Daddy. You ain't gon' wake up for me?" After a while, he gave up. He turned and faced me.

233

"So did you get your boyfriend outta jail?"

"What are you talkin' about?" I asked.

"You know what I'm talkin' about. You know who I fought today."

"TJ is not my boyfriend and I did not get him outta jail. I haven't even talked to him in a week."

Craig's eyes lit up. "Is that right?"

"Yeah." I had a strong attitude. "He's doin' the same shit I told him I didn't like. He's provin' my point."

"What point?"

"That's not your business," I said. I had already told him too much. "Anyway, like I said, I didn't get him outta jail."

"Oh."

"Well, I'm about to go back downstairs. Take as much time as you need." I stepped into the hallway.

"Hold up. Can we talk for a minute?" Craig asked.

I turned around and took a couple steps inside the room. "What?"

Craig sat on my bed. "I appreciate you comin' to the hospital today. It meant a lot."

"It wasn't nothin'," I said. "Tielle called me all hysterical, so I came out to make sure you wasn't dyin'."

"Regardless of the reason, I thank you." He looked at his hands as he opened and closed his fists. I could tell it was painful. "You know I ain't never been in a fight over a female until today?" He laughed. "And what's crazy is, we ain't even together."

"So TJ just approached you and said, 'This is for Tameka?'" I asked.

"Naw, but you know you were the reason behind it."

There was a long pause. "Is that all you wanted to say?" I asked.

"Come here," he said. I could tell he was trying to give me the eye, even though it was swollen.

I took a few steps toward him. "You need to stop, 'cause ol' Jackie would have a fit if she saw you lookin' at me like that," I said.

He smiled and looked away. Thank God TJ didn't mess up those pretty teeth of his. "You crazy," he said.

"Did you really want somethin', or am I supposed to just stand here?" I asked.

"Naw." He looked into my eyes. "Man, Meka, why can't we talk like this all the time? Do you know how good it feels to hold a civil conversation with you? I miss this and I know you do, too, 'cause you haven't left the room yet."

I smirked and ran my fingers through my hair.

"We need to get our relationship together. Yeah, I may be with Jacqueline, and you're doin' your own thing, but we need to cut out all the animosity and build our relationship as Darius' parents."

"I agree," I said. "But that takes work and respect on both ends."

"Understood," he said, smiling again. "See? That wasn't so bad, was it?" He stood up and hugged me.

Why is he on me? I thought. I wasn't ready for the huggy-huggy friendship thing. I still felt like his hugs were the romantic ones that we shared during our relationship. I lost myself in the warmth of his chest as he held me close. *Could we really be friends?* I silently asked myself.

Chapter 27

Interestingly enough, the civil parent thing with Craig was going well. We were two weeks into our newfound friendship, and I couldn't believe we actually made it that long. Everybody else around us was shocked, too. Tielle was amazed that I was really making an effort, and Alexis was disgusted by the idea that me and Craig could actually make amends and be friends. From what Craig told me, Jacqueline wasn't too happy about the time that he and I were spending together. She felt like he was making too much of an effort to be cool with me.

Personally, I was enjoying our family time. Darius was much more responsive at three months old, so Craig and I got a kick out of every little thing he did. He always became so excited when he heard his daddy's voice, and seeing him smile and kick his legs uncontrollably when Craig played with him was priceless. The first time he did it, I realized that I couldn't hate the man he loved so much.

***

Tielle and I went to get Darius' pictures taken. While the photographer was squeezing the rubber ducky to get Darius to laugh, my two-way went off. The screen read:

"In case you were wonderin', I'm out. I'm sho' yo punk ass babydaddy told you he pressed charges. I'll holla."

I handed the pager to Tielle. She read TJ's message and started laughing. "Girl, that dude is too much. He just had to say somethin'."

"Right," I agreed. "I ain't even gon' respond."

We got back to my place, and Lexis, Tielle, and I sat around reflecting on how pitiful our lives had become.

"We don't do shit no more," Lexis said.

"And we ain't got no excuse not to be doin' somethin'," Tielle added.

"Well I got Darius, so I'm excused," I said, laughing.

"You ain't excused when you have a babysitter," Tielle said.

"Who?" I asked as the phone rang.

"My mama. You know she loves Darius," she said.

Alexis answered the phone and handed it to me. "It's your babydaddy," she said in a teasing schoolgirl voice.

I gave her the finger and answered the call. Craig asked how Darius did at his photo shoot, and I told him all about it. I was in the middle of telling him about the pose with the miniature basketball when the doorbell rang. Alexis jumped right up, so I assumed she was expecting company.

I continued talking with Craig, but I was soon speechless when Yari walked into the living room. After my five seconds of being mute, I told Craig I'd talk to him later and hung up the phone.

Yari stood in the middle of the living room floor with her arms in the air. "Surprise!" she said.

"What are you doin' here?" I jumped up and ran over to her.

"I couldn't miss little man's christening," she replied as we hugged.

"I thought you couldn't make it."

"That's what you get for thinkin' on your own. I'm here, right?" she said.

Alexis and Tielle had been planning Yari's visit for weeks. I couldn't believe neither of them slipped up and told me what was going on. We kicked it hard the Friday and Saturday before the christening. I let Craig watch Darius unattended for the first time on Friday. He wasn't allowed to take him to his apartment, though. He had to stay at my place. Call me petty, but I didn't want my child around Jacqueline. I was nervous about leaving him alone with our son, but when we got home early Saturday morning, Darius was clean, fed, and still in one piece.

Unlike the baby shower incident, the christening went well. Even though Jacqueline showed up uninvited again, the stupid broad knew her place. She sat in the back of the church, and after it was over she made a quick retreat to Craig's car.

The ceremony was beautiful. Craig and I were asked to hold hands and vow to raise Darius the best we could and teach him the ways of the Lord. Tielle and Romeo vowed to help us in our endeavors and be willing and ready to take care of Darius if something happened to Craig or me.

I felt a connection when Craig and I held hands. His fingers intertwined perfectly with mine, and his sweaty palms were evidence that something was making him nervous. Perhaps he felt it, too. There was once a time when nobody could get us to unlink our hands, and for the period of time that Pastor Johnson stood there and talked to us, I felt that same way again.

Everybody except Craig and Jacqueline stayed for the regular church service. I didn't walk into my house until after two. Alexis and Yari entertained Darius while I took a nap. I was awakened by a knock on my bedroom door at 6:30. I was annoyed because my alarm wasn't set to go off until seven.

"What?" I yelled, pulling the covers over my head.

"It's me, Meka."

Why are you here? I thought. "It's unlocked," I said.

I heard the door open, then close again, and I felt my mattress give as Craig sat on the bed.

"Lexis said it was cool to come up here. She said it was time for you to wake up," he said.

"I got a half hour left," I said.

He laughed. "You could never wake up gracefully, huh?"

"Not when I'm supposed to still be sleep," I said. "Now go away. Didn't you see Darius downstairs? Go bother him!"

"He's sleep," Craig responded. "And so were Lexis and Yari. Y'all lazy around here."

"Well you need to take a hint and either leave or go to sleep, too," I said, rolling onto my right side.

Craig fumbled around, and his shoes hit the floor. I peaked out from under the covers and saw him pulling his shirt off. I caught myself staring at his broad shoulders and his muscular, chocolate back.

"What are you doin'?" I asked.

He looked over his shoulder. "I'm 'bout to go to sleep. That was one of my options, right?"

"I didn't say you could sleep here. Don't you have a bed at your place?"

"Yeah, but I'm not tryin' to go all the way out there just to come right back," Craig replied. "What? You don't want me in your bed? You want me to get on the floor?"

"Just keep your pants on," I said as I flung the sheet back over my head.

"Girl, I ain't gon' touch you. I'm just tryin' to take a nap."

"Tell your girl that," I replied. "I bet she'd approve of this."

He laughed as he got under the covers. "You got jokes, huh?"

The first fifteen minutes or so were cool. Even though we wanted each other to think that we were sleep, neither of us was. I stayed on my side of the bed, and he stayed on his. As time passed, Craig scooted closer to me and conveniently rested his hand on my thigh. I still pretended to be sleep as I locked my leg in place. After a few seconds, he said, "It feels weird bein' this close to you again."

He must've known that I wasn't sleep, but I still didn't say anything. I just silently agreed with him as I tried to ignore the moisture forming between my legs. I hadn't been in the same bed with him since before I went to Columbus, and to lay next to him after all that time…It felt good, but in a forbidden love sort of way. I laid still, hoping that he'd keep his hand right where it was.

And he did. He gently ran his finger up and down the length of my thigh. My body quivered from the touch of his fingertips, and all my muscles relaxed, inviting him to do whatever he pleased.

"You don't mind me touchin' you, do you?" Craig whispered.

"Un unh." I felt foolish for welcoming him into my bed, knowing he had a girlfriend, but I couldn't tell him to get up. I sensed the closeness and felt the security that we once had, and I wanted to hold onto that as long as possible—even if it was only for one evening.

Craig proceeded, kissing the back of my neck and nibbling on my left earlobe. He was extremely passionate, but gentle, just like I remembered.

"Meka," he said between pecks. "You don't know how much I miss you." I didn't know what to say. "Do you miss me?" he asked.

"Umm hmm," I mumbled as he lifted my t-shirt and kissed up my spine. He unlatched my bra and turned me onto my back. For a moment, he just stared at me with growing intensity, then finally said, "Man, I want you."

I smiled awkwardly and looked away while he kissed my neck. Soon, he was grinding his ten-inch near my pelvic bone. I couldn't believe the shit that was happening. First of all, me and Craig were in the same room getting along. Secondly, we were having this big sexual moment, despite the fact that we weren't together. And

239

thirdly, I was letting him have his way with me, even though he had a chick at home.

Craig slid down to my hips and kissed on my stomach. His kisses moved lower and lower, and the next thing I knew, I was moaning uncontrollably from the pleasure I felt. He worked unbelievable magic with his fingers that he would've normally performed with his tongue, satisfying me just as well. I threw a pillow over my face to muffle the screams that came out.

He reached over and grabbed his pants off the floor. Within seconds, the condom was on, and we were having sex. I can't describe how good it was. I was in another world during the whole thing. My mind was consumed with fantasies of me and Craig renewing our relationship as my body moved in unison with his. Each thrust was deep and sensual, and we were so close at times that I could feel his heartbeat. In between kisses, he caught me by surprise. "I love you so much, Meka," he said.

He kept moving, but I was out of the groove. Those three words got to me. I hadn't heard him say them since we broke up, and I didn't expect to ever hear them again.

He didn't notice that I was stagnant because he was climaxing. He lifted my pelvis off the bed, pushing himself deeper and deeper inside of me and moaned so loudly that I had to cup my hand over his mouth. Once he was empty, he collapsed on my chest and trembled. When he regained his strength, he got up and went into the bathroom. I heard the toilet flush, and soon, Craig was sitting on the bed.

I had my back to him, hoping that he wouldn't see the tear inching down my cheek. No such luck. He playfully leapt over me and prepared to make a random comment.

"What's wrong, beautiful?" he asked after seeing my face.

I cried harder, wondering why he was pulling me in with the couple lingo.

He wiped my tears. "Talk to me. Why you cryin'?"

"I don't know."

"Is this a good cry or a bad cry?"

"Bad." Once I gathered myself, I explained. "You didn't do nothin'. It's me. I'm stupid for lettin' this whole thing happen."

"What whole thing? Us makin' love?" I didn't respond. "How is that stupid? You didn't want to?"

"I didn't need to. If we wouldn't have done anything, I wouldn't be feelin' like this. But no, I had to fuck up my emotions again," I replied.

"Tameka, what we just did was real. There ain't nothin' stupid about what we just felt."

"But there's somethin' stupid about bonin' another chick's man. Three's a crowd."

"So you think I'm usin' you or somethin'?"

I nodded. "And you know what, Craig? I don't blame you. My grandma used to tell me, 'As long as somebody wants to be a dummy and let you use them, use 'em up.' I let you get in my bed. I let you kiss me. I let us go all the way, and that's why I'm the one cryin' now. And just so you know, all that extra stuff you was sayin'…that 'I love you. I miss you' garbage…It wasn't even necessary." I chuckled with disgust. "I was gon' give it up regardless, and that's sickening."

"Meka, I meant that. I wasn't just sayin' that in the heat of the moment. I love you."

"Yeah, and you'll go tell your girlfriend the same shit."

"I've never told Jacqueline that I love her. I don't love her," Craig said.

I didn't get a chance to respond because Yari knocked on my door. "Open up, Meka," she said. "I know damn well you ain't sleep."

"Hold up," I said as I threw on my t-shirt and some shorts. Craig hopped up, grabbed his clothes, and ran into the bathroom. I opened the door for her and walked back over to the bed. She looked around the room, searching for Craig.

"Where's he at?" she asked.

I pointed to the closed bathroom door.

"You think you slick," she said, smiling.

"Why you say that?" I asked, crawling back under my covers.

"Y'all was in here doin' the grown folks," she said in a slight whisper. "You are not slick! The sheets are all messed up; your hair's all over your head; he's in the bathroom; and the room smells like worn out coochie and sweat. Tell me I'm wrong."

As she stood with her hand on her hip waiting for an answer, Craig walked out of the bathroom.

"Is my boy awake now?" he asked Yari.

241

"Umm hmm," she replied. "That's what I came up here to tell Meka." She looked him up and down, searching for any clues to prove that we'd had sex.

"Alright," Craig said. "I'll go get him. That's who I came to see anyway." His attempt to cover up our act was pitiful.

As soon as she heard Craig go down one step, she walked over to my bed and sat down. "So gimme the scoop. How'd this come about?"

I confirmed her suspicions and told her how stupid I felt and how I didn't want to face Craig again.

"C'mon T. You gotta be realistic. You can't get around seein' him. You have his baby. What y'all need to do is sit down and figure out why this happened. And if it's 'cause y'all still love each other, then he needs to break up with ol' girl so y'all can get back together and stop the games," she said.

"I thought you didn't like Craig," I said.

"I like seein' you happy. And if he makes you happy, I'm happy. Just be smart. Don't let him play mind games with you again."

***

Yari left the next day, and the house was extremely quiet for the next two weeks. Lexis went to Florida with Robert on a romantic getaway, and Tielle was at another one of her conferences for radio personalities. Who else was left in town for me to kick it with? Craig. I would never admit it to anybody else, but Craig Thomas had stolen my heart again. Instinct was telling me he felt the same, but I wasn't gonna assume anything until he broke it off with Jacqueline.

Chapter 28

One afternoon, I was sitting on the couch calculating my bills. I couldn't believe it was already the first of October. While I was in the middle of deciding who was getting paid and who would have to wait, the phone rang. It was my dad. Immediately, he could tell I was stressed.

"I'm cool," I said. "I'm just lookin' at all these bills." I threw the statements on the coffee table. "I'm actually glad you called. I was about to pull my hair out."

He laughed. "Is it that bad, baby girl?"

"Worse," I replied. "But enough about that. What's up?"

He really didn't want anything. He was just calling to check on everybody. The major thing he was concerned about was Darius' doctor's appointment the previous morning.

"So how did things go?" he asked.

"They said that so far, there's no sign of HIV," I answered.

"That ain't nothin' but the Lord, sweetheart."

"I know, Daddy. I mean it when I say he's my angel," I said.

There was a long period of silence. I didn't know if he just didn't have anything else to say or if he was thinking about something. Either way, I wasn't going to hold the phone. "Well, I'ma go on and get off this phone," I said.

"Alright," Daddy said. "Hey listen. Add up all your bills for the month and call me back when you get a figure. I'll take care of 'em 'til the end of the year."

"No, Daddy. I'll be alright."

"No, I know there's a lot goin' on with you right now, and the last thing you need is the burden of finding a good, reasonable babysitter for Darius while you go back to work. Plus, I know you don't have a clean bill of health yet. Alexis told me about you looking pale and being tired all the time. Don't let your stubbornness get the best of you."

Thank you, Jesus...and Daddy.

Early in the week, Craig had called and asked me on a date. Well, I guess it really wasn't a date, but he said we needed to talk and we should do it over dinner. He instructed me to dress to impress, so it sounded like a date.

The big day had finally come, and I needed something to wear. On my way over to the closet, I stopped at Darius' crib and kissed him on the forehead.

"Mommy has to find somethin' to wear, baby," I said as I frantically pushed the hangers aside. Nothing looked appealing. I was just about to give up when I spotted a black garment bag hanging in the far right corner.

"My black dress from Tanya!" I remembered. While I was in Columbus, one of my clients at the modeling agency gave me the one-of-a-kind piece. It was sure to blow Craig's mind. If he didn't have any good news to tell me to begin with, after he saw me in that number, he would definitely change his mind.

Alexis came home while I was getting ready. She peeked her head into my doorway at about 6:30. "What time is your date?"

"Seven," I yelled from the bathroom.

"Where y'all goin'?"

"Come in here. I can't hear you over the music."

She walked over to the crib and picked Darius up, then stood in the bathroom doorway. "Oh shit! Don't hurt 'em like that!" she said, stepping back to get a better view of my dress. I laughed. "What you tryin' to do? Give the nigga a heart attack?"

I had to admit I was wearing the hell out of that dress. Every curve of my body was perfectly accented, and I was showing just enough cleavage to make a man wanna be breastfed again. After having a baby, my body was still intact, and that night, even Halle couldn't fuck with me.

"So where y'all goin'? The president's inauguration?" Alexis joked.

"I don't know. He just told me to dress to impress," I replied. "Can you help me with this?" I asked, handing her a bobby pin to put in my French roll.

"Well, you dressed to cardiac arrest," she said, laughing at her own joke. She handed Darius to me and finished my hair. After she

244

was done, she took him back so I could add the finishing touches to my look.

"Where's that one necklace? The diamond one," she asked while I was putting my earrings in.

"You think I should wear it?"

"Why not? That'll set the dress off!"

"I thought about wearin' it, but TJ bought it for me," I said.

"And?" Alexis replied. "What? You can't wear nothin' he got you around Craig? Please. You betta stop trippin'."

So it was settled. I wore my diamond necklace with my droplet earrings and my long black dress. I prayed that I wasn't all dressed up for nothing. What if Craig was gonna tell me he was staying with Jacqueline?

I tried not to think negatively when I heard the doorbell ring. Alexis was in the bathroom, so I got up from the dining room table and answered the door. Craig stood on the other side, looking oh so scrumptious. He had on a black suit with a white shirt and a black and silver tie. His hair was freshly cut, and his waves were smoother than ever.

"Damn!" he said, looking me up and down. "You lookin' good, girl."

I smiled and stepped aside so he could come in.

"You lettin' her walk around lookin' like this, man?" he asked Darius, who was in my arms.

Alexis came out of the bathroom and took the baby. "Go on and get outta here so y'all can come back and take care of this rug rat," she said.

"She might not be home," Craig said as he helped me put my coat on.

That had to be a good sign. I was hoping it meant that he had nothing but good things to tell me over dinner…and I was right. While we sat at an intimate table at Claude's, the same table we sat at on our first date, he told me that I'd never forget the evening for the rest of my life. He then signaled for the waiter to come over with a bottle of wine. As he filled our glasses, another waiter came to the table with a bouquet of white roses.

"For you, Madam," he said.

"Thank you," I replied. I was a little embarrassed because everybody in the restaurant was staring at us. "So is tonight the remix version of our first date?" I asked Craig. "Same restaurant, roses…"

"That's not the same amount of roses," he said.

"Oh. Did I lose one?"

"Count 'em," he said.

I counted thirteen.

"I gave you an extra one because I've never met a woman like you. I mean, it may seem a little too late for me to be realizing this, but I guess I had to search elsewhere to realize what I had all along. Your qualities go far beyond the twelve I used to look for, and I admire that. You have so much on your plate right now, and you're still walkin' around, stronger than ever. Most people would've folded under the pressure. And I know I'm runnin' the risk of soundin' corny, but there was once a time when I told you that I'd never given any female a whole dozen of roses, and I'm givin' you the extra rose to let you know that nobody will ever compare to you—not even Jacqueline."

"She didn't get twelve?" I asked.

"Eleven," he said.

I couldn't control the smile on my face. I felt like I'd won the Miss America crown or something. Craig reached across the table and held my hand. "I'm done bein' wishy-washy, as you put it. I want you in my life. I know I've got some serious makin' up to do for the stupid things I've said and done in the past, but I'll do whatever it takes to get you back." He took a deep breath and nervously awaited my answer.

"Well, I don't know," I said in a snappy voice as I snatched my hand away from his. Craig's eyes opened wide with disbelief. I couldn't continue my joke any longer. I reached across the table and pulled his face towards mine. "I'm just playin'," I said and kissed him softly. He prolonged the kiss, but we stopped when we heard some people in the restaurant saying, "Aww…"

While we ate, he told me the story of how he broke up with Jacqueline. She told him that she expected him to "pull this shit." To prove to me that they were through, he took me to his place and let me search for any trace of her. I found nothing. Then, he let me hear a couple of her "Go to hell" messages on his answering machine.

We left his apartment and went back to my place because I felt guilty leaving Darius with Lexis all night. Craig understood and decided to stay with me. We didn't even have sex that night. Instead, we laid in bed with him enveloping me in his arms.

That night, I learned that penetration wasn't required to make love. Being in love with Craig again and hearing him whisper that he couldn't live without me gave me the same tingles I felt during intercourse, and that was deep—deeper than his manhood could ever go.

***

One day, me and Craig were having a casual conversation when he dropped a big question on me.

"How do you feel about livin' together before marriage?" he asked.

"Shackin' up?" I responded.

"Damn! You ain't gotta put it like that," he said.

"Why you ask that?"

"I'm movin' into my condo on the first, and I wanna know if you're coming with me."

My heart started pounding. That was a huge step. I'd never even entertained that thought, so I wasn't prepared to respond. "Where is this comin' from?" I asked. "You've never asked me to live with you, even when we were at the peak of our relationship. I thought you were comfortable with us livin' apart."

"But Darius wasn't in the picture then."

"So you think we should live together now that we have a child?"

"That's not what I'm sayin'. We're startin' over, and I think livin' together would make our relationship stronger. Plus, it would take a load off you financially."

"I ain't tryin' to move in with you so you can take care of me," I said. "You can cancel that."

"Baby, I'm not sayin' I want you to sit up in the house and not work. I know you ain't gon' let me take care of you like that. I just wanna lighten the burden. And Darius can have his own room 'cause it's a three-bedroom. I know your lease is up in December, so it's not like you have to stay here," he said.

"You've got this all figured out, huh?" I asked. He smiled and shrugged his shoulders. "Stop grinnin'," I said.

"So what's your answer?"

"I guess," I replied. "But it won't be 'til the end of November. I gotta tell Lexis so she can get stuff squared away, too."

"She gon' trip."

"Naw, she'll be cool. She was thinkin' about movin' in with Robert anyway."

"So we gon' be roommates?"

247

"That's what it's lookin' like," I said. "I'll give you a definite answer tomorrow, though."

I talked to Nicole and Tielle that same evening. Nicole was a little leery about me making the move. She felt that Craig would probably return to his old, indecisive ways and I'd regret leaving the comfort of my own home. She made a lot of valid points that I knew would linger in my mind and possibly affect my decision.

Tielle was her usual, cool self when she offered her opinion. She didn't want to say too much, so she just asked a lot of questions that made me examine the pros and cons more closely. Her angle was geared toward seeing where my head was. When our conversation was over, she left me with the impression that Craig's offer could be a step toward something bigger…maybe as big as a lifetime commitment. I didn't wanna take her input lightly, since she had the inside track.

I went to bed that night feeling a little confused. I had one friend with a subtle vote of yes, and another with an obvious vote of no. I couldn't wait for Lexis to return home the next day so she could break the tie. Deep down, I knew I wanted to try living with Craig, but I couldn't find a way to block out the heartbreak he caused me in the past. At about two in the morning, I finally closed my eyes and prayed for an answer as I drifted off to sleep.

The phone rang at ten o'clock the next morning. The caller ID read, "Unavailable." *It must be a telemarketer*, I thought as I answered with an attitude.

"Meka," TJ said.

I couldn't answer. I wasn't expecting to hear from him.

"I need to talk to you. I need to see you," he continued.

"What's goin' on? Why are you soundin' like that?" I asked.

"Can I please just come over there? I'll only stay like twenty minutes."

I reluctantly agreed to the visit. I racked my brain, thinking of why he would need to see me so urgently. The only other time I'd heard him sound like that was about two years prior when he was running from the cops and was scared to death of going to the penitentiary.

I didn't have to wonder long because he was at my door within five minutes. I let him in, and the first thing he did was hug me.

Whoa, I thought as I kicked the door shut. *What is this?*

He finally loosened his grip, but still had me by my waist. "You don't know how good that felt," he said. "I miss you, baby girl."

248

Too Little, Too Late

I frowned. "Travis, is this you? The TJ I know doesn't want anything to do with me."

"I ain't here to argue about what went down with us," TJ said as he walked over and looked at Darius, who was laying on the couch.

"Damn, he's gettin' big," he said. "He's startin' to look like you." He paused for a moment, then turned around to face me again. "You know I was heated when you said that you wasn't fuckin' wit' me no more, right? But honestly, that was the best thing you coulda done for me—for us."

Here we go with this 'us' shit again.

"TJ—"

"Wait a minute," he interrupted. "Havin' to go that long without talkin' to you or seein' you opened my eyes. I mean, before when we broke up or whatever, it was different 'cause we always ended up back together after like a week. This time, you wasn't bullshittin'. You wouldn't return my pages or my phone calls, and that shit drove me crazy."

"I'm sorry to hear that," I said, trying to stay strong in the midst of his effort to break me down. I sat down in the chair.

"Don't be sorry," he said as he walked over to me and kneeled down by my legs. "Do somethin' about it." He reached for my hand. "Meka, I can't do this shit without you. I can't live my life the same. The shit don't feel right. You've always been there for me, and not havin' you around is eatin' me up. And you know I'm not playin', 'cause I'm on my knees and shit."

"Why now?" I asked as I looked into his eyes. He was finally saying all the words I'd been waiting to hear for years, but it was too late.

"The other day I heard them niggas was askin' about me, tryin' to find out where I stay now. It's been years since I robbed dude, and they still won't let that shit go…draggin' you in it… I've been thinkin' about what you said. You were right. It's a endless cycle. I don't even wanna fuck wit' them niggas, but they still comin' after me over some old shit. I'm tryin' to chill."

He was rambling, but I tried to stay with him.

"I always told you I know what I need to do to be with you for real, and that's what I wanna do. That's what I'm here to do. I'm tired of the streets, baby girl. I'm through. They ain't done nothin' positive except get me some paper. Other than that, I can only remember that shit gettin' you raped and infected. I can't take that back, baby girl, but I can tell you what I'm willin' to do now."

249

I couldn't interject because I was crying. I absolutely lost it when he reached in his pocket and pulled out a black velvet ring box.

"You already know what I'm 'bout to ask you," he said as he wiped some of my tears. "I've loved you ever since I first laid eyes on you, and I told you that night that I was gon' make you mine. I never thought I'd say this, but forever with you wouldn't be long enough for me. But since that's all I can get, I'll take it. I want you to be my wife, Meka."

He opened the box and damn near blinded me. The princess cut pink diamond was surrounded by smaller diamonds and mounted on a platinum band...Breathtaking.

"I can't do this, TJ," I said.

"I know everything ain't gon' change overnight, but I knew if I came at you, I had to be for real. I'm not tryin' to scare you off, baby. I'm tryin' to do the stuff we been talkin' 'bout for years." He slid the ring onto my limp finger. "I figure for starters we can move away from here so these niggas won't be a problem. Then—"

"Stop!" I yelled. "Please stop." I fought to speak through my sobs. "Why couldn't you say this stuff a week ago? Why did you have to come over here and do this to me? There was a time when I would've killed to hear you say this to me, and I would've been ready to go to Vegas and get it done right away. But you can't pull this shit on me now. I just got back with Craig last week. Don't do this to me." I clenched the hair on the top of my head in frustration.

"Where is your heart?" TJ asked.

With my face buried in my lap, I simply shook my head back and forth. When he first arrived, I could've answered his question with confidence, but after his proposal, I didn't know what to tell him.

Darius whined as he began to wake up.

"Look. I'm about to go. My twenty minutes are up. I got my point across, so get at me when you find out where your heart is," he said as he stood up.

As I walked him to the door, I looked down at my hand. "Don't forget the ring," I said, extending my hand for him to take it off.

"Hold on to it," he said as he stepped outside. "I'm leavin' regardless, but I'll stay in town until I hear somethin' from you."

After he left, I sat on the couch and tried to calm Darius down. I don't know how I expected him to stop crying when he could look at my face and see the small pond I was creating. I was having a hell of a time with him when Alexis came home. I had never been so glad to see my sister in my life. When she first walked in, she was fumbling with her shoes as she took them off by the door.

"Girl, I stepped in some mud on the way in here," she said once she entered the living room. She looked at my damp face. "Aw shit. What done happened now?" she asked.

I started off telling her about Craig's proposal for us to move in together.

"Well, it's cool with me as long as it's cool with you," she responded. "I already told you that I might stay wit Robert when the lease is up, so I got somewhere to go. Do you really wanna live with him, though? I mean, y'all did just get back together. What if the shit don't go as planned?"

"That's only half of my drama. TJ was just over here not too long ago."

"For what?"

I pointed to the ring lying on the coffee table. She picked it up and looked back at me. "You shittin' me," she said. I shook my head. "So you accepted?"

"No."

"Well why is the ring still here?" She was still admiring it, and even slid it on her finger.

"He wouldn't take it back," I said.

"Did you offer to give it back? I mean *really* tell him to take it back?"

"I told him about me and Craig, and I told him to take the ring back. He wouldn't take it 'cause I couldn't tell him that I've completely given my heart to Craig."

"So you havin' second thoughts about you and Craig now?"

"How could I not? I'm just confused right now. I don't even have the energy to think about who I wanna be with."

"I'm trippin' 'cause TJ came outta nowhere with this," Lexis said.

"The marriage thing is out the blue, but he's been pagin' me and leavin' messages for weeks."

"It's gon' boil down to who you want in Darius' life. Do you want his role model to be a cute thug who loves you or a cute professional who loves you and is his father? Now don't think I'm takin' sides, 'cause you know TJ was my boy and I can only stand Craig for so long, but you need to think of the lifestyle you wanna have. Fuckin' wit' TJ, you'll be runnin' scared for the rest of your life. We both know that most niggas in the street don't let shit rest

251

until they put their enemies to rest. I know he can't expect you to fall for that 'Let's move away' bullshit."

"I can't talk about this no more today," I said.

"I understand. We can talk about it tomorrow if you want." She took another look at the ring. "This thing gotta be like five carats, though! TJ knew what he was doin'."

I went upstairs and stretched out on my bed. For the longest, I just stared at the ceiling. My eyelids occasionally fell, but I didn't get any rest. Sleep, yes, but no comfort. I got up at one and fixed a couple hotdogs and some French fries. I picked over the food and took my medicine, hoping that one of the pills would also work for a confused heart.

Things didn't work out that way, so I moped around the house for the majority of the day. Tielle called and invited me to the mall, but I told her about my love triangle, and she understood why I didn't want to be out and about. She couldn't even offer me advice on who to choose. I thought for sure that she'd have something to say about TJ's career, or lack thereof, but she didn't go there. She just acknowledged that my history with him made my decision harder to make, and that Craig needed to come up off of a ring soon instead of just talking about shacking up.

Craig had been calling all day, but I avoided contact until early in the evening. Before then, I hadn't decided whether I was gonna tell him about TJ's proposal or not. The final decision: No. He didn't need to know until I could tell him what my answer was and be able to justify it. We talked for about twenty minutes and I tried to sound like I was in high spirits, but I was sounding more unconvincing by the minute. He opted not to come over for the evening because he could tell I wasn't in a good mood…

And I stayed that way for the next two weeks. The pages and phone calls from TJ were driving me crazy, and Craig nagging about moving in with him wasn't helping. I was almost on the brink of exploding before Tielle called one afternoon and said she was taking me to dinner. She wanted me to get out the house so I could think about something other than the commotion stirring in my life.

We walked into Bernice's, a small soul food restaurant, on Thursday evening. The place was packed, so we had to wait a half hour to be seated.

"Damn! I can't believe all these people are up in here," I said as we followed the waitress to the table.

"You know how folks are," Tielle said. "It's Christmas season, so everybody's been out shoppin' and they don't feel like cookin'."

"I guess," I said as I slid into the booth. "I'm just happy to be out the house and away from that damn phone."

Tielle laughed. "So did TJ call again before I came and got you?"

"You know he did," I replied. "I swear he's called me more these past few days than he did all last year."

"You know they don't realize they messed up until you're happy and in love with somebody else. Look at Maurice. I'll be damned if that dude don't call me at least once every two weeks just to see how I'm doin'."

"Romeo don't say nothin' no more?"

"He knows I ain't goin' nowhere."

"Is that right?" I said, impressed that Tielle was feeling Romeo enough to say that. Maurice had always been number one in her life, no matter how much she denied it before.

She had a Kool-Aid grin on her face as she placed her hands on the table and flipped through the menu. I didn't pay much attention to her because I was looking at my own menu, but something caught my eye when I looked up to ask her if the catfish was any good. My mouth fell open when I saw an engagement ring on her finger.

"You are fuckin' kiddin' me?" I asked as I grabbed her left hand and gazed at the rock. "When did this happen?"

Romeo proposed to her at her mother's house the night before. As she told the story, I could've sworn I saw cool-ass Tielle's eyes water for a second. I was instructed to keep the news on the hush until she invited everyone to their engagement party, which was scheduled for November 15th—exactly one week away.

Once we ordered our food, I told Tielle how happy I was for her. She sensed that I was about to go off on a tangent about my "you, me, and he" dilemma, so she quickly changed the subject. Still, the thoughts never left my head, and I vowed to make my decision of who I wanted to be with by the end of the upcoming week.

After some serious soul searching, I chose Craig. He wooed me from day one, and I believed he could do it again as soon as I let the past stay in the past. I figured it wasn't everyday that a chick with HIV had a man who still wanted to be with her and take care of his child, too.

And yes, TJ would've offered me the same things emotionally, but it would've helped if he had a job and a stable lifestyle to go along with it. I knew he wanted to change, but he should've made those changes before he proposed. I didn't want to be part of the transition.

I knew I had to tell TJ the news. I'd finally given Craig an absolute answer about moving in with him, so it was time to fill TJ in. I had a problem, though. I couldn't bring myself to call him, and I still wouldn't return his pages. At some point, he was bound to catch up with me, and that point happened to be the night of Tielle and Romeo's engagement party. Lexis and I were rushing around the house, looking for her silver purse so we could leave. We knew that parking was gonna be hell at the Marriott, so we wanted to be early.

"I gave Tiffany my cell number, right?" I asked Lexis. I'd taken Darius to her house an hour earlier so she could babysit during the party.

"About ten times," she replied. "Will you relax? That girl has three kids. She knows what she's doin'.""

I grabbed my keys off the end table and turned the doorknob. I was looking back at Alexis to see why she was still in the kitchen as I stepped outside and ran into TJ's chest.

Fuck me! I thought as I apologized to him and took a step backward.

"Where you been?" he asked.

"Busy," I said. "Actually, I'm about to leave right now."

Alexis came to the door and spoke to TJ. "We leavin', right?" she asked, trying to save me.

"Where y'all goin'?" TJ asked.

"To Tielle and Romeo's engagement party," I said.

"Damn. They doin' it like that, huh? When's our party?" he asked.

"I'll be in the car," Alexis said, squeezing past us.

I fumbled with my keys, searching for a gentle answer.

He nodded toward my left hand. "So is that why you've been avoidin' me?"

"I didn't know how to tell you, but I guess you've figured it out. I'm stayin' with Craig."

You woulda thought I cut his chest open and stabbed him in the heart. I couldn't look in his eyes and see the pain I'd caused. "I just wanna know why," he said.

I explained my reasons, barely holding my tears back.

"Can't say a nigga didn't try, right?" he said, trying to laugh his embarrassment away.

"I'm sorry, TJ. You don't know how hard I struggled to make this decision."

"It's cool. Shit happens, right?"

"You wanna talk for a little bit? I don't want you to leave, thinkin' that I don't love you or care about you anymore. Your timing was just off."

"Your heart doesn't run on a timer," he replied.

That hit home for me and made me question my decision. Nevertheless, I stuck to my guns and stood silently while he finished.

"It's all good. I ain't got no hard feelings." He played with his fingernails to avoid eye contact. "I'm leavin' Monday. I was only hangin' around here to see what you was gon' do. Now that I got your answer, I ain't gon' waste no more time here. If you wanna get at me, you know my numbers."

I didn't know what else to say besides, "Hold on. Let me get your ring."

"Keep it. I ain't got no use for it. You know I don't keep receipts, and I don't want no store credit. That's a bitch move to ask for the ring back."

"Alright," I said, throwing my hands up helplessly.

"You know what? I do want somethin'," TJ said.

"What?"

"A goodbye kiss. You practically a married woman, movin' in with dude, and I'm leavin' town, so I ain't gon' get to do this again."

He thought he was slick, but I played along. It was the least I could do, and a part of me was extremely happy to fulfill his request. I leaned forward and gave him a peck on his soft lips. The peck turned into two minutes of non-stop tongue wrestling. We only stopped because Lexis blew the horn.

"I gotta go," I said, quickly pulling away. I couldn't believe that was the end of us. After I locked the door, we hugged.

"Take care of yourself, baby girl," he said softly.

After he walked away, I jogged to Alexis' car and got in. She backed out of the parking space and said, "I'd hate to be you."

***

We found a parking spot near the front entrance and walked through the gold-trimmed glass doors of the hotel. The ballroom was packed. The atmosphere was sophisticated and warm, which helped me stay calm. I was one TJ flashback away from an emotional breakdown. Lexis and I went straight to the bar and ordered drinks,

255

then we eased our way into the main area to mingle with the folks we knew.

By midnight, I'd consumed at least five drinks and was feeling a little queasy. I intended to drink my cares away, and I was getting pretty close. I sat down at one of the tables, hoping I'd feel a little better, and I did until 12:27. I remember looking at my watch right before I got an excruciating, shooting pain in my stomach. It was the worse pain I had ever felt in my life, making my Columbus experience seem like a minor toothache. The agony only lasted a few seconds, then stopped. I didn't have a chance to recover before my two-way vibrated.

Right away, I knew something was wrong. I flipped up the screen, took a deep breath, and read the message.

Meka, call me ASAP. It's Carlos.

Carlos was one of TJ's best friends, and I couldn't think of any reason he'd contact me except if something was wrong. I took my cell phone out of my purse and called him.

"What's goin' on?" I asked.

"Where are you?"

"At the Marriott out east. Why?" There was a long pause. "Hello?"

"Shit ain't good, Meka," Carlos finally said. His voice was quivering.

"Un unh, Carlos. What's that supposed to mean?" Silence again. "Carlos, you better not tell me what I think you're about to tell me." I was almost in tears. "Where's TJ?" He didn't answer. "Where is he?" I screamed. Everyone within twenty feet stared at me.

"He's gone, Meka," Carlos said. "They shot him."

"No!" I yelled. I held the phone away from my ear.

Alexis was standing nearby, so she snatched it from my shaking hand. "Who is this?" she asked.

Carlos explained the encounter to Alexis. He said that he, TJ, and their other friend, Jeff, were out at the bar. TJ went to his car to get something, but he never came back. When they went out to look for him, they found him in his car, shot six times, with no pulse. He seemed almost certain that Smoke or one of his affiliates had committed the crime.

"Where are you now?" Alexis asked, quickly wiping the tear that ran down her cheek.

"I'm at the hospital waitin' on his grandma to get here. Jeff went to get her."

Alexis stayed on the phone and bombarded Carlos with more questions. Meanwhile, Craig, Tielle, and Romeo surrounded my chair, begging me to talk. I felt cold all over as I shivered with shock. No matter what they asked me, all I said was, "He killed him." They were getting understandably frustrated with me because they didn't know what I was talking about.

Alexis told them about the shooting after she hung up with Carlos. Tielle covered her face with her hands as Romeo put his arm around her. Craig immediately embraced me but didn't say a word. I buried my face in his chest and cried even harder.

***

Alexis got Tielle's attention and they walked to a nearby corner.

"Carlos wants Meka at the hospital," she said.

"For what? What can she do?" Tielle asked.

"Well you know she's close to TJ's grandma, so I guess he wants her there to calm her down. You know him and Jeff don't know what to say."

"She can't even talk right now," Tielle said. "How is she supposed to calm somebody else down? I don't think you should take her. It'll only make things worse." She leaned on the wall. "I can't believe he's dead. We all knew he lived a little foul, but I never expected him to get caught up like this. Not TJ. He was usually smarter than that."

"Sometimes bein' smart can't help you," Alexis replied. She took a deep breath. "Well, I guess I'ma just take her home."

"You need me to come?" Tielle asked.

"This is your party, girl. Enjoy your night."

"The party's almost over anyway," Tielle said. "We only rented the room until 1:30. Besides, I can't enjoy myself when I know my best friend is in so much pain. Let me go get my purse."

"Stay here," Lexis said, firmly grabbing Tielle's arm. "I know how to get in touch with you if I need you."

***

The car ride home was hectic. I begged and pleaded with Alexis to take me to the hospital, but she wouldn't. When we pulled up to the house, I refused to get out of the car. She tried to pull me out, but her efforts failed. After about five minutes of us wrestling, Craig pulled up, got out of his car, and relieved her. I still tried to resist

257

him, but he just scooped me out of the passenger seat like I was weightless and carried me into the house and up to my room.

"Why are y'all doin' this to me?" I asked Craig. "I just wanna go see him."

He didn't say anything. He just lowered me onto my bed. When he tried to release me, I wouldn't let go. I locked my arms around his neck, holding on for dear life. "I can't believe y'all doin' this to me," I yelled.

He sat on the bed and held me in his arms like I was Darius as I whimpered. He gently rocked me and ran his fingers through my hair. His lips lightly made contact with my forehead and remained there. "Let it out, baby. It's alright," he said.

Alexis came to the door. "I just called Tiffany, and she said she'd keep Darius overnight," she said.

Craig simply nodded his head, not wanting to take his attention off of me.

"Is she alright?" Alexis mouthed.

Craig nodded again, then used hand signals to let her know he was gonna stay the night.

"Well, I guess I'll say goodnight now," Lexis said. She walked over and kissed me on the cheek. "You hang in there. Try to get some sleep."

Craig dressed me for bed. When we were under the covers, he pulled my waist toward him and stayed up with me until I fell asleep.

I woke up to a ringing phone the next morning. It was Ms. Pearl calling with the dates and times for TJ's wake and funeral. I could only say goodbye once, so I told her I'd be at his funeral, two days away.

"I can't take this shit," I said as I rolled over and faced Craig. "I feel like the walls are closin' in on me." I clenched his t-shirt and wrapped my leg around his.

"You gotta be strong, baby. It's not gonna be like this forever."

I had stopped believing that. The whole *Annie* theme, where "the sun'll come out tomorrow," wasn't convincing me. I didn't know how to cope with TJ's death, so I chose not to even try. I stayed in bed the whole day, attempting to sleep the pain away.

The day of the funeral, I was doing a little better. I had stopped crying and wasn't having any more nightmares about TJ's murder. At first, I wasn't gonna go to the service because I thought it would only make me feel worse. But after I prayed about it, I decided that seeing him could give me closure.

I asked Craig not to go because I wanted to say goodbye to TJ alone. I didn't need him crowding around me, telling me that everything was gonna be alright because it wasn't. My TJ was dead, and that wasn't alright. I think he understood that he didn't belong at the funeral, but he was worried about how I'd act once I finally saw him lying in the casket. To ease his mind, we agreed that he would wait in his car outside the church in case I needed him when it was over.

Tielle picked up me and Alexis. "Y'all alright?" she asked before we left the parking lot.

"For now," Alexis answered.

Tielle looked over at me. "T?" I shook my head, signaling that I didn't want to talk about it.

When we arrived at the church, a weird aura came over me. My breaths became labored, and my body was overcome with chills. Alexis and Tielle escorted me through the heavy wooden doors. The hallway was crowded with people I didn't know and miscellaneous chatter filled my ears. We made our way past everyone and entered the sanctuary. Straight ahead, the shiny, black casket trimmed was showcased under the bright lights and surrounded by a ton of flowers. My heart sank as I paused in the entryway to gather myself. We had ten minutes to view the body before the family's processional.

"You don't have to go up there if you don't want to," Tielle said.

I swallowed hard, took a deep breath, and started my journey down the middle aisle. The burgundy carpeted walkway seemed like it went on forever, and I kinda wished it would've because I wasn't prepared for what was at the end. All eyes were on me as I approached the casket. I closed my eyes for a few seconds, then opened them quickly and looked down.

TJ had on a midnight blue suit with a matching silk shirt, the first two buttons unfastened. It was exactly how he would've worn it if he was still alive. I lifted my hands from the side of the casket and touched him gently on his cheek.

"I'm so sorry I couldn't be there for you. I tried to come out to the hospital." I wiped my tears. "They wouldn't take me out there. I tried, baby. I promise I did." I stroked his goatee. "I promise."

I rested my hand on his chest and stared at him. *He can't respond*, I thought. *He's gone. Sorry won't cut it now.*

I shook my head in disbelief as one of my tears dropped on his right hand. I wiped it off, and as I went to remove my hand from his,

259

I remembered when I grabbed his hand the night he was shot. Why did I wait so long to tell him that I couldn't accept his marriage proposal?

His words, "Your heart doesn't run on a timer," echoed in my head over and over, and suddenly, it hit me.

"Oh my God!" I yelled. Alexis and Tielle ran over to me.

"What's wrong?" they asked simultaneously.

I ignored them. "Oh my God!" I repeated as I raised my trembling hands to my mouth. "I killed you. I'm the reason why he caught up with you," I said quietly.

They tried to pull me away from the casket, but I wouldn't budge. "You waited around for me, and I fucked you around for a whole week!" I cried hysterically, almost to the point where I couldn't breathe. "TJ, I'm sorry, baby." My knees gave out as I screamed in agony, and the room went black.

Everything else was a blur. Lexis told me I passed out for a couple minutes, and when I came to, I just wanted to lie down. The only thing I vaguely remember is curling up in Tielle's backseat and crying the whole way home, feeling just as responsible for TJ's death as Smoke.

That feeling didn't go away until five days later. Like I normally do when I'm depressed, I stayed in my room, but this time was a little different. I was a complete zombie. I wouldn't talk to anybody; Craig, Lexis, or Tielle had to wash me up because I wouldn't make an effort to do it, and I didn't take any of my medicine.

The fifth day was the worst because the lack of medication in my system was starting to affect me. Unlike the other four days, I couldn't move if I wanted to, partially because I hadn't eaten anything more than a couple of crackers that Tielle forced into my mouth. "Weak" couldn't even describe my state. Toward the middle of the day, every breath I took seemed like it could've been my last, and I feared for my life. I hadn't spoken with Craig since before the funeral, but I found enough energy to tell him to call my doctor.

He, Tielle, and Alexis had been debating all week on whether they should call, but they probably knew I was strong enough to put up a fight and not cooperate then. While they were devising a plan for intervention, I was contemplating on whether I was gonna give up on everything or try to press on. For the first time in my life, I had suicidal thoughts. I thought about overdosing on my pills, but then I figured I could just continue the destructive path of not taking my medicine at all. I didn't wanna suffer long, so I decided that those methods wouldn't have worked for me.

I never had to deal with the death of someone so close to me, and I didn't think there was any way to handle it besides making the memory of the person disappear. And the only way I could make TJ's memory disappear was to make myself disappear. I lived that man. I didn't just love him. I didn't realize how crazy that sounded until three days after the funeral when I pulled my gun out of the bottom drawer of my nightstand and slowly lifted it to my temple. The cold metal grazed my skin as I rubbed it back and forth, bracing myself for what I was about to feel. I took a deep breath as I placed my sweaty index finger on the trigger and closed my eyes. I thought about how one bullet could take all my troubles away. I was tired of being strong and thinking of new ways to cope each time a problem arose. Still, I couldn't do it. How could I use the weapon TJ bought for my protection to aid in my demise? How could I leave my son without a mother?

Needless to say, I returned the gun to its original place that day and didn't pull it out again. I stared at the bottom drawer as I recalled that day and waited for Craig to get off the phone. He was speaking with my new specialist, Dr. Moore.

"When do I go?" I asked after he ended the call.

"You don't," he answered. "Dr. Moore's nurse and some counselor lady are comin' here." He sat down on the bed and tucked my hair behind my ear. "I'm glad you're comin' out of your slump."

I moved my left cheek, hoping that it looked like a smile. Craig was being extremely understanding and supportive, and I knew that couldn't have been easy. He sat in the room with me for days, missing work and watching me shut down because of my ex-boyfriend's death. I barely talked to him, and when I did, I wasn't pleasant. If there was ever a test of his loyalty to me, that was it, and he passed with flying colors.

Chapter 29

Alexis led Dr. Moore's nurse, Lori, and Cathy, the counselor, up to my room. As Lori checked my vitals, Cathy stood near the doorway and talked to Craig and Lexis.

"...So she hasn't been talking at all?" Cathy asked, almost whispering.

"She won't talk, and she won't eat. She'll barely move," Alexis replied. "We've had to wash her up for the past five days."

"Do you feel she may be suicidal?" Cathy asked.

"Naw," Craig said. "She gets in these slumps sometimes. Most of the time, she just needs to be alone. She's done this before, just not to this extent."

"Do you agree?" Cathy asked Alexis.

"I don't think she'd kill herself," Alexis replied.

"How has she been with her son?"

"She hasn't had any contact with him. I didn't want him to see her like this," Craig replied.

"Like we told you before, she hasn't done anything. She won't move on her own, much less hold my nephew. Me and Craig, and Darius' godmother have been takin' care of him," Alexis added.

Before Cathy could respond, Lori walked over to them. "She's very dehydrated, and her lack of nutrients worries me. For a normal, healthy individual, that would worry me, but her HIV-positive status puts this on a different playing field. I called the hospital, and they're going to send some technicians out so we can get her started on an IV. We need to replenish her system as quickly as possible."

"How long will she need that?" Alexis asked.

"It depends. It's probably safe to say two to three days, though. A nurse will have to be here around the clock as well..."

They continued their conversation until the technicians came. While they were setting me up, Cathy suggested that Craig and

Alexis write down a few key points to remember when dealing with someone in my emotional state. Craig couldn't find any paper on my dresser, so Alexis told him to look in my nightstand.

My eyes opened wide as he reached for the top handle and pulled out the drawer. I looked helplessly at my arm, wishing I had the strength to grab his hand and stop him. Before I was even able to move my finger, it was too late. His eyes were fixated on the engagement ring TJ gave me.

"You see some?" Alexis asked. "She usually keeps a notepad or somethin' in there." She walked to the side of my bed and looked over Craig's shoulder.

"Shit," Alexis said through clenched teeth once she saw the ring. Thinking fast, she ignored it. "There it is," she said. "Hand me that yellow pad right there."

He never moved, so she reached over him, grabbed the notepad and closed the drawer. Craig stayed in his state of stupor while Alexis wrote everything down. I chose to take the easy way out for the moment by closing my eyes and pretending I was invisible. There was no way I could explain why I never told Craig about the ring, and I didn't want to hear his mouth about how shady that was.

After everyone left, Craig escorted Alexis to the hallway.

"Did he give her that ring?" he asked, referring to TJ.

"Yeah."

"When?"

"I don't know. Like a month ago, I guess."

"A month?"

"Shh!" Alexis pulled my door so that it was only cracked.

"I'm just findin' this out after a whole month? Mind you, I said 'findin' out' instead of 'bein' told.'"

"Look. You need to calm down. I ain't got nothin' to do with that. And Meka probably didn't know how to tell you."

"That's bullshit."

"Okay, so you mad now. What you gon' do? Leave her again?"

He glared at Alexis. "You know that ain't the case, but you act like this is just a old phone number or somethin'," he said.

"It's only as big as you make it, Craig. You want the story? TJ called her out the blue and asked to come over. When he got here, he proposed. She told him y'all got back together, but he told her to keep the ring until she made a final decision. You don't know what she went through, tryin' to figure out how she could refuse a marriage proposal from a man she still loved. Then, she had you on

263

the other hand, who all of a sudden wanted to act right, but you wasn't offerin' up no ring. It was a fucked up situation to be in. But naw, it ain't over yet. When she finally made up her mind, she told you she'd move in with you but didn't tell him. And she probably still wouldn't have told him, but he—"

"I know," Craig interrupted. "He died."

"No. He showed up at our house the night he died. Meka told him she was gon' start over with your punk ass before we went to the hotel."

Craig looked away, embarrassed that he was so angry about the ring.

"Speechless, huh?" Alexis asked. "Yeah, so is TJ. And you up in here about to throw a fit, knowin' Meka ain't strong enough to deal with no shit from you right now. You mad over a dead man's ring."

"Let it go, Lexis. I have," Craig said, about to walk down the steps.

"Have you? 'Cause if you haven't, you need to get outta my sister's life now. I'm not gonna watch her suffer over some shit she can change. I did it before, but I won't do it again. She can't remove the virus from her body, and she can't find Smoke and lock him up, but she can get rid of a nigga who don't mean her no good. You decide whether you gon' a problem or a solution and holla at me," she said.

He walked halfway down the staircase.

"Count your blessings, Craig. You got the girl and a beautiful son in one package. TJ got killed. Who should have the attitude?"

***

On November 24th, I was feeling a lot better. My strength was almost back to normal and for the most part, I wasn't depressed. It was amazing to see how much of the outside world I had missed while I was confined to my bedroom. I had stayed in my room so long that I'd forgotten about the big event unfolding all me. There were cardboard boxes of all sizes stacked on top of each other lining every wall downstairs. When I looked at my day planner, I realized I was supposed to move in with Craig that day.

Craig, Romeo, Tielle, Alexis, and Robert loaded the truck and were able to move everything in two trips. By six o'clock, my dresser and a couple of mirrors were the only things left on the truck. Robert and Craig carried the dresser while Tielle held the screen door open for them. Meanwhile, Alexis tried to be Superwoman, struggling to carry the mirror that went with the dresser.

"Meka, come here," Tielle said, cracking up. "You gotta see this."

I picked Darius up and walked over to the door. I couldn't help but laugh as I watched my sister damn near buckle to her knees from the weight of the mirror.

"Lexis, why don't you put the mirror down?" I said finally.

"I got it!" she yelled.

In the midst of our laughter, I noticed a black Acura driving unusually slowly. The music was just loud enough to hear the bass thump, and the windows were tinted. I squinted to get a better look as the car drove closer to the condo. No one else seemed to be paying attention, but for some reason, I had a funny feeling about the vehicle.

"I'm goin' back inside," I said. "It's too chilly out here for Darius."

As I walked to the couch, I tried my best to convince myself that I was tripping. My instinct was telling me that Smoke might've been in that car, but my logic told me that he couldn't have found me that quickly. We were way on the other side of town. He could only do that if he had been watching my old place and followed…*Oh shit! What if he followed me to Craig's place?*

I was thinking too much. "Tameka, calm down," I said, taking a deep breath. For all I knew, it could've been somebody looking for their friend's condo. There was probably no need for me to get all worked up about a stupid car.

Romeo walked through the living room. "Do they need some more help?" he asked before he passed me. I was too caught up in my thoughts to answer him. "Tameka!" he called.

"What?" I asked, flinching. Darius started crying.

"You alright?"

"I'm fine," I answered as I comforted Darius.

"Baby, come help Lexis," Tielle called from the doorway.

When he went outside, he must've said something to Craig, because as soon as he and Robert took the dresser upstairs, he came back down and sat beside me on the couch. "What's wrong, beautiful?" he asked after he kissed me on the cheek.

"I'm fine, Craig," I said impatiently.

"Maybe you should lay down and get some rest," he suggested.

"You know what? I think I will lay down." I handed Darius to him. "Tell Tielle to come see me before she leaves, and tell everybody else I said thanks for their help."

It was best for me to go upstairs and be alone. I needed time to think. Who was in that car? And if it was Smoke, why didn't he make himself known? Did he plan on coming back? The questions kept rolling as I tried my best to go to sleep. I tossed and turned for the longest, wishing I could deactivate my brain for the evening.

***

Craig called Tielle into the kitchen. "I need to talk to you," he said as they sat down at the table.

"What's up?" she asked.

"Did Meka seem like she was actin' funny?"

"Not really," she said slowly. "Why?"

"I don't know. She seems irritated."

"Where is she now?"

"Upstairs. Maybe she's just worn out from today. She told me to tell you to come upstairs before you leave. Maybe she'll talk to you about it."

Tielle shrugged her shoulders. "That could be it. It's our job to be here for her, you know? When's she's up, we need to be up. When she's down, we need to understand. And you really need to step up. She needs you now more than anybody else. And she's gonna push you away sometimes, but you gotta hang in there. If you love this girl, show it."

"I do love her. I don't think she knows how much."

"So now that y'all livin' together, what's next?" Tielle asked.

He leaned back in his chair and sighed. "Ain't nothin' left but the ring now," he said. "I can't believe that dude proposed to her before I got the chance to. Now if I bust out with a ring, she'll think I'm doin' it 'cause TJ did it."

"Do you really wanna marry her?"

"Yeah. I've been thinkin' about it for a while."

"Then propose! Do what's in your heart. Life is too short to try to wait for the right moment for everything. I mean, what exactly *is* the right moment anyway?" Craig sat silently. "I'm giving you a female's opinion. You need to show her that you're serious about your relationship. I know for a fact that she's ready to settle down. Before, it was just a matter of who she wanted to settle down with."

Too Little, Too Late

***

"You sleep?" Tielle whispered as she tiptoed into my room.

I pulled the comforter off my head and rolled onto my back. "Hey."

"I'm about to go, but Craig said you wanted me to come up here. What's up?" She walked over to the bed and sat down near my feet.

"I think I'm goin' crazy," I said.

I told her how freaked out I was when I saw the car go by earlier and admitted I was scared out of my mind.

"Well Meka, why shouldn't you be scared? You have every right to jump outta your seat every time you hear a pin drop. Do you realize what you've been through? You're only human, and I think somewhere along the line you forgot that. It's okay to cry in front of people. It's okay to say that you're scared. Fear is an emotion, not a sign of weakness."

"Here I go cryin' again," I said as I wiped my face. "LT, I'm tired of cryin'! I'm tired of hurtin'. I'm tired of bein' afraid. I'm up here in the bed tryin' to sleep my fears away when I should be playin' with my son, whoopin' somebody in spades, or cuddlin' with my man. This shit is frustratin'!"

Tielle waited until I was calm. "So, do you wanna call the police and have them look out for the car in case that was Smoke?"

"I didn't even see a license plate, girl. I can't just have them lookin' for a black Acura with tinted windows. Do you know how many people have a car that fits that description?"

"He might be one of those people."

"LT, you said you didn't even notice the car and you were standin' right beside me. I'm not gonna cause no ruckus over somethin' that just looked suspicious to me."

"Well I'ma tell Craig to look out for it. You never know. You might've been the only one who thought somethin' was strange 'cause you were the only one who was in his presence before. You need to give yourself more credit. Intuition ain't no joke."

***

The next couple of days, Craig and I spent every minute together after he got off work. We were in lovey-dovey mode times three, but I liked it. Enjoying family time and sharing late night talks gave us a tighter bond and reassured me that I'd made the right choice when I moved in with him. I didn't know love could feel so good.

267

On the 26th, he came home from work early, then left right out again. He said he had to run some errands and asked if I needed anything while he was out. I told him not to worry about me because I needed to go to the grocery store to get a few more things for Thanksgiving dinner, which was the next day. He took Darius with him to give me a much-needed break.

**

While Craig was out, he called Tielle from his cell phone. "Guess where I'm headed."

"It must be somewhere special if you felt the need to call me," she replied.

"I'm on my way to get Meka's ring."

"Ring?" Tielle screamed with excitement. "You proposing tonight?" she asked.

"I don't know yet. I might wait 'til dinner tomorrow."

"Oh, you want a audience."

"Whatever, man."

"Well make it good. If I'm gonna witness this, it better be original and romantic. Where's Meka? Home?"

"Naw. She went to the grocery store. I got lil' man with me so he can approve of the rock I picked."

Tielle laughed. "Well, y'all have fun."

**

I walked in the house and put the bags on the floor just inside the door. I had one more trip to make to the car. As I reached into the trunk, I noticed the black Acura I'd seen a couple days before. It was parked on the street, about seven doors down.

They must know somebody over there, I thought as I grabbed the other bags and walked back in the house. I flipped on the hall lights as I walked into the kitchen. When I sat the bags on the counter, I thought heard a noise. I froze in place and listened for about ten seconds.

"Damn, I'm trippin'," I said. I listened to the messages on answering machine while I unloaded the groceries. My mother, Chauncey, and Alexis had called.

When I put all the groceries away, I called Lexis back. "You left some of your CDs at the house," she said. "I was gon' bring 'em to you while I'm out."

"I'll be here," I said.

"I'm comin' from Robert's, so it'll only take me like fifteen minutes to get there. Don't y'all try to squeeze in a quickie or nothin'."

"Shut up," I said, laughing. "Craig ain't even here right now, and I doubt he'll be here in the next fifteen minutes."

After we hung up, I stretched out on the couch and turned on the TV. As I flipped through the channels, I heard one of the plastic bags move.

"The damn bananas," I said under my breath as I walked back into the kitchen. I thought I left the bag on the counter and figured it toppled over. To my surprise, the only bags I saw were by the pantry, and they were empty.

Almost instantly, I had a bad feeling. I knew somebody was in my house. I took a quick glimpse around the kitchen, then hurried back into the living room to get my gun from the hall closet. TJ always told me to assume the worst, then find out if I was right later.

I opened the closet and reached up to the top shelf to grab the shoebox that housed my weapon. I was lowering the box when I felt a strong forearm hook around my neck and hold me in a headlock.

"Guess who, bitch," a familiar, raspy voice said. It was Smoke. He knocked the box onto the floor and dragged me into the kitchen.

"What do you want, Smoke?" I said. I tried to sound strong.

"Oh, you know my name, huh? So it *was* you feedin' the cops my information. I knew I came to the right place." He squeezed my neck tighter, and my air supply became scarce. "You know, I thought you got the fuckin' picture when I called you before. I told you not to fuck wit' me then, but I guess that's what I get for tryin' to be nice."

I found just enough air to tell him what I'd wanted to tell him since December 21st of the previous year. "You made it this way when you fuckin' raped me and gave me HIV, you nasty bastard! Fuck you!" I said, struggling to break free.

"Don't you ever say that shit again! I don't have that shit!" he yelled back. He flung me around so I could face him. "None of this shit was supposed to happen. You fucked this shit up." His finger was only millimeters away from the tear that oozed from my left eye. I tried to break free again. "You ain't goin' nowhere," he said. "Not now. I already got ya boy, so it's only right for me to send you to the same place." He turned me back around.

I looked at the closet through the kitchen doorway, desperately wishing I could get to my gun. It had fallen out of the shoebox and was lying on the carpet, waiting to be used. Scorching tears trickled

269

down my face and onto his arm as I felt myself getting dizzy from the headlock. I silently prayed for Craig or Alexis to bust through the door and save me.

Smoke loosened his grip and pushed me to the floor. My head slammed against the cabinet, and my ears rang so loud that I couldn't understand what he was saying for a few seconds. Once the ringing stopped, I heard, "Hey, you know what? I think we should make the most of our time together before we part ways again," he said with a sly smile. He reached for his belt buckle.

My mind was telling my body to move, but nothing happened. I couldn't see straight, and my head was throbbing from the impact of the cabinet. He kicked my legs to spread them apart and yanked on my pants until they were at my knees.

God, if you're listening, please stop this man. Please don't let this happen again, I silently prayed.

Once he got my underwear down and one leg out of my pants, he shoved himself into me. Out of nowhere, I was able to scream as loud as my vocal chords would allow. He covered my mouth with his left hand, and I tried my best to bite it every chance I got.

"Stop tryin' to fight it," he said. "The more you fight it, the more I'ma keep goin'," he said, banging even harder. "I like it rough."

When I screamed again, he reached by his right ankle and pulled a gun out of his jeans pocket. He held it under my nose. "I will blow your fuckin' brains out right now!" he yelled. "Shut the fuck up!"

I knew he was gonna try to kill me regardless of whether I fought or not, so I chose to go out fighting. If there was a chance I could make it to the closet and shoot him, I was gonna take it. Even if I could fight him long enough for Craig or Alexis to make it, that would do. Things were finally starting to fall into place in my life, and I wasn't gonna let that animal ruin it like he did the first time.

"I hate you!" I yelled and pushed him off of me. The stupid fool didn't have sense enough to pin my arms down that time. The gun fell out of his hand and slid across the tile, stopping near the refrigerator. If I went for it, I would've had to jump over him, so I ran toward the living room to get my own instead.

In mid-stride, I heard a muffled noise. I felt something hot hit me in my back, and I collapsed to the living room floor. My scream was caught in my throat. Smoke stood over me and pleasured himself to his climax as if there was something romantic about our encounter. I struggled to breathe as I laid on my stomach and looked longingly at my gun, only inches out of my reach. My legs felt like blocks of lead, so moving wasn't an option. I was trapped.

"Thank God for silencers, huh?" he said with a smirk. "I never start somethin' and not finish," he continued as he buckled his belt.

As the warm liquid on my cheek inched toward my mouth, I mustered the strength to slide the couple inches I needed to grab my pistol. Smoke was too busy rambling and wiping blood off his Air Force Ones to notice. I got his attention when I fired a shot that hit the wall behind him and another that miraculously hit his penis. By then, he was firing back at me, but I kept shooting and tried to ignore the piercing pain caused by the three other bullets that seared through my body.

Chapter 30

Alexis and Tiffany pulled up almost four minutes later. As they got out of the car, Alexis was fussing about Robert.

"Girl, I'm about to let his ass go. I ain't got time for his fuckin' attitude. I'ma ask Meka if she can talk to the leasing agent for me. I want my place back. I ain't movin' in wit' his ass."

"Yeah right," Tiffany replied.

"I was all excited about tomorrow, but he done fucked up my holiday spirit," Alexis said as she rang the doorbell.

Tiffany laughed as they waited impatiently on the doorstep.

Alexis rang the doorbell again. "Now where is this heffa? I just talked to her." She noticed the next door neighbor peeking through her blinds. "And what's this bitch lookin' at?" She bucked her eyes at the elderly lady who quickly disappeared.

"I see some lights on in the back," Tiffany said.

"Yeah, that's the kitchen," Alexis said, pounding on the door with her fist. "Maybe she's in the bathroom."

"See if it's unlocked. She knew you were comin'."

"Please. She don't keep her door unlocked, especially livin' in this nice ass condo," Alexis said as she tried the doorknob. When it turned, she looked at the door in disbelief, then turned to Tiffany. "Somethin' ain't right," she said as she removed her gun from her Dooney bag and slowly walked inside.

She immediately ran upstairs, yelling Tameka's name every few seconds. Tiffany stayed downstairs and walked around, doing the same. When she reached the living room, she was immediately horrified.

"Oh no," she said, covering her mouth and looking around for any signs of trouble. "Lexis!" she yelled.

Alexis trampled down the stairs and ran toward the living room. She stopped in the entryway once she saw the most devastating sight she could ever imagine. Tameka was sprawled out in a pool of blood with only a ripped t-shirt on. Her pants and underwear were just inside the entrance to the kitchen, and her gun rested near her lifeless fingertips. Four bullet holes were clearly present in her torso and leg, some of which were still gushing, and her once flawless face was covered with fresh scratches and bruises.

Tiffany dialed 911 while Alexis knelt at Tameka's side and held her hand.

"Open your eyes, Meka. You gotta wake up, sweetie," she said, overwhelmed with tears.

"Does she have a pulse?" Tiffany asked.

Alexis nodded, never taking her eyes off her big sister. "You stay with me, Meka. You hear me?"

Tiffany hung up and informed Alexis that dispatch had already received numerous phone calls from people who heard gunshots coming from the house. They already had police units and an ambulance in route. "You need me to do anything?" she asked.

"Grab a blanket out of that closet."

Tiffany handed Alexis a multicolored afghan, and she draped it over Tameka's lower body.

"What's that on her face?" Tiffany asked.

Alexis leaned closer to examine the clear, gooey substance on her sister's cheek.

"Sick bastard! I can't believe this shit!" She stood up.

Tiffany knew exactly what it was after witnessing Alexis' reaction. She glanced at her watch, praying that the paramedics would arrive soon, then knelt down to recheck for a pulse. She wasn't sure how much longer Tameka would make it.

"Fuckin' around wit' Robert. I shoulda been here," Alexis said as she paced above Tameka's head.

"Do you think she shot back?" she asked, nodding toward Tameka's gun.

Alexis checked the weapon, then threw it back down and retrieved hers again. "The clip is empty."

As approaching sirens sounded in the background, she crept to the kitchen entrance and peaked around the corner. Her foot slipped on a patch of blood, and she looked down to discover a trail of crimson fluid that led to a body. The black male who looked to be in his late twenties was lying near the back door, dead. The gruesome sight almost made her sick as she surveyed the damage on his body. The most noticeable gunshot wounds were on his neck and face, which was almost totally blown away. Alexis cracked a satisfied smile, impressed that her sister went down shooting.

"You see anything?" Tiffany called from the living room.

Alexis spit on Smoke's face. "If my sister dies, I'll dig up your grave and kill you all over again."

Swarms of paramedics and police personnel arrived and took control of the crime scene. Alexis informed a detective of Smoke's corpse in the kitchen, while Tiffany told another officer her version of what they'd witnessed. After ten minutes or so, they had controlled some of Tameka's bleeding and started her on oxygen. The policemen agreed to hold off on more questioning so that Alexis could ride in the ambulance and be by her sister's side. Smoke, on the other hand, was officially pronounced dead and zipped in a navy blue body bag.

It was total chaos once Alexis entered the emergency room. She was immediately greeted by the detectives from the scene. They bombarded her and Tiffany with questions, many of which they couldn't answer. Finally, she demanded that they leave them alone. She paced around the waiting area while Tiffany sat nearby.

Alexis was convincing herself that Tameka was going to be okay. She knew her sister had already endured a tremendous amount of pain and suffering, and trusted that Tameka still had the will to fight. Her constant pacing put her in somewhat of a trance, and she didn't snap out of it until Craig bolted over to her with Darius in his arms.

"Where is she?" he asked, out of breath.

"They took her back for emergency surgery," Alexis answered.

"Surgery? What happened?"

"Smoke shot her."

Tiffany saw the look of panic on Craig's face and jumped out of the chair to take Darius from him.

He took a deep breath. "How bad is it? Where'd he shoot her?"

"In her back, twice in her thigh, and once in her chest," Alexis said.

"Oh my God," Craig said, lowering himself into a chair. "At our place?"

"Yeah."

Craig shook his head in disbelief. "This shit can't be real," he said through clenched teeth. "How long has she been in surgery?"

"It's only been like ten or fifteen minutes," Alexis replied. She looked over at Craig. "I don't know what I'ma do if…"

He hugged her as they both cried. Within the next ten minutes, Tielle and Romeo had arrived, and Tiffany filled them in on what was going on.

At 9:37, a doctor walked out into the waiting area, still dressed in his scrubs. Alexis, Craig, and Tielle jumped out of their seats as soon as they saw him. He asked if they were with Tameka James, then signaled for them to follow him around the corner into a more private hallway. He introduced himself, then began talking. "She's out of surgery. We were able to remove the two bullets that were still in her," the doctor started.

"Yes!" Alexis whispered loudly. "That's good."

"But she's not out of the woods, yet," he continued. "We're still very concerned about internal bleeding. We did what we could for now, so…"

"So she still might be bleeding?" Tielle asked.

"Well, she's had an enormous amount of organ damage. We repaired what we saw, but it isn't uncommon to see further complications from more bleeding or infection," the doctor answered.

"Point blank. What are her chances?" Craig asked.

"As of right now, she has about a 45 to 50 percent chance of surviving."

***

I woke up to the sounds of a beeping heart monitor and hissing oxygen tank. I didn't know what was going on, but there was one thing I was sure of…I was hurting like hell. My chest ached on the outside and felt like it was on fire inside. When I tried to touch it to see what was wrong, I realized I could barely lift my arm. I didn't feel like I had a lack of energy. This was different. My body *couldn't* do anything.

My door opened, and in walked Tielle, Craig, and Lexis. Someone was missing, though.

"Dar-i-us," I said.

"He's here, baby," Craig said. He walked to my bedside and held my hand. "He's outside with Tiffany."

"Don't try to talk too much if it hurts," Tielle said.

"Just squeeze my hand once for yes, and twice for no," Craig said. "We'll just ask you yes and no questions."

275

Portia A. Cosby

Alexis was near the door, peeking over at me. I couldn't understand why she was so stand-offish. It wasn't like she hadn't seen me in the hospital before. Tielle followed my eye line.

"Come over here, Lexis," she said. "I think she wants to see you."

Alexis wiped her eyes and walked over to the vacant side of my bed. She forced a smile. "You feelin' alright?" she asked. Her lip was quivering.

I squeezed Craig's hand twice.

"She said, 'No'." He leaned over and kissed my forehead. "You hang in there, beautiful. You beat the odds more than once, and we need you to do it one more time. He's gone, baby. You don't have to worry about him bothering you again."

I was confused. Who was gone? "What?" I forced out.

"Maybe she doesn't remember," Tielle said. "Do you remember what happened, Meka?"

"She said, 'No'," Craig replied. He let my hand go, grabbed his head, and took a few steps away from my bed.

My heart rate sped up. I didn't like the vibe I was getting from them. My eyes probably looked like they were about to pop out of my head because I was looking at Tielle and Alexis with so much anticipation.

"Tell her, Lexis. You know more than we do," Tielle said.

Alexis' body language made it clear that she didn't want to tell me. "Meka, you were shot...four times," she said.

Instantly, my eyes filled with tears.

"I walked in the house and found you in the living room, on the floor...half naked, and," Alexis stopped to gather herself. "And blood was everywhere," she finished.

It was slowing coming back to me. I remembered Smoke raping me, but I only remembered being shot once. I cried hysterically, squeezing Lexis' hand so tightly that she probably lost circulation for a few seconds.

"Where is he?" I asked.

"In hell," Tielle said. "He's burnin' as we speak."

I kept repeating his name periodically, and the beeping on my heart monitor reached a record speed, sounding more like *The Price Is Right* wheel when the contestants spin it the first time. Craig was concerned, so he ran out and got one of the nurses. She obtained approval from the doctor to give me a sedative, and I was soon out for the count.

276

***

When Tielle walked into the waiting area, Romeo was playing with Darius, and Tiffany was flipping through a magazine.

"How's she doin', baby?" Romeo asked.

"Not too good. She didn't even remember what happened until Lexis told her. I don't think she can move, and when she talks, she only says one word every few seconds."

"They kicked y'all out the room?"

"Naw. She's sleep right now, so I came out here to let you know what was goin' on."

Tielle took her phone out of her purse and walked outside to get a signal. When she checked her messages, she heard Dap's voice asking her to call back immediately because it was an emergency. Tielle prayed that this emergency would be something small because she couldn't handle any more bad news.

"What's goin' on?" she asked when Dap answered.

"Where you at? I just saw the news and they said Tameka got shot," Dap said.

"I'm at the hospital right now."

"So it's true?"

"Yeah, Dap. It's true." Tielle was losing her patience.

"Oh shit! So that Smoke guy finally caught up with her?" She was in total disbelief and sounded genuinely concerned. "I feel so bad for givin' him her number, man. Make sure you tell her I really didn't know who he was. I know we don't get along, but I wouldn't do nothin' like that."

"You're the least of her worries right now."

"Is she gon' make it?"

"We don't know."

"Damn...Well, I'm about to go to the police station and tell them everything I know about ol' dude. They still don't know what he looks like, right?" Dap asked.

"They know now."

"What you mean? They caught him?"

"Meka killed him."

Dap searched for the right thing to say. She wanted to start cheering, but she could tell from Tielle's tone that the bad might come with the good. If Tameka died too, there would be no justice. "You alright?"

"Not really," Tielle replied. "But I gotta go. I need to see if the doctors know anything else."

They hung up, and Tielle went back inside. She was surprised to see Robert, who greeted her with a hug. Everyone else looked restless as they slouched in the orange leather chairs, sipped coffee, and looked at the news.

Alexis nodded off and was awakened by a tap on her knee after eleven. She opened her eyes and saw her mother.

"Lexi," Regina said, hugging her daughter. "I got here as fast as I could. How's she doing?"

Alexis lowered her eyelids and shook her head. Regina let out a sigh. "Have you talked to your father?"

"No. I had to leave a message."

"Well, when can we see her?"

"I don't know. I guess when she wakes back up. I already told 'em that we ain't leavin' until we know she's alright, so if I stay here 'til this time tomorrow, oh well."

Luckily, Alexis didn't have to wait that long. One of the nurses came to the waiting area about twenty minutes later. Regina rocked Darius side to side in an effort to lull him to sleep as she listened to the nurse.

"…She's awake now, but she's not doing very well. If you wanna go in and see her briefly, now is the time. We need to let her rest as much as possible. I can only allow three of you in her room at once."

Craig, Regina, and Alexis went in first. This time, they took Darius in so Tameka could see him.

***

I heard footsteps coming closer and closer to my bed. Once they stopped, I opened my eyes. My mother was standing over me, tissue in hand, bawling.

"Baby, why did he do this to you?" she said.

I bit my bottom lip in an effort not to cry again. I couldn't break down anymore. It took too much out of me. I looked over and saw Darius in Craig's arms. I smiled as I watched him twist and giggle with excitement.

"He wouldn't stay sleep," Craig said. "I think he needed to see you."

I tried to reach out for him, but couldn't. My body was deteriorating. I felt worse than when I first woke up, and I wasn't sure that when I closed my eyes again, I'd be able to reopen them.

Craig saw my fingers twitch, so he leaned over so I could give Darius a kiss.

"I love you," I said to my sweet baby boy. I managed a little chuckle because he was fascinated with the IV tubes and determined to grab one. Craig handed him to Alexis after he got a little too close.

As I listened to everyone's motivational speeches and lighthearted chatter, I became extremely winded. I felt my eyes rolling in the back of my head, but I couldn't control them.

"Un unh, Meka. What's wrong?" Alexis asked. "Look at her, Ma! Look at her eyes!"

"Tameka," my mother said, shaking my arm. "Tameka!"

Alexis ran toward the door just before I reopened my eyes.

"Wait, Lexi!" Mom said. She stared at me, waiting to see if my episode was over. "Hold on. She opened her eyes again."

"I'll be back," she said. "I'ma take Darius out here."

Craig didn't take his eyes off me. "I can't lose you, Meka. Don't do this. Stay strong, baby."

I wanted to. I wanted to sit up and crack jokes about ruining everybody's Thanksgiving, scold Alexis for being five minutes late that evening, and tell Craig I owed him for the carpet cleaning bill he'd have; but it was getting harder and harder for me to just keep my eyes open.

"I can't watch this," Mom said. She walked over to the window and kept her back turned.

Craig held my hand, shaking it every time he saw me drift away. "Hey," he started. "You need an incentive to stay strong?" He reached in his pants pocket and pulled out a ring box. My life had officially qualified to be a *Lifetime* movie.

I couldn't believe it was happening again. Only this time, I was ready to accept the proposal. He took the ring out of the box, and my eyes opened wide. It was a beautiful princess cut diamond, but that was its only similarity to TJ's. I could tell that Craig went out of his way to make sure his ring was nothing like my ex's.

"Meka, I've known since our first date that I need you in my life. You've taught me so much about love and acceptance, and I wanna spend the rest of my life thanking you. You've made me a better man. I still have more to learn, so you can't leave me now." He was crying. "Will you marry me?"

279

I squeezed his hand once. He kissed me on the cheek and slid the ring onto my finger. "I love you, baby."

"You too," was all I could say.

I heard my mother burst into a loud cry. I think she knew exactly what was going through my mind…I wasn't gonna make it. I used to hear people say their family members had premonitions about dying, but I never understood how that could be until that moment.

Craig leaned over and kissed me again. "That's my girl."

I wondered where Alexis was. I needed to say goodbye to her and Tielle, and I wanted to let Robert and Romeo know that I would haunt them from my grave if they did either of them wrong.

I opened my mouth to ask for them, but the words got tangled in the fiery pain that attacked my chest. I choked on my own spit and coughed uncontrollably for a few seconds. Although the cough soon went away, the pain didn't. It felt like a bullet was still burning through my bloodstream, circling around my heart. I screamed in excruciating pain.

"Push the button for the nurse," my mother yelled. She ran to my bedside.

Sweat beads surfaced all over my face as I tried to breathe through the pain. Craig pushed the call button with one hand and squeezed my hand with his other one.

I looked deep into his eyes. "I can't do it," I cried. "I'm tired."

"Shh," Craig said. "Calm down, baby. You gotta save your energy."

Mom held my other hand and softly recited the 23rd Psalm. *Maybe she really did recommit her life to Christ.* I felt an indescribable energy that flowed from her hand to my heart, and a calm fell over my body and spirit.

"…Surely goodness and mercy shall follow me all the days of my life, and I will dwell in the house of the Lord forever."

Those were the last words I heard before I looked at Craig and said, "I'm sorry." I cried my last tear, closed my eyes, and found true peace.

***

"No!" Craig yelled. His eyes were scarlet red. He felt Tameka's grip loosen and her hand go limp. "Oh my God," he cried as he buried his face in her stomach and grabbed a fistful of her hospital gown.

Regina simply kissed her daughter's forehead, then whispered in her ear, "You don't have to hurt no more, baby."

A crew of nurses and doctors rushed in and attempted to revive Tameka as Regina and Craig watched from a nearby corner. After almost being trampled by the team running down the hallway, Alexis busted through the door to find out what was going on. When she entered the room, she saw the doctors' last attempt to shock Tameka's heart.

One of the doctors stopped the crew, and the room fell silent. "1:54 AM, time of death," he said as he removed his gloves.

Alexis called out Tameka's name as she slowly lowered to her knees near the doorway. She reached out her hand in a pointless effort to touch her sister. "No! I love you, Meka. Don't leave me. You can't leave." Regina ran over to her, and they cried together, embracing each other tightly. Craig was in the opposite corner, hugging his knees to his chest and sobbing.

The nurses moved the three of them to a private room where they could bring in a counselor to console them. Another nurse had already rounded up everyone else and instructed them to wait in that room. When Craig walked in, Tielle knew what had happened.

"No," she said, already in tears. Romeo held her hand. "Don't you tell me she's gone."

Craig exhaled slowly and took Darius out of Tiffany's arms. He looked into his son's eyes as tears poured from his own. "It's just me and you, lil' man," he said, laying Darius against his chest.

As the counselor walked in, Alexis looked at Craig with the innocence of an impressionable child. "So now what?" she asked.

He put his arm around her and simply said, "I don't know."

They leaned on each other, looking for the answers the counselor couldn't provide and regretting every opportunity they didn't seize; wondering if it was selfish to want Tameka back, even though she was in a better place.

Portia A. Cosby

Wonder what happens next?

Read

LESSON LEARNED:
IT IS WHAT IT IS

Book Two in the
"Situations & Circumstances Series"

Step into Alexis' world and witness what she learns about her mother, her best friend, her man, and herself.

Have questions for the author?
Contact Portia at: feedback@portiacosby.com

Also visit:
www.portiacosby.com
www.myspace.com/portiacosby

Portia A. Cosby

Discussion Questions

1. Alexis and Tameka had a volatile relationship. In spite of that, do you think Alexis stepped up and supported Tameka like a sister should? Do you believe her concern was genuine?
2. Dap seemed to be the root of many of Tameka's problems but always attempted to make peace. What are your feelings about her involvement and her ultimate attempt to right her wrongs at the end?
3. Tameka had terrific friends who helped her through her toughest times. How important was that? Did that help her mindset and allow her to lead a "normal" life?
4. TJ or Craig? Overall, who do you think she should've chosen? Why?
5. Why do you think both men still pursued her after learning she was HIV positive?
6. In your opinion, who loved Tameka more? Who did she love more?
7. Craig said some pretty harmful things about Tameka and wavered about his feelings for her after her diagnosis. Was he just being human or was he being more of a jerk? Do you believe he only apologized because Darius was a reality?
8. Regina was not your typical, loving mother. How do you think that affected Tameka and Alexis' attitudes toward life?
9. What was your favorite part?
10. Who was your favorite character? Why?
11. Who was your least favorite character? Why?
12. What character(s) do you look forward to reading more about?

Feel free to send your answers to **feedback@portiacosby.com**

Portia A. Cosby

Printed in the United States
221234BV00004B/1/P